CULT OF CHAOS

SHWETA TANEJA is an author, graphic novelist and journalist based in Bangalore. Her debut novel, *The Ghost Hunters of Kurseong* (Hachette India, 2013), is a breezy mystery set in the hills. She has written two graphic novels, *Krishna: Defender of Dharma* (2012), which has been subscribed by CBSE for its Schools Reading List, and *The Skull Rosary* (2013), which got nominated for Best Writer at the Comic Con Awards the same year. Her aim is to prod and pry the peculiar and the odd, and to break preconceived notions about paranormal and supernatural with her books. To do that, she regularly drinks Makaibari tea, hogs on popular occult shows and books, and asks all sorts of weird questions (you've been warned). Connect with her online at www.shwetawrites.com or find her on most social networks with her handle @shwetawrites.

Cult of Chaos is Shweta's first Anantya Tantrist mystery. If you would like to ask questions to Anantya or know more about tantriks and her world, connect with her on Facebook and Twitter with her handle @anantyatantrist or follow her blog tantrist.tumblr.com.

CULT OF CHAOS

AN ANANTYA TANTRIST MYSTERY

shweta
taneja

HarperCollins *Publishers* India

First published in India in 2014 by
HarperCollins *Publishers* India

Copyright © Shweta Taneja 2014

P-ISBN: 978-93-5136-444-3
E-IBSN: 978-93-5136-445-0

2 4 6 8 10 9 7 5 3 1

Shweta Taneja asserts the moral right to be
identified as the author of this work.

HarperCollins *Publishers*
A-75, Sector 57, Noida, Uttar Pradesh 201301, India
77-85 Fulham Palace Road, London W6 8JB, United Kingdom
Hazelton Lanes, 55 Avenue Road, Suite 2900, Toronto, Ontario M5R 3L2
and 1995 Markham Road, Scarborough, Ontario M1B 5M8, Canada
25 Ryde Road, Pymble, Sydney, NSW 2073, Australia
10 East 53rd Street, New York NY 10022, USA

Typeset in 10/13.5 PalmSprings Regular at
SÜRYA, New Delhi

Printed and bound at
Thomson Press (India) Ltd.

For
My parents, Sunita and Raman,
Without whom nothing would be

Prologue

A drop of her virgin blood. That is all you need.

The words vibrated in him. A drop. That's all. It would not hurt her. It was just a little drop. She would do that for him. Of course she would, he reassured himself. There was no doubt about it.

The night was searing hot, not unusual for the beginning of July, rather like being inside an oven. His tattoo itched, but he couldn't scratch it. Couldn't sully his hands. He carefully wiped the sweat off his face, and dried that hand on his dhoti. The last thing he wanted was to contaminate the yantra triangle. He crouched along one side and sprinkled an even layer of roughly ground copper on it. The yantra's lines needed to be built up with seven layers – powdered agni, copper, vibhuti from the ashes of a funeral pyre, silver, black-as-night parada, cyanide and broken pieces of a fluorescent light. Their lord loved the number seven. His heart skipped a beat with joy at the thought of his lord as he bent down again, covering the copper layer with vibhuti. He knew the ritual by heart. They had made him do it over and over again, until he could do it with his eyes shut.

A breeze wafted up from the open drain across the road, bringing the sickly sweet smell of decayed flesh.

'Filthy holes full of filthy rats,' he spat.

He'd never be in a place like this under normal

circumstances. But tonight wasn't just any night. Tonight was special. Tonight would mark the beginning of the end of all impurities. Tonight, they would cleanse all evil from the world. Clean away putrid, evil places like these, where vile humans lived with dirty rats, nibbling away at the world, bite by bite.

A drop. That is all you need.

He stood up to admire his artwork. The triangle gleamed in the pale moonlight, seeming alive and eager. It was a perfect yantra, he thought proudly. The isosceles triangle, drawn with a steady hand, was straight and taut, its two longer sides measuring exactly seven haath each. It covered almost the whole of the terrace, leaving him about two feet space to walk around the perimeter. He knew the importance of getting the yantra's direction as well as proportion right. It was like any other science. One needed to be precise with the time, materials and permutations to be successful in one's experiment. He nodded, satisfied, and looked at his watch. An old one that his wife had gifted him. He smiled when he thought of Gayatri. Tonight, he will take her too. *You will see. I will make you eternal too.*

Over to the other side of the terrace, a small body lay curled like a sleeping kitten. Her stomach rose and fell in an even rhythm. One whiff of the chloroform had been enough for two hours of sleep. She had slept soundly while he stripped her and smeared her body with kumkum. Her hair, forehead and ... and *that place* ... were all covered with the bright, fiery red of the powder. Her skin shone in the feeble moonlight, a scent of rose and jasmine rising from her. He sniffed, his eyes softening. He had massaged her body for weeks with the oil specially made for this occasion. Consider it spice in a meal, they had told him. It will make her body more delectable to the one we invoke. He picked up her limp body in the cradle of his left arm. She stirred, mumbling in her sleep.

'So little, but with so much power. You are truly blessed, my child,' he whispered, his lips close to her hair, kissing it gently.

She was the only pure thing in this beastly world. A cradle of pure shakti, the power of unshed blood. She was all that mattered. He placed her delicately on the hard ground, in the middle of the triangle. He spread her legs apart, her womb exactly aligned with the triangle's apex point. Her shakti needed to face the same direction. To invite. The ritual demanded it. He looked at her body, naked except for the kumkum, which looked more like black smears in the moonlight. For a moment, his heart lurched. She was just a child, really. Could he go through with this? The phone rang, making him jump. He didn't bother to check the number. He knew who it was. It was almost twelve.

'Jai Kolahalnath!' he whispered, the doubt of a split second ago already forgotten. He listened for a few seconds and nodded. It had to be done. This was his destiny. His part in a greater story that would unfold. His part in recreating the world. Purifying it. They would remember his sacrifice in the new world. He placed the phone at the apex of the triangle. Its screen glowed for a second before automatically darkening. The phone crackled like a strangled deer. They had started the mantra, so should he. He stepped out of the yantra and picked up the small black velvet package that had been placed beside his bag. Its velvety leaves opened at the touch of his hand, one by one. His heart began to race. Even though he knew what lay inside, he gasped. The exquisite blade, not much bigger than his palm, was pure white, it glowed from within. He held it up in his left hand. It was perfectly sickle-shaped, a broad arc, its middle thicker than the ends. The handle was white as well, only it wasn't luminescent, but gleamed nevertheless like polished marble with intricate ancient motifs carved upon it. *It looks so delicate. Can it be as old as they say it is?* The knife quivered and shook in his hand slightly. It wants to go inside, he thought with mild surprise. He had been told that this could happen, but to actually feel it was something else altogether. The knife had attached itself to his left hand, almost becoming an extension. A thrill of excitement passed through him. He looked at the girl lying in the centre of the circle, her legs apart. It was time.

As soon as he bent down, the blade rushed towards the girl, like a hound with the taste of blood in its hungry mouth. All that power. He felt like a slave to a vastly more powerful master. The knife's arc turned in his hand, its sharp end pointing down, thirsty. *A drop.*

The mobile phone crackled with excitement as the mantra recitation at the other end quickened. They could sense the blade's excitement too. The triangle had started to glow like a yellow neon sign. It was so beautiful. He felt tears in his eyes, his left arm stretched, his body crouched, his head bent in submission.

Her virgin blood.

Finally, after months of practice, years of yearning. Finally, he would be the one to set the wheels in motion. *Tonight.* He closed his eyes and started to whisper the mantra. The last one.

'*Aum Ain Hreem Shreem Kolahala Namaha!*'

I offer you the ultimate gift, my lord. My blood, my born, my seed, my all.

She stirred, opening her heavy eyes. The blade jerked forward, towards her navel, its arc downwards, like a claw.

'Papa?' she mumbled, sleepy, confused, not yet fully awake.

He didn't hear her. His ears were full of white noise, crackles and rushes from some other world. He lapped up the voices, a fish in electric water, gleeful. His eyes glazed. *Finally*! The blade hacked, its marble surface darkening with the blood from her womb. Her eyes flew open with surprise and pain. She wailed, the pain ripping away the shroud of sleep. It was supposed to be one cut, only it wasn't. The blade withdrew of its own accord, still thirsty, and then plunged again. Her shrill scream filled the noxious night as the blade sliced through her. The scream died on her lips midway, incomplete, as something swirled in from the sky, a gush of black blood, only denser.

९

The restaurant was dark and still. The candle in front of me flickered nervously. I was tense. I discreetly sent my senses into the darkness around us. An embarrassed giggle. A whispered murmur. The strong, waxy smell of rose candles mingled with the rotten fish odour of sexual desire. Stop it, Anantya. There's nothing here other than horny people trying to talk politely to get laid. Which is what you should be doing too.

'… begin with the appetizers since it's your first time here,' my date Nikhil Kapoor was saying. 'I would recommend the chicken yakitori …'

We sat in an upmarket Thai restaurant in Rajiv Chowk's inner circle, newly opened and noted more for its decor than its food. The walls and the floor were a glistening black with alcoves of highbacked sofas so you had no choice but to stare at the person sitting opposite you. All I could see was his teeth and a curvaceous singer who oozed a blues song on the small, dimly lit stage before us. It was all very sophisticated and tasteful, if you went in for that sort of thing. Unfortunately, I did not. The candle-lit ambience made me sleepy as did the sway of the penguin-like waiters in their black coats and white shirts. In other words, I was bored.

'… it will have a slightly charred flavour that I hope you won't mind …'

I tapped the toe of my right foot under the table, looking at Nikhil's lips as they moved. Nikhil was a neat-looking guy, in a Dakini sort of way. Waxed all over, his hair gelled and not a strand out of place. His face shone, perhaps a little too much, in the candlelight. He wore a white linen shirt, so severely starched that its creases stood out. A 'missionary' type, I was sure. But I could be wrong and he could well turn out to be kinky in the bedroom. Anyway, to know for sure I would have to get him into some kind of bed. Even a couch would do. Unfortunately, he seemed to enjoy talking more than anything else.

'...for the main course, I will order a sushi ni*gi*ri. The subtle flavours will really *tease* your tongue,' he said in a deliberately deep voice, 'or if you want something tangier, I would suggest you go for their crispy aromatic duck done in hoi*sin* sauce.'

I shrugged. As if I would know, or care, about the difference between the hose sauce and whatever that nila thing was. If it was edible, I would eat it. He smiled again, his unnaturally big, clean teeth shining like the headlights of an SUV.

'If I were you,' he continued in his deep monotone, 'I would choose the duck. They can get it wrong here, but if I give them careful instructions, they will get the tanginess of the hoi*sin* sauce purrfect.'

He smacked his full lips together. I took a large gulp of the wine that he had chosen after a long-winded discussion with the headwaiter, and wished it was soma. I had figured too late that this blind date thing was a bad, bad idea. My kind of date usually started with a cup or two of soma-on-the-rocks at the Bedardi Bar and ended two hours later in a bed of some sort with a species of some sort. It was simpler, the dating style in Bedardi. You went, you saw, you grabbed and you left. You had a night of wild (hopefully what you would call) sex, and then both of you (or more) were off in different directions. There was no talking or nibbling on nila thingies. Who had created these human mating rituals? Why wait and talk about dead ducks? What a waste of a perfectly good evening! I picked up the wine glass again and drained it this time. It did nothing to settle my stomach, which continued to play skull and bones with dread.

'Here, allow me,' said Nikhil smoothly, refilling my glass and handing it back, his headlights ablaze again.

I was just about to drain the wine again when I felt it. The rim of the glass stilled on my lips. A hum, low but insistent, just out of the reach of my human ears, so that I sensed it in my kidneys not my ears. A vibration of shakti. Something warm touched my hand. I jerked involuntarily and splashed my wine on the settee.

'Hey, hey, relax,' Nikhil said, taking his hand away and leaning forward, 'I know how you are feeling. Dakini kinda warned me. She told me that you don't have very much experience of, how should I put it, the romantic kind ...'

There it was again. The vibration strummed in my veins. It wasn't unusual to find shakti in high concentrations at some spots. It is the power that tantriks use for magic after all, and there are quite a few shakti spots around, especially in old worship houses, temples, mosques, ruins of ancient monuments and so on. But this one was slightly different. It felt more like a broken pipe than a steady deep ocean. It reeked of a pure rakshasa. Which wasn't threatening per se. After all, Delhi does have a fair few rakshasas and a lot of them do mingle freely with humans and dine in restaurants. The problem was, the shakti this time felt somehow familiar. Like an old friend's cold dead hand. I squinted into the dim light away from our alcove, nostrils dilated, hungry to know its source. My hand sneaked into my satchel and fingered my septifocals, the vision goggles made of bone that usually perched on top of my head. I wondered if I could take a small peek into the second plane in front of Nikhil. Just a peek?

'… it's all right. I like it in a way. To be inexperienced at your age in this day and age, I mean …'

'Wait, what?' I exclaimed, my attention back on my date. 'What *exactly* did Dakini tell you about me?'

'She told me that you haven't dated much,' he said, his hand snaking towards mine which lay fisted on the table. 'It's all right, you know. I have enough experience for the both of us.'

'Ahem,' I cleared my throat, wondering how to fill in the gap between what he had understood and what the reality was. Technically, Dakini hadn't lied. After all, it had been what … seven years … well, seven years since I had tried to talk to a man with a romantic inclination. Usually I was too busy having sex with one or trying to attack another to have time to sit and talk. So yes, even though I was twenty-three, I had not had much experience of the modern marvel of dating. Until tonight, I had thought a date was a convenient way of fixing the day and time for sex. That it would involve wearing a dress, eating food you couldn't pronounce the names of, and talking about drinks that didn't get you drunk, I had had no idea. Yes, I know, I *know*. Well, that's how cut off from reality you could be if all you had done over the past couple of years was see corpses and tried to figure out whose they might have been and who might have killed them.

'Daahling, you have to try something different, like hanging out with your own species for instance,' Dakini had said. As I had been out of work for almost a month and bored to tears, I decided to go along with her mad plan. I could see her grinning now, gleefully rubbing her huge manicured hands. Earlier this evening, she had spent almost an entire hour dressing me up in a softly flowing red dress with a neckline that plunged to my navel. My curly hair had been tamed with gel and turned into a coif, oh yes, a *coif* (learnt the word from Dakini). And she had put make-up on my face. The result, I could see in one of the mirror fragments embedded in the couch Nikhil was sitting on, was a stranger. My face was transformed. My eyes appeared larger, doe-like, shadowed in grey to bring out the flecks of smoke in my black irises. Dakini had painted my lips a soft red. I looked delicate and innocent and younger than my age. Almost like mother. Except for the scowl, which no make-up could mask.

My hand automatically touched the yugma around my neck, a two-inch locket made of silver and snakebone, which hung on a long silver chain resting in my cleavage. It was in the shape of two intertwined snakes, their heads looking away from each other. It was the only keepsake I had of my mother. That and, as Didi had always said, her strikingly beautiful face. Although that particular asset almost always proved to be a hindrance in my chosen profession.

'… I promise you, we will not rush this,' said Nikhil as he caressed my hand. He had at some point moved closer to me. Our thighs almost touched under the table. 'Building trust is far more important to me now. If you had met the old Nikhil, you would understand what I mean. Dakini has taught me to tap into my Inner Spirit. Sessions with her make me feel so upbeat, so positive about life, living its every moment to the fullest. When she suggested we meet, I didn't hesitate, even though it was a blind date. Of course, as an added bonus, you turned out to be so gorgeous. Are you also her client or something? You should take a couple of sessions with her. You are quite edgy. Just like me, you are suffering the tension caused by stress—'

'Did Dakini happen to tell you what I do?' I interrupted, resolving to murder Dakini for saddling me with this metrosexual mess.

He shook his head. 'She didn't, but, by the looks of it, I would guess you are in the fashion industry. A model, right?'

'No,' I answered, smiling as radiantly as I could, and leaning towards him, fluttering my mascaraed eyelashes, 'I am a tantrik. So all that negative energy you see inside me … I kind of thrive on it.'

He leant away for a second, surprised, and then burst out laughing, his even teeth gleaming in the candlelight. 'Oh! That is good. You almost had me. A tantrik? Yeah, right. I am sorry but you are too pretty to be a tantrik. Where are your dreadlocks? And where's your black dhoti and rudraksh beads?'

Kali's tail! Two years ago, and I swear on all the graves that I have dug, I would have turned him into a warty toad. But I had been in Delhi long enough. I had heard all the chauvinistic comments there were to hear, faced all the leers and, frankly, you just can't turn every human male you meet into a toad (much as you may want to), so I tried to take a deep breath instead. Beauty is a handicap to any tantrik, especially a detective tantrik and exponentially worse if she happens to be female. Although, to be fair, it wasn't really Nikhil's fault. Say 'tantrik' and most folk expect to see a tall, broad-shouldered, grumpy man, hairy and sweaty with dreadlocks, kohl smeared around his eyes – oh, and of course the classic rudraksh beads around the neck and a staff. The only thing I had in common with that image was that I liked to put on lots of kohl too. Never quite understood what the rudraksh beads do anyway.

This is why I rarely accepted cases from my own species and preferred to work with what humans call 'supernatural' creatures. Sups of any kind, be it mayans or pashus, don't judge tantriks by their appearance. They determine your worth by the shakti you wield. Most of my cases over the last few years had involved sups. Ever since word had spread in the city that a pro-sup tantrik was ready to take on their cases, which was a rarity since most tantriks wanted to either kill them or enslave them, I had got all kinds of assignments. I had arbitrated between best friend asuras who become arch nemeses and, in their attempt to finish each other off, almost destroyed a chunk of Lodhi Garden between them; saved a yakshi from a spirit; a chandaali from a greedy tantrik and a tantrik from a vengeful bhuta. I rarely refused a case. The only exceptions were the ones that involved daevas, elite heavenly spirits, who were as my teacher Dhuma put it concisely, treacherous trolls. A couple of days ago, I had turned down just such an offer. However, I was now beginning to regret it. Even dealing with a shifty daeva was better than sitting around a candle eating ducks and explaining myself to Mr SUV Headlights here. I took out my kapala, a skullcup that I used for my rituals, and placed it on the table.

'Perhaps this will convince you?' I said, smiling sweetly. The skull gleamed in the candlelight, throwing long dark shadows into the mirrors behind Nikhil.

'Wow, a skullcup! Is it a real human skull?' Nikhil inserted his hand inside its jaw and picked it up for a closer look. 'Where did you find this one? I saw one on eBay the other day. Nothing less than one lakh rupees. Only the imitations are cheaper. How much did you pay for it?'

Was nothing sacred anymore? I stared at him, shocked, and wondered how many seconds it would take for Lala to attack him. Lala was the old man whose skull Nikhil was molesting at the moment. Lala had begged me to ensure he didn't descend into naraka after his death. He wanted to stay on in this world even if it meant that I used his skull as a sacrificial cup. So, after his funeral, I stole his head from his grave on a full-moon night. Ever since, Lala's skull had been my kapala. And he hated anyone else touching it. How would you like it if someone poked inside your head? I dug out my boneblade, ready with a freezing mantra in case Lala fired up and became too hot for Nikhil to handle. (Although, frankly, a part of me was hoping Lala fired up.)

'Are you Anantya Tantrist?' asked a reedy voice behind me. I turned to see the headwaiter who had discussed wines with Nikhil a little while ago.

'Yeah,' I answered curtly. Nikhil plonked Lala back on the table.

'You have an urgent call, madam,' the waiter said. My old Nokia phone lay on the table. I switched on its screen. It seemed to be working. 'Who is it?' I asked, wondering if it was Dakini. No one else knew I had come to this restaurant. The waiter paused and looked to his right, as if he was listening to someone.

'Mister Qubera, madam. He wants to talk to you urgently, madam.' For someone who stood in an air-conditioned space, the waiter's face was very, very sweaty. Drops of perspiration rolled down his forehead and a droplet glistened at the tip of his chin.

'I don't know anyone ...' I stopped, suddenly realizing how quiet it had gone. So quiet that I could not hear the singer anymore or the tinkle of laughter. The singer was on the stage, but she had become mysteriously mute. The feeling that someone was watching us returned, and intensified painfully. I could kick myself for allowing Nikhil's stupidities to distract me. I ought to have sorted this out before now. The waiter stared at me, his eyes vacant and glassy. He pinched and pulled the skin on his neck, like a shirt collar. Stupid, stupid rakshasa. Someday he will get into big trouble and get himself killed. Probably by me.

'You have to come,' he urged, bending down and grabbing my right arm with his clammy palm, his hand cold and hard as stone. 'It's urgent!'

'What is the meaning of this?' Nikhil hollered, his face pink with anger. 'How dare you touch her? Where's your manager? I want to speak to him!'

'Sit down, Nikhil,' I said quietly, my hand reaching for the boneblade in my satchel. I was glad I had brought it along, although I had left my belted scabbard at home. Fashion can be lethal for a tantrik.

Nikhil pushed the table away with a loud screech and rose to his intimidating six feet. Not that that would save him from a disgruntled rakshasa. He lunged, grabbed the waiter roughly by the shoulder and bellowed, 'Let go of her!'

'Urgent,' the waiter whispered, sinking to his knees, his face still blank, his eyes empty, his left hand still frozen on my right arm. Poor guy. He didn't have a choice really. I turned in one swift movement and slashed the waiter's torso from his throat at the right collarbone to the solar plexus with the boneblade. Blood erupted and splattered my face and hair. A loud screech echoed somewhere behind me. *Aah*.

'Aaaaaaaaaa!' screamed the eloquent Nikhil, his hand dropping from the waiter's shoulder as he sprang back. The waiter slumped to the floor in a pool of blood.

'Nikhil…' I raised my palm towards him. Unfortunately, the hand I brought up was my left, with my boneblade pointed at him. 'Stay with me.'

'You stay away from me!' he screamed, his eyes as big as saucers, stepping backwards, away from our cubicle.

I just didn't have time for this. He shouldn't leave the bubble, not until I had completed my mantra. Springing up from the sofa, I leapt on the table and grabbed hold of Nikhil's gelled hair and yanked him back towards me.

'Don't hurt me! I have friends in high places!'

'You listen to me carefully now,' I whispered, bringing his ear close to my mouth. 'You have to stay close. If you make one move away from me, I will slash your neck and use your skull as a kapala.'

'You … you are a tantrik!' he screeched.

'Remember,' I replied soothingly, 'how just a minute ago you thought I was too gorgeous to be a tantrik? Why don't you stick with that thought, be a good boy and sit on the sofa for a minute? It will not …'

I felt a cold, hard hand on my butt. 'Nice dress, hottie,' mouthed the waiter, his face blank, the wound on his chest oozing blood, his pretty, white shirt drenched.

'Seriously?' I cried. 'Grrhat. Come. Out. *Now*. I am warning you. This has gone on long …'

I spun around just in time to see a fist zooming in my direction. Nikhil's punch landed in the middle of my stomach. Winded, I lost my balance and fell backwards, my blade flying. I landed on the cushioned seat with the skirt of my dress over my face, and the table between us collapsed with a loud crash.

'Help! Someone help me!' Nikhil cried.

'Stop being an *idiot*!' I furiously pulled the dress off my face. I felt like grabbing his neck and twisting it with my bare hands.

'Mmfh!' replied Nikhil. He stood rather weirdly, like he had suddenly decided to adopt a yoga pose, his hands stretched behind his back, his eyes bulging and his lips pressed together. There was raw terror in his eyes. *Great*.

'Hello, Grrhat. Nice to see you again,' I mouthed, getting up, straightening my dress, now sticky with blood. I ignored Nikhil's terrified expression and bent down to where the waiter lay slumped on the floor. I twisted one of the snakes' heads on my yugma. I wore it for more than just sentimental reasons. The locket had two snake-shaped vials which were really useful to keep the two essential items for any tantrik – something that heals wounds and an extra dose of shakti to use in mantras. For the first potion, I used rakpiss or a rakshasa's piss, which could heal any wound and neutralize most poisons. In the second, I kept rakta, the blood of a chandaali, which was like caffeinated shakti. A single drop could perform the most powerful magic.

I unscrewed the knob of the rakpiss vial with my mouth and carefully poured one drop onto the waiter's open wound. The waiter had been under a rakshasa-version of Vashi mantra so that my friend Grrhat could control his body and actions. So when I had cut the waiter's body, it was Grrhat who felt the pain. Tendrils of black smoke erupted as the wound absorbed the rakpiss. I let the waiter slump back to the floor, capped my vial carefully and turned around.

'Would you like to show yourself on the human plane, or are you too busy enjoying how Nikhil feels on your crotch?'

A muffled chuckle vibrated around us. The sound was grating, like a horse's chortle going through a sieve. I felt naked without my boneblade, which was under the now broken table. 'And thanks for ruining my date, by the way.'

'It's not like you were having any fun,' croaked a rough voice, coming from a skeletal dark face with hard, green eyes that was solidifying before me. Grrhat's face, like the rest of his body, was pure, adamantine bones. A big, all-black skeleton. Rakshasas are powerful, intelligent sups who can choose how to present themselves on the first plane, the plane which human eyes see, and don't need any maya potion for that. Grrhat always tried to look scary and ended up looking like a charred scarecrow. Like today.

'You were so slow catching on today that I almost decided *against* hiring you.'

'I already told you, Grrhat, I am just not interested in the case. Which part of my "no" didn't you understand?' I asked, turning to pick up my satchel from the sofa. I wished I had my blade with me. I so wanted to teach him a lesson.

'You might want to put that bag of yours away. The last thing you want is for lover boy here to scream and alert the locals.'

'I know you have put a kriti around us. Nobody around us will be able to hear or see anything you or I do.' A kriti was a rakshasa speciality, a bubble of solid air that could be built at will by the rakshasa and he could control all humans inside it. Sort of like a yantra, a closed circle. Grrhat loved to show off this particular trick because only a pureblood rakshasa could do it.

'Beautiful, isn't it? Gives us a little privacy.'

'Well, I would have liked to have more space,' I replied. 'This one is so *tiny*.'

The crooked grin fell off his face to be replaced by a black scowl. Rakshasas were sensitive about the size of their kriti (ring a bell?), and this bubble barely covered our cubicle and a few feet around it. Not big at all. I had met some purebloods who could build a private chamber for you in the middle of a bazaar.

'The game is over, tantrik,' he growled, pulling Nikhil closer to him, holding him in full body contact.

Nikhil looked like death had just pinched his butt. I could understand. A rakshasa's touch can be quite a shock the first time. For one, it's a whole different species. Not like humans are different from, say, frogs. It's a species made up of more than five elements. Evolved from another plane, alien perhaps. Therefore, physical contact with a rakshasa could feel like anything between a slight tingle through every nerve in your body to touching what you thought was water, but turned out to be a pool of electricity. Gut-wrenching. As I said, it's slightly different. (That's also the reason some humans become addicted to sex with a rakshasa. Nikhil, unfortunately, didn't seem kinky enough to enjoy it.)

'Look, I appreciate you chasing me all over the city with this assignment. It makes me feel special. But I am not interested.'

'This time, my little friend, I give you no choice,' he answered, placing his blackened claws around Nikhil's neck. Nikhil's eyes bulged. 'You agree to meet him, or your lover here gets it in the neck.'

'You wouldn't dare,' I replied, stiffening.

'Oh, I have more powerful friends than the *tants* now.' His misshapen teeth shone maliciously. 'They can cover up if a neech or two go missing.'

'Like I said, Grr ...' I tried using his nickname to soften him. 'Daevas are bad news. I don't want anything to do with them. If you had any sense, you would stay away too.' For a second, I thought he would let the boy go, but he tightened his grip instead.

'Just meet my boss once and we'll call it square.'

'Why are you so hell-bent on this? How much money has this daeva promised you?' I pressed my hand to a jagged edge of the broken table leg. Wet blood started to trickle into my palm. I fisted it.

'You think it's about the money?'

'You wouldn't save your dying mother if there was no money.'

'Fine. It is about the money. But there's other stuff too. Something's happening, Anantya. Something bad, and we need your help.'

'Hah. Something apocalyptic, I am sure. It is never less than that, is it?' My fist became wet as the scratch continued to bleed. The twinges of pain were too low to send any warning signals to my brain. I had done it too many times. 'It's amazing how often the world has been threatened and survived. I should find out where it keeps its survival guide ...' Without giving him time, I changed tracks.

'*Aim hreem* ...' I began.

'What are you ...'

I unfurled my fist, blood trickling off my palm and falling to the ground. *Madya. The offering. The wine made of blood.*

'... *bhuta aa! Kar de kreem! Tundeyah!*' Mantra. The invocation.

I pointed my bloodied left hand towards Grrhat, positioning the tips of my thumb and little finger at the base of the little finger. Mudra. The direction of the spell.

'Stop!' screamed Grrhat.

'DUCK!' I shouted to Nikhil, who took my advice for once and bent just in time. Black tendrils of flame burst forth from my fingertips, singeing my hand, straight into Grrhat's surprised face. On the sweet spot. Tunde, the spirit I had conjured, was a low-level bhuta, and not very powerful. Without my blade, this was the best I could manage. But it was enough for Grrhat. Tunde really hated rakshasas (a story I have to tell you sometime) and therefore made sure that whenever he was summoned, he went for overkill. My finger-lock released Tunde like a spray of smoky whips on Grrhat. The kriti that Grrhat had drawn around us would easily contain Tunde should he attempt to suck on the other humans in the restaurant.

'By the balls of Betaal!' screamed Grrhat.

If it were possible to read the expression of a black skeleton, I would say Grrhat was livid. He fell back, his grip on Nikhil loosening as the fiery whips of black spirit clawed his face and body.

'Never, ever, try to twist my arm, Grrhat,' I said, my hand still upturned as the inky scourges emanating from it curled around Grrhat's face. 'It reminds me of my father and I don't like that at all.'

'… was a joke!' he croaked.

I smiled for the first time that evening. The low-level spirit couldn't possibly kill a powerful sup like the rakshasa, but it had certainly wiped the smug smirk off Grrhat's face. It would irritate the hell out of him, like an ant in an elephant's trunk.

Nikhil, who had found his voice, made ample use of it, 'AAAAAAA!'

'Bhuta, bhuta!' the waiter shouted as he tugged at my foot.

My hand jerked and I lost control of Tunde, hitting Nikhil's shoulder. I quickly pressed my treta ring, and hauled Tunde's whip-like form back into my fingers, scorching my hand with his fury. With two humans around, this was too dangerous.

My playtime was done. Free from the bhuta, Grrhat grabbed Nikhil and began to disappear, taking the circle of kriti with him.

'Don't!' I shouted.

'If for nothing else, you will come for your lover. For directions,' said Grrhat, chucking a golden paper scrap in my direction. I caught it as he vanished, his grin the last to go. That's when I realized that my hand had begun to itch. The hand which held the paper. A sticky, yellow-brown residue oozed onto my hand. Yaksha poop. I tried to breathe. For those of you who don't know (and I am hoping you never get to know) what yaksha poop is, you lucky bastards! Tantriks know it as 'God's fart'. Fill a whole lake with human shit instead of water and you haven't even begun to describe the stench. It's hell's garbage but sweeter, in a bad way. It hits your nose like a pile of rotting corpses in a closed room. I mean, it physically hits you. There have been studies which claim that yaksha poop can be lethal to human beings. I threw the card on the floor and fell on all fours, my eyes stinging, my nose protesting, my mouth gagging. Thankfully, it had been just a little drop, to irritate me I was sure. The golden paper shone on the ground. I squinted to read through the fog on my senses.

Lord Qubera
Lord of Men (LoM), Lord of Yakshas (LoY) and Regent of the North (RotN)
Qubera Enterprises
Max Mueller Road, Lodhi Gardens, New Delhi
In the business of financial reconstruction plans and windfall gains since eternity

An assortment of noises rose around me – gasps of horror and disgust – as the smell infiltrated their sensibilities. There were a few screams, some retching, but I didn't stick around to hear it all. The restaurant probably wasn't going to do any business for a long, long time. I fished out my boneblade from under the sofa, stuffed it into my satchel along with my stiletto heels and straightened my now destroyed dress. Barefoot and breathing rapidly through the mouth, I walked out into the scorching night.

२

'You realize she's a female?' asked Lord Qubera, his long golden eyelashes fluttering on his fleshy cheeks as he blinked.

I cringed, wishing I had sunglasses. As with the eyelashes, the rest of Qubera's bulk was covered in gold bling. Rings, medallions, necklaces, bracelets, you name it, he was wearing it. Really, he looked like a walking, talking pawnshop. Even the wave-like pattern etched on his chest, which was part of the binding ritual that let the daeva's spirit inhabit the fat human body, was tattooed in gold.

'She's the best, O Rider of Men,' answered Grrhat, who stood before Qubera with his back towards me.

He bowed deliberately so that his tight butt almost touched my nose. He had changed into his favoured guise, a black muscular body and a regal silver-embroidered coat. I would have been aroused if I did not have other things on my mind. For one, my hands were tied behind my back with mayan rope to ensure I couldn't mumble a mantra. Then, I was still dressed in the tatters of what used to be a beautiful dress and, of course, my body smelt of yaksha poop. And, believe me, I could have ignored all those things but for the fact that I was in what could only be termed a humongous jewellery box.

Qubera's office had turned out to be a swanky newly constructed building behind Lodhi Gardens. But even the gold frills on all the windows and doors of the building couldn't have prepared me for what the yaksha warriors, who escorted me in, called the 'Grand Hall' – a monstrosity of hundreds of richly engraved golden pillars, in the centre of which was a pond. I wasn't sure if the hall was underground or on one of the upper floors of the building because I hadn't been able to sense the direction in which the elevator had gone, but about this there was no doubt: it was glaring gaudiness of gigantic proportions. We sat on a jewel-encrusted raft gently floating in the pool. Opulently dressed yakshas and yakshis – palm-sized forest creatures – fluttered all around, some singing, some dusting, some spraying perfume.

'But ... but, she has breasts and a fertility hole. She is a mere mode of pleasure for man, a womb for his seed. How can she help us?'

'Times have changed, O King of Kings. Let me assure you, she is better than most of the other neechs.'

'You mean there aren't any real tantriks out there anymore?'

'There are, Lord of all Riches. The Central Association of Tantriks can supply as many tantriks as you require, but none of them are as apt as her for this case, my lord. She may be a female in body, but in her mind, she's an alpha male. If anyone can do this for us, she can.'

'To hire a she-tantrik? Inconceivable! What is the universe coming to? We—'

'Mister Qubera,' I interrupted, furious, 'it's not as if I came here crawling on my knees to serve you. I have just about had enough of your bitching ...'

My voice echoed in the large hall. Yakshas and yakshis, green, red and brown, who had been flying silently about their business, stopped in mid-air, all eyes on me, ready to rip out my throat at a single signal from their lord. But I didn't really care. The last thing I wanted was to stand here and explain why I did what I did to this massive flesh of ostentation.

'Why, we nev—' began Qubera.

'I am more than happy to lea—'

'*Ahahaha … aajajajajajaja … aaaa … aha …*'

I shook my hair, trying to rid myself of the yakshi who had planted herself in it, whispering tuneless songs into my right ear. She tumbled in front of me, bright pink in colour, wearing a blue miniskirt and lots of jewellery.

'Stop buzzing around me like that!' I snapped.

'Does thy beautiness want me to pause my song?' she asked, her eyes very wide.

'No, I want you to stop!'

'Then just say so,' she pouted and scrambled to her feet, muttering something that sounded like 'hoity-toity' or 'horrible smell' and retreated. A purple yaksha in a dhoti hovered on my left, armed with a perfume bottle, ready to spray rose water on my face.

'Don't you dare even try,' I said furiously. 'I have smelt enough of you today and am just about ready to kill a few.'

'But you smell of poop,' he answered, wrinkling his tiny nose, conveniently forgetting that the poop was yaksha poop. For a second I thought I would get another faceful of rose-scented squirt, but miraculously he seemed to read my expression and retreated. I turned to look at Qubera.

'Look, I have no wish to stay. I will be more than happy to leave as soon as you release him.' I jerked my head in Nikhil's direction. He stood in the middle of the pond, his body encased in liquid gold and frozen, an expression of mild surprise on his face. Lotuses floated around his statue and alongside our exquisite raft.

'Hmmm...' Qubera nodded, his multiple chins rippling slowly. 'She-tantrik, we have decided to give you a chance. After all, the world is moving on and we must move with the times. You shall be happy to know that we have decided to hire you.'

'Not like I have a huge choice,' I muttered under my breath.

Grrhat quickly bent forward to light Qubera's hookah (also bejewelled), which was held under him by two yakshas, and whispered something in his ear. He took a long drag and stared at me through the smoke.

'Do you know who we are, girl?' asked Qubera, taking another drag from his hookah. I looked at him in stubborn silence. 'Reply, female! Why don't you answer?'

'My name is Anantya,' I said, 'not girl or female.'

'Wha ... you ... you dare...' Qubera's Adam's apple jumped up and down in fury. A fat finger, attached to a fat arm, rose, flashing gold bracelets, and pointed at me in silent fat fury.

'Lord of Rubies, please...' Grrhat pushed a glass of wine below Qubera's quivering chins and spoke in the formal, older dialect. 'Your body's health is of utmost importance. You know we need to find it as soon as possible. If we don't work with her, we will have to go to ... the others. Would you want to do that, Lord of Vast Treasures of Mountains?'

Qubera turned to look at Grrhat and then shook his head, taking a long gulp of his wine. I wondered who the others were that were making Qubera so uncomfortable.

'You are right, Grrhat. Anger doesn't become us. Tell her who we are,' he commanded.

'Yes, my lord.' Grrhat straightened up and indicated Qubera with his long, black hand. 'This is King of all Kings that were, are and will be, Master of the Northern Winds. Caretaker of the Vaults of Gods and Men alike. You are standing in the presence of his Highness, his Respectfulness—'

'I know who he is,' I cut in, irritated. 'He's Lord Qubera. God of Wealth, one of the Diggpalas, Ravana's uncle ... Daeva of Treasure ... yada yada yada.'

'Told you she's smart,' Grrhat muttered, looking down at his black nails.

Plop. A mongoose, which sat cross-legged on the divan beside Qubera, spat out an egg-sized ruby. Qubera smiled, pleased. The flattery had hit the sweet spot. All spirits, be it the so-called 'good' daevas or the 'evil' danavas, basked in compliments. It doesn't really matter that you don't mean any of it. If you mutter compliments, they will be ready to give you a boon to destroy the world.

'Girl,' started Qubera, and then reconsidered. 'Anantya, we mean. We have called upon you for a task of utmost importance. As you know we are the caretaker of the treasury of daevas, asuras as well as manavas. Upon our shoulders lies the tiresome responsibility of making sure that the priceless things that the Lords of the Heavens have amassed over the centuries stay safe and secure, and out of the hands of evil-doers. There are secrets that we know. Secrets that belong to Earth's heart. Secrets that must not be spoken of. What we are going to tell you today is quite confidential and we want you to give us your word that you will not breathe a syllable of it outside of these four walls ...'

Qubera's arm moved hypnotically, ornaments jingling and a curtain of liquid gold rose all around us. Suddenly, we were not in the middle of a pond, but in a small lamplit room, its golden walls shimmering and casting glittering shadows on the three of us. There were no yakshis and yakshas here and Nikhil's statue was out of sight as well. Qubera sucked on his hookah, his golden eyes glazing over and turning red as he exhaled sweet-smelling purple smoke. Then his voice changed and became deeper, as if coming from a deep hole. (I must hand it to him for the cool special effects.)

'… a millennia ago, there was a time when the universe was threatened by the darkness of Vritra, a demonic force viler than anything that had ever been created. He was born burning and hungry. In his fury, he consumed the worlds, one at a time, gorging until all creations of the gods started to uncreate themselves. Solar systems splintered and spread, running thin into the vast space, earths drowned in the seas of emptiness. Stars extinguished and became dark and silent. Everything was being consumed in Vritra's black fury. The cosmic thread of the universe frayed. Humans and trees and rakshasas and asuras and daityas, all species prayed to the gods to save them. This prayer was heard by Indra, the King of gods, Bearer of the Thunderbolt, the only one strong enough to rise up against the tyranny of this danava. Lord Indra hurled his thunderbolt on Vritra, the Demon of Darkness, who disintegrated. The rishis, who witnessed the battle, cried out that he would become whole again unless he was dismembered and trapped in different hells. The universe had to be saved …'

'I thought this was an emergency,' I whispered to Grrhat, as Qubera continued as one in a trance, his hands raised. 'Why isn't he coming to the point?'

'He's an eternal, Anantya,' Grrhat whispered back. 'Be quiet and listen. It's important that you know.'

'… and so Indra tore the danava's flesh and trapped his powers into a Net of Light, locking it in with the Key of Light.

This Key, he announced, can unlock the darkness of Vritra. The suns, the moons and the stars were to be the bars of this prison. As Vritra's influence in the universe diminished, the stars started to sparkle again, life breathed and cheered. The whole world was flushed with radiant light. Daevas, gandharvas, apsaras, men, rakshasas, asuras all came together to sing our Lord Indra's praises.'

Qubera stopped, looking at us, his eyes pinpoints of golden red.

'Uin!' Grrhat gasped and covered his mouth with his hand. Qubera smiled smugly.

'Bloody black booty-kisser,' I muttered under my breath.

'This delicately woven cloak of pure light,' Qubera continued, 'still protects us all from Vritra's power. When the Key had turned and the powers of Vritra locked away, Lord Indra came unto Lord Qubera, King of Men, and gave him the Key that opens this prison of light. The Key to the dark powers of Vritra himself. Since then, for millions of years now, Indra's Key of Light has been safely residing in our vaults.'

He finished with a triumphant flurry, hitting a wine glass and spilling its contents on the divan. I looked at both of them and shook my head. I wished my hands were untied so that I could hit at least one of them, daeva or not.

'I still don't know what I am supposed to do,' I said after it became obvious that there was nothing more forthcoming.

'Oh, yes. That,' said Qubera dreamily. 'As we mentioned, Indra's Key has been residing in our vaults since that time. Until a week ago, that is.'

'So, am I supposed to find out who stole it from your safe and bring it back?'

'We already know who took it,' answered Grrhat, taking

out his mobile phone and showing me a photo of a young woman with sharp features. 'The Lord's vault has surveillance cameras. The lady who took it is one Lavanya Mohan. She's a known dealer of antiques, especially those with a magical history. Most of the Delhi mayan industry knows of her.'

'How did she break in and steal the Key? Aren't the vaults of Qubera unbreachable?'

'You are right, there,' answered Grrhat. 'They are safe from all three types of break-ins – physical force, magical trickery and emotional attack. She could enter because,' Grrhat hesitated and looked at Qubera, who nodded encouragingly, 'she didn't break in. She just walked in. She had the right combinations for entering the vault. She simply entered, took the Key and walked out.'

I shrugged, which sent a tingle through my hands which were numb from being tied. 'If she didn't steal it and knew how to enter, someone must have given it to her.'

'That's not possible. From what I've heard, only Lord Indra and Lord Qubera knew the exact combination to the vault.'

'Maybe Indra's in town?'

'Impossible,' squeaked Qubera, a little too vehemently. He took several furious drags of his hookah.

I squinted at him, trying to figure out what he was not telling me.

'If Lord of All Gods was in town, Lord of Men would know about it,' answered Grrhat. 'He's still in the heavens, reigning from his throne in Amravati. We don't know how she got access to the vault, all we know is that she now has the Key in her possession. The Key has immense powers in the right hands. If Lord Indra hasn't sanctioned this, which could be a possibility, we are afraid that the very existence of this world has been jeopardized.'

'Why not ask Indra? You can ask the daeva even if he's in Amravati. All you need is a simple tantrik ritual to connect with him.'

Grrhat shook his head. 'You see, Anantya, that would be like shooting yourself in the foot. Lord Qubera cannot ask Lord Indra if the person who entered the vault was an envoy of his Highness. It could give the impression that Lord Qubera was, how do I put it, unduly interested in Lord Indra's vaults?'

I sighed. Bloody daevas and their complex lives. 'So you don't want me to find Indra's Key and bring it back to you?'

Qubera shook his head vigorously, jowls shaking.

Grrhat answered for him. 'It does not belong to us. We are not owners, merely caretakers. We just want to be sure that it is not abused in any way, that's all. We want you to find out to whom this lady gives the Key.'

This wasn't getting us anywhere. 'Okay. You already know the woman, you know where she works. Then why not go to her house, ring her bell and ask her politely what she plans to do with the Key? You have an army of minions at your disposal for this. Why a poor detective like me?'

'We … can't. That is simply not possible.'

'Then I will ask her for you guys.'

'No!' Grrhat exclaimed emphatically. For just a second I saw panic in his black eyes. 'That you simply cannot. You are to stay *away* from the lady at all costs. All we want you to do is follow her, from a safe distance. Find out who she meets and deals with. Our sources say that the exchange will happen tonight or tomorrow night. You need to follow her for two days and just report back to us with the names of those she speaks to. We need you to be discreet in this.'

I looked from one to the other. It sounded like a mundane task, one that any of the gazillions of airborne yakshas could easily do. Then why had they gone to such lengths to choose me? Kidnapping a human to blackmail me sounded a bit heavy-handed for a simple task like this. Grrhat suddenly found his nails fascinating, conscious that my eyes were boring into his face. There was more to this than met the eye, so I decided to play along. Curiosity. Someday it will get me killed.

'Fine,' I said, 'but only if you release Nikhil.'

'We will let your lover go as soon as you complete this task,' answered Qubera. 'We will also reward you handsomely.'

'Your lover is a guarantee that you will not speak of us to anyone,' Grrhat said.

'What? You don't trust me, Grr? I thought we went way back. Don't worry, he's not my lover. Yet.'

The curtain of gold vanished in a puff of gilded smoke. We were back in the hall with Nikhil's liquid gold statue in front of me. Grrhat ignored me and signalled to a yakshi. I was sprayed with something extremely fragrant that made me sneeze. Perfume. I turned around in fury. The yaksha, the same purple guy who had the perfume bottle earlier, was standing with a group of yakshis and giggling.

'Keep away from me!' I growled. They giggled some more.

'Here,' said Grrhat, handing me a cream-coloured envelope, 'this is an invite to a party tomorrow night. She will be there. You tail her and tell us who all she talks to.'

Suddenly I was free. Before I could even clench my hands to restore circulation, he signalled to a group of warrior yakshas who flew to me and hoisted me up unceremoniously. They zoomed to the end of the hall, with me spread-eagled awkwardly between them, and threw me in the lift.

'Wha—'

'Bye, Anantya. I hope you solve this quickly for the sake of your lover.'

I was still sprawled on the elevator floor, when the doors slid open again. A girl in a gold miniskirt, whom I had met on my way in, eyed my greyed underwear and then turned away, pretending she had seen nothing. I picked myself up and hobbled to the exit. The sky was streaked with the rosy blush of dawn. My stomach growled tiredly. I realized that I hadn't had that duck meal Nikhil had recommended.

'He's not my bloody lover,' I muttered, walking out.

My phone showed two missed calls from Madhu, my pal who worked in the Special Crimes Division of the Central Bureau of Investigation. My first case had happened by chance when he came to me for help with a mysterious poison that baffled his unit. That was when I realized that I enjoyed solving problems. More importantly, the cases kept me from killing myself or those around me. A good idea, generally speaking. I had worked on many other cases for him since then and none of them had been easy. Any other day, I would have grabbed his call at the first ring. Today, I sighed. Some nights just don't end, not even when the next day dawns.

3

'Khol khal tod phod samapta shakti banke jod.'

I whispered the mantra and blew the white powder at the pyramid. For a moment it hung suspended in the sunlight, morphing from chaos to skull to dog to boat to turtle to girl. It reached the glistening black surface of the pyramid and spread, feeling its way tentatively. It stilled and turned snow white, a bright glittering ring around the structure. I held my breath. Without warning, the powder recoiled, as if on a spring, changed into a hail of icicles and flew straight for my face. I spun around as the shards hit my nape and back.

'Balls of bulls.'

The huge black pyramid glistened in the morning light, its smooth surface impenetrable. It was breathtakingly beautiful, a perfect triangular cone of black diamond. No, it wasn't diamond, I corrected myself, squinting in the sunlight as I walked around it. It looked more like black velvet, plush and evenly spread. As I watched, the texture changed again turning into silk, a black hole ominous and dark, a ball of fur, an ink splash, murky black glass with screaming ghosts inside. The texture changed constantly, as tantalizing as it was confusing. Unbelievably, this exotic, exquisite edifice was situated on a dilapidated terrace, strewn with cable antennas, broken furniture and other decaying rubbish and surrounded by equally shabby terraces all around.

'Ngggh-nghh,' cried the constable who was being carefully wrapped in a blanket by two hospital attendants behind me. His head lolled as gooey, yellow slime trickled from his mouth on to his khaki shirt.

'Don't touch him,' whispered one of the ambulance attendants to the other furiously. 'Can't you see he's cursed!'

Large ravens circled above us, cawing out loud in anticipation. The pyramid couldn't have chosen a worse place to pop up. There was no way to stop wild rumours from spreading like mayan fire here, bang in the middle of the busy neighbourhood of Kotla Mubarakpur. Late last night, while I was powwowing with the goldie god as he puffed on his diamond-studded hookah, someone had called the local police station about the pyramid. The police sent a night constable who had been discovered later, shaking uncontrollably, his body brimming with electric current. The attendants eyed me suspiciously as they bore the constable away. I could wager half my wealth that, before the day was out, the curse theory would be all over the city. There were already a couple of camera crews from the local news channels panning in our direction. I rubbed my nose with the edge of my blade.

'So when are you going to tell me?' asked Madhu Tripathi, flicking the remnants of what looked like glass shards from his dirty brown shirt. He was a stocky, barrel-chested half-human, his head planted squarely on his trunk, like a neatly packed box of cartridges. Bushy whiskers and eyebrows completed his bulldog look. A bald pate was the only bit of him not covered with hair.

'Tell you what?'

'Why you are dressed in ... umm ... almost nothing?' he asked, one bushy eyebrow rising high.

'Long story,' I replied curtly.

'And the smell?' he insisted.

'God's fart.'

It was easier to give him an answer because not doing so would only lead to a barrage of questions. Madhu had joined the CBI as a starry-eyed junior about fifteen years ago and had been moved from desk to desk until he arrived at the dusty desk of Special Crimes. It was the most unpopular, underpaid and uncared-for department in the CBI because no one really knew what Special Crimes did. For Madhu, it was just the opportunity he had been waiting for. He specialized in cases no one could make head or tail of; cloak-and-dagger operations that never had a straight explanation, happenings that involved sups, or disasters by tantriks and charlatans, boring stakeouts, unsolvable crimes, murders where there were no bodies. He managed to solve most of them.

'May I ask how?' His eyes, hawk-like beneath bushy eyebrows.

'No.'

'I … see. And have you figured out what this thing is?' He picked up a shard with his fingers.

'Trouble.'

'Am I going to get only one-word answers out of you? Remind me again why I am paying you.'

'You aren't.'

I walked around the pyramid, careful not to touch its wall, tapping the tip of my blade on my nose. The Sifter, the white powder I had blown in the direction of the pyramid, was a naga-made concoction. When sprinkled on an object with a concentration of shakti, it changed colour. The darker the powder became, the more shakti the object had. It was a popular concoction sold in the night bazaars of old Delhi, especially to people seeking curios. In my rambles through these alleyways, I've had several opportunities to use it and even discovered a couple of items in the antique market which had made it go from white to pitch black. But I had never come across an object that had changed the powder's structural composition. Changing matter, as any charlatan who has tried to convert lead to gold knows, takes a humongous amount of shakti from the atmosphere. Most tantriks couldn't do it. The pyramid glimmered, now a wall of black oil.

What was it?

'It's definitely not solid,' said Madhu from behind me, as if he could hear my thoughts. 'I shot a bullet through the wall and it was kind of ... well, absorbed.'

'Absorbed? And when you touched it?'

'It felt like liquid rubber and gave me a tingle, an electric shock of sorts. Though it did much worse to the constable. I wonder why.'

'Because you have skin that's resistant to magic,' I began. For someone who had magical blood in his arteries, Madhu was surprisingly unaware of the basic aspects of his lineage. 'The skin of a raksh—'

He clutched my arm and whispered furiously, 'Don't use the r-word here.'

Surprised, I turned to see two policemen behind us who suddenly appeared intensely focused on the sky above. Madhu was deeply uncomfortable about the fact that he was half-human and half-rakshasa. His father, a direct descendant of a royal clan of rakshasas, was so proud of his lineage that he named Madhu after a rakshasa king of ancient times who had died valiantly in battle with fake-god (according to rakshasa myth) Brahma. Madhu, however, opted to keep a lid on his ancestry, preferring to live a normal life in the human world. His decision to work with the CBI in Delhi made him persona non grata in his extended family circles. Which reminded me.

'By the way, I was with that brainless uncle of yours. Grrhat.'

'Grrhat? Where? Is he in trouble again?'

'Well, I am not sure yet. I should know soon,' I replied, slipping my septifocals over my eyes. Even the little shakti I needed to put into my vision goggles exhausted me. I desperately needed a caffeine fix to buzz me up. I pricked the tip of my right index finger with my boneblade. A drop of blood oozed out. Blood is the cocaine of mantras. It gives them a lot of zing. I sipped my blood, focused on my spine and muttered the Drishti mantra. The septifocals changed colour, washing the world in a haze of indigo. The pyramid looked the same on all six planes, black. I double-checked, just to be sure. The only supernatural activity I saw was on the red Muladhara plane. Small figures peppered the rooftops around us, although none were anywhere near the pyramid. That was not unusual, since many supernaturals lived in the city, disguised as humans. The pyramid, however, was not made of any spirit or bhuta or supernatural being.

'What in Bhairava's name are you?' I whispered.

The black wall gleamed in response, changing from velvet to liquid charcoal and then putrid gas. For a second it turned translucent grey, sunlight shining through it as if it were a glasshouse. That's when I saw it.

'Corpse of owls. There's someone inside.'

'What?'

'I am going in.'

I pulled out a vial of kataka and took a sip. Kataka worked like the rakshasas' kriti, and created a defensive shield around one's body so that one is immune to attacks by mantras and magical voodoos. It was a rare potion and not widely known. Thankfully, I lived with a naga who knew all kinds of crazy potions, although some of them were a pain in the ass to swallow or digest. As I uttered the protection mantra, my tongue grew heavy.

'Ugh!' My eyes bulged as the drop got to work in my system. Veins popped from my neck. My skin turned blue. Scorpion bites screamed all over my skin. A minute later, I was ready, wishing some of these potions could be made sweet like homeopathic sugar pills. 'Wait … here,' I managed, handing the vial to Madhu in case he decided not to obey me. I tottered and fell towards the wall. Before he could react or protest, I entered…

…dark, so dark. No light, so dark that even darkness becomes light. It's still inside, like a mother's womb, so quiet, so silent. My finger and arm were on fire. Black fire, paining, burning, creating, uncreating, cooling, freezing the blood. Can't take it. So much pain, so much suffering, at the edge of madness, at the knife-edge of darkness. Pull away, go back. Not now, not…

…someone pushed me forward. I fell on the floor inside the dark pyramid, shivering, my hands on the floor. The effects of the potion started to subside slowly.

'Are you—' Madhu, who had followed me inside, stopped and looked up. 'What in Bali's name is this?' he exclaimed in raksha, the ancient rakshasa language.

I had never heard him use it before, but modern language had no words for what we were seeing. The inside of the pyramid was still and quiet, like a cemetery at night. We were witnesses to a frozen tableau, which involved two shrunken bodies. One of them was an adult male human in his forties in a black dhoti with a solid, red triangular mark on his forehead. He was bent down towards a small naked girl, who lay spread-eagled with her legs wide apart. The man held the hilt of a blade plunged deep inside the girl's chest. His expression was that of a person in the throes of passion. His mouth was open, his eyes wide with excitement. The girl, who must have been about nine years old, had an expression of horror etched on her face, her eyeballs bulging. Her naked skin had sprung away from the incision like a curtain as the blade had moved from her womb to her chest, where it gleamed now. They looked like wax models, complete with lifelike expressions of horror and ecstasy.

Thump. I sat down heavily on the floor, holding my head as visions of a past thundered inside. Red and black. Black and red. *Anantya, you are a gift to humankind, to tantriks. You are a pure being of shakti. Your shakti flows from your pure virgin vessel. You thrum with power. Anything you touch can become pure. You are shakti herself. You are the desire of all men. You are my desire, my power, my shakti, my goddess, my everything. I ... I want you, I crave you and your shakti.*

'... ntya? Are you okay?' Madhu touched my shoulder gently.

I blinked rapidly and realized my eyes were wet.

'Huh, yeah. Just the after-effects of the potion,' I said, my throat heavy. My hands felt tainted and impure as if I had been the one who had cleaved the little girl.

'I don't suffer any such after-effects,' he pointed out.

'That's because you are half-rak—' I began hoarsely, but he held up a palm. Madhu was born with a natural kriti around his body. It wasn't perfect, because he was a mixed-blood rakshasa, but his natural immune system was a lot stronger than mine. Both physically and emotionally.

'Do you want to leave?'

I shook my head. No, I wanted to find out who this bastard was, and then give him his due. I wanted to bring him back from whichever plane he was in, alive, dead or a spirit, and punish him for what he had done to the girl. I knew I could find him. A black anger rose inside me; I spurred it on.

'What are those spots in the air?' asked Madhu, pointing at the beads of black frozen above the girl's body, as if whoever had drunk from it had done it so swiftly that even gravity could not claim it.

'It's her blood,' I said, swallowing the lump that had formed in my throat. 'It spurted out and splashed when she was sacrificed.'

'Splashed? And then the blood froze?'

I nodded. 'She was hacked for her shakti, Madhu. Like a log of wood to feed a fire. A harvest – food – for whatever was being brought in.'

The signs of an elaborate sacrifice were all there. The kumkum on her forehead, her legs spread in the direction of the pinnacle of the triangle, the blood that had flowed from her to the pinnacle and spread around, becoming part of the triangular yantra.

I bent down at the edge of the triangle for a closer look at the residue – ash or 'diamond dust' was the term that tantriks used for it. It shone. This was the source of the pyramid wall. Something horrendous had visited the closed triangle a few hours ago. Something that had created the pyramid, drained all the life energy from both those humans, and then escaped.

'But didn't the Central Association of Tantriks announce it was illegal? Human sacrifice, I mean?'

'When has something being illegal ever stopped anything

from happening in this country? Anyway, sacrificing a human is the work of Black tantriks. If you have turned Black, you don't follow laws made by anyone but your guru,' I said, using my blade to clear a line in the diamond dust of the triangle. 'A Black tantrik will sacrifice anything for his goal, anything at all.' With a small clink, the pyramid walls fell away, like a pack of cards. With them fell the droplets of blood that had been suspended in mid-air, gravity kicking in. I squinted. People standing on the neighbouring roof terraces shouted, pointing towards us. Thankfully, the walls of the terrace were high, so no one could actually see the corpses in their dreadful dance of death. Not yet anyway.

'How did you do that?' Madhu asked, shielding his eyes from the hot July sun.

'The wall was just an after-effect of whatever the thing was the Black tantrik had summoned in the night. Maybe the experiment failed and the spirit he had conjured up attacked him and drank him dry as well.'

'And the spirit escaped?'

'Yeah, hopefully it fell back into whatever hell it had sprung from,' I answered, getting up and dusting my hands. 'Sacrifice of a female who hasn't reached puberty is one of the strongest tantrik rituals. The Black tantrik here was aiming high. For a higher spirit I mean, like a daeva or danava.'

'But he's dead! He wouldn't kill himself if he wanted to possess a powerful spirit, would he?'

'He was probably a newbie who tried to do Black magic which he couldn't control or understand. It's not that uncommon. They learn the tantrik art for a year or so, and all of them aim for the star spirits ... the daevas and the danavas. No one wants to experiment with the less powerful bhutas. And, before they know it, they are eaten by the spirit they call. However…' I surveyed the scene. The clean cut on the girl's body, the blood trickling into the pinnacle of the triangle, the blade that looked like a glowing light in the middle of the girl's chest. It was disturbing, this ritual. It was clean, too clean, too perfect. It didn't seem like someone had made a mess of things.

'This doesn't look like it failed, does it?' observed Madhu with his disconcerting habit of reading my thoughts.

'Let's hope we are wrong,' I answered.

'Maybe it failed because of this cellphone,' Madhu said, picking up a small phone with a contraption on its side that lay at the pinnacle of the triangle.

'That's odd,' I said. Even if the tantrik loved his mobile phone (and who doesn't nowadays), to have it inside the yantra was surprising. Tantrik rituals are usually dictated by strict rules. Deviate even one tiny little bit and the whole ritual could go drastically wrong.

'It seems to be in working condition too. I will take it to forensics and see what they say,' said Madhu, putting it into a plastic bag.

I walked around the dead bodies, glad I hadn't eaten anything for a while as my stomach clenched in revolt. I felt like kicking the head off the man's body. I took a deep breath to calm myself. His body had started to shrink as the sun stole the moisture from it. His chest, facing the girl, had something tattooed on it. I crouched on all fours to look up at his chest to see the sign. It was a fresh tattoo, the skin still peeling, of what looked like a snake. No wait, a cobra, a three-headed cobra, its red eyes gleaming. This close, the man looked like he had attained nirvana. His eyes were still alive, alight, glittering gold in the sunlight, as if whatever he had experienced last night was still there. Mirroring them was the edge of the blade, still plunged into the girl's heart.

'Hey, come here,' shouted Madhu excitedly.

I got up, careful to avoid both bodies and walked towards him. Madhu had found a backpack and was rooting through it. Old clothes, a velvet bag, broken sachets of kumkum, haldi, copper, silver and gold lay inside along with something that looked like powdered dried bones, hair of an animal, a human thigh bone, condoms, lubricants and herbs. And finally a wallet. Madhu rifled through it as I picked up the black velvet bag, warm and soft to touch. It had a beautiful crest embroidered on it, that of two intertwined roses. I opened it carefully, each flap was shaped like a petal. Inside was the impression of a sickle. I crouched by the bodies and gently pried the hilt loose from the dead man's grasp. Although the blade was embedded deep inside the girl's body, it slid out easily as if it was merely lying in melting butter. The blade was clean, bloodless. The main motif on its ivory handle was that of two intertwined roses, the same as the design on the velvet sheath. In my hand, which was still slightly singed from when I had summoned the bhuta on Grrhat, the sickle strummed with shakti and quivered. I tightened my grip on it and turned to look at Madhu, who was on his haunches and looking through the wallet, his back to me. *Blood, I need more blood. Much more than a drop. Kill, kill!* The blade clattered to the floor. Madhu looked over his shoulder at me, his eyebrows knitted together in a frown.

'What?'

I shook my head, picked up the blade using the velvet sheath, making sure I didn't touch it. This was definitely not a basic blade. It seemed to have been designed for ritualistic sacrifice, a blade that demanded blood sacrifice from its owner. An ancient, powerful weapon.

'Our man here is a Vikram Sharma,' said Madhu, fishing

out a driving licence, 'forty-six years old and lives, or rather used to live, in Gurgaon. So he drove all the way here, twenty kilometres. Why? He could have found a place in Gurgaon to do this ritual. Why here?'

'So that no one would recognize him?' I answered, coming towards him and showing him the blade. 'Don't touch it,' I said as Madhu's fingers reached for the blade. 'It might be cursed. Let me play with it for a day or two before you hand it over to forensics.'

We stared at each other silently for a moment. Madhu threw a quick glance at the constables behind us and then nodded. 'One night only,' he said as I slipped the sheath with the sickle blade into my satchel. 'Let's go pay his home a visit.'

Madhu called his forensics team, instructed them to take over and collect evidence as well as the bodies. He asked the police inspector posted outside to check for any recently filed reports of a missing girl. Then he instructed the inspector and his two constables to keep mum about the case.

'You sure you want to come along?' he asked when he had finished.

'Wouldn't miss it for the world.'

He smiled. 'Which is why I called you here in the morning.'

I nodded, feeling a faint twinge of guilt at the thought of Nikhil, now a feature in molten gold in Qubera's Grand Hall. Well, I couldn't do anything about it until the party tonight. Might as well help Madhu with this case. The sun was high in the sky, hot and relentless. I wiped the sweat off my brow, kick-started my bike with Madhu sitting pillion and zoomed through the trail of curious bystanders.

When Madhu told Gayatri Sharma that her husband's dead body had been discovered on the terrace of a house in Kotla, her reaction was a weird grin.

'Would you like some tea?' she asked after staring at Madhu for two long uncomfortable minutes of silence, her legs slightly apart, in a flimsy, floral nightie. She scratched her head, and stray strands worked loose from an untidy bun on top of her head. Madhu nodded his assent, more to escape her basilisk stare than any real need for tea. Gayatri's rabbit slippers made squelchy wet sounds on the tiled floor as she led us in. The Sharma home was an apartment on the fifth floor of a posh building in Gurgaon. It looked like it hadn't been cleaned in a while. The curtains were drawn shut haphazardly, the living room was stuffy and dusty. It was quiet, a little too quiet. And hot.

Madhu wiped his bald pate with a handkerchief and whispered, 'Why do I get the feeling something's wrong with her?'

'Maybe it's the shock. Or maybe it's an uncontrollable attraction to you.'

Gayatri re-entered, delivering me from Madhu's beetle-browed glare. The tray slammed on the low table, slopping half the watery tea onto it. She wiped the sweat off her face.

'He was upset, I know,' she said in a voice that was surprisingly deep for someone so small. 'Ever since, you know, ever since I tried to jump off the balcony.' She said it in a matter-of-fact way as she scratched her head.

I noticed that her nails were long with crusted, black dirt beneath. She sat herself down in a rocking chair opposite us and started to rock. The squeaking from the chair echoed in the silent room. Sweat dripped down her skin, leaving oily yellow patches on her arms. She continued to stare at Madhu as he picked up a cup and took a sip, and nearly gagged.

'Ni … nice tea,' he said, replacing the cup on the spindly table and wiping his mouth with the back of his hand. She grinned, her lips stretching almost to the ends of her small face. *Squeak, squeak.*

'Mrs Sharma,' tried Madhu, 'I am really sorry about your loss, but we need some answers to what really happened. When did he leave the house?'

'Night. He left in the night with her.'

'Who her? The girl?' I asked. She ignored me, continuing to rock on the chair, faster. *Squeak, squeak.*

'Would you know who the girl with him was?'

'She was not with her, so he took her, and then he was gone,' she said in a tuneless, singsong tone, the rocking chair moving faster and faster. 'It is a staaaart! Heeeeeee issssssssss comiiiiing!' *Squeak, squeak, squeak.* Faster, faster, faster.

'Ma'am!'

Gayatri began to hiccup and wheeze like she was having trouble breathing, her body rocking back and forth on the chair. She pointed to Madhu. 'Aaaaaaaaaaaaai liike yooo!'

Before we could react, she sprang from her chair like an electric bolt had struck her and leapt at Madhu.

'Liiiiike yoooooo!' Her deep voice boomed, pushing him back into the cushioned sofa until they both lay flat on it with her on top. Despite her small size, the voluminous nightgown completely covered Madhu's huge girth and barrel chest. I lunged, trying to prise her away from Madhu, but my hands slipped. That's when she started to sort of melt. Like wax in heat.

'Youuuuuuuuarenexxxxxxxxxxxt.'

'Blind mother's ass! She's a sup!' My hands were caked with mud, the sort that potters use to make pots. Unbaked, wet mud. What in naraka's name was it? A mud monster? A bhuta? I wasn't sure.

'Can you take her off me? She's tightening her grip,' growled Madhu, from under her.

'It's just mud, it won't hurt you. Where is the real one?' I stormed into the apartment, turning back at the sound of a massive crash.

'Holy son of a shithole!' Madhu was sprawled on the floor. The mud on his body was already drying up, taking on his shape, rather like a full-body mudpack, except it seemed to be shrinking as it dried and squishing him. He gagged, his whiskers stiff, as the mud rapidly dried around his nostrils and neck. I tried to scrape the sludge off his face, with no success. It was already as hard as rock. I reached for my satchel and retrieved my mandala, a pack of bone-based geometric shapes used to cast mantras, and quickly selected the shape of a circle inside a square. I held it in both my hands and focused.

'Bhuta pishacha darke bhag!'

Nodha, the repelling mantra, left the mandala like a blast of air and shot towards Madhu's caked body. He made a gargling sound deep in his throat as the mud monster bloated up. For a second it looked like it was peeling off him, just like a beauty face mask, but then it leapt back on him, and hardened again.

'Balls of bulls,' I exclaimed.

Only Madhu's eyes still moved, reflecting horror and pain. I dragged his stiff body into the bathroom located at the other end of the drawing room. Then I angled him inside so that his head was positioned right beneath the shower, which I turned on at full blast. If it was mud, it might dissolve when wet.

'Mufgghghgh,' screamed Madhu through the mud-mask. Veins in his eyes popped red.

'I know, I know! Your screaming does not help.' I took out a vial of tiger blood from my pouch and put a drop on the monster. The drop spread on the mud monster like an ink stain. I knew by the way it loosened a bit that it liked the blood. I emptied the whole blood vial on Madhu's face and neck. I heard ragged breathing, which was a good sign.

'Get me … out of … this fucking spa pack!' he managed to say as soon as the mud had melted enough for him to speak. At least he could breathe for a bit.

'Stay here,' I commanded. Not that he could have moved.

I ran into the kitchen and ripped open cabinets. Oil, I needed oil. I found a small jar of olive oil and nothing else. Bloody, health-conscious freaks. If only this had been Chandni Chowk, I would have found vats full of all kinds of oils. Then I saw the gas pipeline. I ripped the line open and let the gas float. I ran into the bathroom and dragged Madhu and the mud into the kitchen. The pungent gas had already spread. I took out a matchbox, ran out of the kitchen and threw a lit match inside, crouching with my back to the kitchen. *BOOM!* Heat seared my back, burning and ruining my dress some more. I turned. The kitchen walls and floor were blackened and charred. Fragments of coloured, baked ceramic were spread all around.

'How … how … did you know this would work?' asked Madhu, coughing, trying to stand up in the middle of the disaster area, dusting ashes from his torn jeans.

'I didn't. Just thought I would try to do what a potter does. Bake it.'

Madhu gave me a horrified look. 'It was a bloody experiment? You dropped me into a gas explosion because you thought it *might* work? I could have been killed!'

'Some thanks I get for saving your sorry ass. It worked, didn't it?'

He got up and walked out of the kitchen to take a deep breath. We found the real Gayatri a few minutes later, in a second bathroom that had been locked from the outside, the same three-headed cobra symbol that had been tattooed on Vikram's chest, on the doorknob. She looked unkempt, underfed and really, really angry.

'I am going to drag that bastard through hells he has never imagined!' she exclaimed weakly as we helped her out of the bathroom into the more spacious living room. She sat on the rocking chair.

'Umm … Mrs Sharma, he's already dead.'

Squeak, squeak. She started to rock harder, in the same disconcerting way that her mud-monster double had. I reached inside my satchel and grabbed my matchbox. One has to be ready for any pottery shit the world throws at you. Then she stopped, stared at both of us this time, her eyes wide.

'Good,' she said after a pause.

A security guard rang the bell to find out if everything was okay. He was smoothly dismissed by the new Mrs Sharma, whom I had started to feel good about.

'We have a few questions to ask of you.'

'I am hungry. I will eat something and then answer.' She walked into the kitchen and exclaimed, 'What the hell happened here! I am going to kill that scum again!'

I confessed. She nodded curtly and then started to wolf down brown bread, the only edible thing that seemed to have survived the blast. It was only after she had got six slices of bread under her belt that she started to tell us her story. Her husband had been fired from a company two years ago. He tried starting a business but that had not taken off. As she was working at the time and able to keep the home fires burning, he decided to stay at home and take care of their daughter.

'Then, a year ago, he decided to become a disciple of a swami. In those months, I was travelling a lot for work. In a way I was thankful,' she said, biting into another slice of bread. 'At least he wasn't depressed or anything. A spiritual guru couldn't be so bad, could he? But it turned into an obsession. He would stay in the ashram for weeks on end and leave our daughter at my parents' place. I tried to talk to him about it, but every time I did, he'd look at me with glazed eyes, as if he wasn't really listening. He changed his looks, shaved his head and started wearing a black dhoti. Each day when I came home from work I'd notice something different about him. One day, a mark branded on his skin, another day, he'd applied haldi all over his face. There were some other times when he would just begin sketching figures on the walls of the drawing room. We had a huge fight and I threatened to leave him, but he promised to change. For a few months, he was good. He was attentive to our daughter and really nice to me, cheerful, almost happy. But then ... one night ...'

She stopped and stared at the floor for a minute, then took a deep breath and continued, 'A month ago, I walked in and saw him ... bathing our daughter. There was some ... something about that scene. It was not fatherly, the way he was looking at her, the way his ha ... his hands were touching her. His eyes had a sort of a glitter, not of love but almost ... sort of ... lust.' She stopped and swallowed, her voice heavier. 'She is ten now, my daughter. I kind of lost it that day. I moved out with her, leaving him alone here and forbade him to even talk to our daughter. He came to my parents' place and apologized. We spoke a lot that day. He promised to give up the ashram. I thought we could go back to being a real family again. I came back, but left my daughter at my parents' place. I couldn't ... I just wasn't sure! It was a scene that was stuck in my head.'

I clutched my locket, my heart clenching. 'And when you came here with him, he imprisoned you?'

'Yes,' she said, her face crumpling. 'He would only open the door to put in food twice a day. Some days he would forget. I heard voices outside, of people coming and going. I wondered why my parents hadn't suspected anything or called or done anything. Everyone had forgotten me.'

'And did you hear of anything he was planning to do?'

'He kept on telling me that I would eventually understand. That it was for all of us that he was doing this, and that I would understand in the end.'

'Do you remember which swami or ashram he followed?' Madhu asked.

'I don't. But I can ask my parents. They might remember.'

A really weird thought began to form in my head. 'When was the last time you spoke to your daughter, Gayatri?'

'Two weeks ago. He came back in a good mood and made me speak to her. She is at my parents' place.'

'Call them. Call them now,' I ordered urgently. 'Ask all three to come here now.'

She looked at me with panic in her eyes and dialled her parents' home. It was as I had feared. Her parents didn't know anything. She and her husband had come to their house to pick up the daughter just yesterday. That's when I told her about the impersonator, her mud clone.

'Oh, my god! Where's my daughter? Has he done something to her?'

We asked her for a photo. I didn't want to tell her about

the little dead girl. Not yet. But it was as I had suspected. The photo of her daughter was that of the dead girl we had seen earlier today. The only difference was that here she was smiling, her face beautiful, her eyes lit up with laughter. Madhu tried to be as gentle as possible, but she broke down and sobbed. I was thankful when her parents arrived. Madhu finished the police formalities and told them they would get both the bodies as soon as the post-mortem was completed.

'An educated man, Anantya. How could he do this to his daughter?' he exclaimed as we left her apartment.

My eyes burnt with exhaustion and pain. 'For power.' I ignored the flashes that were beginning to build up in my head. *Father, how could you? Brother, how could you?* But then I knew. I knew that a power-hungry tantrik would stoop to any level to get what he wanted. Mother, daughter, friend's sister. Nothing mattered but the goal. Tantriks were trained to have tunnel vision. For a tantrik, his daughter was above all a virgin sheep to be sacrificed.

'You should have told her the truth,' I said.

Madhu hadn't told her the circumstances in which the father and daughter had been found. Only the fact that both of them were dead.

'I just ... didn't have the heart to.'

'She will ask. She will figure it out. She deserves to know,' I answered. Like I had deserved to know.

8

He stared at her unblinking, his long black tongue, moist, forked and flickering. Round, knob-like eyes reflected her naked body in their eerie, red irises. He gazed down at her naked skin, and through her naked skin, to the muscles, to the bones, into her very soul. She smelt his desperation, his desire for her power. For her shakti, her bloodshed. He cupped and squeezed her left breast ritualistically, his iridescent eyes entranced, his hands rough like dead bark, and cold like icicles. His claws dug and scratched and tore away at her skin, desperate, hungry, wondrous. Her skin curdled and oozed out buttery blood. It felt warm, the deep red liquid, with a tangy metallic smell, on her chest, between her legs. The warm smell mingled with the rank odour of her fear.

'You are mine,' he said, not a question, a statement, soft, polite.

She nodded, helpless, in pain, in desire, in submission. He smiled, his decayed teeth glinting. His other head reared up. And then the third. All three sank down and bit her. Her neck, her breasts, her navel, her inner thighs. Three cobra heads, their six bloodshot eyes shining like rubies. They bit on and on, again and again. The bleeding excited them. She screamed in pleasure and pain, her tongue ululating in a tuneless song.

Jaadugar tu jaadugarrrr ... tu hai mera dilbarrr ... brrring ... brrrring...

The phone rang insistent and angry. My left hand snaked to it, sweaty. The phone almost slipped.

'Ugh,' I barked, my tongue papery. The three-headed cobra stared at me with malicious, ruby eyes. I forced my eyes to open.

'Tell me what happened, dahling!'

'Unh?'

'Come on, tell me!'

Slowly, deliberately, I sat up. My shoulder screamed in protest. The book on my chest fell on the rumpled bed. I was home, at the haveli. That was good, wasn't it? I lay back in the bed for a few more moments, staring at the hot sun as it streamed through the broken pieces of corrugated tin sheets high above my head. The haveli was more than a hundred years old and located in the busy, old neighbourhood of Chandni Chowk. Although it had about twenty-four rooms, only four of us lived here – Zee, a cat called Angi, a ghost called Nawab Sahib and I. Its central courtyard – with boards and tin sheets for a makeshift roof – was my domain. From the entrance to the end, where the rasayana lab was, it was about half the length of a football field. My mind reverted to the horror of the morning. The phone crackled.

'Daks. It's only twelve,' I croaked into it, nose wrinkling at my own foul breath.

'So?' asked Dakini, her voice a fresh bloom of flowers. 'You need to behave like a human and sleep at night and not in the morning. Tell me, na. How did your date go? I hope you didn't scare him off—'

'Daks, I just got home a couple of hours ago.' I remembered now. I jerked upright in the bed. How could I have forgotten him? I know he wasn't all that important but … thanks to me, Nikhil had become a centrepiece in Qubera's flamboyant abode.

'Really? So the date was *that* successful? I knew it! Yesss!

Isn't he a dish? So hawt-looking and such a hunk! He's pure gold, dahling, pure gold.'

'If you say so,' I muttered. Nikhil's brand-new, gold-plated look swam into my view. I scrambled off the bed and tiredly crawled to the kitchen.

'Tell me, tell me more. How was he? In bed?'

'We didn't have sex, Daks. I went on a case after the date.'

My stomach grumbled; I hadn't put anything in it since I left the restaurant. It seemed such a long time ago. There was a small, rarely used kitchenette at the other end of the hall. I fished out the crumbed pan that lay in the messy sink, gave it a quick scrub and put it on the gas with water, three teabags, powdered milk and lots of sugar. Then I picked up a biscuit bin and took one out. If I had to lie, I had to eat a little first.

'I had to leave ... early. He went off ... somewhere.'

'Where?'

'Didn't tell me.'

I munched on a biscuit morosely. Usually I was more upfront with bad news, but this wasn't the time to go into details. Anyway, Qubera's case would be over by Saturday night, and Nikhil freed. Given that he was magically gilded, he would probably not remember any of it. All I needed to do was follow Lavanya and get back to them with a list of everyone she meets tonight and tomorrow. Then Nikhil would be free. Easy peasy. Nothing to worry Dakini over.

'I tried to call him, but didn't get through. I bet he is completely in love with you. Was my dress a hit?'

'Yes, sure looked like it,' I muttered, looking down at the remains of what had been a dress last night. I was still wearing it. My old cotton bra peeked through the tears. No wonder Madhu had been surprised when he saw me this morning.

'I knew it!' she said, still on her jubilant trip. 'He belongs to such a hi-fi family, Antz. You will become a rockstar. I have to call him and ask—'

'Stop it, Daks. Take a deep breath. Like you tell those poor rich sods you counsel.' I couldn't take it. Anymore of her enthusiasm and I would either scream or tell her the truth. Bad ideas, both.

'Fine, don't tell. I am going to meet him at a party tonight anyway. I'll wheedle out all the goss from him there.'

'What party?' I asked, pretending to be interested to get her off the topic of my disastrous date.

Daks's social calendar was usually full with one party or another. Once you got her started on a party, it would be the discussion for the rest of the conversation. I poured my strong chai into a used cup and headed to my rasayana lab at the end of the courtyard. The blade, its back curved, lay gleaming in the middle of a cluttered worktable along with bottles and jars of various shapes and sizes. Instead of walls, my lab was separated from the main space by cupboards and piles of books – all the things I generally needed at one time or another for something I was working on. This was the place where Zaazee, my roommate, and I made potions. The bare space in the corner was reserved for the more elaborate tantrik rituals that required yantras to be drawn. I made a mental note to clean it up when I had the chance. Then I turned to a dusty cabinet by the wall, a huge one that had all kinds of stuff crammed into it and piled on it – glass jars brimming with goat testicles, powdered bones of a rattlesnake, skins of frogs, various kinds of stones which couldn't be exposed to air, water or other elements, precious metals, and other things I had collected over the years as a potion maker.

Madhu had allowed me to take the blade so I could examine it and perhaps figure out where it had come from, but so far, I had been unsuccessful. I had already tried everything I could think of on the blade – acids, antacids, chemicals to test all kinds of metals, bones, hardened skins, claws. Nothing had revealed to me what it was made of. It did nothing except lie there like a talon, gleaming softly and screaming for blood in my head whenever I touched it. I picked up a small dusty bottle from the cupboard, its black and green liquid swirling as I carried it to the table. Darzit was a concoction that helped reveal the past experiences of a magical object. Perhaps it would be able to tell me where this thing had come from. Or give me some clue. I picked up the blade, feeling its almost liquid, buttery weight. The two intertwined roses etched on its handle glowed. There was no sign that it might have been through violence of any kind. It looked so innocent, an object of beauty. It felt so right, like it was created to belong to me. Like it did belong to me instead of having come into my hands just by chance. It was a heady sort of feeling. And, just as before, as soon as I touched it, it became an extension of me, desiring its share of bloodshed. Human blood, I was sure.

'Now start talking,' I commanded, as I put a drop of darzit on the blade. The blade's edge sizzled and absorbed the black drop. It didn't change colour or reflect anything, simply absorbed. As I bent closer to get a better look, something spat the drop back on my face. The blade gleamed its lopsided smile.

'Did you even hear a word of what I said?' grumbled Daks.

'You said you were going to a party,' I replied, carefully wiping the darzit off my face.

'Antz, seriously, here I am telling you about the biggest shindig of the decade and you don't even pay attention! As I was saying, the host is like an absolute hunk. He owns this cellular network multinational. He has serious style, Antz! He's already being touted as a politician in the making, with the ruling party offering him a Rajya Sabha seat. Money, style, looks, you name it, he has it.'

'Who?'

'Haven't you been listening at all? I told you, Vajrin Mahendra is one of the richest and most influential men in Delhi right now. At tonight's party, he's unveiling some new gadget that will completely change the way we use our phones. Or so the invite said.'

'Ah, that party? I will be there too,' I answered. I looked at the blade morosely, wondering if I should try and hit it with a rock of something. You never know what would work.

'You will be?' she asked, surprised. I could hear her mind ticking. She knew me. If I said I was willingly coming to a socialite party, there was something drastically wrong.

'What's up, Antz. There's something you aren't telling me, isn't there?' she asked suspiciously. Finally she was catching on.

'Uh-huh. Nothing. Want to see Nik—' I almost choked but forced myself to say it. 'Nikhil. Gotta go now, see you there at the party then.'

'You learn to liesss,' drawled Zaazee as I disconnected. He was sprawled on our much-abused sofa in the centre of the courtyard. His lithe, python-like dull gold body was ballooned in the middle. A huge chicken, by the looks of it. I gave him a dirty look, which he didn't notice, because his green eyes were glued to the television.

'You smell like vulture shits,' he said, flicking his long tongue on the remote to change the channel.

'Zee, get your filthy tongue off the remote,' I retorted,

ignoring his jibe and taking my clothes off. I took a quick bath, scrubbing myself with an Ayurvedic soap, hoping to get the smell of yaksha poop off.

'Where the hell were you this morning, when I needed you?' I asked when I had changed into an almost-clean T-shirt and salwar.

'You become celebritiesss,' answered Zee, increasing the volume.

The telly flickered to life with a loud anchor who shouted in near hysterics about a mysterious black pyramid that had manifested in Kotla in the middle of the night. The channel threw up possibilities that ranged from a threatening alien attack to a Black magic ritual gone wrong. In the second possibility, they might be closer to the truth than they realized.

'... later in the day, the police cleared two bodies, both dead under mysterious circumstances – that of a father and daughter. They are investigating to see if the mysterious beggar woman by the pyramid is responsible for their deaths ...'

'Lizard's piss!' I exclaimed.

A witness had told the channel that a suspicious-looking woman in filthy rags had entered the premises almost naked and had managed to destroy crucial evidence while the police did their best to stop her.

'... was she sent by the enemies to baffle the police further?' The story finished without any mention of the CBI being involved. I had to hand it to Madhu, he knew how to remain in the shadows.

The image of the girl lying in the congealed pool of blood screamed in my head. How had the tantrik learnt a Black ritual? Black rituals that involved human sacrifice were not something you found in library books and the like. The Central

Association of Tantriks, which was created five years ago, had declared human sacrifice illegal in the country for all tantriks, but it had already been an unwritten law in our profession since time immemorial. In spite of that, sacrifices did take place time and again because tantriks got greedy for shakti and knowledge of Black rituals. It was an easy way to gain real power, real fast – the reason why tantrik novices were the ones who got attracted to it the most. Gayatri had mentioned that her husband had taken on a guru, but no sane guru would give you knowledge of Black tantrism if you had been practising the art for only a year. It was suicidal and stupid. It took time and practice to understand how shakti could be tapped, used and directed. A virgin girl sacrifice would generate a lot of shakti, which, without adequate knowledge, would only destroy you. As with the novice. But a stupid novice with the right knowledge could be very, very dangerous. There was something else that bothered me about the dead bodies of this morning. Dark rituals always happened in secret, in hidden basements or inside caves deep in the forests. Never on a terrace in the middle of a city. Why had the Black tantrik chosen that particular spot? And who was his guru? Had he given him the blade for the ritual? Without this blade, this ritual might not have been possible.

Zee's tail flopped into my lap, waiting. I obliged with a scratch. He sighed contentedly, his eyes still glued to the telly. Zee was a cat trapped inside a naga's body.

'If anyone from your naga clan finds out how you purr when scratched by a tantrik, they will take out a fatwa against you.'

Zee didn't respond. For all I know, he already had a fatwa against him. Zee had left Patala, the city where most of the nagas lived. He never told me why. A year ago, I found him in a gutter in the city, mortally wounded and left to die. I brought him back here and he never left. Both of us were outsiders in our own way and I liked his company. He had started a business of making potions, and, considering he was a naga, a natural at potion-making, it had become quite successful. His maya potion, which could turn sups into humans for a day, was one of the most reliable in the city. It was one of the few that had no embarrassing lags like change of skin colour in the middle of a metro ride. I quietly updated him on the early-morning case. The virgin sacrifice, the dead tantrik, the cellphone, the mysterious blade which was driving me up the wall and the meeting with the mud monster.

'Was fathers?' he asked quietly. I nodded, my throat too tight to speak.

'That's why you had nightmaress,' he said. It wasn't a question. Even without knowing my past (we had a contract of never talking about each other's past), he knew.

'I will find out why,' I replied, my lower lip quivering. 'I will find the bast—'

'Kaminon! Khuda kasam tumhari boti boti noch ke giddon ko khila doonga! KANEEZ!'

Baam! Baaam! We looked at each other exasperatedly. Obviously, Nawab Sahib, the resident ghost, was up. Considering the haveli was in the middle of the city, and prime property, I had got it for peanuts. The reason for that was Nawab Sahib, the dead owner of this haveli who had been brutally decapitated a couple of centuries ago by the lover of his newly-wed bride. Since then, he had turned into an acheri, the ghost of a murdered man, and haunted the haveli, refusing to leave the place. Hapless occupants who had attempted to live here since then had either gone crazy or killed themselves. I could handle a vengeful ghost without any issues. And the sinister reputation meant that I didn't get any nosy neighbours. It wasn't Nawab's murderous streak that was a problem for me, though. In that he was more bark than bite. The problem was his tantrums.

'Nawab, what the hell is it now?' I shouted, standing at the foot of the stairs, by the doorway that led to the first floor, his residence.

'*Kaaaannnnnnnnneeeezz! Hamari bandook pesh kijiye. Kaun najaiz gadhon ki aulad humare dahleez-e-sehen mein gandagi phaila rahen hain? Humare! Nawab ke? Hum inki boti boti kar ke—*'

Something whizzed past through the permanently shut, small triangular window above the main door and fell with a crash on the street in front of the house. It was immediately followed by loud jeering noises. He rushed to the window.

'NAJAAYAZ BADTAMEEZ KAMINEY!'

I wish his mother had whacked him on the butt when he was little. I wouldn't have had to deal with this then. I picked up a small vial from the table. 'Nawab Sahib, if you don't want to live the rest of your long, ghostly life in this little blue bottle, I suggest you shut up and let me work.'

He stopped and leered at me with his kohled eyes. Nawab Sahib used to be a short man with a pot belly. Becoming a ghost hadn't improved his looks much, and now he also sported a permanent gash from his neck to his chest. He wore his hair fashionably long and was always dressed in a rich, silken achkan with paan stains.

'*Kaneez, aap bahut badtameez hain. Hamare aangan mein koi ma ka lal ... eech!*'

He wafted down the stairs towards me. '*Aap tasveer kab se bana rahen hain?*' he asked, indicating the tattoo sketch I had drawn. I angled the bottle in such a way that it glinted.

'*Aap mohtarma hain isiliye zubaan-taale hain. Hamare zamane mein badtameezon ko tang ke saza-e-maut pahuncha dete the,'* he replied and floated up to his rooms, grumbling.

I wondered whether I should do something about the neighbourhood kids. I was okay with their harmless playing around with ghosts, but the last thing I wanted was someone to start snooping around in my lab. Perhaps a repellent charm wasn't such a bad idea.

'Where did you find this sssymbolss?' asked Zee.

'On that dead man's chest.'

'Sssss not good,' he answered sharply. Zee was alert, his hood flared, something he did when he was threatened or scared. I looked at him inquisitively. What was the matter with him?

'Why? Do you know what it is?'

He started at the symbol, his body still, frozen, as only a reptile's can be.

'What is this symbol? Tell me!'

'No, I dontsss,' he answered, shaking his hood in a very human-like manner.

I stared at him, surprised. He had never lied to me before. 'Really? Are you sure you don't?'

'It's best not spoken ofssss,' he answered, his hood still spread, ready to strike. He slithered away, heading to his hideout, a dark corner behind a pile of crates.

'Oh, come on!' I called after him. 'Don't be a superstitious sod! You are seriously scared of a symbol?'

'It's not just any symbol, Anantya Tantrist,' he said in a human voice, which was strange twice over. He never called me that. And he hated to 'turn', which was what he was doing. Nagas have a human form that they can change into whenever they desired. Sometimes, turning could happen involuntarily too, depending on the threat of a situation. The naga turning did not quite work like rakshasas taking on a human form. Rakshasas could turn into pretty much anything in the first plane. Nagas, on the other hand, were half-human. They could change into only one form, their own. I had never seen Zee in his human form, because of how much he hated to turn. By the time he had turned completely, he was hidden in the shadows at the other end of the courtyard.

'This symbol,' he spoke from the shadows, his voice older, flatter, huskier as if it was someone else's, 'is an evil one. It belongs to one of the foulest, oldest, most ancient powers of the universe. It is the symbol that opens the door of Patala's deepest pit, the seventh hell, a place where the Demon of Chaos lives. A danava so ancient that younger generations of Patala have even forgotten it exists.'

'But how would a tantrik know about it? Maybe he picked up the symbol from somewhere and doesn't really know its legend?' I countered, hopeful.

'It doesn't matter, Anantya Tantrist.' His green eyes glittered like jewels from the shadows. 'You see, the symbol alone is powerful enough to bring ill-luck. It is an omen of evil times.'

ॐ

I tried to smooth the creases from the wrinkled invite before handing it over. The bouncer stared at it for a long second, picked it up with a pinch of his fingers, stared some more and then glowered. I gave him a sweet smile. He looked down at an invisible list and then looked back up and asked, 'What did you say your name was?'

'Anantya Tantrist.'

He glanced again at the non-existent list but was distracted by a perfume factory in a short, purple, fitted tube-dress with hair straight out of a glossy magazine. He gaped at her for a moment, my invite totally forgotten. A group of photographers zoomed in like vultures to a carcass.

'One smile, miss!' shouted one, his camera flashing in a frenzy.

The perfume factory turned and smiled, her lilac lips curling just enough, her shoulder-length hair bouncing. Everybody froze, fascinated. She had the most enticing eyes, like pools of liquid nitrogen, clear like the moon, and the colour of soft snow. My heart (and I am not attracted to women, mostly) started to pump blood faster into my arteries. I looked around to see that the men around stood perfectly motionless, their tongues hanging out, their eyes wide.

'It's her, Miss Mohini!' someone who stood further away and wasn't taking in the effect of her eyes, exclaimed. She turned back to the bouncer whose glower had turned into a vapid smile. He undid the velvet barrier rope, shouldering me out of the way. I noticed he hadn't asked to see her invite. She walked up the stairs, her dress shaping her buttocks and casting a svelte shadow on the crimson carpet, and disappeared through the doors.

Yes, there was a red carpet, complete with bouncers, flashing cameras, people who had no business to be standing there and others who desperately wanted to get into the party. Obviously, Dakini hadn't been exaggerating this time. It was a farmhouse in Sainik Farms, where politicians and industrialists with connections built palatial houses and lockers to keep their illicit income. The farmhouse was done up in classical style, with wrought-iron gates, a drive-in and a mix of statues of Kamasutra-inspired apsaras and copies of Greek gods. Holders of the invite arrived in monster-sized limos and Rolls Royces and other cars I couldn't recognize. They were all dressed like they had come from a costume store or a whole other planet.

I had arrived on Chhotu, my fifteen-year-old mobike, bought second-hand from a bike shop in old Delhi. Her bright-green paintwork had faded into a pasty, peel-off grey. As if nervous in this company, she had announced herself with a huge black belch of kerosene, causing some youngsters standing along the red carpet, waiting for friends who held their invites, to jump away and cough. No valet had come forth to claim Chhotu. Not that I would have given her to anyone.

'Your name's not on the list, miss,' said the bouncer, his arms crossed on his vast chest.

'I have the bloody invite, don't I?'

'Yes, but your name is not on the list, miss. We are allowed to let in only—'

I wondered whether turning him into a toad would speed things up a bit. If it wasn't for that psycho Qubera who had kidnapped my date, I wouldn't be standing here, really. But I would be darned if I had to explain things to a steroid-pumped dinosaur. I crossed my arms and scowled.

'Why don't you call up Vaju and ask him yourself? Mention to him that Antz is standing on his doorstep. I bet he will be delighted to explain to you why he decided to give me an invite.'

If you want to enter somewhere in Delhi, one of the following things usually works: either you are dressed half-naked and wearing stilettos and your hair looks like a wig, or you know how to drop names. I was dressed all wrong for this party of course. After last night's fiasco, I wanted to avoid anything that would make my breasts pop out in the middle of action. So here I was, in bright printed culottes and a sensible black halter-top. My satchel held my arsenal, my hair was bunched up on top of my head and the only make-up I had was kohl to darken my eyes. I was wearing my comfortable chappals, my bracelet and my mother's yugma. My boneblade was in its waist-belt scabbard and my septifocals lay on top of my unruly hair as a hairband. I touched it to reassure myself. If I wanted to run, I could. Which is just the way I like things to be. I was dressed for work, not for nibbling on fancy snacks. But then I knew how to drop a name right: first name if you want to make an impact, or better still a nickname if you wanted people to fall at your feet. The velvet rope plopped open like burning wool.

I walked into the party of the year. The main hallway was neo-classical with tall columns, a staircase with an elaborate balustrade in the front and Italian marble flooring. An usher gave me a fur coat and opened a door to the left.

'The ballroom is this way, madam,' he said.

The door opened into a huge space lit up with icy-blue lights. The ballroom's walls, ceiling and floor were covered in ice – looking like an igloo meant for a daitya. Blue lights lit up tables made of ice and gave the whole ambience a soft baby-blue glow. It was hard to believe that I was in Delhi in July when temperatures tended to soar to 40 degrees Celsius. Awed expressions mingled with tinkling glasses, trance music and giggles. Even though it was only 9 p.m., early by Delhi standards, drunken laughter indicated that the party was in full swing.

I located the bar and ordered scotch-on-the-rocks. The bartender expertly juggled his bottles, mixing multiple drinks simultaneously in tall glasses. He gave me a glass with skull-shaped ice cubes. I took a huge gulp and started to look around, trying to locate Lavanya Mohan. Frankly, my heart wasn't in the task. My mind's eye kept seeing Zee's glowing jade eyes in the shadows, the last I had seen of him before he had disappeared. Zee had never been this dramatic before. I wondered if he was watching too many damn soaps. Anyway, I had to find out what the tattoo on the dead man's chest meant. Perhaps his widow would know, although I seriously doubted it. The tattoo had been fairly new, a week old at most, probably done while she was locked in the loo.

A tall guy drew up a high stool next to me and whispered into the barman's ear. His weight shifted from one foot to the other beneath a long maroon coat with fur collar. Wavy hair fell on his face as he nodded briefly in my direction. He wore a thin chain around his neck with a golden locket that had an ossified firefly trapped inside. It reminded me of Nikhil, similarly trapped in a gold sheath. I responded to his smile with a grimace. The barman handed him something small and he left.

'Looks like you need it too,' said the barman, winking as he handed me a small pouch. 'This one's on the house.'

The pouch contained a small thumb-sized vial of red liquid. I undid the stopper and it spilt onto my palm. It was diluted, but there was a strong waft of shakti on it. Charak. I flipped my hand, letting it drain to the floor. No wonder the party had begun to swing way before its time. Charak was diluted chandaali rakta, the blood of one of the most powerful sups, a chandaali. Over the centuries, tantriks had started to farm chandaalis to control their rakta, full of shakti and very helpful in rituals. Even I carried rakta in my locket along with rakpiss, using it every time I needed to do a complex spell. Charak, however, was another deal. Cheaper and meant mostly as a recreational drug to sharpen your animal instincts and increase sexual potency, it was highly addictive. A lot of tantrik rookies tasted charak before they performed rituals, especially the ones that required high levels of emotional power. It increased awareness, made you hyper-conscious of your surroundings, and alert. Charak had been introduced to the high-society manavas in Delhi about five years ago when tantriks came out into the open and the clans got together to form the Central Tantrik Association, a front for tantriks to interact with the Indian government. Now it was a regular feature in fancy parties and pubs. A couple of NGOs were trying to get charak listed as an addictive drug with the Narcotics Control Bureau and banned, but that hadn't taken effect so far. As long as CAT had its way, I couldn't see it happening any time soon.

I got up and started to circulate, trying to locate Lavanya Mohan. Grrhat had told me she would be there by nine. It was fifteen minutes past. About time. I spotted Qubera on the far side of the hall. He wore a brilliant white suit with gold embroidery, multiple layers of gold chains around his neck and arms and dangling medallions. For some reason, he had opted to wear gold-rimmed sunglasses. He was busy nodding, his multiple chins jiggling, to an elegant woman in a sari with long black hair which she was wearing sideswept and kept running her fingers through. I noticed a couple of fascinated men stop dead in their tracks to take a good look at her. Grrhat stood behind both of them. He caught my eye and slightly flicked his head. I turned to see a group of young women. They stood in the middle of the hall. One of them was Lavanya Mohan. I would have noticed her before if it hadn't been for the fact that her face was half hidden by a fur coat which had its collar turned up. From where I stood, she appeared to be in her thirties, dressed smartly in an outfit which skimmed her slim figure without clinging. I beelined towards her with my drink in my hand, wondering if I should have downed that shot of free charak offered to me. The quicker I solved this, the sooner I could be out of here and the faster I could move on to the blade which had hacked into that little girl.

Suddenly the lights went off, leaving everyone in velvety darkness. Gasps and giggles filled the dark as people nervously switched on their mobile screens to see. I stopped in my tracks. A single spotlight lit up the middle of the stage, where a tall, broad-shouldered man stood with his face in the shadows. His eyes glittered like diamonds.

'No need to be afraid, ladies,' he whispered in a husky, warm tenor. 'I am here to protect you.'

The crowd cheered as the lights adjusted to reveal Vajrin Mahendra's grin. He had a sharp, angular face, a perfectly shaped nose and a chin that looked like it had been lovingly chiselled by an artist. He wore his hair longish so that the soft waves ended just above his broad shoulders. There was a single grey streak in his hair, which looked more like a bleach-job than real age. He wore an elegant black suit with a narrow blue tie, not banker blue, but a stylish blue. He could give movie stars a run for their money. And as if that wasn't enough, his chin and cheek dimpled every time he smiled.

'That also includes those of you who have managed to gate-crash and are having drinks at my expense,' he added, looking in my direction. 'I don't distinguish between my gals ... or my boys.'

His cheeks dimpled as the crowd cheered.

'We have a special show planned for you tonight, so those of you who have already made too many forays to the bar, I request you to stay conscious for just a while longer. Red drops will help with that.'

'Kiss me, Vajrin!' someone from the crowd shouted.

'Lady, much as I would love to take you up on your offer, I am afraid it will have to wait. Why don't you charm the barman and wheedle a drop from him to help hold that thought?' He winked amidst peals of laughter.

I reoriented myself to keep Lavanya in sight, not sure what I was supposed to do. I didn't know what Indra's Key looked like. How was I supposed to just follow her and figure out who she might strike a deal with? Qubera's instructions to me were vague to say the least. Still, one had to do what one could to save a frozen guy.

'Now, before all of you head to the bar again,' Vajrin continued, 'I would like to show you a way of making all your dreams come true. Hey, don't laugh! Hear me out. I am a practical guy and not some sadhu making dramatic promises. Your dreams emerge from your mind, a powerful tool, as ancient Indian tantriks have known for centuries.

They started to tap into the powers of the mind when science had only just started to wear diapers. Mind power can bend the rules of physics, the rules that work this universe. What can't happen if you put your mind and will to it? Unfortunately for mankind, by the time the yogi, who had centuries of practice behind him, came out of that cave to announce to the world that universal powers were theirs for the taking, humans had already moved on to the cellphone!'

Vajrin waited for the laughter to die down. Lavanya had moved to the back of the room, behind the bar, far away from the stage. I extracted a Luv-Kush from my satchel, and tore them apart. Luv-Kush were a set of twin bugs, listening devices, which relayed sound energy from one to another. I opened the claws of Luv (or maybe it was Kush, I can never tell them apart) and strolled towards her, the bug between my fingers. Just a tap and it would be done.

'… technology has become a new way to look at this world, to control it. Tantrism has been forgotten as we stare into smartphone screens and tweet. But that doesn't mean it isn't just as powerful as it ever was, does it? So we, the innovators in the industry, thought, why not combine the two? Why does there need to be a divide between technology and tantrism? And so we started to develop a new gadget with endless possibilities …'

Someone jostled me, spilling my drink.

'What the …'

But the guy didn't pause. It was the man from the bar, with the firefly locket. He elbowed two more people on his way to Lavanya and fell at her feet. They began arguing, the boy was seriously high on charak, his hands shaking with its power. A crowd had gathered around them. I deftly threaded through the commotion and placed one half of the Luv-Kush duo on Lavanya's neck as she turned away from the boy kneeling before her. The bug was tiny, its claws barely touched her skin.

'... ME ALONE, YOU!' she screamed suddenly. 'I have had it with your kind!'

The bouncer manifested right behind her to take her away. I started to follow, glad we were leaving the party, when my way was blocked by Grrhat.

'I told you not to go close to her!' he barked.

I pressed my blade to his neck, furious. 'Don't you dare question me,' I said. Vajrin's voice boomed, drowning Grrhat's words. I let the blade fall, letting him go.

'iMagic! It's a smartphone on the one hand and, on the other, a yantra, a circle of power around you. This circle protects you from bad energies; at the same time, it reads your mind and invites the good energies of the universe into your body. The yantra will read your will and bring whatever you want into your life. All the good things. Whether you want career opportunities, good health, offspring or, like me, hot women all around you, you name it, and it will be yours.' As if on cue, Mohini walked on to the stage and, as the crowd applauded, kissed Vajrin full on the mouth. Vajrin surfaced for air after a while, smiling widely, and said, 'I mean, look at me. I only have the prototype and see what I have by my side already!'

His hand was possessively placed on the small of the girl's back. She smiled and stood with her back arched so that everyone could get a good look at her assets. People went berserk with excitement, their hands in the air and hooting.

'On a serious note,' continued Vajrin, 'it wasn't an easy task to complete. We had experts from the technology department of CAT working on the gadget for years before they could do this. It took a whole year of manufacturing. It wouldn't have been possible without the expert tantriks, our research team. And now I would like to welcome on stage the tantrik behind it all, the visionary swami who has put in years of sweat and research into this device. The man who has already made a reputation of sorts in the tantrik world as a magician, a miracle worker, a healer, a scientist, a researcher, a spiritualist, a swami, all combined. Please welcome ...'

I played with Kush and opened its claws. All I needed to do now was start the mantra and I would be able to hear...

'... Swami Narahara ...'

My face paled. I turned to face the stage, slowly. Yes, it was him, very much. He looked taller somehow. His bald head – with its long ponytail, the shikha, beaded with rudraksh – was still too small for his body. He wore a black dhoti and a gold-edged black patkan, or shawl, and carried a bone staff with the Kaula triangle on top of it. I dug my nails into my palms to calm myself, my hands becoming fists. *Nasty*. That was my nickname for him when we were kids. *Nasty Nara*. I would say it every time he pushed me to the ground. Every time he called me names or ganged up with his cronies and beat me up. It seemed such a long time ago.

'... the man who heads the technology department in the Central Association of Tantriks!'

This was news but not really a surprising one. It was inevitable of course. Although the association was a coalition of all types of tantrik sects, both red and white, the most influential amongst them continued to be the Kaulas, the White tantriks of Banaras, and Nasty was a favoured Kaula. With the blessings of CAT, the Kaulas had managed to move to Delhi, become internationally famous and gain the patronage of powerful people in both the government and the business community. Within a year, they had expanded into two huge campuses in Manesar and Noida, Delhi's sister cities. No other clan of tantriks had gained as much as Kaula after CAT was formed. Nasty more than anybody else.

'The Central Association of Tantriks is the conglomerate of tantriks from across the world,' began Nasty. 'It is an organization committed to bringing the benefits of tantrism to the common man. Our knowledge combines all the traditions of the clans of tantrism from across India, and even China, Indonesia, Malaysia and other countries. The association is committed to working with governments across the world to combine technology, culture, religion and human aspiration within the tenets of tantrism.'

It sounded like PR he had mugged up. The chatter levels around me increased, people started to return to the bar, treating Nasty's speech as a loo break. I smiled grimly. He wasn't used to being ignored. If he were a child, he would have simply hurled stuff at people. What would he do now?

'iMagic is a new direction for the technology department. It's an experiment with old knowledge which has been passed on to us through millennia of talented Nathas. Now I won't take you through the exact process of how we have done this …' He shuffled through papers.

Someone tittered from the back of the stage. I barked a laugh. Much as he wanted it, Nasty was not really made for the limelight.

'Bo-ring,' someone sang out from the back of hall. Laughter broke out. Nasty froze, his face mask-like, his facial muscles working. He raised his right arm, pointing the staff in the general direction of the voice.

'Dear Swami, there are ladies here,' interrupted Vajrin smoothly. 'We don't really need a display of your abilities.

Don't we trust his powers, friends? Why don't we get some drinks instead? Whoever wants to understand in detail how iMagic was created, read the fucking brochure!'

People started to laugh out loud. Vajrin elbowed a still fuming Nasty off the stage, announcing that there was a spectacular show of tantrik prowess planned in about half an hour. The mood lightened as a bunch of near-naked dancers took to the stage and started to gyrate in acrobatic positions that would have given competition to the Kamasutra. With trembling hands, I completed the mantra to connect the Luv-Kush and tried to eavesdrop on Lavanya Mohan. But there was silence on the other side. I decided to leave so that I could find Lavanya.

'Antz! Where have you been? I have been looking all over for you!'

Dakini shouldered her way towards me, a hearty grin on her face. Heads turned to look at her. She hardly noticed, or didn't care. She was a transgender who loved to dress up, usually in a dramatic fashion that looked glamorous on her coffee skin. For tonight's party, she had chosen to wear a green wig with an orange sequinned mini-dress and two huge sunflowers in her hair. Her eyes were heavied with long orange eyelashes and made up in a glittery, loud black. She engulfed me in a heavy, rose-perfumed bear hug. Dakini was a head taller than most men, thanks to the daitya blood in her. Her heart was huge, and so was her tendency to gossip.

'Isn't this party such a grand ... ?' she asked, in her unabashed, carrying voice, giving me an air kiss with her deep-coloured lips. 'Vaj sure has taste. And did you look at the shameful way that Mohini clung to him? She's calling herself his personal curator now, wink-wink. Apparently handles his *cultural* interests. She's an art dealer, or at least

that's how she introduces herself. I remember her gate-
crashing a couple of fashion parties in the city last season. But
then, she looks hawt in a trashy kind of a way, doesn't she? I
tell you, Antz, these PYTs are desperate to score at least some
brownies with him. He's the next IT-man in Del-hi.'

She did a sort of jig, her manicured hands waving. I forced
myself to smile, my mind still on Nasty. He had disappeared
from the stage as far as I could see. There were whispers in
my ear from the bug, something Lavanya said. Instructions
to the driver to leave for home.

'But tell me something, darling, what in hellcat's name are
you dressed in?' She pinched my halter and wrinkled her
nose. 'You know you could have just buzzed me and I would
have got you this gor-d-geous dress I have. It would have
looked really amazing. Dress reminds me, what the hell
happened with your date last night? Where is Nikhil? I haven't
seen him here though he told me he was coming.'

The conversation was veering into uncomfortable territory.
I made a quick getaway with the age-old loo excuse.
Unfortunately, Dakini decided to accompany me. I saw that
graceful woman who had been talking to Qubera walking
towards us, and asked Dakini about her, more to distract my
friend than to know. The woman looked like she was in her
late twenties, but something about the way she carried her
deep-blue chiffon sari made her look older. She seemed
familiar, beautiful sharp features with big black eyes and
cupid's bow lips. And the kind of figure schoolboys draw on
bathroom walls when they are fantasizing about what women
look like naked.

'Ahh, that! Don't you remember her? That's Rambha Devi,
the actress who was like this huge star in the sixties? *Kamal ke
Phool*? *Love in Ladakh*? Don't you see any movies?'

I shook my head. Hadn't found much time to sit in front of a television in my life, forget the cinema. Perhaps Zee would know. He always sat in front of the 'telly' as he called it.

'She hasn't aged a bit. Must be what in her sixties or seventies by now and doesn't look a day above twenty-five. I tell you some of these doctors are actually modern magicians. Or maybe she's found soma, the elixir of youth, eh? It looks like someone's been giving her a hard time.'

Dakini was right. Rambha walked past us, unseeing. I could see that her eye make-up was smudged. Had she been crying? What the hell had Qubera been talking to her about? I looked back to see where Qubera was. He was missing, so was Grrhat. I decided to leave as well, and said so.

'Oh, come on. Don't be a bore. Let's at least have a drink first. You cannot—'

'Dakini, my darling girl. Do introduce me to your unusual friend here.'

We turned around to see Vajrin Mahendra standing before us. At close quarters he looked even more dashing than on stage. His eyes were moist and deep, his hair was silken. My fingers itched to touch him.

'Name's Anantya Tantrist,' said Dakini, giving Vajrin a smacking kiss on the cheek.

'I got an invite from Mister Qubera,' I said, my voice defensive. I didn't want him to think that I had gate-crashed his fancy party.

Vajrin nodded, smiling a dimpled smile. 'I am glad that Qubera has some good sense left in him. I wouldn't have known that we had such pearls in our city if it hadn't been for him.'

The bugger knew what kind of effect he had on women and was playing me. He took my left hand and kissed it with his beautiful lips.

'Aah, you practise tantrism, do you?' he said, looking at the cuts and abrasions on my fingers. 'A beautiful lady and a tantrik?' An electrical charge passed up my arm. I clenched my teeth together. There was more to Vajrin than met the eye. The power he exuded wasn't human. 'I should probably stay away. Tantriks seem to have a temper.'

'Well, you sure chose the wrong one for the stage,' I replied.

He chuckled. It sounded like spring breeze. 'I wonder if you are the right one. Wait for a while and see the next act of the evening. It might feel like, how should I put it … a revelation or a reunion? It was nice to meet you, Anantya … Tantrist. I hope we meet again when there's more time to chat.'

He winked, threw a kiss in Dakini's direction and left. Dakini sighed.

'Isn't he a dish? If you hadn't become so pally with Nikhil, I could have fixed you up with him. He definitely has more class.'

She dragged me to the bar, where we ordered a Patiala peg of scotch each and I listened in to Luv-Kush. There was no conversation there. Vajrin was back on stage. I stared at him and wondered if I should put on my septifocals, and see what he turned out to be in the second or seventh vision planes. He moved with the grace of a tiger, sexual magnetism at every turn.

'Now for the last act of our magical evening, friends. Some of you have been questioning the idea of tantrism. Some of you might even think of it as superstition. I understand. If you haven't seen something, it doesn't exist, right? Now I am going to show you something that you might think belongs in the movies, not real life. How many of you have heard of vampires?'

Most hands shot up. Not mine. Vampires had become part of the popular culture recently with books and films dedicated to them. There had been a case recently when a boy had reported a vampire sighting and I had gone to investigate, only to discover that it was just a little ghoul.

'What you are about to see could be scary and dangerous,' Vajrin whispered. The lights dimmed and silence engulfed the hall. You could only see his eyes staring out from the smoky darkness. 'But I am ready to show you this so that you believe. You believe that the power of iMagic, the power of tantrism, is the power to control the universe, especially evil powers that might affect all our lives. May I request older people to step back a little? Heart patients and pregnant ladies, please stay away.'

There was pin-drop silence in the hall. Everyone looked around, excitement shining in their eyes, all waiting for a glimpse of the danger that the creature would bring. The sophisticated, diamond-wearing, designer-clothed party-goers had become a predatory gang of wolves on the hunt together. Vajrin Mahendra sure knew how to entertain Delhiites.

'... I have to confess, Antz,' said Dakini.

'Huh?'

'I have been a really bad girl, you know. I should ... but I'd hoped it would work out ... I so want it to.'

I looked at her perplexed. She was standing in front of me (I was seated on a high bar stool), her large manicured hands were tightly wrapped around my smaller grubby ones. I noticed her nails were painted purple. Her eyes were ... worried, looking deep black in the blue frozen lights. 'There's someone I want you to meet. I hope ... I hope you won't think of me as being too much of a bad gal.'

She moved to one side. My heart skipped a beat. Riju stood in front of me, smiling his soppy smile. The smile that used to make me laugh. I used to call him a rabbit because of the way his teeth protruded when he smiled. I froze as he moved towards me, hands extended for a hug.

'Anu!'

My hands curled into fists in my lap. What the hell was happening? Why was this night turning into a reunion nightmare? First Nasty, and now Riju? Riju. The joker. Yogi Riju, I corrected myself. He had moved up the ladder since I had last seen him. He looked ... different, too. Grown up. He wore a black dhoti with a patka as was required of anyone at the level of Yogi or higher. Somehow, the garb made him more serious, more ... official, although he was only a few years older to me. Even the way he used to carry himself, like his head was too heavy for him, had changed. He stood taller and more confident. He used to be skinnier, but now he looked fleshed out. A gold medallion of the triangular Kaula signet sat on his hairy chest. His hair had turned prematurely grey; he used to wear it in short brown spikes.

'What the hell are you doing here?' I asked, my voice harsh, as memories poured in. Us smoking pot together. Our first. Riju had been like a brother, an elder brother. The only one I could call my brother. Who had been there with me always. I had shared everything with him, my fears, disgusts, experiences. Then it had all changed, when I had left the ashram. When he had turned his back on me. NO! I didn't want to remember. Not that. I got off the bar stool with a jerk.

'Anu, please! Listen, please!' he said, trying to stall me.

'Stay away from me!' I shrugged him off.

His hands dropped, his eyes moist. Too much had happened in our past. Besides, he wasn't Riju, I reminded myself. He was an official of Kaula Ashram. He was not my friend. No one from the ashram was. I looked at Dakini in anger. She had a sympathetic expression in her eyes.

'And we are done too,' I whispered. 'This so wasn't—'

There was a lump in my throat suddenly. I couldn't think of anything more to say. I picked up my bag and started to move towards the exit, something threatening to crash inside me. Riju, who had smiled and let go of me, in favour of the ashram. No, I couldn't ever forget or forgive that. That chapter of my life was closed. It didn't matter. Bloody Kaulas, they never leave you alone.

'Antz!'

I didn't look back, heading towards the main door, my head down. I wanted to get away from here as soon as possible.

'ANTZ! STOP!'

I banged into something cold, colder than the frigid place I was in. Someone exclaimed behind me. I looked up to see a beautiful, god-like creature. His cold but delicate hands held my shoulders through my fur coat. I could feel a tingling through my coat, on my skin. He smiled, his eyes staring deep into my eyes. A numbness began to flood through me. His eyes were pools of desire. I smiled. I was happy. Here was someone who would take care of me. Finally. It was a good thought. I let myself go and kissed him on the mouth, wanting, desiring this god-like creature from the bottom of my heart. Someone tugged at me. I clung on. I didn't want to let go of this blissful, beautiful feeling. But the pull was strong and I was pried loose from the heavenly creature. Then someone slapped me.

'Antz, Antz! Stop it!' *Slap!* Something above me was glittering. My eyes were glazed. Another slap. My head lolled, moving from side to side.

'What … happened?'

'You just kissed a bloody vampire that's what happened,' replied Dakini as her concerned face solidified in front of me. 'What the hell were you thinking? Clinging to him like a leech?'

I shook my heavy head. The spell had shattered, leaving what felt like a hangover. As I was saying, I had never met a vampire before. Well, obviously I didn't know everything in the world.

'… as you can see, it's really easy for them to control your emotions and enthral, especially the female of any species. But even males will not escape their spell. I will show you just how in a minute. Stand back, everybody.'

I stood up, precariously steadying myself with Dakini's help. That blood-creature had been strong. I looked back at him. There he stood, smirking. He licked his lips with a long tongue. I touched my lips, which were still numb from the kiss. People were giggling at us. Blood rushed to my cheeks. Of all the stupid things to do. I had just ended up making a complete fool of myself. I took out my boneblade and stared at it, wondering if I should plunge it into his heart.

The vampire gasped, like he was suffocating, which was funny as vampires are actually dead and don't really breathe (or so I've heard). That's when I noticed the Vama. He stared at me, his eyes like coals. He stood there, practically naked but for a red loincloth. Vama, a Red tantrik clan. His forehead and arms were covered in ash, his long hair was dirty and matted. He wore a necklace made of what looked like the bones of human fingers, but that was just for effect. The real symbol he wore was a huge scorpion tattooed on his chest, with its tail disappearing into the small loincloth. It was his soulbeast. For a Vama, a soulbeast was like a mate you share your soul with, the animal you become and with which you wield your power. Vamas choose their soulbeast really seriously. The scorpion looked alive, as if it was crawling on his belly, up towards his neck. The Vama expertly pulled the vampire, with something that looked like a long red claw. I noticed that his hand had scorpion pincers etched on each finger. The Vama's muscles rippled as he walked, his body had been oiled to perfection. I had met Vamas in the jungle during my student days, but never seen one in the city. They avoided crowds, stayed in isolation, as they practised forbidden magic. He looked alien, like something from another world. Which was how people seemed to be treating him too.

'... welcome, Mattreya, who has captured this vampire and brought him here tonight for all of you to see. You don't need to worry about the vampire as long as this man is on our side. The evil that lurks in this vampire's heart is like a cancer ...'

Mattreya was followed by two younger men, one fat and the other thin and tall. His apprentices, I reckoned, as both were without tattoos and hadn't chosen their soulbeast yet. I recognized one of them as the person who had taken charak from the barman, the guy with the firefly locket. The same guy who had been talking to Lavanya earlier. He now wore only a loincloth.

'... it has become his very nature to drink human blood. It cannot be cured by any amount of goodness. Now Mattreya needs a volunteer, who will help him? Who will willingly give her arm to the vampire to help demonstrate to everyone how a tantrik can protect you?'

Everyone took a few steps back. The apprentice walked towards the stage. Whispers spread like wildfire in the crowd. I stood on one side, spellbound. What was he planning to do?

'Ah, we have a volunteer.'

Mohini offered her arm to the vampire. The vampire, overcome with hunger (and he did look famished), lunged towards the girl, snarling to show his extended canine teeth. The crowd gasped. A few of them took photographs with their mobile phones, which were immediately confiscated by the bouncers. The vamp now looked more like a hungry animal than a civilized god. I touched my lips.

'… the only kindness we can show him is put him out of his misery, like a fatally injured animal …'

Mattreya came forward and stared at the crowd. He raised his hands in the air. The action made him look like a scorpion, standing on its tail. Everyone stood still. He begun to emit noises from deep within his throat and then looked at the audience with burning, poisonous eyes. People surged forward, curiosity sparkling in their eyes. A couple of women, whose diamonds glittered in the darkness, pointed their fingers at him.

'Does it hurt?' a middle-aged woman asked Mohini. She smiled, weakly. We could see her visibly weakening as the vampire continued to suck her blood.

'Stop it!' cried someone from the audience.

'But Mattreya, like iMagic, won't act until he hears your will. Mind power, the shakti in all of you, that's what works here. You have to say it, you have to command! You will have to tell him that you want to kill the creature. Tell him quickly before he sucks all of the girl's blood. Kill or save? Kill or save!' Vajrin's voice echoed in the silent hall.

'Kill!' shouted someone from behind. Everybody turned around, horror etched on their faces. For a second I thought they would say no, but then the chant started. It built up slowly and steadily until it reached a crescendo.

Kill, kill, KILL!

The decision was made. Mattreya raised his clawed hands towards the ceiling. He looked at us, his discoloured, crooked teeth in a snarl as he yanked the vampire away from Mohini. Blood dribbled from the vampire's mouth.

'Bhagute, bhutey, bhukanatha, namaha!'

Mattreya's claw-like left hand rose again and sank deep into the vampire's neck. There was a collective cry. Those who had been standing too close to the stage were splattered with blood. There was a second's silence and then everyone started to clap in unison. A monster had been destroyed. Nobody seemed to care that it was another monster that had done it.

'This is what iMagic can do for you. Destroy all the evil in your path. Conquer the universe so that nothing can come in your way.'

I couldn't quite see the connection between killing a vampire and owning a device, but it definitely left the crowd on a high note. The Vama picked up the head of the vampire by its hair and showed it to the audience. They cheered and clapped.

'Mattreya! Mattreya! Mattreya!'

The vampire's body lay on the stage, wilting in plain sight as blood gushed from it. Someone behind me retched. I turned around to find Dakini throwing up over her stilettos.

'Why the hell would someone do this in a civilized party,' she bellowed when she regained her voice. She wiped the puke from her face. 'I think I will leave right—'

'HOW DARE YOU DO THIS? INVITE SOILED, OBSCENE, RED FILTH HERE?'

Nasty stood in front of Vajrin, his right hand outstretched, staff pointed threateningly. Riju tried to hold him back, but

Nasty was furious, his dark eyes burning in the dim light. This was going to be interesting, I thought, amused. First a Vama glory show and now a Kaula standoff. The clans of Vamas and Kaulas hated each other's guts. It had been murder, every time they met. The establishment of CAT had brokered an uneasy truce between them. At least no one had killed the other since, publicly that is. They could never trust each other completely because they just didn't trust the other's tantrism style. Kaulas were White tantriks, who used sexual energy to tap into shakti. They hated sacrifices or blood. Vamas, the Red tantriks, revelled in killing, choosing soulbeasts, sacrificing animals and hoarding the shakti created from those. They were completely different kinds of magic. And Vajrin had invited both to his party. He sure would make the headlines the next day.

'Death-bringers like him should stay in the wild, which is where they belong, gorging on meat from innocents!'

Mattreya stood behind Vajrin. I could see from the way his fingers were itching that he was quite riled and this could lead to a tantrik showdown. The vampire's not-quite-dead body continued to twitch on the blood-drenched stage. The guests stood still in anticipation. Oh, Nasty would get a nasty surprise as fallout for this outburst the next day. CAT didn't like tantrik ego clashes in public, especially since they were trying really hard to build a positive image for themselves. The Kaulas had closed rooms and secret organizations to kill Vamas.

Nasty seemed unstoppable though. 'This is a slap in the face for the Association! We have never been insulted like this. I wish I could turn you into a slimy mass of worms! It was a mistake! You were a mistake! I will complain about this to the Council ...'

Vajrin's beefy guards lined up, ready to drag Nasty out of the premises. But Vajrin signalled to them to back off.

'... you have some obligations to Kaulas. It's not for nothing that we brought you here. You are stuck with us whether you like it or not. If you carry on in this vein ...' Nasty was red in the face and screaming now.

'Narahara, I have done nothing. Nothing *yet*, that is.' Vajrin's voice was strangely calm, considering Narahara had had the gall to threaten him in his own house, in front of about three hundred people. I wondered what kind of dope Nasty had on Vajrin.

'I am the one who is responsible for your behaviour. I am the representative of the Council. I *am* the Council for you and you will heed my command, or else—'

'I know who you are, Swami Narahara,' replied Vajrin smoothly, as he placed his arm around Nasty's shoulders and propelled him away to a dark corner, 'as do all my guests, but it's a lovely night and we have just announced a beautiful device together. Why don't we drink instead of fighting, eh?'

As if on cue, the music grew louder. The audience lost interest and moved towards the bar, some of them got on the dance floor. They were back to their drinking and partying as if all of that had been just part of the entertainment for the evening. My phone rang. It was Madhu. The music had become too loud for me to answer it, so I headed out. I found a quiet spot outside and lit up a beedi, taking a deep puff. There was something about the small pleasures of life. Pleasures in a beedi. Pleasures in blood, drinking it, seeing it bleed from a sup and how it gave people a high. Humans were slaves to pleasure. It had always been like that. The people in the party tonight loved all types of highs – be it charak or bloodletting. I remembered Mohini, standing around, licking the splattered vampire blood off her arm. I stubbed out my beedi and called Madhu.

'Anantya, you had better come here now,' he said without a hello. He gave me an address and hung up. Lavanya had just reached home and probably wouldn't be meeting anyone in the middle of the night. Still, I couldn't afford to take any chances. I made a quick call to Prem Chhokra, a young dasyu who'd be a perfect shadow to stakeout Lavanya Mohan's apartment in case she decided to conduct a midnight rendezvous. The dasyu was smart, had great night vision and could fly. And he was desperate for a spy job. I removed Luv (or maybe Kush) from my ear and revved up Chhotu. It was a small job, safe enough to keep Prem Chhokra out of trouble. My bike belched forth a joyful snort, as if it was also glad to get away from the party scene.

6

The moon hung like a sickle in the sky. The night was dark and stuffy, as if the heat rose up from the very core of the earth. It was early July, the time when everyone looked skywards, hoping for dark clouds. There was nothing there but dust and heat. I turned on to the dirt road as Madhu had directed, riding past the main entrance of the Indian Agricultural Research Institute, or Pusa Institute as it is popularly known. For someone who liked to make a lot of noise, Chhotu had become quiet, almost as if it didn't want to disturb the dead silence of the forest around us.

The forest on Pusa hill is a green belt in the middle of Delhi, land used by the Pusa Institute for plant research. The trees here were stunted, the dirt road dark. I could barely see beyond Chhotu's feeble purple light (there's a whole story behind that but now is not the time).

After a while, the road opened up into a circular clearing and I saw the Do Not Cross police strip within the shrubbery. A spotlight lit up the area and reflected off Madhu's bald head, shiny with sweat. Two spooked policemen stood outside the cordoned area. One of them wiped the sweat off his face as he checked my ID. The clearing was a huge bare rock surface, as smooth as a pebble. All around it were dark trees. But for the occasional croaks and cawing of the ravens, there was silence. Madhu signalled to me.

It was as if the Kotla bodies had time-travelled to this rock tonight to confuse us. Just for fun. The bodies of the man and the girl child were in the same position, with the man bent over the girl, wearing the expression of a monomaniac. The girl looked horrified as her body was rent asunder by the blade in the man's grip. I could barely see her darkened blood flowing into the apex of the triangle but I knew it was there. There was only one thing missing.

'Definitely a cosier location than the last time,' I said. 'No pyramid this time?'

'Not a pyramid, a tetrahedron,' came a low-pitched voice from behind us. I hadn't noticed anyone other than Madhu and his two henchmen until then. A tall, sort of vertically elongated man stood behind us.

'Its base is triangular, as opposed to a pyramid's base, which is a square. It was here all right when we first came in, but I removed it exactly…' He looked at his wristwatch that glowed a green neon in the dark. '…forty-six minutes ago.'

'This is Shukra, our forensics consultant,' introduced Madhu. 'He will be helping us with this case. He was the one—'

'Shukracharya the seventy-sixth, from the illustrious line of scientific guides to the asuras,' said Shukra, holding out his thin hand with his fingers held down to show me a ring bearing a Sanskrit-inscription. He waited for a few seconds, as if expecting a kiss on the ring. I crossed my arms and stared at him, wondering if I should deliver a swift kick on his royal butt. Since I didn't move, he let his hand fall and bowed slightly. 'No need to be formal, of course. You can just call me Shukra. We will be working on the same team after all.'

Shukra was only slightly older than I was, but his pinched

face, manner and tone of voice reminded me of a Kaula Council grandfather I had always hated. He was dressed like an old man too, in a formal white shirt, black suspenders, a long coat and trousers that floated on his thin legs like balloons. I couldn't understand why someone would wear a coat in this Delhi heat, but then His Grace would have some regal reason for it I bet. I looked at Madhu who either didn't notice the exasperation on my face, or chose to ignore it.

'As I was saying, he's the one who received the bodies from the Kotla Mubarakpur incident. He's been studying them since last night and has given me some good insights. When I heard about this one on the wireless, he wanted to come too. He has figured out that the pyramid was a result of—'

'There are many things that forensics notice that could be missed by those not trained in the art of observation,' said Shukra. 'So it was essential that I accompanied you. Take, for example, the tetrahedron…' He pushed his glasses, a thin, black, metallic frame, up the bridge of his sharp nose. 'Or as you both put it "the pyramid". You would never have figured out its exact nature if I hadn't been here tonight.'

'And do enlighten us about the exact nature of the said pyramid,' I said, dripping as much acid from my tongue as I could manage without scalding myself. He missed the sarcasm altogether.

'It's all quite elementary actually, as a famous detective put it. That is, if you are proficient in the power of deduction. Whatever experiment was being conducted by the man there…' He trained a red laser dot from a small torch on the dead man. '…was something that involved a massive quantity of electrical charge. Not very difficult considering it's just before the monsoon and the weather is dry. There's a lot of static up there. This is not the handiwork of a demon, like someone else had suggested to Madhu, but quite simply a clever use of excessive atmospheric electricity … or an attempt at it, at any rate, because being dead as a result isn't frightfully clever. After all, to the unscientific,' he said, nodding curtly towards me, 'large concentrations of electricity do look like spirits. Tonight, when the phenomenon occurred, it was sometime between eleven thirty p.m. and twelve fifteen a.m. …'

'An assumption?'

'Of course not.' He looked affronted. 'Yesterday's victims died at around the same time. Tonight, this had to be performed sometime before twelve thirty because that was the time when the lady called the police.'

'What lady?'

'The one who relayed the distress call to the police. The wife of Rohit Kanwal, the dead man.'

'His wife was here?'

'Pardon me, but you do tend to interrupt a lot,' said Shukra.

I ignored him. 'Did she see what happened? Why was she here?'

'Yeah,' Madhu answered, 'we are presuming it was her. She was the one who called the police and filed a report on her husband, explaining how she had lost sight of him while in pursuit. I heard it on a constable's wireless and, since the situation sounded similar to the Mubarakpur case, came here. She must have eventually become curious and tried to touch the blasted thing. When we arrived, she was on the ground, unconscious, almost dead. Electric shock, the doctor has said. She's in a nearby hospital now. Someone from the local police is there to inform us as soon as she wakes up. Shukra removed the pyramid by using some instrument …'

'An insulator, which is exactly what you should have done last night instead of almost killing yourself and Madhu.' He looked smug as he pushed his spectacles up his nose. His head, I noticed, looked like a rectangular box with bushy hair planted on top. 'The powder here,' he said, touching the pile of 'diamond dust' on the triangle, 'is made of copper, mercury, gold and silver, which are highly conductive elements and so act like conduits to the static electricity. I think that's how the surplus electromagnetic waves created an illusion of a tetrahedron around the triangle, making it seem solid, when actually it was a wall of moving, residual electricity. Considering it was made purely of electric discharge, it would naturally give a shock to whoever touched it. You see, science has all the logical explanations if you only cared to look.'

'Ah. You are that kind. All science, no spirits.'

'Most of the "demon did it" superstitions are concocted by those who don't understand the scientific reasons of tantrism. I concede that there are some tantriks who are actually scientists, much like my ancestors who performed highly evolved scientific experiments. But unfortunately, all those experiments are interpreted by the riff raff, or mere manavas, as dark magic. I told Madhu yesterday itself that he didn't need a tantrik on the case. What he needs is a scientist.'

'Why don't you indulge a tantrik's ignorance in this case, Your Grace …'

'Just Shukra will do. As I said, I don't hold with royal privileges.'

'Your *Grace*,' I insisted, and walked around the triangle, my hands clasped behind my back. 'So just tell me how it goes. If all this guy wanted was a bunch of electricity to tap into, why not use a generator? I mean modern science has something as mundane as electricity-generation down pat, right? Then why hack a girl's body with a sickle?'

The pinnacle of the triangle had an object that had bothered me the last time too. Last time. I seemed to be already thinking as if this incident was going to recur.

I picked up the cellphone near the apex. This, I couldn't understand. Once could be a mistake. Twice, however, could just be the beginning of a pattern. A bunch of ravens rose up overhead, cawing in alarm. Long misshapen shadows played grotesquely on the two bodies.

'Perhaps he actually believed that he was performing a tantrik act,' said Shukra, readjusting his infernal glasses on his nose, his eyes serious. 'One's beliefs can control the mind to a great extent. Although in reality he was only tapping into the static electricity in the atmosphere, in his mind he probably imagined it was a powerful demon. I think if we start looking at the case from the perspective that it has a scientific answer, we can work out an explanation.'

'And how do you explain, scientifically that is, this phone? If it was all a lightning bolt, as you put it, how do you suppose this cellphone wasn't damaged by it? Madhu,' I turned to him, 'this is exactly the same type of phone that we saw yesterday, at exactly the same place – the pinnacle. I don't think twice is a mere coincidence. Did you find out who Vikram Sharma had contacted before he sacrificed his daughter? That could give us a lead to the death ... deaths.'

'Yes, I did follow up on that,' said Madhu, his bushy whiskers trembling in a stray gust of wind. 'The last call was to a private number. We are still working out whose number it is. Shukra, would you happen to know what this gadget plugged into the phone might be?'

'Ah, that's an amplifier,' answered Shukra, directing his laser torch to the tip of the phone I held. 'If Miss Anantya had let me explain before she butted in with her conclusions, I would have mentioned that as well. Now, you may know, an amplifier amplifies waves of electricity. My theory is that the cellphone in your hand served as an antenna to the static electricity and channelled it, rather like a copper wire, which then spread through the triangle. I will, of course, have to check its innards to understand exactly how that happened. But I am almost sure that it played an important role in tapping into the electromagnetic waves and directing them around these two people.'

With a sinking heart, I focused on the frozen tableau again: the two shrunken bodies, a man bent over a small naked girl, the blade in the girl's chest, her skin rolled back from the vertical incision from womb to chest – the path of the blade across her body. I walked around and came to stand in front of the dead man's body, and leant down. The three-headed cobra symbol was tattooed on his chest, its red eyes small dots of blood. But it looked like it had been drawn hurriedly, almost as an afterthought – like he had forgotten about it. I gently extracted the blade from the girl's chest. It came out just as effortlessly as the last one had and felt just as dangerous.

'Madhu! She is tampering with evidence that could be crucial,' whined Shukra. 'We haven't even taken photographs yet. This is why I wanted to be here before amateurs started poking around, leaving their fingerprints all over the crime scene!'

I ignored him, experiencing the heady rush that the blade gave me. It was the same blade, clear, translucent, sickle-shaped. A blade to harvest human blood. The handle had the engraving of two intertwined roses, identical to the earlier one. One such blade was a rarity, but two in the hands of two separate humans? There was a connection, I was sure of it.

The scene was exactly the same. The blade, the bodies. The only difference was the time of day when we saw it: it was night this time. I looked up and saw the moon, sickle-shaped, the same shape as the harvest blade in my hand. Many, many ravens rose up flapping and croaking, beginning to circle overhead, their shadow changing the girl's expression of horror into a smirk. As if on cue, the blade also smirked, its edge shining as the moon above. I held the blade aloft in both my hands; it covered the moon perfectly and began to shine with an eerie white light, like a sickle-shaped fluorescent bulb.

'Why didn't I think of this before?' I was awestruck. 'This is a true moonblade!' No wonder it rebuffed all my attempts to look into it. This was one of the most potent sacrificial blades in the history of tantrism. And to think I had one in my hand all of last night and hadn't realized that. What kind of an idiot was I?

'How did you make it shine like that?' asked Shukra.

'A moonblade?' asked Madhu in confusion.

'A blade that legends say is a soulmate to the moon. A powerful blade that juices up through the moon during a sacrifice,' I said. Shakti's ass, I was actually holding a moonblade! As I felt its cool white reflection on my face, I wondered how many human sacrifices it had made. 'You see, tantriks believe that the world, the universe in fact, is powered by shakti. Some,' I continued, looking at Shukra whose thin lips were pressed together in a thinner, tighter line, 'might call it energy. It's the same deal. It's female power. Life, death and everything in between happens because of it. Tantriks are always looking for more ways, more powerful ways to tap into shakti, to store it, channel it and use it. The moon is one such source. Its cold light is a powerhouse of shakti.

That's why tantrik rituals are done in the night. Not because they want to keep it a secret.'

'Where does this blade fit into all of this?'

'Moonblades are made for human harvesting. They were traditionally used in reciting mantras to call upon and even bind daevas to humans. If you notice, this moonblade is the exact shape of the crescent moon that's out in the sky right now. That's because it is at its most powerful twice a month, on the day when its shape perfectly replicates the moon in the sky. That's when it can perform to its full ability.'

'So if this blade is so rare, why is it in the hands of people who aren't established tantriks? How did these people get the blades?'

'I don't know yet, but I know of someone who might be able to find out.'

'Ah, a convoluted story made entirely of confusion,' exclaimed Shukra. 'It's a sickle not a blade, made of phosphorescent material that can shine. Don't go connecting it to some feminist mumbo-jumbo from aeons ago.'

Anger uncoiled in my head. I jumped up, moving snake-like, moonblade in hand, and put it against his neck. I could feel it thrill in my hand, itching to taste blood.

'Don't ever,' I said through clenched teeth, blood pounding in my veins, 'use the f-word again if you want to live.'

'Anantya!' exclaimed Madhu, trying to haul me back. 'Don't be ridiculous! Back off. Now!'

Shukra, who, to his credit, hadn't budged at all, readjusted his spectacles. 'Miss Anantya, all I am trying to do is make this as rational as possible. So there's no need to take it personally. I am not against fem—' He saw my expression and stopped. 'You are merely assuming that this is a moon knife. What's your proof?'

'Don't think that things you don't understand do not exist …'

Kill, kill, kill!

'I …' I whispered, shocked. Whose thought had that been? It had rung inside my head, clear and bright. With extreme effort, I forced my hand away from Shukra's neck. I should have known better than to wield such a powerful object. I gently placed it on the boulder, feeling shaken.

'Stop it, both of you!' Madhu's whiskers bristled. 'We are on the same team here. Solving this case is more important than arguing about whose perspective on life is better. Why don't you, Anantya, take the blade as you did the other, and try and find out if they are actually moonblades as you suspect and, if they are, what their relevance to the case may be.' He turned to Shukra. 'And Shukra, start your photographing, fingerprinting and the other things that you forensics guys do. I want to know the causes of death for both these bodies as well. Analyse the materials used to make the triangle's lines. And also analyse the cellphones and see what's inside. I will try and push my technology team to trace the person whose number was last called from this phone. I don't want to hear about "possible scenarios". I want to know the real deal. We need to figure out what's happening here and more importantly,' he hesitated as if voicing the possibility might jinx it into existence, 'plan what we need to do in case it happens again.'

Ignoring everybody, I quietly picked up the velvet pouch that I found in the bag, presumably the dead man's, wrapped the moonblade in it and rose. For a second, I stopped, staring at the dead girl, her expression of horror filling the sky. The ravens were still circling and cawing, excited by the smell of dead, rotting flesh. I felt ashamed. Ashamed that I had been more focused on my anger than the pain she went through. I moved to my bike and made a call to Prem Chhokra to find out if there had been any movement in Lavanya's house, which he had been watching over for nearly an hour now. When he assured me that nothing had moved, not even a leaf, I tried Kaani's number. When he didn't answer his phone, I decided to head to Qutab Minar. Guru B's place was open all hours, although only for people who could bring him the right dakshina. Which meant I would have to go to HaveMore Dhaba first.

The silent garden behind the canteen was bare, except for the mausoleum in the middle of it. Even guards don't like to disturb the dead, I thought. What the hell was it about that Shukra fellow that had irked me so much anyway? It wasn't as if I hadn't met assholes who considered tantrism pure fantasy fiction. I had had enough of rational thinkers who thought reality was only what they experienced. No, that didn't bother me that much. Nor was it the casual arrogance of blue blood. No, there was something else here. It was the way he looked at things. His stubborn conviction that there was no way other than his scientific methods. The way he had looked at me with those big black eyes when I had held his collar. Not fearfully, but daring me. And then he had used the f-word. The one word I couldn't stand. The smug, arrogant bastard.

But hating someone doesn't give one the right to want to kill them. The desire to taste his blood was planted in my head because of the moonblade, but to be honest, there had also been a tiny bit of me in it. A tiny bit that desired the taste and sight of blood, that wanted to deal death. Didn't I enjoy being a Red tantrik? Wasn't I looking forward right now to sacrificing this rabbit for the incantation? How was I so different from that man who had sacrificed someone for something too? The ritualistic act of sacrifice had been the same. Only, he had done it to a little girl, his daughter, while I did it to animals. I wondered if hell would categorize us both as monsters.

Someone whistled tunelessly in the distance. My ears cocked as I crouched in the shadows, motionless. Dawn was only two hours away and I wanted to finish this and be on my way back by then. I really didn't want, first thing in the morning, to be standing around explaining to a guard why I was hanging around the Qutab Minar complex, attempting to break into the tomb of a long-dead Mughal general. Not that it had been a problem before. The guards at the Qutab Minar were mostly either fast asleep or nodding off by this time, and rarely ventured to the dark area behind the canteen. The grave inside was a stone cuboid that contained the dead body of Muhammad Quli Khan, a general of Emperor Akbar. It was a forgotten remnant of a dead civilization. That is before Guru B had chosen that spot as his workstation over three hundred years ago. Unfortunately, some decades ago, the spot had been 're-discovered' by the British and converted into a local tourist attraction. Instead of putting up a fight or showing some form of resistance to protect his space and land, Guru B had simply yielded to the colonizers and, later on, to the government of independent India and quietly gone deeper underground.

After assuring myself that the whistling was not getting any closer, I slashed the rabbit's neck from side to side and let the warm blood spill over one side of the grave. To ensure that only people with magical knowledge could enter, the portal to Guru B's workspace needed a blood sacrifice. I pressed a carved stud on the tomb. Somewhere below me came a soft, well-oiled swish. The stairwell was open. A sudden draught of cool air hit me as I descended into the darkness. Behind me, the aperture slid shut.

'I've brought peacock meat,' I whispered.

I had three more flights of stairs to go but I knew he could hear me. The place was teeming with Luv-Kush bugs and other listening devices that I didn't even know about. Guru B was rather paranoid, which explained his sophisticated and complex security systems. I had stopped at HaveMore Dhaba at the Mehrauli night bazaar to pick up some illegal peacock meat on my way to his place. Each step on the staircase was about a foot high and I had to jump down to the next one. The walls grew colder the further I went and my teeth started to chatter. Because of the kind of stuff stored here, Guru B preferred to maintain low temperatures in his vaults – sub-zero mostly. I accepted this without question. He had more experience with archiving written material than any librarian across the globe (except perhaps the Vatican's curators). I reached a tiny, neat, capsule-shaped room, which had smooth white walls.

'Combustible items to your left and all other things to your right,' said a mechanical voice in the pod as two shelves appeared out of the wall on either side of me.

I placed my box of matches and beedi in the left compartment. After a moment's hesitation, I placed my satchel, my locket and the septifocals in the other box. The only things on me, other than my clothes, were a small piece of paper and the peacock meat, of course.

'What's the purpose of your visit?'

'Delivery,' I answered, showing a small camera eye the bag of meat. A series of sprays full of sneezy sanitizers buzzed on me and I was released – clean and disinfected. I walked along a long white corridor with glass bookshelves on both sides. There were books written on parchment, vellum, papyrus, paper, insects, animal skins and various other materials. Guru B, who had had a long life, had dedicated his entire collection to the study of tantrism, Indian sorcery and science. Ashwa, my friend at Bedardi Bar, had once told me that he had even managed to save some books from the legendary Nalanda university before the library had been burnt down by a savage attack from the west in the twelfth century. If anyone had the answers, he would. The corridor I walked along was just one of the many arms in his web-like underground 'resource centre', as he liked to call it. Although I was not really into books, the place had never ceased to amaze me.

Guru B was an old tantrik. And eccentric. He spoke to his manuscripts and rejected all offers of help from the tantrik clans. But everybody has their weakness, and peacock meat was his. Since he lived underground with his millions of books, Guru B ended up surviving on food pills or uncooked things. Gas and anything that could start a fire was a strict no-no.

'Here,' said Guru B, handing me a coat as I entered his study, a long white room with a low ceiling. He was seven feet tall and wiry thin with skin that appeared to be the texture of shiny brown gift-wrapping. He looked like he was lit up from inside, with piercing, grey eyes. His flowing white beard framed a gaunt brown face. Black-rimmed spectacles were perched on the thin nose jutting out at a sharp angle from his face.

'Why the visit?' he asked, his voice hoarse. Probably due to eons of disuse. I had visited this place only twice before and never seen anyone here but him. I offered him the meat. He promptly placed it on a beautifully carved ivory plate on one of the desks and sat down to eat it with a fork and knife. There were five desks in all, arranged precisely parallel to each other, each flanked by a pair of chairs on either side. At the far end was a lounge chair and a small stool.

'I want to know more about this symbol,' I said, showing him my sketch of the three-headed cobra tattoo.

He looked at it, chewing, expressionless. 'Why?' he asked when he had swallowed the morsel.

'It has cropped up in one of the cases I am working on. It was tattooed on a dude who sacrificed his young daughter.'

He stared at the sign, his irises sharpening into pinpoints. 'Is he alive?'

'No. Tonight we saw another man who died the same way, sacrificing a young girl. He had the same tattoo, although it was a poorly executed replica.'

'Understandable.' He wiped his beard with a napkin. The plate was spotlessly clean, like the meat hadn't even been there. 'Come.'

As I mentioned earlier, the library is a labyrinth of tunnels. We walked through some of them. I wondered how many years it had taken him to build this library. Guru B looked like an old man, but just how old I could not have said. Three hundred years or three thousand? Ashwa had introduced me to the old man and he had proved useful more than once. There was nothing he didn't know about tantrism. I wondered what Shukra would say if he ever came to this place. Fall over in surprise, I bet. The old man stopped suddenly and I collided with him. He gave me a stern look and then fished out a large hardbound book from a shelf. In the clinical white light, the book sparkled green, like an emerald.

'*The Cult of Chaos*?' I read the title aloud, transfixed by the three-headed cobra symbol on the cover. It was etched in molten black, the eyes of the cobras were rubies, six of them. It seemed to surge from the cover.

'Now that's a name I haven't heard in two hundred years,' said Guru B, stroking his beard. 'Manohar Banwari. He was the one who named it back then. An exceptional scientist. He was the leader of the Cult of Chaos in the early nineteenth century. The cult simply called him "the Chief". They believed that the natural order of things is anarchy, madness, turmoil, pandemonium. That humans, mayans, pashus, bhutas, everyone is supposed to mingle and coexist without boundaries, without physical planes. That boundaries between realities were made by the newer gods to segregate the species. Many more boundaries and rules were added as humans created civilization.'

He started to retrace his steps and I followed. 'What does the symbol mean?'

'They were convinced that civilization is not the way we were supposed to live. That chaos is the true state of being. All the species living together, intermingling in a horror of love and blood and violence. The cult had one aim, turn the clock back and evict the false gods. Restore the universe to its original self – that of formlessness and chaos.'

'Must have been misfits,' I muttered. This time he did hear me.

'Not really. They were all prominent members of the society. Scientists, doctors, businessmen, politicians and other influential people. You will be surprised how many humans actually think they are doing the world a favour by destroying it. To answer your first question, the symbol is their cult god.'

'Then why did a naga, who I bet doesn't know about this two-hundred-year-old human cult, literally jump out of his skin upon seeing this symbol?'

We had returned to his study. Guru B removed his spectacles and wiped them as he sat back in his lounge chair. I fingered through the pages, feeling them, as if they might hold the answer.

'Because the cult affected not only humans but other species as well. The symbol wasn't created by the cult. It is older than the Cult of Chaos. An icon of an ancient creature, a spirit from the beginning of the universe, older than the gods themselves. The cult called it the God of Chaos. There are references to this creature in all mythologies across the world. He has been named Kolahal, the god that breeds chaos, and Ahi in different times, during different ages, by different cultures. He is so old that humans have forgotten his existence, although other species haven't, not yet. According to the nagas, Kolahal was locked in a deep dungeon of Patala by one of their earlier kings. The door to that dungeon, in which the God of Chaos now resides, still bears this symbol.

'The cult found out about Kolahal and wanted to release him into their world. For years, they tried but failed. Every time a ritual was perfected and sacrifices performed, the god would arrive and invariably end up destroying the human who was to be the vessel, the body for Kolahal. Finally, after years of failure, they discovered a foolproof way to bring Kolahal into this universe and were successful. Millions of lives were destroyed, some human cities were razed and laid to ruin. But worse was to come. Kolahal destroyed the fine lines that divided the world of the dead from the world of the living. This not only affected creatures on earth, but also those over and under it.'

'The Patala?'

'Yes. In the dark recesses of the underground world, the plague of Kolahal spread like wildfire. Half of Patala's population was devoured by the chaos demon. But somehow, it was leashed and locked into the vaults of Patala with the symbol, this symbol of the cobra with three heads, painted on it as a reminder to keep that door closed.'

'You said that many cities were destroyed and millions of people killed. Why did we forget this destruction? It happened only two hundred years ago.'

'Because that's what humans do. Humans have short lives, like moths, lit one night, dead the next. They rarely pass on knowledge from one generation to the other. In stories, Kolahal become the Black Plague. But the Patala remembers and still shudders at the destruction Kolahal caused.'

'No wonder Zee turned at the sight of the symbol. Guru, could the symbol mean that the Cult of Chaos has become active again?'

'It could. Or it could just be a coincidence. Let's hope it's the latter.'

'You mentioned that Kolahal was brought in through a ritual which the cult found out about. Would you know what kind of ritual they used?'

Guru B didn't reply, staring at the blank wall for a while, stroking his beard. His smooth brown face emitted a soft glow.

'This book doesn't mention the ritual, but I have lived a long time and one hears things. Whether they are true, I know not. Like any other spirit, Kolahal cannot survive on this plane without a human body. As a rule, the leader of the cult offers their god his own body, to possess, to use and to claim. As soon as the god is in the leader's body, Kolahal's powers can be controlled and channelled. Mayhem and destruction can be directed, sometimes by the danava and sometimes by the human that he possesses. But sooner or later, Kolahal will completely take over the body, consume its soul, seize its powers and then do what he does best – destroy. Erase the boundaries between the spirit and the living and the dead. The boundaries between civilization and wilderness. The boundaries between jungles and cities. The boundaries between the sky and the earth. All will be erased, all consumed.'

'And the ritual that brings him in?'

'The ritual involves sacrifices of six humans, preferably virgin girls until the new moon rises. This is to appease Kolahal's six mistresses who are his powers. On the seventh sacrifice, Kolahal will present himself. The power of each of these mistresses is stored, saved for her god, mostly in the body of the cult's leader. When Kolahal is called into the world on the seventh day, the human vessel, the body of the leader, needs to be prepared to take on the danava's powers. Only when Kolahal is married to the power of his six mistresses will the power of the danava be fully realized. But it's the blackest of arts and also a tricky one. Tantriks are weaker today than they were two hundred years ago. I don't think anyone can do this now. The art has been dead for quite some time now. You don't need to worry.'

'But the ritual does sound like the same shit I have been seeing,' I said. 'Virgin girls, check. Ritual at midnight, check. Fifth night is the new moon. Two sacrifices have already happened to please two mistresses. Four more mistresses in four more nights. And the fifth night for Kolahal to come into the world.' That sounded like wholesale trouble. 'Would you know how it can be stopped?'

'Hopefully,' he said, stroking his beard, 'the attempts to carry them out will fail. The rituals are very tricky to perform. If that is the case, we would only have seven dead manavas, and not the end of the world as we know it.'

No, I couldn't just let the young girls die. To me, it was not just about saving the world. I needed to save the little ones.

○

'Cult of Chaos, huh?' said Madhu. 'And you think they are performing a ritual to bring in this Kolahal or whoever he is?'

'Possibly,' I said, yawning and stretching until my hands touched the police jeep's roof. Madhu and I were on our way to meet Mrs Kanwal. The widow of the second dead tantrik had regained consciousness a couple of hours ago. It was nine o'clock Saturday morning and I had slept for only two hours sporadically in the last forty-eight. Even the thought of a sacrifice to destroy the world could only bring on a yawn.

'Sounds rather dramatic to me, but say we do believe it, does that mean that the same pattern of deaths will continue until the new moon? You mean there will be five more deaths like these?'

'Only if it's the same ritual,' I replied, fingering a lock of my hair. If the sacrifices were the same, someone was trying to bring this Kolahal guy into the world. The question is – who? The moonblades held that answer, I knew. Someone had given these moonblades to the two dead tantriks.

We reached the hospital and climbed up three floors to the private wing. Geeta Kanwal turned out to be a thin, pale woman.

'My husband, what happened to him?' she asked as soon as we entered the hospital room. 'And please don't make up lies like the last policeman did. I deserve to know the truth about what my husband did.'

She had a steely look about her. The veins in her hands were distended and still had an IVF needle in it. She was in her thirties but looked much older. Madhu recounted the entire night's events, honestly this time, including the fact that her husband had sacrificed the young girl. The only sign of emotion she betrayed was a quiver of her lips when we told her that her daughter was dead.

'She wasn't my daughter. She was a bas ... his illegal child borne by a maai, a housemaid, you understand!' she said. 'I had seen him get familiar with his dau ... that whore's daughter over the last two months ... he was the father of the girl ... I thought—' She swallowed hard. 'I thought he was doing something with her, which is why I followed him when he took her out in the night. But he was actually just trying to save our boy. Stupid, stupid man!'

'Save your boy?' I asked.

She looked down at her clasped hands and then back at me. 'My son has terminal cancer. We found out a year ago, and since then, we have been looking for a doctor who can tell us how we can save our boy. I guess my husband was trying to do the same in his own twisted, religious way.'

'You mean he was sacrificing another child to save yours and you *understand* that?'

'Anantya,' Madhu said in a warning tone.

Her eyes hardened and her mouth became a thin line again. 'Are you a mother, miss?' I didn't reply, but she took my silence to be an answer. 'Then you wouldn't understand why my husband would go to any lengths to save his child. I would have done the same.'

My stomach churned. There was no doubt in her eyes and no love for that little girl lying with her guts open to the sky.

And humans had the nerve to call daityas ruthless. She told us that by the time she found her husband's car in the forest, there was nothing around but the pyramid. That's when she called the police and then tried to touch it. She didn't remember anything after that.

I swallowed my anger because the need to get some answers came first. 'Mrs Kanwal, your husband was performing a pretty advanced tantrik ritual. Would you know where he found out about that?'

She shook her head. 'I don't know. He did have a lot of books in Sanskrit. It is part of his job as he is …' She stopped. For a minute I thought she would lose her composure, but she swallowed and said, '… was … a Sanskrit professor. He might have read about those rituals somewhere in his studies.'

'Do you remember anyone he might have met, any strange place he may have visited which would strike you as odd?'

'No, there was nothing. All he did was go to the university and come back for Anuj ever since he was diagnosed with cancer.'

'If not in the last year, perhaps before that?'

'No. I am sorry. If I remember anything, I will tell you.'

We turned to walk out. I ground my teeth in frustration. All our leads were coming to dead ends.

'There was one odd thing which he did,' she whispered as we almost reached the door, as if she had only just remembered it. 'He did go and stay at some ashram for a month, though that was part of a research for a paper he was working on.'

'Do you remember the name of the ashram?' I asked, turning around.

'No, but I did see that swami he was working with last night in the news. He was speaking about a phone—'

She and I almost spoke in unison, I ended with a question

mark and she with the surprise of remembering the right name.

Swami Narahara!

'Sexual intercourse, or sex as modern society puts it, is like a delicate silk thread. A single piece of thread is of no particular use, but weave it into a pattern and it becomes a thing of beauty and a marvel. In Kaula philosophy, you can create your own definitions of what ecstasy means. Do you want to just reach a place where your thread can sew a button, or use it to heal a festering wound? Or do you want to create an endless piece of silken cloth that will encompass the whole universe? Neither is wrong, it is just the way you want to achieve your personal ecstasy. The Kaula path teaches you both ways. And you can follow either. For both will lead to the master thread, the one that takes all those individual lost threads of the world and binds them together to create flowers so that we can spread fragrance and happiness in the universe through our collective ecstasies. That's the tantrism life. That's the tantrism belief. We can …'

'Is it me or did that make no sense at all?' asked Madhu, going mono-browed.

'Don't even try to understand,' I snorted. 'It's meant for lost souls who have a lot of money and time on their hands. You have neither.'

'Ouch. Someone is being cynical. For all you know, the fundas might actually work. We need to keep an open mind.'

'Keep it too open and your marbles will start to fall out.'

'But it seems to be working with all these people,' he exclaimed, sweeping his hand in an arc.

Madhu was right. It was a hot Saturday afternoon, but the reception area of the Kaula Ashram in Manesar was teeming with people of all nationalities who didn't seem to mind the sultry weather. They were chatting, signing forms and talking to immaculately dressed counsellors and receptionists. The reception itself was spacious enough to take in more people. It was an ugly twin-dome structure with a high ceiling. The walls and the ceiling were painted a dull gold with sculptures of nude apsaras (exaggerated bosoms and bottoms) high up on the walls, looking down at those who entered. Between the apsaras were tall windows on both sides. At the far end of the hall was the reception desk made of pure sandalwood. The heady smell of the wood filled the space. Enclaves had been created where beautiful women, each dressed in a black sari with a white Kaula triangle drawn on her forehead, introduced newcomers to the ashram and told them of their programmes. I knew what they were doing because I had done the same thing in the Kaula Ashram at Banaras a lifetime ago. However, that ashram was nowhere close to being as slick as this one.

Ever since Kaula Ashram had become a part of the Central Association of Tantriks, it had changed its philosophy. Leaving its hardliner approach to tantrism, it had begun to tout a bastardized version, a new-age spirituality, turning the ashram itself into an international spirituality centre. It started to attract people from all over the world who thought sexual intercourse would bring them peace and solace. It was a good business model, actually. Take the things which most humans feel guilty about and package them with spiritual bull that touts them as essential for the world and good for the soul. Who wouldn't want that? I am not saying that Kaulas were fake. The tantrik school did have the knowledge to use intercourse to gain shakti, but this slick front, the Kaula Ashram in Manesar, was more like a one-night stand with tantrism. They rarely introduced visitors to how they could actually use sexual intercourse to gain power. The touristy part of it was a lot of spiritual claptrap with liberal doses of good old-fashioned sex. It brought the ashram and its Council oodles of foreign money to play with. The result, this palatial ashram in Manesar, the sweet spot to waylay tourists on their way to Rajasthan (the richest tourist trail in the country) from the Delhi airport.

'Number fifty-eight.'

I sprang up, desperate to get it over with and get the hell out of here. Madhu seemed equally uncomfortable, although I didn't know why. The last time I had been in the ashram was seven years ago, when I was only sixteen. To put it mildly, I hadn't left them all those years ago with a goodbye note. Perhaps I should have warned Madhu, given him a sort of heads-up about my past connection with the ashram. But then, I am private that way.

Before heading here, we had called Gayatri Sharma, the wife of the first tantrik. As soon as Madhu had mentioned Kaula, she had started to cry. Yes, it was Kaula Ashram all right. Two virgin girl sacrifices on two separate nights by two different people, one of whom had a connection with the Kaulas, and the other had worked with Swami Narahara of the Kaula clan. So here we were, the one place I had vowed to stay away from.

The receptionist, a pretty young lady in a black dhoti dress and nude make-up, handed us a pamphlet on tantrik sex, the holy kundalini way.

'Couples this way please,' she said, pointing towards her right.

'We are not …'

'You are …'

Madhu explained that we wanted to meet Swami Narahara.

'But Swami Narahara does not meet anybody without prior appointment,' she answered, smiling politely.

Madhu took out his CBI badge and shoved it under her nose. The smile faltered, but was swiftly replaced by another.

'Please wait a moment,' she said musically. I started to drum my fingers on the desk impatiently. A flock of tourists, who were busy photographing everything, noticed my action and began clicking pictures of me as well. One scowl sent them skittering away. I was still in the outfit from last night, black halter top and culottes, and my hair was frizzier than usual. I fiddled with my locket. The smiling lady came back and told us to follow another smiling lady. Years ago, a lifetime ago, I would have been one of them, a smile on my face and a clinically prettified dress on my body.

We followed the new smiling lady through a door behind the reception hall, leading into a corridor and then to another. The path was dimly lit, long shadows at our feet, the walls gleaming a dull gold. Finally, she stopped at a door and knocked discreetly. The door opened and she gestured that we may enter. In front of us stood a man wearing a black dhoti, his hair short, shot through with grey. He smiled a toothy smile, a gold medallion with the Kaula signet shining on his hairy chest. I remained in the shadows.

'Welcome, Mr Madhu Tripathi. I am Swami Narahara's personal assistant, Yogi Riju. Please follow me.'

Riju's office was spartan with just a computer on a work desk, a lamp the only source of light and two chairs for visitors. The walls were covered with bookshelves from floor to ceiling, making the room look smaller than it was. Some things don't change. Riju was always a bookworm, preferring pages to playing. He sat down, breathing heavily, and waved us to sit as well. I took care to stay in the shadows behind Madhu so that he could not see me.

'Pardon me, I haven't been feeling too well,' he said, wiping beads of sweat off his forehead. 'Swami Narahara would love to meet you, but unfortunately he's in the middle of a class. Weekends, you know. If you had called ahead, I would have managed to get you an appointment. In his absence, I will be more than happy to answer any questions you may have.'

'We want to know about two men who we are sure had associations with the Kaula Ashram.' Madhu took out photographs of both Vikram Sharma and Rohit Kanwal and placed them on the table.

Riju stared at the photographs for a second and wiped more perspiration off his forehead. His face looked tired, and his chest, I noticed, had black-and-blue bruises all over.

'They both died recently. We have reason to believe they were both part of a programme headed by either Swami Narahara or someone else from your clan. Can you please check your registers and give us a list of the people who took courses at the ashram over the last couple of years?'

Riju hesitated and then shook his head. 'I wouldn't be able to disclose whether they were students as the ashram signs a confidential contract with all our clients. I am sure you are mistaken …'

'Perhaps you should let us do that database check, Yogi Riju,' I said, coming forward so that he could see my face in the lamp's soft glow. 'After all, the ashram has nothing to hide, does it?'

'Anu!' he exclaimed, standing up. Madhu looked from Riju to me, his brows furrowed in confusion.

'But you ... you shouldn't be here!' he said, flustered. He mopped his spiky-haired head, which was freely sweating now. 'If someone recognizes you ... you ... I'll be in trouble.'

'Don't worry about me, dear Riju. I knew of the trouble I'd be causing when I entered the ashram. If you can give us the right information, we'll be on our way and no one will be any wiser. I don't want to cause you any trouble.'

'What trouble?' asked Madhu, looking at me mystified. 'Why would you cause him any trouble?'

I ignored him. 'These two men died performing a Black sacrifice, Riju. They killed two innocent girls. If someone is teaching that in the ashram ...' I let my threat hang there as Riju took in the enormity of it.

'Impossible! We would never! Swami Narahara would never!' he exclaimed.

'I am not trying to suggest that he did. All I want is to be sure that he didn't.'

'But it's against the Council rules to reveal names of the ashram clients to any outsider.'

I stood up and put both my hands on the table, leaning forward. A part of me was glad to see Riju cower and shrink in his seat. 'Are you calling me an outsider now, Riju?' I asked softly.

He stared at me, petrified, a deer caught in the beam of an oncoming truck.

'Look, I want the ashram's name cleared as much as you do,' I lied. 'Just show us the registers and we'll be on our way.'

Riju grasped his medallion with sweaty hands and seemed rattled. Finally, he nodded. 'Yes, fine. I will check the database to clear Swami's name. But we,' he looked at the door and thought for a few seconds, 'we will have to be careful. You have to understand that I am going out of my way and what I am about to do is against the ashram rules. And it's only because it's you, An ... I mean, Anantya,' he finished, head lowered.

'Mr Riju, if it will get you into trouble, I can come through official chan—' Madhu began, and I put a hand on his shoulder. Sometimes, Madhu could be so naïve.

Once the Council found out that we had a lead on one of their swamis, it would be red-taped for years. Kaulas had enough political clout to ensure that the CBI would never be allowed to enter their premises ever again. Hell, Madhu and I may not be able to step into Manesar again. Riju's offer had come unexpectedly. I thought he would snub us and send us away. Instead, he was giving us the red-carpet treatment. I sure seemed a natural at emotional blackmail. I did feel a stab of guilt at cornering Riju like this, but it had to be done. The poor chap had never learnt to say no. I had loved that about him when we were kids. I could convince him to do just about anything then.

Madhu looked from me to him, his brow furrowed. I sympathized, but had no intention of recounting to him my sordid history with the Kaulas. We waited as Riju checked the ashram's database on his computer.

'They are not in here,' he said, after a few minutes.

'Are you sure?' I asked. 'Did you check Nas ... Narahara's personal clients?'

'I ...' Riju hesitated, and then leant forward. 'Swami Narahara's clients are not in the database. He prefers to keep his client list in physical files in his office.'

'Ironic, don't you think, considering he heads the department of technology for CAT?' I said.

'He took the decision two years ago,' answered Riju, shrugging. 'Ever since he started the research for iMagic. Since then, he has not electronically stored any information about anyone he might be associated with.'

'Well, it looks like we have no choice but to inform the Council about this,' I said softly. We stared at each other. 'Or maybe Tazaak.'

'No, you can't do that,' Riju whispered, his full lips opening wide. 'He won't like that.'

'Do I look like I care? This involves serious Black magic, so the Council needs to know. If Narahara is involved in something like this—'

'He isn't!'

'We will wait and talk to him,' replied Madhu to no one in particular.

Both Riju and I knew that would be impossible. To think that Nasty would invite us into his office and let us go through his personal files! The very idea was laughable. Riju stared at the computer screen for a few seconds. Then he seemed to come to a decision.

'Well,' he said, getting up, 'I would not like to disturb Swami for something as simple as this. He's innocent and if the only thing that can convince you is his client list, I will help you with that.' He got up, picked up a pair of keys. 'But we will need to hurry. We have just about half an hour before his class ends.'

We followed Riju through another door that led to yet another series of long softly lit corridors. Not surprisingly, Nasty's office was nothing like Riju's. It was as big, bigger if possible, than his massive ego. The office was half the size of the reception space with tall windows on both sides. Sunlight would stream in if the windows weren't covered by the thick, purple-red brocade curtains. The walls were black and covered with artwork. There were raised sculptures in relief holding Kamasutra poses – men and women gyrating together in stone. Orgies were highlighted with gold and purple. Madhu stared open-mouthed.

'Is that even possible?' he whispered to me, pointing to a particular position that had two men and a woman, entwined and bent at impossible angles like they were made of rubber. I nodded. When spiritual frenzy was tied up with the orgasmic, the results could be surprisingly supple. 'It's a position in tantrik sex. Most of these are.'

I had even been a participant in some of them. Madhu gave me with the same do-I-really-know-you look he had been giving me ever since Riju had referred to me as Anu. I shrugged.

'You will need to hurry,' said Riju nervously. He muttered an incantation and touched a wall, which turned out to be a hidden cabinet.

'If Swami Narahara finds out about this, I will be—'

'We are looking for last year's batch,' I said. 'And, Riju ...'

He looked up, his eyes full of worry.

'... thank you for understanding,' I managed to say.

He gave me the rabbit smile that said the same thing it always had: anything for you, Anu. I looked away. The feeling of shame and guilt fused with rage within me. He handed us the files and we pored through them.

'See, I thought so,' Riju said after a while, smiling his rabbit smile. 'Those two names are not in there. Swami Narahara could have never been involved with Black tantriks.'

'Can I see it?' I took the files from his hands before he had a chance to refuse. I glanced through them quickly. The dates ended halfway through the year. 'That's not the file for the entire year. Where's file two?'

'Oh, isn't it?' He turned back to the cabinet and started to shuffle through the folders.

I looked at his back, narrow-eyed. Was he being sly, hiding things from us? Madhu looked at me quizzically. My distrust of Riju must have been obvious to him. Riju was a nice lad, but I had a feeling he knew things he wasn't letting on. I needed to figure out another way for us to talk.

'What do people come to the ashram to learn? Sexual positions?' asked Madhu, picking up one of the small-sized statues on the table, again a pose from the Kamasutra, and examining it.

'Oh, no! I mean not only that,' answered Riju. 'We teach them how to direct the shakti that intercourse creates and achieve divine experiences through it.' He was sweating even though it was quite cold in here. 'There are many things you learn. The basics of tantrism, some rituals, mantras and yantras to focus your energy on. We also do marriage counselling to increase sexual connection between couples.'

'So nothing about getting more powerful and controlling the world?'

'Oh no. The Kaula Council is very strict about what they impart to clients, especially novices. We cannot go beyond basic rituals which will help them stay positive in their approach to day-to-day life.'

'So ... nothing in your curriculum about human sacrifice?'

'That's impossible, of course. Sacrifice is the way of Red and Black tantriks. We are Whites. It's illegal for us and the punishment is banishment or even death. The Kaulas are against any kind of sacrifice or violence to a living soul. Those kinds of things are the mark of dark magic.'

'Would you call raping your own daughter, for a tantrik ritual, violence?' I asked casually, even as the image exploded in my head. Kaulas, or White tantriks as they considered themselves, didn't condone animal sacrifice for shakti. They tapped into shakti reserves through their women – daughters, wives, sisters. The tantrik used his seed, his sperm, his white power, and tapped into the woman's shakti. White was a woman's shed, which gives power to the male tantrik.

'Anu! You cannot really bel—' he started.

'Let it be. Let's not start with the past. It takes too much time,' I said.

I would rather forget it all. It was over, it was behind me. Madhu looked at me worriedly. I knew I wasn't making much sense, but then the Kaulas and their holier-than-thou pretensions did that to me. Positive, my round ass. We all fell into an uncomfortable silence and flicked through the new file together, impatiently. We had been in Nasty's office for twenty minutes and should leave soon. When Madhu found the page on Vikram Sharma, I almost cried out 'hah'. Vikram Sharma had enrolled under Swami Narahara two years ago as a novice. As part of his studies, he had taken basic classes of tantrik sex for harmony within his marriage. Nasty had listed him a high achiever and passionate about the Kaula cause. A few minutes later, we found the other name too. Rohit Kanwal. Again, here for a month to research on a paper, just like his wife had told us. Under Narahara.

'But … but … this is impossible,' cried Riju. 'They couldn't have learnt the sacrifice ritual from Nara. Anu, you know it's forbidden for Kaulas. He loathes even animal sacrifices, forget human! He would never even consider looking towards the Black arts … he won't!'

'This cannot be a coincidence,' replied Madhu. 'I am afraid we need to arrest Swami Narahara. We shall wait—'

'THIEVES!'

We spun around simultaneously. Swami Narahara rushed towards us, a bull in black, his staff with the Kaula triangle pointing straight at us. In slow motion, I watched as he picked up a glass of water from his desk, his lips moving, muttering. As I ducked, I extracted the mandalas from my satchel.

'Ghani bhavati!'

The freezing Shayaya mantra zoomed towards us, but I was ready with a Dhatu mandala, to protect us from elemental attacks. It deflected the full force of the mantra, which hit all the windows on both sides with icicles. I was thrown back by its force, as were Madhu and Riju whom I had managed to partially protect. The windows shattered with a deafening noise. My right hand, which held the mandala, screamed in agony, shaking uncontrollably.

'Swami!' Riju cried in pain, crawling towards Nasty and prostrating himself at his feet. 'Forgive me! I was just trying to prove your innocence!'

Nasty, keeping his staff pointed at Madhu and me, kicked Riju's face with his bare foot. He fell back with a thud, landing beside me, his chin hitting the floor and starting to bleed. With my boneblade I wiped the blood dribbling from his broken lip and, before I realized what I was doing, muttered a calling spell under my breath.

'Aim hreem bhuta aa, kar de kreem, Jaalikah!'

The silken web of Jaalikah, a spider-like spirit, shot towards Nasty, glistening darkly in the sunlight like black filaments. He tried to stop it with a counter mantra, but it came too late. Jaalikah's smoky threads wound around Nasty. He wriggled furiously as the web tightened.

'Guards, arrest them! They are … uggh,' he screamed. Jaalikah wound her misty tendrils tighter and tighter until

Nasty looked like a spindle of black thread. The black web bound his mouth. His eyes bulged and his face contracted. I smiled, standing up, boneblade in hand.

'If you come any closer,' I said calmly to the two guards who had entered the room, 'I will squeeze his windpipe dry before you can act. And don't underestimate Jaalikah.'

They stopped as I strolled towards Nasty, who had now fallen on the floor in Jaalikah's tightening embrace. 'Nasty, do you want to order your guards to arrest us and take us to the Tazaak, so that I can tell them about the Black magic you are involved in. And I have proof.' Tazaak, or the Tantrik Authority responsible for policing tantrik activity in the country, was brutal to Black tantriks. Although most of them were in the Kaula's pockets, there was one thing that they took real seriously – allegations of human sacrifice. Death was the minimum sentence, but it could go further than that. Something I wished for Nasty with all my heart.

'You chandaali cun—' he whispered, choking, his eyes pools of hatred.

'Stop it, Anantya!' shouted Madhu. 'This is no way to behave!'

'He hit us with a deadly mantra, Madhu! If I hadn't defended us—'

'Just … just calm down, Anantya. Let's … let's just talk about this, please?' Madhu said in a hoarse undertone.

He was tense. Despite being a hard-core investigator for humans, he hadn't seen this side of tantrism. The brutal sides of Nasty and me were identical in so many ways. I would have snorted, but I knew he wouldn't take kindly to that.

'Aren't we going to arrest him?' I asked instead.

'I don't have a warrant yet,' replied Madhu.

Some days I swear I think laws are made to allow the guilty to go scot-free.

'But I am not setting him free. You can go ahead and ask him whatever you want to.'

'I am from the CBI, Mister Narahara,' Madhu said to Nasty, whose whole face had become one ugly expression of hatred. 'I have some questions for you.'

He looked at Madhu up and down and smirked. 'You have no jurisdiction here, Mr I-am-from-the-CBI. The ashram comes under the Tantrik Authority, not you fags.'

I tightened Jaalikah around him. Not because I felt that would convince him to talk, but just because it felt so good to see him gag. He spluttered for a few seconds, veins popping in his face.

'Anantya!'

'Fine, fine,' I muttered, loosening the web. 'If you don't cooperate with us, Nasty, we can always go to the Council. When they get to know that your students are learning forbidden arts under you—'

'Lies!' he spluttered.

'They … they are right, Swami,' stammered Riju. 'Your students, they were … were involved in Black magic.'

'Impossible!' he shouted.

'And, as you know, you have no business teaching Black magic to novices,' I said. 'Or to anyone, considering you are a Kaula. Wait till the Council sees the proof we have gathered. All your dreams of reaching the top will suffocate and die. As you know, Nasty, it only takes one red mark.'

When he hesitated, I knew I had him. The only thing that made him quail was that his untainted record would now get smudged. Learning or performing any form of Red or Black tantrism was strictly forbidden by the Kaulas. Even the smallest whisper that a tantrik had the slightest inclination towards human sacrifice would shatter any chance he had to get any position on the Kaula Council. And, although Nasty was an asshole, he was not entirely stupid. Not to mention he had more ambition than all his Kaula cronies at the ashram put together.

'What do you want to know?' he growled.

'That's better.' I smiled, loosening the constriction of the web slightly. I still didn't trust him enough to free him. With my blade pointed towards him, I bent close to him and showed him the photos of Vikram and Rohit.

'Both of them died performing identical Black rituals which involved sacrificing a girl. In both cases, they were sacrificing their daughters. And in both cases, they studied under you.'

Nasty stared at the pictures for a while, and then replied coolly. 'Yes, they were my students but not full-timers. They merely attended a couple of classes. And no, I didn't teach them any Black tantrism. They could have learnt it from somewhere else.'

I took out pictures of the scene of crime and showed them to him. 'Do you recognize this ritual?' I asked. To his credit, he hesitated for a second before he lied.

'No. I have no understanding of the Black,' he answered curtly, and then smiled, his crooked teeth gleaming. 'Perhaps your teacher would know more. She knows the Black, doesn't she?'

Madhu stood up. 'This will be enough for today. Thank you for your time, Mr Narahara. I suggest you do not leave the city and get yourself a good lawyer. We will be back with a warrant.'

'You do your best, you fag,' cried Nasty. 'And you, filthy chandaali, I will find you and slowly squeeze your vagina dry for this. And I will enjoy every bit of it.'

I allowed Jaalikah to give him one last hug before I left

him. He fell on the floor, exhausted. The thud was music to my ears.

'Anantya, we will have a talk later about anger management,' whispered Madhu as we left. The guards still stood there, an expression of indecision on their faces.

'You should have just arrested him,' I said accusingly.

'He's right. CBI has no jurisdiction over the ashram. We will have to go through the Tantrik Authority. Only they can issue an arrest warrant with the evidence we have. Which, frankly, is sketchy. We found out that both the men who died were his students. So what? They could have learnt the ritual from anywhere or anyone else. Yes, it's a big coincidence, but it won't be nearly enough for me to get a warrant.'

'Madhu-sir, please,' begged Riju, who had been following us without either of us realizing it.

'This is not Swami Narahara's doing,' said Riju, sniffing, holding a large black-and-red handkerchief to his bleeding lip. 'Anantya, can't you see the ritual has the Black written all over it? Sacrifice is not our way. They don't even teach it here anymore. Our ashram's reputation is at stake here. If this gets out, the bad publicity will keep us away from those who need our help. It's … it's the Vamas. They do the Red magic. They know how to sacrifice animals, so why not humans? They are trying to give our ashram a bad name. Please give us some time. We will figure out who's doing this and—'

'If that boss of yours has anything to do with these little girls,' I said softly, 'I will find out and I will relish hacking him into tiny little pieces before feeding him to jackals.'

We were escorted by the guards to the gates of the ashram. Riju took me aside.

'Anu … I mean Anantya…' He hesitated, staring at his hands. I noticed that his arms were black-and-blue as well.

He looked weaker than last night. His eyes had dark shadows, his thick lips quivered. His nose was already swelling where Nasty had kicked him. 'Will you promise me something? Promise me you will stay away from this. Forget this case, find something else to do. Please don't cross Nara's path like this. You … you have already used up one lifeline where the Kaulas are concerned. Don't give them a chance … to … to harm you.'

I pursed my lips. 'I will not back off from this, Riju. And don't worry, I can take care of myself.'

'Look, all I am saying is…' He nervously played with his medallion, his hands sweaty. 'If you cross them again, they will not be as lenient as they were then.'

A cruel retort came to my lips but then I saw his face, the way he trembled, his eyes huge like a cornered rabbit, and sighed. 'You don't need to worry about me, Riju. I am a big girl now.'

That made him smile his rabbit smile, which brought some sunlight to his face. When we were kids, Riju had always protected me. From Nasty, from the didi, from trouble. He had always shielded me from everything. Like the brother I never had.

'I know. I am so … so proud of you, Anu.' His hand reached out and softly touched my hair. 'I just … I just wish we … it could have been different, you know. That we could have … can't we be … friends still? I … I would really like that.'

The memory of my only friend in the ashram turning his back on me returned. The way my heart had sunk. That betrayal had hardened my heart. But it had been seven years since, and I was much stronger now. I laid my hand on his naked shoulder. It was soft and hairy.

'Princess,' he whispered, his eyes shining, calling me by the name he had used when we were kids, 'we can, can't we?'

'How did you get these marks on your body?' His chest had angry contusions, some fairly recent and still red, but most of them older, black-and-blue.

'Experiments,' he said, his hand falling from my hair. He touched his medallion nervously. 'I help out Swami in many of his rituals.'

'Rituals that involve him beating you?' I waited for an answer, but it never came.

Riju looked at the reception, where the pretty girls sat in their black outfits. The silence said it all.

'Why are you still taking this shit?' I cried, angry. Why was he so weak? Why couldn't he just leave?

'I ... I have to go.'

'Come with me,' I offered, knowing it was madness, sure death. Even I wouldn't be forgiven by the clan for making him betray them. 'I am stronger now. I can protect us both!'

He looked back at me, his eyes full of longing and something else. A strong emotion I couldn't put my finger on. 'It's too late, my princess,' he whispered, and turned and walked back into the hole he had come from.

'Both of you deserve each other!' I yelled after him, turning furiously. The last thing I wanted was for Madhu to see my wet eyes. How can you save someone who doesn't want to be saved? 'A total idiot ... completely and thoroughly.' I walked out of the gates. Madhu didn't say anything this time. It was over, whatever semblance of friendship we had had. Riju was over.

ट

'My, my, I haven't held something this precious ever since I died,' Kaani whispered, as he led me in. I stared at the lapping black tongue sewn on his back. It was the size of a porthole, slobbering as it moved. 'Both are different and both are true blades, truest friends of the moon.'

'Yes, yes, I know. But can you tell me more about their most recent ritual?' I asked impatiently, trying to ward off the tongue. I brandished the moonblade, hoping it would back off. The broad, black tongue licked the blade exuberantly, and then erupted in electric excitement, throwing wads of drool on my face and chest.

'Euugh,' I cried, wiping the slobber off my face. I had come to Kaani's place straight from the Kaula Ashram. Kaani was a Kinnara, a blade-maker – the best in Delhi. He was the one who had created the boneblade for me. We were at his home, a small, stuffy, dark room, crammed with just too many things, mostly dead things. Various types of skins lay on the floor in layers, like ragged carpets. The sofas, tables and nooks and crannies of the small room were filled with remnants of the dead – bones and other debris taken out of animals, humans and other beings.

Death was something Kaani didn't mind, after all he had died once and it hadn't been too bad. The Kinnaras had a choice at death. They could choose to continue to live by binding their soul to another body. When he had died, Kaani had asked the shaman from his tribe to bind his soul to a corpse. But dead human bodies came at a high premium and he could only afford an adulterer's burnt body at the time. He hadn't lost hope though. Every once in a while, when he had managed to save enough money, he would upgrade his body, one part at a time; in the process he now resembled something straight out of a horror movie. His blackened, charred body now had two scorched human arms, and three extra arms – one was a feathered wing of a garuda, one, the delicate wing of dasyu and one claw-like arm of an unknown animal, all protruding from various sides at various angles. His latest addition, the daitya's slobbering black tongue, was on his back.

He stared at me through burnt-out, empty eye sockets and then grabbed my arm with his clawed one, a talon pressed hard into my wrist, piercing the skin. Blood spurted out. I was used to Kaani's odd behaviour, so I didn't budge or bat an eyelid. If you got on his wrong side, or even flinched at something he did or said, you would be summarily dismissed, ejected from his home and never allowed in again. I couldn't afford that, not when he might be the only one who could possibly decrypt these blades. The room filled with the tangy, metallic smell of my blood. A second later, the moonblade, which I still held in my other hand, began to quiver like it had been kick-started.

'You understand now? It's a true blade,' he said, staring at me with his hollow eye sockets. 'It craves blood like a fish craves water.'

Man, why in naraka's name do all talented people have to be so dense? I clamped down on an irritated quip that came unbidden to my tongue. 'Umm. No, Bladebirther. I don't understand.'

'You tantriks lack the knowledge of olden times.' He let go of my arm and turned away, taking the moonblade with him. His tongue got a chance to slobber at me again like a giant dog. Although I tried to take a discreet step back, I was too late, and it licked me from breasts to hairline.

'In our times, a tantrik would not just view, but look deep into the being's soul and know. You depend too much on sight nowadays.'

Hah, easy for him to say, he didn't have any. Anyway, he would come to the point eventually. He was a Kinnara and they were famous for two things: their art of blade-making and their poetic style of yapping. I knew he was dying to gloat to me about the enormous amount of knowledge on blade-making that he had amassed.

'A true blade is sacred; it knows the true value of blood. It knows, nay craves, for the shakti that lives in all blood, that makes it throb. The rasa, the prana that causes the whole world to be born. The absence of which makes things wither and die. Oh, this one knows the value of that pure prana, the liquid light. It was born to crave it.'

'I already know what a moonblade does, Bladebirther. Can you tell me something about the one to whom it last belonged?'

'For that,' he touched the blade to his forehead and started to walk to the back of his room, 'you will have to follow me and listen to its story.' He opened a door at the far end and gestured with his human arm, inviting me in. I sighed, wishing this Kinnara could understand urgency. This morning, Shukra had smugly informed Madhu that the cause of death of all four corpses was 'high charges of electrons'. In other words, electricity. His Grace was still adamant about his 'no-demon' theory. *What proof do you have?* Shukra's taunting voice rang in my head. Other than a name of the cult whose tattoo was etched on both men's chests and a Kaula tantrik who might have taught them in the past, I had nothing much really. Even if I could prove that Nasty had taught the two men this ritual, it didn't help. Nasty hadn't murdered any of the four. Both the murderers and their victims were dead. With such a sketchy case, Madhu was not likely to be able to arrest Nasty. And I so wanted Nasty's guilt to be proved. Hell, I was wishing that he would turn out to be the leader of this Cult of Chaos so that he could be beheaded by the Tazaak. If only it hadn't been them, I might have been doing a better job of solving this case. Bloody Kaulas. I just … didn't have enough … what is that word … neutrality, when it came to them.

'Brains of a bull!' We were in a long, low-ceilinged room with bones of every description hanging from the ceiling and protruding from the walls. They were not only human bones, but bones of various other beings both big and small; there were bones in jars of viscous liquid, bones piled up on each other, bones suspended from the ceiling like birds in flight. Bones on tables and delicate bones lying on the floor, which crunched underfoot. It wasn't that I was unaccustomed to seeing bones. It was how they were illuminated with an eerie, mossy glow. And Kaani seemed to love his bones like they were his babies. I suppose it was only to be expected – after all, he was a boneblade-maker. The only other lover of bones I knew was my teacher, Dhuma. But even her collection paled before *this*.

Kaani navigated the clutter expertly and sat on a seat at the far side. I tiptoed and side-stepped as best as I could, heaving a huge sigh of relief when I finally managed to reach his side without doing too much damage. He sat on an asana made of a daitya's ribcage that glowed green, and indicated that I be seated as well on a similar asana on the opposite side. I gingerly lowered myself on to the skeletal torso. My bones and the ribcage of the asana protested, sworn enemies.

'Long, long time ago,' he began in a soothing voice, 'when the world was still new, Ida, my forefather, went to hunt for bones one night, as was the custom of our tribe. It was a dark night. He walked towards the charnel grounds, where the animals fought and killed. As he reached the place, a bobbing light, as radiant as the brightest star, distracted him. He followed the light, fascinated, and saw it turn into a celestial beauty. Her naked skin was luminescent like cold light in the dark night. Ida's heart throbbed with craving to possess her. He drew his boneblade and shot it straight into her heart. The blade pierced the celestial one's naked breast. Instead of blood, moonlight spurted from the wound. He rushed towards her and caught her. She gazed at him with love in her eyes. "While the boneblade remains lodged in your heart, you are completely mine," he said, for that is the magic of my tribe. The celestial one, who revealed that she was the Moon Goddess, begged him to let her leave.

'But Ida didn't heed her wish. For three hundred and fifty moonturns, he kept the Moon Goddess as his wife. Although Ida loved her dearly, when he grew old and tired, he let her go. He withdrew the boneblade from her breast and, with tears in his eyes, he said, "Go, my love, go and shine on the paths for wayward ones." The Moon Goddess took seven of his glowing teardrops in her hand. And lo! They turned into seven blades, six white as milk and one black as hell. "These are my seven sisters," whispered the Moon Goddess, "the moonblades. Use them wisely, oh husband of mine. Together they can either protect or destroy your world, for they can pierce the veil of my father's darkest desires and bring those who reside in heaven, the powerful moonspirits, to follow and obey you."'

He raised all five mismatched arms, the tongue bobbing excitedly on his back, as his voice rose in a sing-song quaver. 'The holiest blades known to our world, owned by Ida to summon the moonspirits that reside in heaven.'

'You mean to say that they can summon daevas to earth?' The Kinnara called daevas the moonspirits, older powerful spirits who lived in the sky.

'Your crudeness, though high, remains lower than your ignorance. It's a blade created to slash the very fabric of night. The seven sisters can not only call a daeva, as you put it, but can actually own, control, bind and lead it, make it do anything that the blade-wielder wishes of it. The last time I saw a blade like this was in the seventeenth century—'

'Bladebirther,' I interrupted, 'please reveal its past and tell me what kind of a ritual it performed last and who its owner was at the time?'

'Be sure, Anantya, for this is the moonblade. The one who dips into the past of the blade of the moon will become part of it a bit. She will remember you, she will crave your blood.'

I nodded. It didn't matter. I had too many enemies already. What difference would one more make? He picked up something from the side with his charred human hand and threw it somewhere between us. A pit, which I hadn't noticed before, started to burn green. It didn't look like fire, but I could feel the heat of its flame on my face. It looked like liquid splashing around.

Considering the antiquity of the blade, a Revealing ritual

was not an easy one to do, which was my reason for coming to Kaani. Every blade used for a tantrik sacrifice retains its memories. It becomes a living being, having been used and abused through the ages by tantriks, rakshasas, asuras and many other beings. In other words, etched into a blade's very soul is its activity – the ritual, the user, the power it brought into the world. The older the blade, the stronger and deeper its memory and the more difficult it is to dredge up its past, which was why my attempts yesterday to unlock its history had failed. If I saw the blade's experiences, I would have a better understanding of what happened up there on the terrace and on that great flat boulder in the middle of the forest. And hopefully, the blades would tell me who their owner was too.

Kaani threw a small bunch of hair in the liquid pit, followed by the moonblades. The green flame surged up with a roar as it licked the blades. He stood up and started to dance around the fire, creating noises from the back of his throat. The song was not so much words as noises, like the chirping and croaking of a bird, the critter sound of bugs, an amalgam of jungle sounds. He leapt forward and backward, facing the flame as he moved around the fire, the tongue on his back bouncing in a hypnotic wave. I marvelled at his grace. Even though his workshop was so full of bones, not once did he crush or crash into anything. Perhaps he was right, the ones who could see relied too much on their sight.

He danced towards me, grabbed my hand and pricked my finger with a black boneblade. As a drop of my blood fell into the pit, its liquid fire turned purple, and then darker, a shade deeper than black. It glistened like molten lava. Before I could read his intentions, he shoved my head into the oily fire. I stopped breathing as hot liquid filled my nostrils. For…

…Innumerable countless wombs stomachs breasts lips eyes ears

hearts tongues nails blood ... so much blood, all girls and women, best of girls and women, always females, sacrificed to please the one we belong to. The goddess of the House of Belles sacrificed little fingers, little tongues, for power to him, to adulate him, to celebrate him, sometimes to tell him that we are but subjects, just meaningless little creations that will wither and die, that will cease to exist, but he, oh, he's an eternal, a being of such power, oh, daeva of daevas, the moonspirit like an elephant amidst dry grass, he's the cloud, the sky the universe the stars forever twinkling in the dark and light skies, he pulsates with energy with pure power with shakti, and we adulate him, we are but small insignificant beings, we sacrifice our virgin daughters' breasts and blood and eyes and hearts and lips and wombs to his highness, we dance and crave for power, his power, to save us from flood and fire and death. We have done it down the ages and we will cut some more. Oh eternal, the one who flies, the one who creates, the one who never dies, we are your seven sisters and we call you. Come to us, one by one, part by part, six parts then a whole. Come to us as we call you, all seven of us, we crave for you, we bring you to this world. Come the spirit of the countless twinkling stars, come the spirit of darkness that is chaos, come to us, we give, we sacrifice blood and breasts and hearts and power and shakti and...

...jerked out of the viscous liquid and staggered. I was covered with greasy, purple fluid.

'That was something I'd never do again,' I said, breathing hard.

If Kaani had eyes, he would have given me a told-you-so look. The moonblades floated in the slimy liquid, calm, quiet, gleaming innocently. The images they had shown me came to me unbidden in dribs and drabs from their history. Screams of terrified children as blood gurgled out of their mouths. The sisters bound together to the same fate, with the same destiny, travelling together forever. The Moon Goddess, the owner (or was she a sister too?) of the moonblades, pulsating through the universe, growing it, nurturing it, changing it. I rubbed my eyes, as if something unclean had touched them. *He pulsates with pure power. Six parts and then a whole.* Making it seven. *Eternal being of such power.* A spirit, a daeva, a powerful eternal who could only come through human sacrifice. I knew who it was. Kolahal. What Guru B had told me about the Cult of Chaos seemed to be coming true. My only hope that the rituals were not a success had also been dashed to pieces. The moonblades had *felt* confident that whatever they had set out to do the night before had happened. Now they were waiting for their five sisters to join them. Five more blades, five rituals, five nights until the new moon. It was only possible, if … I sat back on the protesting ribcage, drained. What if the two novices had deliberately died, sacrificing themselves as well as their daughters to the greater cause of bringing in this Kolahal?

What I still couldn't understand was if this daeva, or part of it, had been called to earth, where had it gone? Spirits that are invoked would require a body, or a vessel to inhabit. If a daeva was successfully summoned, where did it go? There was nothing in the pyramid. Neither had there been a break in that black pyramid through which someone could have escaped – of that I was sure. There had been no exit.

But there was no time to mull over that. If two had happened, there would be a third sacrifice tonight. It was evening now and somewhere out there, a lunatic was getting ready to sacrifice his daughter. I had to find out where the sacrifice would happen.

'Bladebirther, what's the House of Belles?' I asked, replacing the moonblades in their velvet pouches. After glimpsing their soul, I didn't ever want to touch them again.

'The last known owners of these blades. The moonblades were exchanged for safe passage by my tribe and given to the House of Belles. It's a house of divine dancers, reputed to have been started by Indra's apsara, Urvashi herself. They were dancers in the courts of royalty and kings. The house withered away a century ago and the moonblades were lost.'

'Oh,' I said, slinging my satchel across my body. What a waste. A dead house of beautiful apsaras. What could I do with that information? Couldn't these novice tantriks have used something simpler? Why in Kali's name did they have to go and use up blades that were exotic and unique? Without a blade owner, how could I find out where the next sacrifice was going to be performed? The moonblades were a useless lead. This was just another dead end. I stamped in annoyance. The only lead I was now left with was Nasty. Perhaps I needed to tail him. There was just one more thing I wanted to ask Kaani.

'Bladebirther, when I held this blade, it urged me to kill. Was it the blade's desire, or mine?'

'The moonblade is like the reflection of the moon in a pond. The desire is yours, not the blade's. The blade merely intensifies it.'

Great, now I had begun to harbour murderous intentions towards my friends and acquaintances. I thanked Kaani, paid him well and left, a gloom following me. I needed a strong drink.

Q

Kutte kaminay main tera khoon pee jaaunga! Kutte kaminay main tera...

'Prem, pick up your damn phone!' I whispered furiously. Prem Chhokra gave me an apologetic look and pressed a button on it.

'Helloo, Ma, can't talk now. Yes, yes I will be back home for dinner, but don't wait up, okay?'

I sighed, wondering if it had been a good idea to hire Prem Chhokra at all. Not that he had done a bad job, only he was such a kid. Prem was a dasyu, a four-winged creature with a slender human-like body, just more wrinkled and jet-black in colour. Bat-like, his arms extended into two of those wings while his spindly legs made the other two. Up in the sky, he could be mistaken for a huge eagle or a bat. Right now though, he hung upside down from the branch of a gulmohar tree, his outer wings tightly wrapped around his body. He had a gash on the inner wing caused by brahmi, a herb lethal to these aerial creatures.

'So, why didn't you call me instead of trying to break into Lavanya Mohan's house?' I asked again.

Evening light lashed at us, the ground emitting heat and fire, as if annoyed with us. We were outside Lavanya Mohan's apartment, which is where Prem had been since last night after I gave him the Luv (or was it Kush?) bug to eavesdrop on her conversations. She had met no one since the party, no one until now that is.

'I told you! First, she started to argue with someone. It sounded like a manava. I was outside, listening in, just like you said, minding my own business. This Luv-Kush you gave me is of the baddest quality! I didn't understand a word of that conversation. Then there was a lull for a while and suddenly she started to screech. And the bug *died* on me. I tried to call you to find out what I should do, but you didn't answer, did you? So I thought to myself, what would Amitabh Bachchan do if he hears a lady shouting for help? What would Dharmendra prahji do? I knew what I had to do. I had to go and rescue her from whoever was raping her. I flew up to her balcony window, but she had smeared brahmi juice there! Of course, I was distracted by the screams, so I didn't see the poison. Before I could see anything, my tissue started to burn and I had to abandon the mission.'

'Good decision. Prem, you are not in some B-Grade Bollywood movie. This is the real deal. You don't try to be a hero here. You just kind of hide and try to survive, while the world around you blows. That's the only way to live long enough,' I said slowly.

He blinked. 'But ... but she was in trouble. I could hear arguments from the apartment. We have to help her, Anantya! The beautiful angel is really, really scared. You should have seen the amount of herbs around her window. To repel all kinds of sups. Some serious protection.'

I chewed my lower lip. Grrhat had warned me to stay away from Lavanya Mohan at all costs. But if Prem heard screams, it could be something serious. I had to go in. Disguise seemed to be the best way to do it.

'I will go and check on her. You stay here, hang around

and alert me if you see anything weird. And I mean it,' I said, pointing my boneblade at him. 'Stick to the tree, or else!'

'You can't do that!' he whined, his large leathery black wings unfurling and fluttering. 'I want in too! You promised to take me when you hired me. I want to be a hero too. It's the hero who rescues the heroine.'

'You can't shape-shift,' I countered.

He put a winged hand under his chin. 'As if you don't have some extra maya potion in that bag of yours. Come on, how will I face my heroes if I stay clear of danger?'

The bugger knew me well. I took out some maya potion and gave him a swig. He plopped out of the gulmohar and turned into a respectable-looking old man with a hobble. As soon as he was ready, I flicked my boneblade on my index finger and whispered the Dehavyu mantra

'*Dikhau chhupau mayavu dehavyuh!*'

Without looking into a mirror, I knew that my face had altered. I had wrinkles around my eyes, mouth and forehead. My hair was now salt-and-pepper while my body sagged to become middle-aged. Shape-shifting into a whole other person took a lot of shakti, but altering your facial features a little bit required just a drop of your blood and a hair. I had a lot of both. I quickly bagged my septifocals and boneblade.

'Chhee ... how can you people walk on the ground? It's just too slow,' complained Prem in a wheezy voice as he tottered, his face wrinkly like his wings had been. I helped him along by putting his arm around my shoulders. You can turn a flier into a human, but that doesn't mean he can walk well. Dasyus rarely use lower limbs to walk. He updated me about the extras, what he had learnt about Lavanya as we hobbled towards her apartment.

'I checked her profile on the internet. She is quite well

known in the antique circles in Delhi. So popular that her clientele includes people like Rambha Devi and that socialite, Vajrin Mahendra. Now if only I could get a client like Rambha …'

'Vajrin Mahendra, eh?' I asked distractedly.

'Yeah, and many others. In the Mayan circles, she is a dealer who pays really well for any pashu antiques. Swords, crowns, talismans, urns, potions, name it and she will buy it off you. I knew of a rakshasa who managed to sell her a locket for thousands of rupees just because it had been lying around in his hole for ages. You know she keeps appearing in the news too. She attends like all the high-society parties. She's a real heroine. Always in a sexy little dress and big melon-like…' He looked at my frown. '… ears. She's quite a big shot.'

'My mantra will not last longer than thirty minutes, so we should hurry.'

Lavanya lived on the fifth floor of an apartment building in Greater Kailash. A fancy one, complete with a gate and guards.

'How will we get in?'

'I don't know. We will just ring the bell, I guess.'

'Bond. James Bond,' Prem said in a thick voice, to the security guard who asked us our business. 'And this is my girlfriend. She cannot speak, but isn't she hot?'

Furious, I hit his hobbling leg. He winced. The guard didn't react to any of this, waving us through with a glazed expression on his face.

'What?' cried Prem as we waited for the lift. 'I had to make up a story, no?'

The lift opened and a wave of perfume hit us. It was a familiar one, although I couldn't remember where I had smelt it before. A lift attendant emerged. He stared at us, hesitated and then smiled.

'Please, maydam,' he said, holding the door of the lift open. Then he smiled again, showing yellowed teeth. I stared at his back as the lift doors closed. There was something weird about him. He seemed cocky, almost arrogant, and was whistling softly.

Even though I had taken out my mandala to repel anything I might find on the door, we didn't need it. Lavanya's door was ajar and the strong, tangy smell of blood engulfed us. Something was seriously amiss. I hurried in, which is why I didn't see the attack coming until it hit me full in the face.

A ball of green fire came hurtling towards me, blasting me and Prem, who was behind me, backwards into the corridor.

'Stay down!' I shouted, positioning myself between the fire and Prem.

It was mayan, this green fire. It would not affect me, but would toast Prem into kabab. I chose a Dhatu mandala and was about to mutter the mantra when another blast of fire, this time yellow, hit me straight in the face.

'Ugh!' I fell on my back, angry heat burning my face. That's the thing with pure mayan fire. It alternates in all seven colours so that it can burn everything and every being on all seven planes of existence. I shook my satchel as it caught fire. Bugger! I felt a cooling leathery blanket on me. Prem had just hugged me, dousing the flames. Shock had killed the effects of the potion, turning him back into a dasyu.

'Say thanks later, ma'am!' he said, grinning, and tumbled into the apartment. He attacked the source head-on. I gripped the Dhatu mandala and muttered the Kavacha mantra.

'Raksha bhaksha kavacha!'

The attacker was on the windowsill overlooking the balcony, across from the main door. Wavy hair flopped on his face in the flickering light of the blaze. He looked at us, his eyes full of malevolence, and threw another ball of fire towards us, before jumping off the balcony. I lunged towards Prem, shielding him as the mayan fireball fell on a table in the middle of the room. The table immediately combusted, and the fire spread to the carpet beneath.

'Follow him,' I screamed, hurling Prem onto the balcony.

Prem only waited long enough to glance back at me and then flew in pursuit. I ran out to the corridor, and retrieved the skullcup from the ruin of my satchel. The fire had to be stopped. Mayan fire spreads like a forest fire, burning everything magical and non-magical in its way. I didn't have much time. I ran into the hallway and tripped on something in the doorway to a bedroom. My skullcup slipped from my hand. I got up on all fours and saw a body beneath me. In the light of the burning fire, now violet, I saw that it was Lavanya.

'Shit of shaolin mothers!'

I felt her pulse, there was nothing there. She was dead all right. The skullcup had rolled under a bed, well out of my reach. The fire was blazing now, in alternating colours, like a disco ball. My hands groped blindly under the bed. Why the hell don't people build beds with enough space under them? I heard sounds outside the apartment. Humans! I needed to get out of this place, fast. I stretched until I felt the skull's cool touch on my fingertips. The yellow fire which burns humans returned and my skin began to burn, but I ignored it. I scooped Lavanya's blood from the floor with my hand and dribbled it into the skullcup. It was fresh and I might as well use hers, considering it was just lying there, going waste. The blood looked black in the fire that was purple now. I dipped my boneblade in it and, as it started to swirl, shouted the Shayaya mantra, to freeze the mayan fire around me.

'*Ghani bhavati.*'

I stretched my arm and started to pirouette. The blood in the cup swirled with me. Drops of blood sprayed all around, spreading outwards within that room and then the living room. Lala, slippery with blood, dropped from my hand. The blood droplets fell like crimson dew on the raging fire, eating away its ire. The fire was out within a minute, but someone was already outside in the corridor, yelling. I saw Lavanya's dead body for the last time, her face covered in blood. She was naked, covered with what looked like bites but so many of them and so deep that blood had oozed out of the wounds, pooling on the floor around her.

The apartment was a mess and I noticed that not all of it had been caused by the fire. Everything had been taken apart. Furniture smashed, the cupboards broken into and clothes, expensive artefacts, dolls, fancy shoes, urns, statues of apsaras, everything was strewn on the floor. Someone had ransacked the apartment, looking for something. Had it been the same tantrik who had attacked us with the mayan fire? What had he been seeking? And why kill Lavanya is such a brutal way? I hadn't seen his face, but I had clearly seen what he was wearing as he had jumped off the ledge into the night. Nothing but a red loincloth. The red loincloth of a Vama, a Red tantrik.

'Miss Mohan, are you all right?' someone shouted from outside. It would only be a minute before they realized the fire was out and that it was safe to enter. I couldn't afford to be found in the room with a dead body. Dealing with the authorities wasn't one of my strengths. I gathered my satchel, making sure I didn't miss anything and ran towards the balcony, the only way out, and looked down. Five floors. I wasn't very good at jumping and couldn't fly for the life of me, but I had another way out. Good old Vedara gum. I took out the sticky potion from my bag, thankfully not completely ruined, and rubbed it on my hands and feet. Then I started to climb down the building. I crouched and planted my feet and hands firmly on the side of the wall. I resisted the urge to scratch my palms. The gel was ticklish as hell. I descended one step at a time as the gum created a lizard-feet-like vacuum between my hands and feet and the wall. Taking a deep breath, I clamped down on the tickle-induced laughter and made my gradual descent. Sometimes, I was thankful for having Zee and his knowledge of potions in the house. Just sometimes, mind you.

'When does it start?' I asked for the nth time. It had been an hour since I had come to the Bedardi Bar and there was still no sign that the Vama would come. It was early by Bedardi standards, but I was dog-tired and just wanted to get it over with.

'Do you want me to poison that for you? It settles all jumpiness,' offered Maaki, pinching his pincers and indicating my soma-on-the-rocks.

'Aren't we touchy today?' I grumbled.

Not a good idea to be a smartass with Maaki. If he hadn't known me well, and wasn't – sort of – fond of me, he would have just picked me up with one of his long pincer hands and tossed me out. He glared at me with a few of his round, shiny eyes for an alarming second and then turned to attend to another customer.

Maaki was the owner of Bedardi Bar. He also happened to be a giant spider-like creature, with pincers for hands. The only one of his kind I had seen around the city, other than his partner Joro that is. Joro and Maaki ran Bedardi together and kept it open at all hours. Joro, who was a she-spider from Japan, manned the tables while Maaki took care of the bar. What with six of his eight limbs available for mixing drinks, Maaki was tailor-made for bartending. And some of the beings that turned up at his bar, like me right now, desperately needed a quick drink.

The bar itself was little more than a hole in the wall. A hole, that is, in the wall of an old building in Chandni Chowk. Quite close to my place, which was another reason I liked it so much. A few tables, some of them broken accidentally, some deliberately to suit the kind of creatures that sat on them, were scattered randomly about the place. Bedardi was one of the few places in Delhi where CAT legally allowed sups to assume their own forms. In all other places, they had to disguise themselves as humans, constantly sipping from a vial of maya potion. And Maaki ensured that everyone left their illusion spells and maya potions behind by installing an anti-maya spell at the doorway. I liked that. No pretensions, no masks. At least no magical masks. Also, there was a certain level of freedom. Maaki didn't like CAT or Tazaak poking around too much in his space and they seemed to respect that.

The place was filling up fast. I saw a daitya couple, hunched over, deep in conversation in a corner, their large heads touching the ceiling. A group of small dasyus were in another, their wings flapping excitedly at hummingbird speed, which is how they communicated. By the look of their outfits, I guessed that they hadn't really seen a city before. I could understand wing-flapping sometimes, but in this case, it was just a constant buzz.

I downed my soma-on-the-rocks, headed outside. There were a few things you couldn't do inside the bar, smoking a cigarette was one of them. Not for health reasons, mind you, but because Joro just couldn't stand the smell of it.

A lone streetlight cast a long shadow in the alley. Bedardi Bar was in a blind alley leading off a small lane in Chawri Bazaar. It was quiet here, quite a change from the din inside. I took out a beedi and lit up, taking a long drag as I thought of my visit today to the one place I would normally have given a wide berth. It hadn't gone too badly though. At least this time I had faced Nasty without cowering, without being raped. But that was a small win. It hadn't helped me find out where the next sacrifice for Kolahal was going to happen tonight.

With the possibility of another girl being butchered, I so didn't have time to follow up on Qubera's Key, which was turning out to be messier than a boiled wart.

I ground the beedi butt on the street with my chappal, wishing it was Grrhat's stupid head. I lit another and took a long drag, waiting as its acrid smoke hit my lungs. When we had lost the Vama who had attacked Lavanya Mohan, I had called Grrhat and told him about Lavanya's murder and how we had been attacked. The first thing he had asked me was if I had found the Key. 'I don't know where it is,' I had replied. Ever since the party at Vajrin's, Lavanya had kept to her apartment and met no one. No one had entered except for that Vama who had killed her. I had requested the bugger to release Nikhil; after all, I had kept my end of the bargain, my task had been done. The dead didn't need watching. 'Find the Vama and I promise you we will release Nikhil,' he said. The shithole of a cockroach. If he knew something more about this, which seemed to be the case, oh, he was in for a good time with a couple of bhutas. All in all, it had been one of the shittiest days I had had in a while. And trust me, I have had many.

So here I was at Bedardi Bar where Mattreya was performing tonight. One of the Vama's apprentices looked suspiciously like the one I had seen at Lavanya's window. The young boy, I had later remembered, had even offered me charak at Vajrin Mahendra's party and had been the only one to whom I had actually seen Lavanya talking.

'A rupaiyya might get you rain, daughter,' said a woman wrapped in dirty clothes, her back bent. She smiled, showing me her broken, crooked teeth.

I smiled back.

'You waste your talents here, Maiyya. You know city people will pay you a fortune for telling them what's on their minds? You could be oodles rich.'

She cackled and showed me her uneven smile again. 'How can I sell things that I didn't buy?'

'Have it your way, Maiyya. You can always charm money from people, can't you, you hag,' I said, winking, taking out a few rupee notes from my jacket pocket and putting them into her tin can. Maiyya was the resident beggar outside Bedardi Bar. There hadn't been a day when I had not seen her here. I lit up two beedis and gave one to her. We smoked silently.

'Your mind is like a storm in the middle of the sea.' She touched my hair with her hand, startling me. She had never done that before. Her fingertips sent an electric charge through my body. I continued to suck on the beedi, ignoring it, but on alert.

'Darkness comes close to you, my child.' Her soft voice was close to my ears and I could smell the dank sweet smell of garbage off her. 'Again you need to fight. But don't give up. When you fall, the goddess will pick you up. For storms are fleeting, much like water in the middle of a bare desert. Maya, maya, everything's maya! Rains will start! Rains will start! But before it does, it will get hot! For that's how life goes on. Goddess has her eye on you, my child. She remembers.'

She moved away, her bent frame a looped shadow in the night. A powerful being watching my every step? That was the last thing I wanted. I stubbed out the beedi and went back into the bar. It was stuffier and louder than a few minutes ago. I was about to ask Maaki again when he silently pointed to the other end of the bar, where a stage had been set up for creatures crazy enough to perform to such a mixed crowd. The Red tantrik was on stage. Behind him stood an apprentice, but he wasn't the one I wanted. I was looking for the pretty one, the one with the wavy hair. I took a long sip of another soma-on-the-rocks.

'Mattreya,' I whispered, tasting the name with my tongue.

'Rare to see a tantrik here, isn't it?' said someone from behind me.

I turned and smiled. It was Ashwa, my drinking buddy. He made an impressive figure with his tall, broad body covered with a black-as-night cloak. He stood a whole three feet taller than me, his face in the shadows of the cloak's hood. 'Isn't there some exclusive tantrik pub in the city now where all tantriks go?' he asked, taking a sniff from a smok-joint, a waft of strong smoky smells which was his favourite 'drink' in Bedardi.

'Yeah,' I snorted, 'it's called Cup and Sorcerer. But that will be too White for our Vama friend here.'

'I meant you.'

'Me?' I laughed out loud. 'But I am an untouchable. I am a girl!'

Most tantriks, especially the kind who aspired to positions in the Central Association of Tantriks, stayed away from Bedardi. It was considered to be a low-class place, where all the sups hang out with the lower lot, the pariahs from the magic community, the slaves and the outcasts. The richer crowd went to other places, more recently the Cup and Sorcerer.

'Humph,' he replied. I turned to face the stage.

'... can we stay quiet faced with such blatantly unfair treatment!' Mattreya's gruff voice carried to us. He was on stage, wearing a necklace of human finger bones, standing like a scorpion about to bite, his body covered with ashes. 'Your ancestors were free beings. They were free to decide what to eat, how to look and who to breed with. They didn't have to accept the authority of the humans. How can you accept being herded and made to "behave" and pretend to be like someone else? Will humans ever agree to drink maya potion every day to look like all of you? Whose blood is darker and doused with ancient magic? Yours!' The scorpion etched on his belly squirmed as his eyes burnt like coals.

'You,' his gruff voice shouted, 'that are beings of the night, created in the form of maya herself. Why should you hide your bodies and faces? Rise up my friends! Rise up and break away from the tantrik shackles! From today, never fear a tantrik. Never do the bidding of a tantrik. Pledge to never, ever bow down to the cat! Don't be mice, be ferocious beasts. If we join together, we can break these shackles. If we unite, we can teach those humans a lesson!' He raised his hands as a dramatic finale to the speech, wearing only the red loincloth. The response from the crowd was a mixture of claps, crashes and jeers. I snorted.

'You are a manava yourself!' cried a pingala, a six-legged sup from the deserts of Rajasthan, voicing my thoughts exactly. 'You want to release us from one tantrik clan to be made slaves of you Reds? Get off the stage and let us drink in peace!'

'True! True! He's a sham!' Someone threw a glass towards the stage, but Maaki deftly caught it in one of his long hands.

'I will show you what it means to be a tantrik.' Mattreya pointed his open-fingered left palm towards the pingala who had spoken. Its throat expanded, becoming a bubble, its yellowed crusty skin spreading on the balloon-like inner skin. 'It's a power to control your fate. It's a power to control others around you—'

'Stop it right NOW!'

I stood up, boneblade in my left hand and the mandala in my right. He ignored me and continued to mutter a spell under his breath. I positioned my mandala and shouted '*Raksha bhaksha kavacha*!' My mantra withstood the blast of his easily. Almost too easily, as if the Vama had sent a weak mantra after me. The pingala behind me trembled in fear and screamed for help.

I burst out: '*Vajti ghanti apahanti*!'

The Apahanti mantra boomeranged Mattreya's attack. It hit him on the face, he staggered and fell back with a loud clank. I got ready for a full-fledged fight, a welcome relief after the frustrating day, but instead he stopped and bowed to me. It was over as soon as it had started.

'As you can see,' he said, addressing the others and completely ignoring me, 'even a female tantrik is more powerful than all of you. It's the control of her shakti that makes her so.'

'You—' I pointed my boneblade at him, furious and on the verge of shouting out another spell, when I felt a cold hand on my shoulder.

'Choose wisely,' whispered Ashwa from behind me.

'She's a Kaula!' someone cried from the end of the bar.

'The female doesn't want any mayans to get their freedom back. Throw her out!'

I looked at Mattreya who was sneering.

'I am no bloody Kaula!' I spat out. 'But I don't want to sell my blood to a cheap Vama either. If that's your wish, however, I am out of this.' I walked back to my bar seat to the accompaniment of boos and hisses. Ashwa came and sat behind me, smoking from his drink. The crowd turned as Mattreya's disciple came up on stage.

'This power to control is exactly what my guru wants to bring to all of you,' the fat Vama shouted. His other apprentice was still missing. 'Learn the art of tantrism that your ancestors knew so well! Learn the ancient arts of the asuras. We are on the side of the magical races. We want to free them from the clutches of a few greedy manavas by teaching tantrism to all. So that even the tiniest and most defenceless of you can defend yourselves. Don't you want to be as powerful as tantriks like her who protect you?'

'Thanks for stopping me, by the way,' I said, thoroughly irritated. Ashwa grunted.

'... sign up, friends! Sign up for the classes by the great Vama Mattreya, who has come from the lofty Himalayas with knowledge from Shiva himself. For just a small amount of money, you can learn it all!'

'They will never learn will they? Always looking for a fucking saviour.'

Ashwa grunted again. I sighed. Serves you right, Anantya Tantrist. Why the hell couldn't I keep a neutral stance, like Maaki, for instance? He hadn't even moved from his position behind the bar, not even for the duel. I waited for the crowd to clear out, some of them after having signed up with the charlatan. Then I made my way to Mattreya and his fat disciple, who stood at one end of the stage, counting their money. The disciple gave me one terrified glance and scrammed, leaving me alone with Mattreya.

'That was a good show, Mattreya,' I said, taking out a beedi to chew on. I couldn't smoke it inside, but I could bloody well taste it. 'Smooth trick, attacking that pingala as if he was a mere bystander. If it hadn't been for the fact that your mantra was so weak, I would never have guessed.'

He smiled, his blackened lips gleaming in the dimmed stage lights above us. 'You walked right into it, woman.'

'Yeah, what can I say. Have a bad habit of coming to the rescue.' I spat out the beedi. 'Perhaps I should have a share in tonight's earnings as well.'

He grinned again. 'Only if you play along again sometime.'

'Or,' I said, 'you could help me find someone.'

'And why should I help you?' he jeered.

'Because if you don't, I will tell the Tazaak about this little side business of yours. Promised to teach tantrism to sups, have you?'

The smile peeled off his face. 'I am doing nothing wrong,' he said, defensively.

'Last I checked, teaching magic to sups was against CAT regulations.'

'I won't teach them for real,' said Mattreya, furious for an instant. Suddenly, he grinned again. 'But we are friends. Tell me, who is it you want to find?'

'I saw an apprentice of yours at a girl's apartment tonight. A tall boy with wavy hair, not like this fat one. He wore a locket with a dead firefly. You wouldn't know where he is, would you?'

'And why would you want to know?' he asked, his eyes dark like coal.

'The girl was murdered just about when your apprentice jumped out of her window after sending mayan fire towards me and a friend.'

'Hah!' Mattreya laughed, shaking his matted hair. 'Can't be Jugnu. Boy can't kill a mouse.'

'Your apprentice and can't kill a mouse?'

Mattreya looked at his clawed hands. 'Yeah. He was a waste of time.'

'What do you mean "was"?'

'Boy has left me. Didn't turn up tonight. Young blood. They make more promises than they can keep. But he's not your man. Jugnu is not Vama at heart.' He thumped his chest loudly with his tattooed hand.

'Let me be the judge of that. Where can I find him?'

He looked at me with unfathomable eyes, taking his time to reply. 'At Vajrin Mahendra's house.'

'Vajrin's house?' I repeated.

'Boy is his nephew by blood,' he answered.

Mattreya slung his jhola over his shoulder, ready to leave. I stalled him by clutching his arm, which had a pincer tattoo. He instinctively flexed his muscles.

'I hope you are not lying to me, Vama,' I said, staring into his coal eyes, 'for the Tazaak will be after whoever killed that woman.'

'Why would I lie?' he whispered, his breath foul, leaving me standing there alone.

I went back to the bar and asked for another soma-on-the-rocks. Vajrin Mahendra. The businessman's name kept cropping up. Lavanya had been involved in some of his deals, and now it turned out that his nephew had killed her and attacked me. I had to find this Jugnu and soon.

On the television screen, a CAT representative loudly proclaimed Delhi's urgent need for more protection from supernatural attacks. He was part of a forum that discussed the four mysterious deaths of the two pairs of fathers and daughters. 'We need to save our children from the attacks. To be vulnerable is to die,' he emphasized. Another panellist was convinced that it had been an alien attack. The CAT guy and the alien-theory guy engaged in a shouting match as the moderator made feeble attempts to control them. It was eleven o'clock and I was still in Bedardi, getting drunk, without any lead on where the sacrifice would happen tonight. Pathetic.

I hefted my satchel over my shoulder as I got up. The soma had hit me harder than it would have on other days. My head swam. I stopped, took a deep breath and very, very carefully, placing one foot in front of the other, wobbled to the door. I could feel Maaki's compound eyes boring into my back but didn't turn around.

My stomach roiled, bile rising to my mouth. My tongue tasted foul. I gulped to swallow back whatever was threatening to erupt. I didn't want to puke, not here with half the sups in Delhi watching me. No one here respected a being that couldn't hold her liquor. I stumbled out into the dark humid night. A soft slithering breeze followed me. Halfway towards the main lane, I stopped, my stomach retching bile into my mouth. I took a deep, calming breath. Taking a shortcut that would lead directly to my house, I stopped and leant back against a grimy wall in an alley. It was one of those narrow alleys between houses in Chandni Chowk, dwarf lanes that few know about. Balconies loomed above, making a canopy of sorts. It was darker here, and silent, except for a faint slithering sound. I belched, a hot breeze ruffled my sweat-sticky hair. A little rest and I could continue my walk. With shaky hands I took out a beedi, put it in my mouth and lit up.

Cold, red eyes gleamed in the match's yellow light. Unlike the match, the eyes were motionless, red rubies, six of them.

For a split second, the three-headed cobra and I stared at each other. The hoods, three of them, one olive-green, one black and one tan, flaring. Its forked tongues flickered, its eyes cold. Then my stomach heaved and watery remains of the soma-on-the-rocks spurted out of my mouth all over the cobra's hoods. The cobra recoiled, its three long tongues flickering furiously. The matchstick fizzled out and we were plunged into darkness.

90

My mouth felt like I had been chewing wool. In the blackness, I heard the monster cobra hiss. It was more of a snarl than a hiss. I steadied myself with one hand on the wall behind me, not daring to breathe, much less retch. As my eyes adjusted to the gloom, the lane came alive in shadows. The monster cobra stood facing me. I couldn't see all of it, but I could make out that its body covered the entire ten-foot width of the narrow lane. The black scales shone softly on its body, which extended all the way to the end of the lane. Balconies loomed over us, grey behemoths obscuring the night sky.

The reptile lunged towards me, its three massive mouths open, its fangs dripping poison. I hugged my knees, somersaulted and landed on my back, directly beneath the cobra, in its blind spot. I had missed the bite, but not the spray of poison that spritzed my left shoulder. Even my alcohol-numbed body felt the stinging pain shoot up my collarbone to the back of my shoulder. The serpent gathered itself to prepare for another strike, using its tongue to see, smelling me out. Running was out of the question.

Moving as little as possible, I unscrewed one of the snakebone vials on my yugma locket, the one filled with rakta, and hurled it as far away as I could. The locket looped upwards and, with a small clunk, fell to the ground some distance ahead. The tangy, metallic smell of rakta filled the lane as the blood splattered everywhere. For a second, the monster froze, confused, sniffing the blood with its forked tongue. It slithered in the direction of the locket, hissing in excitement. I jumped as high as I could, praying to the goddess that I could reach the balcony, which lay a few feet above my height. I missed, and threw myself sideways, my arms entangling in the low-hanging mesh of cable and power lines typical of the streets in this part of Delhi. I managed to hoist myself just enough to clutch the end of a parapet with my right hand; I clung to it, feet dangling several feet above the lane.

The cobra raised its monstrous triple heads, facing me. Its tongues flickered. In the greyness, it seemed to smile, recoiling, ready to attack. I slashed my right arm with my boneblade, scooping the blood that trickled on my boneblade and, still suspended from the parapet, shouted, *'Jal bhun bhasm ho ja!'*

A stream of red fire hissed from my boneblade straight into the monster's oncoming faces. Smack on the sweet spot. The cobra hissed, livid, as its right hood caught fire. It lashed at me blindly, but missed. Its massive tail hit me on the side as it twisted, and I fell. I plunged the boneblade into whatever part of its neck I could see, blindly clinging to the hood in the centre as the fire spread. It lashed out in anger and panic, writhing, left, right, up, down. I sank my boneblade into its neck again, screaming the Visphota mantra. The maddened monster screamed in agony and thrashed in frenzy.

I was catapulted to the far end of the lane, my back hitting the wall hard. Flames from the serpent lit up the whole alley and filled it with smoke. With sheer willpower, I rolled on to my back, as the cobra monster rose again. In the firelight, I saw its face. Two of its heads had caught fire but the third looked straight at me, its red eyes cold with fury. It lunged open-mouthed towards my face. I ordered my body to move but something somewhere had broken and I just lay there. Without my boneblade, I had nothing. In slow motion I saw its fangs, dripping venom as it approached. I threw myself to the left with all my strength. The cobra's teeth sank into the edge of my right wrist. I cried out in pain, but the cobra didn't let go. Its other two heads burnt bright yellow and orange.

The lane vibrated, confusing the cobra. Agonizing pain seared through my wrist. I took a deep breath. Not now, Anantya. Not now. Deal with it first. My boneblade was still stuck in its back, but I wiped the blood still trickling from where I had slashed myself and mixed it with the venom, which was already crusting on my wrist like pus. I shaped my hand in a mudra with my middle finger locked with my thumb. With the remnant of my power, I shouted the mantra.

'Hawa hawa, tez ho ja!'

A gust of wind escaped my fingertips, making my hair fly madly, and zeroed in on the burning parts of the cobra. The fire, which had almost started to die down, blazed brighter as the blast of the draught stoked it. The three-headed monster cobra hissed in fury as the flames engulfed its entire body. I carefully crawled to what was left of it: three separate cobras, one olive-green, one black and one tan, writhing, glowing embers in the dust. They were babies, only about a foot or two in length, squirming in pain as they too were rapidly reduced to ashes.

I staggered, fell and then dragged myself to the other end of the lane, which side I couldn't remember, to locate my yugma locket. My mother, she would know what to do now. She always did. I crawled and crawled. My mouth had gone really dry and my tongue was swollen. I reached for my locket, my fingers scrabbling in the dust where it lay, gleaming a dull silver. My fingers curled around its snake heads. One of them was still closed. I tried to open the vial, but my hands slipped.

'Mother ...' I whispered, wincing as the excruciating pain knocked me back. Then I remembered how I had puked on the snake. I giggled and turned on all fours as I convulsed with a coughing fit. I collapsed halfway, my right arm numb and useless. With the remainder of my energy, I unscrewed the cork of the snake locket and poured two drops of rakpiss on to the bite wound. It sizzled but I couldn't feel anything. The rest I drank and then fell back on the ground, exhausted. If the rakpiss wasn't effective now, there was little else I could do.

The damp darkness smelt metallic. It pulsated. A soft hand touched her cold, clammy skin. Her limbs burnt. Her eyes flickered open and a young face came into focus. A little girl looking down, smiling, her eyes glittering like twin stars.

'... all we need is a drop ...' the girl with a raven's body croaked, hopping a few steps before taking off, its black feathers melting into the darkness. A sense of panic built in her. She didn't even know the girl's name. How would she call her back?

'All we need ...' They were three now standing around her. Innocent eyes, stark naked, with blood running down their bellies and thighs.

'... is a drop of your virgin blood ...'

A raven flew down and climbed on her chest, pecking at her wet cheeks. She struggled, but couldn't move. More ravens came in, slipping a little on the wetness as they landed, hopping over to where she lay, then onto her body, pecking. One stood on her breast, its eyes red as rubies, its luminous beak, sickle-shaped and sharp, bent towards her eyes. 'A drop ...' it croaked.

She shrank back as the beak flashed, piercing her shoulder. Pain engulfed her. 'A drop ...' croaked one. 'Just a drop ...' said the other with jet-black hair and large doe-like eyes. 'You owe us that much, don't you?'

Three moonblades glittered above, extensions of the ravens. They all came down together, nipping, slicing, cutting her eyes, her breast, her womb. Butter-smooth, the moonblades tickled her flesh, almost like a balm.

Wet and moist and slippery. My eyes felt like wool, as did the taste on my tongue. Something licked my shoulder. My swollen eyelids flickered open. A black cat stood on my chest, staring, her eyes round disks of yellow. Her fur shimmered with an emerald aura in the darkness. '... hello ... Angi ...' I whispered, turning on to my side to ease myself up. I struggled to my feet, and Angi leapt to the ground from my shoulder. It admonished me for a few moments, yellow eyes staring, and then trotted off. My shoulder was sore and so was my tongue. Gingerly, I walked around, picked up my satchel, found my yugma locket and septifocals and put them on before staggering home.

The three-headed cobra had confirmed that I was on the right track. That someone had become nervous about my visit to the Kaula Ashram. I smiled, wiping the sweat and grime off my face. I will see you again soon, Nasty.

The earthquake had saved me from turning into giant cobra food, but had caused mayhem in central Delhi. A few buildings had collapsed. Some of them had developed cracks. By three in the morning, the TV was screaming about the shifting tectonic plates that lay beneath Delhi. I could tell them about Kolahal and that the seismic upheaval had been triggered by the brutal killing of a little girl as a sacrificial ritual, but somehow, I didn't think that the crazy media guys would buy that. Nonetheless, the sky confused even the expert climatology consultants. The stars had disappeared. The sky looked bloated. Streaks of boiling red sprayed across it, heavy and tired. Kolahal had clawed his way into the world.

The call I had been expecting came just as my mind had given up to the darkness of exhaustion. The third sacrifice had happened somewhere in Daryaganj. Madhu and Shukra were already on their way. I calmly refilled the vials that had been broken in my bag, replenished my locket with rakpiss and rakta. It lay heavy on my chest like an iron ball of guilt.

It was still dark. The air felt sluggish, a miasma of filth. Even Chhotu advanced listlessly as if reluctant to be out on the road. I was almost glad when I reached the abandoned warehouse near Ghata Masjid Road. My vest was flat against my body and made my nipples stick up uncomfortably. I didn't realize it until the old man who stood chatting to Madhu turned and greeted my breasts instead of me.

'Ajee, we did wonder,' he said, wiping his mouth with a towel. Although it wasn't yet dawn, this man was dressed in a crisp, all-white garb, with an equally crisp, all-white beard flowing down to his chest. 'Why pay so much if you had to use the place just for an experiment? After all, it is only a ruined building. The publishing house burnt down a few years ago. It was a protest against one of the books that they had published about our religion. Hota hai. You write wrong things and someone will protest in this country. Since then, half the building has collapsed. We would have repaired it, but what with education for children and our begum's love for clothes and jewellery, we never seem to have enough money. When Malli sahib came with his offer to use the building, how could we refuse?'

We were surrounded by a group of other men, most of them curious bystanders, some taking pictures of the warehouse, and one attempting to take a photograph of me. I obligingly took out my boneblade to pose. The man replaced his phone in his pocket.

'… scientist, the devil called himself. A scientist. We would have refused, but our begum wouldn't let us. She fell for the shaitan. The money he offered was quite a lot, a lot more than we have ever seen. But he told us that he had a funder in Amreeka and could afford to pay more. Who refuses if Allah himself has granted us his grace? I fell for it, sahib, mind you. I didn't want to, but I did. All he wanted was for me to ensure that nobody entered the place because the experiment was top secret. We weren't supposed to say anything. Doing Black magic in our own backyard! Devil of a …'

I left Madhu patiently nodding, and walked past the police cordon tape. The warehouse looked like it had only just been burnt down. The grimy bulbs glowed weakly and only added to the dingy atmosphere of the place. Tables, chairs, photocopier machines and half-burnt books were strewn around. Towards the middle, there was a section that had no roof. It was exactly under this hole that the triangle had been made. Right beneath the stars, for the moonblade needed to look at its sister above to power up. I wondered how many months of research had gone into finding the perfect spot so that this guy, who now lay dead and frozen in front of me, could perform the ritual. Shock jolted through me when I saw the girl lying in the triangle – on her face was not terror like the other two, but acceptance. It was the same face that had come to me in my nightmare attached to a raven's body.

The successor of the great Shukracharya gave me a curt nod before returning to his work, his reedy frame bent down at the apex of the triangle. He had a metal box in his hands that buzzed every now and again. I walked around the triangle, examining the grim scene. The triangle was the same size, made of diamond dust; the body of the naked girl lay in the middle of it with the moonblade inside her, the man's dead body bent over it, still grasping the hilt. In the semi-darkness, the bodies looked polished, like unfinished wax statues patiently waiting as the master craftsman took a nap. Naked, still and powerful. I swallowed hard, my mouth so dry that it was almost painful.

Croak! Croak! The black ravens sat on the ledge above by the gaping hole in the high ceiling. There was something unnatural about their stillness.

'It was electricity after all,' said Shukra, pointing to the cellphone as soon as Madhu entered. 'I ran a test at my lab this morning. This cellphone served as an amplifier, which directed the static electricity available in the atmosphere inwards into the triangle. That, in turn, built up such a massive discharge of electricity within its walls that the two people inside died instantly. The triangle's outlines, as I had mentioned before, served as the conductors, spreading the electric discharge and at the same time containing it within the tetrahedron, almost like an electromagnetic bomb.' His voice echoed and faded into white noise in the background as I continued to stare at the ravens, which stood still, too still, looking at the scene below. Did I imagine it, or did I see the eyes of one turn red? Just like in my dream?

'Then why sacrifice a girl for it?' Madhu asked, his arms folded across his broad chest.

It was the same question with which I had shot down Shukra's theory last night. I didn't bother to contradict His Grace, choosing instead to stare at the birds above.

Ravens, as you might know, are one of the most intelligent birds out there. They like to take care of their community, but they never synchronize their flying patterns as some migratory birds do. They looked below, all staring together, in the same direction, towards us, again and again.

'Have you noticed how each time we find a sacrifice, we also seem to see ravens around us?' I asked quietly, my hand snaking to the scabbard on my belt.

'What?' said Shukra, stopping mid-word. 'Not very surprising. Ravens are carrion birds and so dead bodies will attract them. Anyway, as I was saying ...'

'Hmm ...'

'... I have an answer to that as well,' Shukra was saying. 'Just as I suspected, I'm afraid. Look at what I found inside this man's bag. *Is Tantrism a Science? Logic in Tantrik Rituals*, *Secret Science of Tantrism*. I have read some of these books and they are quite potent. They explain tantrism as a logical science, as a science of cause and effect and even teach you how to create rituals that could tap into energy using scientific mediums. I know some scientists who are part of the technology department in CAT and are trying to disassociate themselves from magic per se, and now call themselves scientists who reform the world through scientific rituals.'

I turned around, distracted for a second. 'Isn't that the one written by someone from Kaula Ashram?'

'Narahara?' Madhu asked, frowning. 'The same names seem to keep cropping up in our investigation, don't they?'

I took the torchlight from his hand and shone it into the nook above. The black coat of one of the ravens gleamed in the light, casting a misshapen shadow behind it. It was not the shadow of the bird, but something larger, like a ragged cloak. Someone I knew?

'Not Narahara but the Kaula Council tantrik who set up the technology department, Maharishi Amritananda. He's a real innovator in the space, trying to figure out the older scientific reasons behind codified tantrik rituals. I am a huge fan of his work. But that's not the point,' said Shukra. 'It doesn't prove that he was actually involved. This,' he indicated the triangle with his long, thin hand, 'is mere foolishness in the hands of people who read his book, misunderstood it and tried mixing tantrism and science. But the book proves one thing, Madhu.' He jerked his head at me. 'This sure isn't any hocus-pocus or demonic doing. As I said before, it's mere science gone wrong. So I suggest you relieve Miss Anantya of her duties. I don't think her misleading arguments will help the case.'

'I will decide when she has to go, Shukra,' answered Madhu, pinching his whiskers. 'You do your work.'

'I quite agree with Shukra here,' I said from behind.

They would have fooled me, if it hadn't been for the eyes. I didn't even bother with my septifocals this time. Instead, I took out my mandala, choosing an intricate one that had been created by interlacing fine bird-bones with mayan threads; Jaala, it was called. I pointed the mandala towards the ravens. In my left hand was a thick brown powder.

'The Kaulas are definitely responsible for this mess. But before we figure out how, Madhu, can you direct your torch up into those eyes?'

'What?'

'Now!' I said quietly and firmly and then blew the powder through the mandala. The granules filtered through the mandala and converted into a heavy, velvety smoke on the other side, starting to swim in wave-like movements towards the darkness. They shot upwards, towards the ravens that had been spotlit by Madhu's torchlight. Their long misshapen shadows loomed on the crumbling first floor of the warehouse. The shadows merged again to form something that looked like a beast.

'Keep it pointed there!' I shouted and then yelled, *'Kaali parchhayee chipak jaa!'*

The mantra took the shape of a web and was flung up towards the shadow of the first raven that tried to rise up and fly. The shadow splayed on the ceiling, frozen in place. An ear-splitting whistle filled the night. The other ravens flapped away, cawing in confusion. But they couldn't go far without their buddy. All their shadows had coalesced into one creature's shadow. And it was now trapped. I could smell its panic at the sudden inability to move. It was the raven's shadow that had given away the fact that the raven was in fact a yatu. The shadow had not been that of a bird. Yatus, you see, are creatures of shadows and have no physical bodies. Undisguised, they look like a whirlpool of black smoke.

'Craaak!' the raven whose shadow I had snared screamed again, its red eyes bulging.

'It's no use!' I shouted so that the ravens could hear me loud and clear. 'Why don't you just give up and come down. To talk.'

'Why is she bullying the ravens?' exclaimed Shukra.

'Catching an eavesdropper,' I answered.

'Craak!' said another raven, as it dive-bombed towards my shadow, trying to attack my face, its beak clacking. But it couldn't get close enough. It was yanked back by its shadow like it was on a leash. The raven froze in mid-flight. I had this one. The other two flew downwards, slowly, morosely.

'Who are you? Tell me!' I ordered.

'CRAAAAAAAACK!' The bodies of the ravens melted and became shadows. It was as though a long cloak of night had spread above us, stuck to the wall. Their croaks filled the dark night.

'She's completely mad,' Shukra muttered, 'and all of us are going mad too.'

'We can wait while my Parchhayee eats you up or you can talk.'

'CRAAACK!' they said together, in deafening volume.

'Shukra, give me a piece of wood,' I ordered.

Thankfully he didn't question me. He picked up a stick. 'Will this suffice?' He nervously adjusted his glasses.

I nodded and took it. 'I am going to puncture your shadow if you don't start talking soon,' I said. Hit them with a bullet and they will escape, but wood can slice right through them.

'AACK! AACK!' In the blink of an eye, they had fused together to form a being – something as different from a raven as can be. A shadow, misshapen, like black smoke in a gust of wind.

'I was here just to eat, I swear, I swear! A yatu has to eat!' the smoky form said.

'Ah, to eat, is it?'

'Yess, yess, to eat. Dead meat. That's all me wants,' it said, pointing to the dead bodies.

'You seem to like these particular dead bodies a lot. I remember seeing you two nights ago in Kotla and then again near Pusa. Weren't you there?'

'Aack! Aack! Me wasn't in any of those two places you said about,' it answered unconvincingly, its eyes darting from one to another. 'Shukra, believes me! She traps innocents for spite. Tantriks are not good. Not good.'

'This is the kind of prejudice that I have protested against since the very beginning!' Shukra said, readjusting his glasses. 'Just because it's a creature of some sort doesn't mean it was involved in the deaths.'

'I am a real bitch, yatu. So, if you don't want to be eaten by white light, talk. NOW!' I brandished the stick.

'CRAAACK! Not to do that, not to do that! Will talk, will talk!'

'Why are you here?' I asked. It squirmed in protest but with two torches trained on it, it was trapped.

'Was send by me Shadow King to see what's happening and then tell him all me sees.'

'Were you there before too? In the last two deaths?'

Its smoky head bobbed up and down in agreement. 'Craak! Was, was. Me was there. Waiting. Waiting and seeing all and then me would go and tell everything to me King. Came here before the dead manava. He came in, his eyes roving, glittering in moonlight, carrying his own born. He picked up magic box and said something to it. He said the words and then blood gushed out of his born. Oh! The smell, the smell was delicious! Me wanted to eat it, to lick it, to drink it. Next thing me know the blood starts to burn, as if all black, something evil comes into the place. It becomes darker and darker until I cannot see, and a wall is built around it. The noise it makes! Like millions of metal feathers flocking together! Me scared, but me doesn't leave. Me waits for someone to see, someone to discover, someone to shout. Then yous come, yous take off the wall and look around at the dead. Everything me tells to Shadow King like a good yatu who tells it to his boss.'

'And who's your Shadow King?'

'Me cannot tells that! Tribe rules, me cannot break of me lord. He will kill me.'

'Then tell me who's his boss.'

It shook its head. 'Me don'ts know. Me swear to the death of rats, me don'ts know.' It cried as I waved the piece of wood I held.

'AAACK! Me just hear a name. King was telling it to another. That's all me knows. Please, please—'

'What's the name you heard?' I asked, ignoring his tirade.

'Something with Nss … AAACK! Yes, yes mes remember. Narahara! Narahara!'

I took out an empty bottle from my satchel and, using my mandala, trickled the yatu's shadow into the bottle. The inky black form of the yatu became greyed, lighter. I slipped the bottled shadow into my bag.

'You are free now.'

'But, miss. Me's shadow!' it croaked.

'I keep your shadow to make sure that you don't go back to your King and say something about our little talk tonight. If you do, I am going to light up your shadow from a distance.'

Trembling like a blob of puss, it flew away. Shukra was uncharacteristically silent as we walked out. Even though it was dawn, the sun hadn't broken through the film of darkness. The sky looked grey and tired, streaks of dirtied red and black across it like fingers. Fingers of Kolahal. I knew. A god that needs blood to be born will need more blood to sustain it.

'It's over, my friend,' I whispered, looking up into the grey, grumbling sky.

'... this is the third in the series of grisly deaths that have been reported across the city. A source tells us that they could somehow be related to a prominent tantrik clan in the city, although that is yet to be confirmed by the Central Bureau of Investigation which is the investigative agency behind this ...'

It was ten in the morning, five hours since we discovered that Nasty was the guy behind the sacrifices. All we needed to do was arrest him and then find out who else might be involved. But no. I sat in front of a small television in a room at the CBI headquarters, waiting for Madhu. We hadn't headed out immediately to the Kaula Ashram because of something that Madhu called protocol, which basically is documented crap. Madhu had tried to explain the protocol (aka written shit) to me when I snapped at him. Apparently, since it was a Sunday morning, and since justice sleeps on Sundays, getting a warrant was impossible. So Madhu had to get permission from his boss, who had to get permission from the Tazaak, who would then allow us to enter the Kaula Ashram to arrest Nasty. He had bluntly refused my generous offer to sneak into the ashram and ensure that Nasty remained there. As I said, complete *shit*. Frustrated, I sat outside his office and slept while Madhu ran around like a headless chicken. Right now the case was stuck in the borderline debate. Whose jurisdiction is this? I twiddled with my blade.

'... bizarre fire led to the death of a prominent socialite of the city, Miss Lavanya Mohan. A lift attendant was found dead from a poisonous snakebite in the basement of the same apartment complex. The police are now looking for clues in her apartment which could shed some light on what might have happened ...'

Madhu came over and sat down beside me, mopping the pouring sweat off his head. He fidgeted with his whiskers, wiped his bald head again and put his elbows on his thighs, sighing and staring at the floor.

'Go on then, tell me. What is it?' I prodded. He told me that he had just finished talking to someone called Jasmine at the Kaula Ashram in Manesar.

Jasmine had come across Madhu's visiting card on a side table in Yogi Riju's room and had called to inform him.

'Anantya,' he began, looking straight into my eyes, his swimming with concern, 'Yogi Riju ... he ... he was found in his room an hour ago. He committed suicide by consuming poison. He left a note by the table. A note confessing that he was the one who had told all three men about the ritual of sacrificing their daughters. That he's responsible for all those deaths.'

Riju Das wore nothing but a clean black dhoti like he had just bathed. He had carefully removed all his jewellery, including the gold medallion with the Kaula signet. He lay on the single cot with a slight smile on his face, his lips just about covering his overbite. He looked like he was asleep and having a pleasant dream. I sucked in my breath, bracing myself for the flood of memories. Riju. The person I would hide with to avoid Didi's wrath. The friend who had taken a beating on my behalf when, instead of doing the dishes, I threw them down a well and ran away. I wished I had not turned away from him. *Don't give them a chance to harm you.* But you let them harm you, dear friend. I wished I had taken him away from the ashram when we met yesterday. Was it only yesterday? It seemed like years ago already. I wished I had insisted that he left with me. That I had held his hand and given him a hug one last time. How I wished I had let the fury go and spoken to him. Now I couldn't tell him how much he had meant to me.

I turned my head away, blinking rapidly, unable to stem the surge of emotion that I thought I had purged forever.

'It wasn't suicide,' I said aloud, proud that my voice didn't betray the massive lump in my throat. I swallowed. 'He ... he didn't kill himself.'

'And how do you conclude *that*, madam?' Shukra, busy taking blood samples from Riju's corpse, his spectacles precariously perched at the end of his nose, countered.

'I ... it's just too convenient,' I answered, losing the will to argue anymore.

'See?' He turned towards Madhu. 'Miss Anantya considers herself an investigator. The first rule for a detective is evidence. There's a bottle of a liquid on the bedside table, neatly labelled sarpa vish, or snake poison. Even a single drop is lethal. Then there's a dead body on the bed, which shows no signs of external aggression. Though rigor mortis has started to set in, which places the time of death approximately twelve hours ago, the blood still flows in the veins, a common feature of this poison. To top it all, we have a suicide note, confessing the crimes of the past three nights, in what we have been able to establish is his own handwriting. In it, he writes exactly what I have been suspecting all along – that it was a pseudo experiment with electricity, with a random tantrik ritual thrown in. And here is Miss Anantya who feels that this explanation – the only concrete one we've had so far, mind you – is all "too convenient". Perhaps she has read too many thrillers and expects this case to throw up—'

'That's enough, Shukra,' said Madhu quietly. 'Why don't you take the body to the morgue, do an autopsy and *confirm* the cause and time of death.'

Shukra's lower lip quivered. 'I will as soon as I test this sample.' He gestured to the assistant waiting outside. The girl walked in slowly, her hands trembling. She looked vaguely familiar. Perhaps that was because she looked like a novice who had never seen a corpse before. For a second I pitied her. I couldn't remember when I had ever been like her. I have been seeing dead bodies since I was a little girl, starting with my mother's. Each death had its own flavour of pain. I wanted to tell her that it didn't get better.

'Dust the room for fingerprints, Ruki,' Shukra ordered, carefully placing the syringe on the sidetable, 'before the people here destroy all evidence of the suicide.'

She turned a shade of grey when she looked at the dead body, but obeyed all the same. All this while, I stood leaning on a cupboard opposite the bed, concentrating on breathing evenly.

'… can't seem to put my finger on it. Anantya, are you listening to me? Anantya?'

I looked up, startled to see Madhu, frowning, holding the letter in hand. It had been put into polythene to protect it from other fingerprints.

'Read this,' he said quietly. 'Maybe you will understand.'

I took the evidence from his hand.

*I, Riju Das, take responsibility for the deaths of Vikram Sharma,
Rohit Kanwal, Sasaka Kukreti and their young daughters that have
unfortunately occurred these past few days. All three of them were
students of Swami Narahara, but it was I who taught them the
know-how of one of the darkest sides of tantra – human sacrifice.*

*Swami Narahara has nothing to do with these unfortunate
incidents. I hope the Kaula Ashram and my friends find it in their
heart to forgive my sins. I go on my own accord, to atone in another
world, in another life.*

Yogi Riju Das

'Where's Narahara?' I asked, returning the letter to Madhu
like it had scorched me.

'Swami Narahara is in Banaras,' answered the attendant
who had telephoned Madhu earlier this morning. She leant
against the doorway to Riju's room, a polite expression on
her pretty face. 'Thankfully, he was summoned on an urgent
mission by the Ashram Council, and didn't have to witness
this unfortunate incident.'

I stared at her for a second. She wore the standard black
dhoti off-shoulder dress that Kaula Ashram's attendants
usually did, her shoulder blades jutting out sharply. She
looked older than the girls I had seen at the reception though.
More mature, more responsible. Something about her tone
gave me the impression that she and Nasty were more than
just student and teacher.

'Weren't you the one who discovered Riju's body?'

'Yes. I was the unfortunate one. When Yogi Riju didn't
appear for the special staff meeting that he had never failed
to attend before, I was sent to his room. That's when I saw
him. He was quite dead.'

'Did you call the doctor when you discovered him?' I
asked.

She had a perfect smile on her face as she talked. I wanted to hit her with a mantra and shatter her even, white teeth. 'There was no need. He had stopped breath—'

'So you assumed he was dead and didn't even call a doctor to confirm it? What did you say your name was?'

'I ... Jasmine,' she answered, pouting, her expression turning stubborn. 'There was no need to call a doctor. He had obviously stopped breathing.'

'And you can judge that a man's dead just by looking at him? So instead of calling a doctor, you pick up a letter on the bedside and call your seniors. And all this while you don't call a doctor? How interesting. The letter with its contents was of course more important to you. So, did you manage to call Narahara in Banaras as well?'

'I—'

'Why the hell didn't that Madhu return my call?' The booming voice interrupted my interrogation. Jasmine took the opportunity to slip away from the room with a quiet 'excuse me'.

'I want to speak to that girl again,' I told Madhu, thoroughly pissed.

Madhu, however, ignored me and went outside to greet whoever was still shouting.

'... NOT ANSWER THE PHONE WHEN I CALL? You dare to ignore your own boss, Mister Tripathi. If you weren't from the minorities, so to speak, I would have you suspended immediately. But you fags are favourites of the higher-ups ever since that sorry Act was passed—'

'As I said, I was busy.' Madhu's usually calm voice sounded strained. 'What were you calling me for, Nandan?'

Nandan was Madhu's boss and didn't step out of his cushy office unless there was a photo-op. Seemed like someone important in Kaula Ashram had been busy. I found myself alone in the room, staring at the bed where Riju's dead body had lain a few minutes ago. It was like a drama script. Riju had been the culprit, who had ultimately paid the price for teaching Black tantra to novices. Narahara had been conveniently out of the picture when Riju confessed and died. There were no loose ends. It was way too neat. And real life was never neat. It was messy.

'... comes under their jurisdiction now. Not for us to investigate. I suggest that you wind up and formally hand over the case to the Tantrik Authority.'

'But Shukra has already taken the body and we are still working on the case ...'

Crap of crows. Tazaak, the Tantrik Authority, was sympathetic to the Kaula clan. They would be mere puppets in whatever scenario the Kaula Ashram wanted to play out. If the Tazaak took over the case, it would be tidily packed up and buried for a long time to come under dungeons of red tape and tantrik codes. I had to do something. The syringe of Riju's blood sample glimmered on the table. I quickly grabbed it, dropping it in my bag.

'... you have one day to finish the post-mortem and hand the body over to the Authority. Close it, fag boy, if you still like the cushy office you have back at the CBI.'

I saw Riju's cellphone lying on the table beside the bottle. For a moment, I wondered if I should nick that as well, but decided against it. If something went missing, Madhu could get into trouble. For now, the blood will have to tell me the truth.

'... he has agreed to personally supervise the investigation. He's big, Madhu, and I don't want you to mess it up. Be polite and tell him everything you know, you understand me?'

'Who is?' I asked as soon as I stepped out of the room. I had met the CBI chief only once before and it had been a moment of instant mutual hatred. Nandan Tilak still looked the same, a big, brown baby pig with a tiny moustache and tiny porcine eyes which glared at me from the folds of a fleshy, double-chinned face. One of the chins was quivering.

'What is she doing here?'

'She's helping me with the investigation as you very well know,' said Madhu, a tad defensively.

'In that case she is no longer required here as the CBI is handing the case over to the Authority. I suggest—'

'Maharishi himself!' exclaimed Shukra who popped up unexpectedly from behind the baby pig boss. He looked quite different all of a sudden. He looked ... what was the word? His age. Highly strung and excitable, like a regular twenty-something-year-old. He stood behind Nandan, a head taller, his head bobbing.

'We are going to meet His Highness, His Holiness Maharishi Amritananda himself!'

'Rakshasa fuck,' I exclaimed before I could stop myself. Amritananda of all people. It seemed like my run of bad luck was having a field day today. His presence meant that the Kaula Council had become personally interested in the case. His presence also meant that I had to get out of here, and fast. I didn't want to meet him. Not yet. Not ever. I clutched my satchel.

'Madhu, I have to leave.'

'Why?'

'Looks like the case is finished. Taz ... Tantrik Authority will definitely not hire me to do ... and anyway, Riju's dead, he has confessed and all ... so ... well, my work is done,' I finished lamely and walked away as fast as I could without actually running.

'Anantya! Stop, yaar!' Madhu came after me, his hairy hand closed on my shoulder, spinning me around. 'Why have you gone so weird? Is there something I should know?'

Here was my chance. To tell him the truth, the complete truth on why I didn't want to meet Amritananda. The truth bubbled inside me. Trust him, Anantya. He's a friend. He will understand … No. No one would.

'Nothing. I just want out of this mess,' I answered.

He knew I was lying to him, his entire barrel-chested self could sense it. Madhu nodded curtly, looking at me disappointed. It was a first and I felt the hurt physically. 'As you wish. Can I request you to come and debrief Authority about the moonblades and then you can be out of this?'

'What's the hold up?' asked Nandan from behind. 'Is your hire giving you trouble, Mr Tripathi?'

'No,' said Madhu, his arms crossed. 'We are coming.'

'Then let's go. It's not a good idea to keep Maharishi waiting.'

'His Highness is full of graciousness,' gabbled Shukra exuberantly, as we started to follow Nandan and Madhu to another room. I don't know which was more irritating – when he behaved old beyond his years or this bouncing around like a five-year-old. 'To take out time from his research into the worlds where science and magic overlap and decide to look at the case himself for the sake of a dead colleague—'

'Stop ass-licking, Shukra,' I snapped. 'He's involved because of Narahara, you fool, not to investigate for some greater good thingy.'

I had to get out of here. I couldn't meet Amritananda. That would be a huge disaster. I didn't want my past to break loose and come pouring down on the new life I'd built.

'Maharishi Amritananda is a great soul. He has developed

a new direction for tantrism. He's the one I mentioned, the one who studied tantrik rituals in depth and explained their scientific roots. Didn't you see his book in that student's bag? It's read by every scientifically minded tantrik worth his salt today.'

I laughed out loud, startling a woman who stood at the entry to a hallway. 'Hah! Your Maharishi is simply saving his own cushy ass by covering up for his baby's mistakes.'

'What do you mean?' asked Nandan.

'I mean Narahara, Nandan,' I replied. 'Narahara is Amritananda's son. So you see, Shukra, Maharishi is involved so he can cover any tracks that lead to his own born. After all, Narahara is the only legitimate child he has to groom for the Council seat in the ashram. Any spot of Black tantra on even a colleague of his will close that door forever. Amritananda will do whatever it takes to protect Nas ... Narahara.'

'Those are serious allegations, Anantya,' began Madhu.

'His son?' exclaimed Shukra, cutting him off. 'Swami Narahara is Maharishi Amritananda's son? I didn't know!' His voice echoed in the hall we had just walked into.

'And did she tell you who she is?' asked a smooth voice from the far end of the chamber. The same oily, coaxing voice from all those years ago. To sacrifice for the greater good. For the Kaula clan, for the betterment of humans. For a superior world. It was like someone had passed an electric current through my body. My hands balled into fists, my left hand automatically reaching for my boneblade.

'Maharishi! To be in your esteemed presence.' Shukra abruptly ran forward and fell flat on his face at Amritananda's feet. Before Amritananda could draw back, Shukra had kissed his chappal. Nandan hurried up to them, muttering apologetically. Maharishi's two chic, female bodyguards in black dhotis sprang forward with their swords, ready to wrench him off if necessary. Maharishi stopped them with an almost imperceptible flick of his hand. I am sure no one noticed that his smile had faltered for a second. I saw it because I knew him so well. His lips thinned slightly with displeasure and his studiedly calm eyes turned a darker grey. Then the smile was back in place. Some things never change.

'... have read all your books. The very idea that tantrik rituals involving blood could be explained scientifically is something that no one but you could have thought about ...'

'Shukra, get up!' whispered Nandan urgently, hovering behind him like a ruffled hen. I would have been laughing aloud if I hadn't been so incredibly pissed off. 'I apologize profusely for his behaviour, Maharishi. It's most unwarranted.'

'That's all right,' said Maharishi Amritananda graciously, bending down to help Shukra rise. 'May you live a long life.'

For effect, he hugged Shukra, staring at me over his head. I deliberately cut my hand on the boneblade to feel pain. This man still had the power to upset me. I took a deep breath to control myself, and focused on his appearance. He hadn't changed much. His beard was shiny and black and his face radiant and youthful. He had a perfect face, evenly proportioned, with a good nose and light grey eyes. His expression had a gentleness to it, like the priest at a confession box to whom people could unburden themselves and find a sympathetic ear. Even after years of sedentary living, his body was muscular. He wore the Kaula black dhoti and the small golden triangle that hung on his immaculately waxed chest signified his lofty position in the ashram. Nothing else. Nothing flashy or in bad taste. No. There was no outward evidence of the darkness that lay within him.

'You look different, dear Anantya,' said Maharishi as he glided towards me. 'Older perhaps? It's been a long while, my child.'

'And you look the same, Maharishi, like a college-going teenager,' I said with all the sarcasm I could muster. 'Must be because of those new bodyguards you've got yourself.' I looked at the stunners who had positioned themselves behind him.

His lips thinned but he held the smile. 'Always so angry, my child. Nandan, does the CBI know that the person advising you on the case is actually someone who was dismissed from Kaula Ashram in Banaras with serious allegations?' he asked softly.

'Oh. No, my lord! I had no clue about that! Madhu,' asked Nandan, turning to his junior, 'did you know anything about this?'

Madhu shook his head, frowning. I felt sorry for him suddenly. Perhaps I should have told him before. But no. My past was my business, not his.

'Oh, I see. So she lied her way into the CBI too? I am not surprised. You see, she was a favourite in the ashram once. She had many influential people wrapped around her charming little finger. Oh, she can be charming when she wants to be. Look at how beautiful she is? And she knows exactly how to use her beauty. But, fortunately for us, she tripped herself up in one of her own games. If I were you … Madhu, is it? I would be wary of trusting her with any confidential information. She has a tendency to leak and tweak, all for her own benefit. I bet she hasn't told you that she's my birth daughter?'

'You have no right!' I shouted. 'We broke that bond a long time ago!'

His boyish chuckle filled the hall. 'Darling, the one thing you cannot break is a blood bond. You of all people should know that.'

I turned to Madhu, who looked both hurt and angry. 'Madhu, I wanted to tell you—'

'When? After we had finished investigating?' he asked, angrier than I had ever seen him.

Maharishi smiled. Was I the only one that saw the malice behind the smile?

'It's not really her fault, Madhu, she can't help it. She was clinically declared a pathological liar. I cannot tell you the details, because the incident is ... well ... Kaula business, and you know how secretive tantriks can be. But you are most welcome to come to Banaras and ask our able doctor, Bhattacharya. I gave her an easy way out by asking her to leave the ashram. After all, I am her father. Which father would want to accept that his child is a spiteful liar? My heart was broken. Now I hear that she has started to dabble with back-alley tantrism. I heard that she discarded the name we had given her and changed it to the rather flashy "Tantrist". That's when I knew I had truly lost my little girl.' He sighed for dramatic effect. 'But I am really surprised that the CBI failed to do a background check on a tantrik. All you needed to do was connect with CAT, and they would have recommended a more reliable tantrik, better qualified than a mere woman—'

Madhu's phone rang loudly, startling us all. He didn't answer it, but stood concentrating on a spot on the floor.

Maharishi smiled and said, 'Why don't you answer that? Phones are like crying babies. They need to be attended to.'

'You were saying, Maharishi,' said Nandan, his head bent in deference as Madhu walked away to the far end of the hall, phone glued to his ear.

Maharishi spread his manicured hands wide. 'We say this to all civilian lawmakers and businesses alike. If you need a tantrik, go with CAT recommendations. To hire a woman, that too a renegade, seems to me like the CBI is taking quite an unnecessary risk, especially in a sensitive case like this one. She could be misleading you by applying her own tantrik ideas, which are not officially approved. She has been known to associate with some radical Red tantriks and even dabble in the lethal Black tantrism. If you ask her now, I bet she's got some wild theory about me. Seeing patterns and conspiracy theories where none exist is one of the symptoms of her mental condition. Poor baby, cannot help it. Her head is messed up with all kinds of electrical impulses that make her so—'

'Arrgh! All lies!' I shouted, surging towards him, my boneblade in my left hand. Before I realized it, I had sliced my right thumb and as the blood splashed on the boneblade, I attacked with the Rudhira mantra, the blade angled towards my hateful father.

'Pak, paka, rudhira!'

The blood dripping from my hand arced towards Maharishi like a meteor shower. As they landed on him, they sizzled like hot oil. He fell back in pain as blisters bubbled on his skin. His face turned ashen and, for a second, to my joy, he actually looked scared.

'Suffer!' I screamed in hate. 'May you suffer in the deepest pits of naraka, like I did!'

His bodyguards leaped forward, spinning me around and flattening me to the ground. Swiftly, they twisted my arms behind me. My boneblade fell away and I felt the pressure of a sword's tip on my nape.

'Don't you dare do anything stupid,' the bodyguard whispered.

My bleeding stopped as soon as I retracted the mantra. That's all I wanted to do, wipe the smugness off their faces. I heard a click as someone cocked a gun.

'Should I shoot her, Maharishi?' asked Nandan.

No ... wait,' he groaned, getting off the floor. He grimaced, looking more elegant in pain than I ever did even when I smiled. But his pristine body was speckled with burns wherever the blood had hit it. It wasn't over. It would fester. It was like a disease and he would have to undergo skin grafts to cure it completely. Rudhira was an illegal mantra in the CAT rulebook for a reason. I smiled grimly.

'What in Bali's name happened here?' asked Madhu who had only just returned to the chamber.

'Your friend went nuts and attacked the Maharishi,' answered Shukra.

Madhu looked at me bleakly. I knew our relationship, if ever there was one, was now well and truly over. But I simply had to do this. The last time I had seen my father, I was just a frightened child. He should realize that he could no longer scare me. I grinned a crazy grin.

'There will be repercussions for this, Anantya,' said Maharishi, dusting imaginary specks off his dhoti. 'I will file a formal complaint against you at Tazaak and hope that you will be institutionalized again so that no one is hurt by your erratic behaviour.'

'You have to do your duty, father dear,' I cried out, beaming from ear to ear. 'You always do. Even if it betrays those who love you.'

'Well,' said Maharishi, 'as I told you, making up stories is her speciality.'

'I thoroughly apologize for this,' said Nandan. 'Madhu can be hasty in his decisions. She's just a consultant and nothing more. And not even a consultant anymore.' He looked pointedly at Madhu.

'You need to trust me on this case, Madhu,' I said urgently to my friend. Somehow, suddenly, I needed him to understand my behaviour, my motives.

'Oh, and there's one other thing,' said Maharishi. 'I was told that Mr Tripathi came into our ashram the other day and wanted to speak to Swami Narahara. Well, let me assure you that the allegations against Swami Narahara are all untrue. The reason Anantya's so against Swami Narahara and wants him to take the blame for what happened is because he was always the more talented one. You see, he's my son and her half-brother. So this, I assure you,' he waved his manicured hands at me, 'is mere sibling rivalry. There's no proof that Swami Narahara was involved in these hateful rituals. Yogi Riju, unfortunately, has confessed to it, as all of you know by now.'

'Riju was framed and I will prove it!' I shouted angrily.

'You will do nothing of the sort, Anantya,' said Madhu, his voice sharp with displeasure. 'Just stop with your conspiracy theories about the cult and all that. Everything points towards Riju as the guilty one. It was his cellphone to which all the calls from the other phones went to, his number. He's the one who asked these three men to take the lives of their own daughters. You are just too emotionally involved in this to look at it rationally.'

'You have to believe me, Madhu!' I cried. 'This isn't over. This will continue! The yatu—'

'The yatu was a fluke,' he countered before I could speak.

'Women!' muttered his boss from behind. 'So delusional, all of them.'

But Madhu ignored him, still looking at me with

disappointment in his eyes. 'Why?' he asked. 'Why should I believe you? So that you can feed me more lies, like you did before? This is over. Maharishi, since she attacked you here, you can do whatever you wish with her as per the rules of your ashram. We will close this case and forward the file as well as the dead body of your colleague to the Tantrik Authority.'

There are some bridges that can't be rebuilt. Trust is one of them. I turned to look at the retreating CBI boys. I could feel my father's smug smile behind me as he watched the others leave.

'Just the two of us, after a long, long time, Anantya.' His smooth voice bore sinister malevolence.

۹۲

'Again!'

The whip, made of hair torn from widows and sharpened with glass, flayed my back. It felt like all their sorrow had turned each hair into thin iron rods, flexible and lethal. I winced with the pain, pain that I wanted. Pain was good. Pain helped to forget some things. And I so needed to forget. So needed to let go. I hung upside down, naked, strung up by the ankles to the ceiling, as a low fire burnt below. Sweat, pain, blood and noise emitted from me, falling into the fire below.

'... spit it out! Spit it out! Spit it out! Spit and shout, spit and SHOUT, SPIT AND SHOUT! Aiyiyiyiyiyiyiyiya!' Dhuma's ear-piercing ululating bored through my pores like millions of tiny swords. She danced and jumped and twirled around me – hop and run and bend and twist. In one hand, she held the scourge with which she whipped me at intervals, and in the other a small damru on which she played an incessant rhythm. *Tak! Thak! Tak! Thak! Tak! Thak!* The rhythm squeezed out my frustration and anger in drops of blood and sweat. I could see flashes of her naked body, grey with layers of ash and rivulets of sweat.

'Aaaaaaaaaaaaaaaaaaaaaaiiiiaaa!' Dhuma shrieked, thrashing me again.

Sunday afternoon rushed to me, as sharp as the whip that

just landed on my back. Riju's dead body. Madhu's parting shot. But most of all, Maharishi Amritananda. It had been seven years since I had last seen him. I thought he had forgotten and finally let me go. He and his hideously beautiful smile. After my CBI cronies had left us alone, his pretty bodyguards had tied me up with mayan rope.

'Will you finally finish this off?' I had spat at him.

He had laughed, the sound gliding mellifluously around us. 'I never wanted to kill you, my dear. You are way too emotional,' he had said, shaking his black beard, gently as one of his bodyguards applied a balm to the rash I had created. 'If only you had agreed. With your shakti, your emotional power and my knowledge, we could have achieved so much more.'

I saw red then, but controlled my anger. 'Dear father,' I said, smiling, 'like it or not, I would rather pay to have sex with a rakshasa than be an incestuous Kaula whore.'

His eyes had turned a dark, slate grey, the only indication of his anger. But his voice held no hint of it. 'You have so much of your mother in you, *Princess*,' he had whispered, his face so close that I could see flecks of black in his grey eyes. 'So much of your mother. She was the same when she was younger. Don't you want to see your mother before she leaves this plane?'

My shock must have shown on my face, because he laughed softly and replied, 'Oh, no. She's not dead. Is that what you were told? She must not want to see you again, I guess.'

'That's not true, I … I saw her dead … where is she?'

He looked at me, fingers gently combing his beard.

'*Where* is she?'

'Someplace safe,' he whispered, smiling softly. 'She will remain safe as long as you help us out.'

'If you touch her again, I will grind your bones and feed them to the rats,' I said through gritted teeth, my voice quivering in rage.

'Colourful choice of words. I see that ugly aghori brute is teaching you more than just the Red arts. Now, about the deaths. Riju is dead, the case is closed. Stay away from it.'

'Riju didn't do it. Someone else from the Kaula Ashram framed him.'

He sighed as he stood up and walked around, his footsteps hushed on the marble. 'Princess, princess.' He looked at me, stroking his beard. 'You underestimate Swami Riju. Believe me, we are well rid of him. Tazaak will close the case soon and it will be over. You don't have to get involved in this mess. It was not Narahara. The poor boy's only ambition is to reach the Council. Even in that, he had to be trained, had to be sponsored. Don't ruin his chances by helping our enemies.'

'Ruin his chances? Or yours?' I had asked. 'I will find out who did this and take the proof to CAT.'

Maharishi's eyes were cold. 'You will again just end up a pawn in a game that involves many others. Someone in CAT wants to frame the Kaula Ashram and I intend to find out who. I don't want you involved. You have no legal right to investigate this. If you do, Tazaak will only arrest you. Now, be a good girl, and go and get the filth on your skin cleaned. It won't be long before you lose your beauty if you abuse it like this. Let the Tazaak handle it.'

'You mean let you handle it. But you forget, dear father, I am not your pretty whore anymore.'

'You will be if you want to see your mother ever again,' he had whispered softly, eyes darkening again.

They had let me go then. For seven years, I had been under the impression that my mother was dead. Apparently, she wasn't. And she had forgotten to tell me. Great. I wondered why Maharishi let me live. Why hadn't he killed me all those years ago? After all that had happened, why save me? And for what? In a way, I had wanted this to end. I had wanted us to confront each other. But he had just let me off with a warning. Almost like he cared. Tears sprang to my eyes, plopping into the fire below. Lies, all lies.

'Harder!' I screamed, wanting to forget, wanting to hurt, wanting to lash out at someone.

'Some more, some more,' coaxed Dhuma, splashing a freshly sacrificed goat's warm blood on my face and body. My body spasmed, burning, sweating and crying out. 'Spit it out, shout and spout, spit and shout! Shout, shout! Spit it out!'

She hit me again with the whip. I felt the pain but there was not much more left inside of me. I felt drained. I hung tired and humbled. Spent. The damru had stopped and so had the ritual, although the fire below me still burnt, low and flickering, but steady. I could see the remains of bones in the fire, all the skin that clothed them consumed by the fire.

'Kraudha, the demon of anger, eats you,' said Dhuma. Her eyes seemed to change colours in the light of the fire. One went from grey to black and the other from blue to green. She was an old, hunchbacked woman, with huge breasts that hung low, her nipples almost touching her flabby, pot belly. Her hair was in filthy dreadlocks and fell like discoloured cotton around her face. Years of religiously covering herself with ash every midnight had given her skin cracks and a permanent grey shade. She smelt of ashes and shit and crusted blood. Two of her attendants, fleshless skeletons, untied me and lay me down on the mud floor. I heaved a sigh of relief. My ankles ached and my body was drenched with goat's blood, but my anger and frustration had left me. I felt tired and drained, but cleansed.

'You cannot give control like this to Kraudha,' she repeated, giving me a glass of water mixed with some herb. Her nails were blackened and chipped.

I took a sip. It was like swallowing liquid fire. I spluttered. She grabbed the glass and forced the rest of it down my throat. My throat burnt, my body ached all over, but for the first time since this morning, I felt relaxed. Cleansed. Utpu was a ritual that worked like a spa for the soul. I lay on my back and looked at the rough, thatched roof. Skulls of every size and shape hung here, like wind chimes, slowly swinging back and forth. Dhuma's hut was located next to a cemetery in Mehrauli. She liked to live next to a place where she had easy access to a steady supply of bones and corpses whenever her rituals demanded it. Her favourites, of course, were skulls.

Jadoogar, tu jadoogar! Tu hai mera dilbar ... I ignored my cellphone. I hadn't returned any of Grrhat's calls. There were several missed calls and messages from him asking for an update on the Key. But right now, I just didn't have the energy to deal with anything. Instead, I thought about Dhuma and her life. Dhuma was an aghori and, if you went by CAT's definition, a controversial Red, and by certain definitions Black, tantrik. Tazaak had been hunting down aghoris in the city, but no one dared touch Dhuma. For one, most of them thought she was harmless and merely crazy. A mistake that. Dhuma was one of the most powerful tantriks I had ever met. And the only other woman tantrik I knew of.

'It eats you up. You can use it to power you, but no, you let it eat you!' *Thwack*! She hit me on my head.

'Ow!'

She trotted to a corner of the small hut, which was where

her makeshift kitchen was located. I could smell soup. Dhuma was many things to many people, but to me, she was the mother I never had. Oh yes, I did have a mother. A mother who was apparently alive, but had forgotten to tell me about it for seven years. But Dhuma was, in the truest sense of the word, my mother. She had taken me in six years ago. I had been mad at the time, crazed with grief after a year of travelling through the country, through cities, through jungles, my eyes glazed with charak. She had turned me, changed me, got the drug addiction out of my system through painful training and made me what I am today. She had taught me tantrism, her style. Taught me how to delve into my own shakti. Taught me dignity, taught me to be confident and love my body. She had untaught everything that the Kaulas had drilled into me for years. Everything that said helplessness, that said *need*. I had been thrown out of the Kaula Ashram for speaking the truth. She had taken me in without any questions. She had built me from a snivelling, broken teenager to a self-respecting, independent woman. She had healed me, helped me, encouraged me and then powered me up. I would have gone right round the bend if she hadn't been around. So no, to me she was the sanest person around.

'What the hell did you just give me? It's making me grow feelings of all kinds!' I grumbled, sitting up.

'A good cry or good sex helps get Kraudha out of you,' she said, putting a dirty, broken cup with some soup next to me. 'Have. It has chicken and semen of a bull.'

'Eugh. No thanks, Dhum. I don't think I need anymore of those hormones inside me,' I replied, and promptly got poked with a stick.

'You have, else I force you,' said the mad old woman, her breasts swinging like pendulums.

Was I feeling sentimental about her? Must have been the drugs she gave me. 'Crazy old chudail,' I grumbled as I sipped the soup. Though it looked runny and muddy, it was lip-smackingly delicious.

'You use Kraudha to help you, not help him! It is useless if you don't control yourself and use the anger!' said Dhuma, coming over to sit beside me. She waggled her stick.

I smiled. For the first time, since the week had begun, I was feeling relaxed. Almost renewed. Utpu did that. It was almost like alcohol but without any of the side effects. Dhuma usually refused to do it, but after one look at my face earlier today, she had not argued. I started to tell her about my father. About meeting him. About my friend Riju ... My throat constricted again as I remembered. She whacked me.

'What?' I growled.

'So much work to do and you sit here drinking soup?' She whacked my head again.

I was properly annoyed now. 'Why should I care what happens to the world? Let it burn!'

'What d'you want? That someone hugs you and tells you that they love you? That they bow to you and say you are goddess and recognize you for the work you do? What d'you want, huh? That your father becomes someone else? That your mommy opens her arms to you? Stop living in the past and start work. You cannot change things that are long gone. But you can change things that will happen. You can save people. Those little girls who came into your nightmare. You can find out who killed your friend. But nothing will happen if you don't move your ass.'

Thwack! I don't know how she had found out about these things, but I was thankful that I didn't need to say them out aloud. She rose to walk out of the hut. I had just been dismissed. She was right of course. It was time I stopped thinking about the past and started focusing on how to thwart Kolahal's mistresses. I nodded to her, as I scrambled into my clothes, and then left for home to prep my bag.

Back home, I walked straight to my lab, refilling all the potions in the padded corner of my satchel. Getting ready. Getting ready, but for what? Where did the cult fit into all this? Riju had said nothing about the Cult of Chaos, the cult that wanted Kolahal to enter this world. Did it mean that he didn't know? Why was I so sure that Riju's death was murder anyway? The note had been in his handwriting. There was no proof, was there? Just like Shukra had said.

'Oi!' I cried, almost crashing my flagon of precious rakpiss on the floor. Now I knew! If Shukra was right, Riju died around ten at night. In his letter, he had apologized for the deaths of three interns. But we had only mentioned two when we had spoken to him. The night that the third sacrifice had taken place, he was probably writing his confession and drinking the poison. Curiously enough, he had added the third name in his suicide note, *in the past tense*. So, while he might have known of an impending death while he drank poison, he couldn't have known for sure that the death would actually happen. Either he knew way more than he had divulged in his letter, or … someone else had included the third name, after the third sacrifice and after Riju's death. Riju had been a mere pawn in someone's evil plan. But whose? Nasty or someone else too? My father's presence had confused me. Did he know this was happening? How many Kaulas did? What kind of game were they playing? And what should I do now? Call Madhu and tell him about this? Yeah, right. He would take me seriously after this morning's fiasco. Tazaak didn't want me around for sure. They would most probably be doing their best to put a lid on the case as soon as possible. I could probably connect with some others in the Kaula Council. It was quite possible that they weren't aware of any of this. My father had a knack for hiding things from the Council. A virgin girl sacrifice was serious enough to make all of those oldies sit up and pay attention.

'Working hardsss,' said Zee, his pale gold snake body coiled on the sofa, his green eyes glued to the telly.

The TV played news about the mysterious static increase in the atmosphere that made people's clothes stick to their bodies and their hair rise in protest. People were also falling ill because of this strange climatic phenomenon. My own hair was all over the place like a demented crow's nest.

'I need you to find out what kind of a poison this is,' I said, placing the syringe of Riju's blood on the sofa. 'Find out who made it and where one can get it around here.'

He peeled his eyes away from the TV for a second to stare at me, the short golden beard motionless on his lower jaw.

'Pleases or smiles might speeds up the processss,' he hissed, then went back to using his tongue to surf TV channels.

'Sure.' I shrugged. '*Please* ... do this for me, your highness.'

'Good.'

If anyone could tell me what the poison was, and where it came from, Zee could. I called Prem, who had called me earlier when I was with Dhuma.

'Anantya! I am in love!' he screeched as soon as he answered the phone.

'What? What the hell are you talking about?'

'I finally met her, Anantya! So beautiful, so elegant, just

like she is on the big screen. And hasn't changed a bit even after so many years! She convinced me that my real talent lies in acting. I thought I would call to tell you that I cannot work on the case anymore. I would have really liked to, but she gave me really good advice when she said I should follow my passion. So I just called to tell you. Actually, funny how destiny works, I met her because of you.'

'Who are you talking about?'

'My idol! My first love! See, I was outside Lavanya's flat, right? I saw her visiting. Poor woman didn't know Lavanya had died. Doesn't see much news. Understandable for someone like her. I couldn't let her go without telling her how much I loved her work! I said hello. I just had to!'

'Wait, wait! You saw whom in Lavanya's flat?'

'… that got us talking and as soon as I told her how much I adored her she told me that she could get me in the movies! I am in love, Anantya, in lo … oh, wait, someone's come to visit—'

'Prem, who the hell did you meet at Lavanya's flat?'

But he was off the phone, speaking to someone. I heard a female voice.

'Aaiye! Madam, it's you! I gotta go, Anantya. Well, I never …'

The phone disconnected. I shouted 'hello' a couple of times more, but the connection was gone. Gah. I kick-started Chhotu and set off, wondering as the evening heat hit my face how Prem Chhokra would look in a movie.

93

It was the kind of stench that got in through your pores, eating away at your nerves. It was the smell of festering wounds. But there was another thing that bothered me about it. It was the quivering smell of fear. It came out of the cave, crawling on my skin like worms. Instinctively, I took out my boneblade and walked cautiously towards the mouth of the cave.

Although I had been to dasyu hangouts in other forests, this was my first time at the cave, the ghetto of dasyus on the border of Delhi at the foot of the Aravali hills. Dasyus had yet to be recognized as mayan, or independent sups, by the CAT. By the Association definition, they were still pashu or mere magical creatures, and therefore weren't allowed to roam the city on their own, unescorted by a tantrik. The classification meant that dasyus were regarded the way a human would look at a dog or sheep. As pets, or worse, ugly wild animals. It was unjust, but hardly anything that CAT did could be considered fair.

I waited, listening intently to the sounds, which was the problem. There were no sounds. The cave was silent, too silent. Usually, outside a dasyu cave, you could hear a buzz, a vibration that can only be made by hundreds of leathery wings flapping simultaneously. It was so quiet that I could hear my heart pounding. The silence bothered me more than the smell.

'Hello? Can I come in?'

No one replied. The cave's mouth had no door, but it was considered polite for a biped like me to ask for permission before entering a dasyu ghetto. The sun had already set, it was getting dark outside. I could see nothing beyond the mouth of the cave. I waited for a few seconds and then walked into the darkness. I considered switching on a torch, but decided against it. Artificial light was considered rude to beings who could see in the dark just as well as humans see in sunlight. It was like gifting a kilo of shit to a friend. Like I said, rude.

The floor was damp with mulch, which was usually the case in any dasyu nest. Dasyus usually chose places that had high natural ceilings and plenty of stalactites. A stream trickled at the bottom. I carefully avoided it. The thin stream of water I knew was considered holy and I didn't want to risk contaminating it by stepping in it. The smell and silence were overpowering. There was something weird going on here. I pulled down my septifocals, wore them over my eyes, and whispered the Drishti mantra focusing on the Anahata plane, the green plane, which showed all living matter that was around, all flesh.

'Balls of bulls!' I exclaimed, dropping my boneblade in shock. 'What in shakti's name happened?'

My voice echoed around the cave. I took off my septifocals, the shadow of what I had just seen still imprinted on my blinded eyes. As far as my eyes could tell, dasyu bodies lay strewn around me. Slashed, sliced, slaughtered. The stream that ran through the cave was awash with freshly cut pieces of leathery wings, bones, flesh and blood. It was fresh because I could still see the distinct heat signature that came off the bloodied pieces. My human eyes had adjusted to the cave's darkness now. I took a deep breath and told my pounding heart to take it easy. That's when I heard the first furious wingbeats.

'I swear on my father's flight, I will kill her!'

'Noooooooooo!'

Sharp claws dug into my back, pinching and clamping, hoisting me like a rat in their clutches. I shrieked as my feet lifted off the ground, and I rose higher and higher. The dasyu was big, at least twice the size of a fully grown man.

'... filthy, two-legged beasts ... dare attack us in our homes ... justice ...'

I struggled to reach into my bag as my hands and feet flailed helplessly. My fingers seized a sachet of herbs in the bag and I hit the dasyu holding me right in the face with brahmi. He yelped in pain and let me go. I plummeted down, plunging towards the sinister stalactites below. I heard rather than saw the others, flying in, their wings flapping angrily. Four of them grabbed me in freefall and held me spread-eagled in mid-air. Sharp claws started to rip at the flesh on my arms and legs.

'Filthy, sloppy two-legged!'

'Killer of wings!'

'Destroyer of flight! Land crawler!'

'Murderer! Death bringer!'

I gasped as claws and sharp things stabbed and pierced my skin. Pain spread like fire into every corner of my being. Then there was a reverberating echo of a deep, guttural flutter and suddenly I was free, splashing flat on my back into the bloodied stream. I winced as I heard an ominous 'crack'. My head swam with stars and cuckoos.

'Who are you?' asked a dasyu, leaning in.

'Arrgh ... friend of ... Pre ... Prem. Wanted to talk to him,'

I said, grimacing, blinking my eyes to clear away the flecks of blood in them.

He looked at me seriously for a few seconds, as he mulled over what I had said. 'So you are the two-legged he was working for?'

'Yes, Anantya Tan ... Tantrist,' I answered with an effort.

'You his boss? Can you prove?'

'Yes.' I found my bag and with shivering hands fished out my phone, every move I made sheer agony. I showed him Prem's call. He took the phone in his claws, squinting at its screen. He flapped his wings, communicating to the others, shaking his head. The others replied with equally rapid fluttering. It felt like we stayed like that for hours. Me, bleeding into the stream, and the winged dasyus in conversation. Finally, they seemed to arrive at a consensus. I saw the dasyu standing in front of me, his clawed hand extended towards me in an unusual manava-like gesture. I took it, thankful, and stood up, crying out as pain shot through my back. Something there was broken.

'Aaargh!'

'Are you hurt?'

I thought I would shake my head, but didn't. I nodded instead. What the hell. The bunch of them had just attacked me.

'I say sorry for this,' he said, shaking his leathery wings yet again. 'I am Simbara, the head of the ghetto.'

An old dasyu waddled up to me and reached for my face with his clawed hand. I shrank back, wildly reaching behind me to grab something to attack him.

'Please, let him. He is hakim.'

I nodded. The hakim gently flipped me onto my stomach and put something that felt metallic on my back. I was prepared for pain, but felt a dry chill instead, like someone was gently rubbing my back with dry ice. The same thing was poured on my leg. In the heat, the freezing sensation was almost welcome. The polite dasyu gently picked me up and helped me upright. There still was some pain, but I could manage to stand now. Whatever the hakim had applied had worked faster than rakpiss did. I made a mental note to find out what it was. Not that they would disclose their healing secrets to a two-legged ever.

'Who did this?' I asked Simbara, pointing to the strewn bodies.

'A two-legged storm attacked us a few sundowns ago.' Sundown was about ten minutes, which is how the dasyus measured time. A few sundowns could be anywhere between an hour and half an hour. Just about the time I had taken to get here after Prem's call.

'Here,' he said, returning my phone as well as my boneblade. 'You will need to see something. Can you climb these rocks?'

I nodded. We climbed up a steep slope inside the cave, towards the summit. The path he chose was narrower than the main cave and took us upwards. To my surprise, my body was already responding like it was never broken. Smooth, whatever it was that the dasyu hakim had used on me. I started to crawl through the crevice Simbara had vanished into.

'What happened here?'

'We don't understand. Maybe you can tell.' He had a shaky voice like he had had no practice using his vocal cords of late. We emerged from the tunnel into a clearing. A tin-roofed, makeshift shed stood on the right. It had caved in and collapsed.

'Prem liked the open. He was,' he hesitated, looking for the right word, '… different. From the rest of the ghetto. Always fighting with father and mother, and had magic things that manavas had invented. Box in which you see what's happening in other places.'

'You mean a TV?' I smiled. 'Yes, he is special that way.'

'Was, tantrik. He was.'

'What?'

'About ten sundowns ago, we heard noises here. Loud, human noises and screeches. We came here and discovered a two-legged and … can … can you tell us why someone did this to him?'

He pointed to something to the far left. I caught my breath sharply. Prem's body was spread across the rock, his leathery wings thumbtacked with nails made of thin, silvery bones of fish or insects. I went closer and swallowed hard. Each of the nails had been carefully inserted into the delicate bones of his wings. His face was frozen in an expression of horror and pain. 'He was still alive when our guards first entered. A two-legged beast stood over him, shrieking. The beast then turned on the guards. Its weapons were lethal. Poison darts. There was mayhem. It kept on screaming something about a "Key". We ran, terrified. The beast slid into our holy place, still screaming in fury, and let loose poisonous arrows to kill. We tried to escape, but it kill, kill, kill and laugh, laugh, laugh. It left suddenly, through the cavehold from which you entered. What did it want? What is this Key?'

He looked at me, blinking, expecting me to tell the truth. I decided to lie. Everyone who knew anything about Indra's Key had been killed. Lavanya and now Prem. I didn't want to risk what was left of this ghetto going the same route.

'I don't know. When did it leave? This two-legged monster?'

'Just a few sundowns before you came in, which is why the ghetto attacked you. But you not the same. You smell different. You smell sane. It didn't.'

I nodded, looking at the anguish and terror etched on Prem's dead face. Not surprising, considering that whoever had killed him had slowly nailed in each and every bone in his translucent wings. They are delicate things, a dasyu's bones. I blanched, and inhaled deeply to calm myself. I wished I hadn't been wallowing in self-pity and had called him sooner. In time to save him. His last words rang in my head. *I finally met her, Anantya! ... I met her because of you.* Who was the woman he had met? What had Prem found out just before he had been killed?

'We need ...' He licked his lips in a human-like gesture. 'Don't mention this to CAT. We don't want any trouble with two-legs.'

'You don't want to inform CAT that a raving lunatic just murdered your people?'

'No.' Simbara shook his head. 'We cannot afford fight between two-leggeds and us. We have just applied to CAT for conversion of our status from pashu to mayan. We want our younglings to live in the city, and not be stuck in these caves. This,' he used his claw-hand to sweep across Prem's body and his hut, 'is something we would rather forget. Mere foolishness by an eccentric youngling.'

'I see,' I said, even though I didn't. 'Because you are too afraid to offend CAT, you will let Prem's murder and the death of all your people go unaccounted for?'

'I only want what's best for the ghetto, Miss Tantrik.'

A deep quiet anger started to burn inside me. It was intermingled with guilt for bringing Prem into this mess. I entered what used to be Prem's home, a tin-shed that had collapsed. Things were smashed and scattered on the ground, things were even pried off the walls. It looked like a hurricane had hit the place. In spite of that, the place was so Prem that I wanted to cry. It had been colourful and alive, unlike the caves that most dasyus preferred to inhabit. Piles of videotapes and audio CDs of various movies were strewn around. Tattered posters of old Bollywood movies hung on the wall. Something shiny caught my eye, under one of the videotapes. I bent down and reached for it. A locket in the shape of a firefly that had been fossilized in gold while it had been alive. I had seen this locket twice before, around a neck I would like to throttle. Can't kill a mouse, eh? Jugnu had not only killed one but scores of dasyus. I ran my tongue over my boneblade. It was time to find the two-legged beast responsible for Prem's murder.

Like everything else in the haveli, the terrace was dark, dingy and dirty. I carefully navigated the clutter of iron rods and broken furniture to reach the centre, where I had cleared the debris to make a clean space for the rituals I performed under the sky once in a while.

There was a surreal quality to the day that had gone by. First Riju's death and then Prem's. Even Prem's funeral had had an abrupt, unreal feel to it. The dasyus had peeled Prem's body off the rock and without further ado flung it into the Pit of their Winged Gods, an empty junkyard by the ghetto. The dasyu race believed in using their dead to feed the incarnations of their Winged Gods – eagles and vultures. They had fluttered in synchrony for a few minutes and then silently flown away one by one until only I remained. Somehow it wasn't enough.

The tray in my hands almost slipped as I snagged my foot on a stray wire. I steadied myself and took a deep breath – which was a very bad idea considering the things I was setting on the floor. Although I had taken the precaution of clamping my nose and taken that breath through my mouth, the smells hit me. I used my gloved hand to put the four items within a pentagon drawn on the floor, careful to stand outside its lines. A kilo of long-dead sea fish marinated in rotten eggs. Yaksha poo that had been embalmed with grains of sugar in a closed container for a year. Piss and shit of daityas tossed together with bomb worms. Livers of three drunken men whose corpses had been left rotting in the Delhi heat for a week. Any one of them would have worked for a gandha. But I didn't want just any gandha. I wanted a specific one. I muttered a mantra and whispered his name.

Rajni Gandha.

I repeated the mantra, this time slashing my index finger and letting a drop of blood fall in the pentagon.

Rajni Gandha.

He was the oldest and the most experienced one. The task I had in mind was not an easy one. I sat back and waited. It was not a good night to invoke gandhas. The sky was dark and overcast, and the air felt prickly, as if it wanted to pinch you everywhere with its scalding fingers. On a clear night, any one of the four things would have been enough even to summon Rajni Gandha. But this wasn't a good night and I didn't want to take any chances.

I lit up a beedi and sat down, leaning against the parapet wall and waited. Fifteen minutes later, a distortion in the pentagon, like seeing stuff through a heat haze, told me that Rajni had just floated in. I gave him a few minutes as he breathed in the foul smells I had laid out. Gradually, the stinking food lost its bruised colours, fading, becoming grey and then finally turning into black mulch. The gandha began to vaguely materialize, and sat down in the shape of a misshapen wart with a humongous pair of protruding nostrils. It lay on its back and made a gross guttural noise – a combination of a fart and a burp. I waited.

'Would you care for some deodorant dessert?' I asked, getting up from my corner.

His nostrils flared and he exclaimed, 'Badboo ki saugandh! A tantrik trap! Mare huye phool. Gulabo will whiff me to death!'

'You should have been careful, Rajni.' I stubbed out my beedi and rose. 'You of all the people know there are no free lunches. Or dinners for that matter.'

The nostrils flared again, like he was disconcerted. 'What is it you want, tantrik? This is the third time I have been tricked by your kind and I am in no mood to give in.' If he had arms, he would have crossed them around his fat, translucent middle.

'Oh no, you cannot say that after you have spent the last fifteen minutes gorging on my treats.'

'I … I couldn't … help myself. Please, please let me go! My wife is waiting. She has already warned me, Gulabo has, and will flay me alive this time if I am taken again. I am an old gandha. Not much use for anything.'

'Wife? When did you adopt human customs? But don't worry, today's your lucky day. I don't plan to capture or abuse you. All I have is one little task for you and then you are free to go. Do the task in an hour and there will be a bonus of five smells to take home. Gulabo will like that, won't she?'

The gandha thought about it for a while, breathing deeply.

'Ten.'

'Excuse me?'

'Ten smells and we call it a deal. I have two little smellies to think of too. Family is big and cost of living in this city is increasing by the day.'

'You know I can make you do this by force. You have already smelt my offerings and are bound to do me a service.'

'Yes, but I can take days to do the task. You smell of that piss-like thing that most tantriks have. What is the manava word for it? Ah yes, impatience. I don't think you have days to wait and play with gooey nose-picks while I fly around, do you?' If he had teeth, he would have given me a big fat grin right about now. He was right. I knew I was beaten and so did the smelly bugger.

'Fine, ten smells. Twelve if you do this in an hour. And believe me, the kind of smells I can give you will make you come back and beg me for more work.'

He bowed. 'Kinder you are. What stink work can I do for you?'

I took my boneblade and slashed my middle finger, letting two drops of blood fall on one of the pentagon's points. The blood caught fire and the whole of the pentagon burnt with black flames. Rajni's nostrils flared.

'Who are you, tantrik? I have smelt your essence before … but now you are different.'

'I am Anantya Tantrist. We met years ago although the circumstances were quite different then.'

'Ahh …' Rajni answered, his enormous nostrils flaring. 'The little unfortunate one. Now you smell different. There are new wafts. Wafts of anger, juicy and new, not the old burning anger which always keeps smouldering inside you. And the fear is less, but there, icy in its tanginess. Last time I smelt this blood, it was like that of a sheep about to be taken to its sacrifice. You breeze in more … confidence. But,' he sniffed, 'your blood smells of guilt too. Something recent.' He sniffed again. 'Something that happened only a day ago. A death which cannot be undone?'

'Look, I am in a hurry. Can we do the psychoanalysis later? Figure out where this man is.' I threw the firefly locket into the pentagon. 'I want to find out where he is. Not the area, but exactly where he is.'

He sniffed loudly. 'Manava. New blood, a mere twenty-one years have passed in his life. But don't underestimate him because of his inexperience. He pulsates with power, newly gained but unsure. Ancient blood flows in his veins too.'

Five minutes later, during which he sniffed the locket and the air in all directions, Rajni was a gandha on steroids. He held the locket loosely in his hands, or what I assumed were his hands. Rajni was formless, only burning vapour with a pair of nostrils. He hovered, waiting. I broke the pentagon with my boneblade to set him free so that he could direct me to the Vama. The first thing he did as soon as he leaked from the broken pentagon was rise until he drew level with my face, and hit me hard on my nose with his sticky, gooey body. I felt like I had been sandbagged with a trashcan.

'What the hell was that for?' I cried, rubbing my nose as my eyes watered.

'So that you can whiff me,' he answered.

'It didn't have to be so hard.'

'You mean just the way you trapped me when you could have just called me politely and offered me work?'

'I didn't have your number,' I grumbled, gingerly massaging my nose. It felt different. My nose I mean. It had started to twitch and was kind of 'pulling' me towards him.

'You know the recipe,' he said, hovering above my head. My nose jerked up, to align itself with him. 'I follow the trail. Your nose follows me.'

Chhotu grumbled as I set off into the opaque night, my nose twitching relentlessly, first left and then right, telling me where to go.

The twitch on my nose practically barked orders. At one point, it nearly drove me up the wall, literally, when there was no road ahead. Much to the gandha's annoyance, I neatly navigated around the block to go in the direction it wanted me to. I wished then that I had liquidated the gandha and used his olfactory sense myself, instead of relying on his airy butt.

We (Chhotu, my twitchy nose and I) eventually reached the wide, smooth roads of Civil Lines. Suddenly, my nose stopped twitching. I parked Chhotu in a nook by the sidewalk, and looked around. The street was wide, with huge bungalows on both sides, all with wrought-iron gates. Some had sentries posted by them. I smelt something like the liver of a dead alcoholic, and noticed a bluish visual distortion hovering by my side.

'He's inside,' he whispered, his voice carrying the smells he had absorbed, making me recoil. He pointed to the bungalow on my right.

'There are many others inside, but he's not with them. He sits outside, in the garden,' said Rajni, and added urgently, 'My smells?'

'Later tonight. On the terrace,' I whispered curtly.

'Don't be late. My family's starving,' he answered, and melted into the dark night.

Taking out my boneblade, I walked around the parapet wall, all set to deal with any obstruction in my own special way. At a place where the wall was broken, I quickly vaulted over and landed in a crouch on the soft grass. The building in front of me had most of its lights on. I could see shadows of people walking around, and sounds of occasional laughter breaking the silence. The yellow lights streaming out of the open windows shone on an unkempt and overgrown garden. If Rajni's directions were correct, the Vama would be somewhere to the right of the house, sitting outside. I stayed close to the parapet wall, keeping low and to the shadows.

'Help!'

Someone barged into me from behind, hard. I stumbled

but managed to stay upright. It was a naked woman, with her back to me.

'What the—'

'Ghost, ghost!' she yelled in an unsteady voice. Then she doubled over, retching, and began to puke. 'Aouuu!'

I took two steps back into the shadows, alert. Two guys, equally naked, came running and attempted to grab hold of her flailing arms.

'Get away from me ... saw someone!' she shrieked. Then she started to giggle hysterically.

The two men led her back to the house. I thought for a moment that no one had noticed me, but I was wrong. I heard the soft swish of shakti. I hurled myself to the ground as a light shone above me, lamp-like, suspended in mid-air.

'Who are you?' asked Jugnu, standing a few metres away from me, his legs apart, his bone staff illuminated in a blue light and directed towards me. 'You!' he said, recognizing me, his pupils becoming dots of fury, his bone staff readying for an attack. 'Aren't you the same tantrik—'

I didn't give him a chance to complete his sentence. '*Aim hreem bhuta aa, kar de kreem, chusitah!*' I shouted, nicking my index finger. A smoky liquid oozed out of the edge of my boneblade, making a loud slurping sound. Jugnu muttered a mantra and a defence circle lit up around him, a light-blue fire. His defence was strong, but not as strong as my chusit, which was a dark bhuta that sucked on light and fire. The chusit wrapped itself around Jugnu, making suckling noises like a hungry infant.

'Yes, the same one whose friend you just killed, you two-legged monster!' I said, turning my boneblade so that the chusit was forced to drink in more of his prey's light. Jugnu's blue defence circle glimmered weakly as it waned. 'The one who is going to kill you.'

He gasped and cried out, 'I didn't kill anyone! You did, you chudail! Show your true self to me!'

With his defence still on, Jugnu formed a shape out of thin air and send it hurtling towards me. Halfway through, it took on the shape of a firefly, flashing in the dark. I held up a mandala with my right hand to protect myself from the firefly's attack, but all it did was twinkle as it circled me before zooming back to him.

'Is that the best you can do?' I sneered, twisting my boneblade and infuriating the chusit. 'I will make you scream for killing Prem!'

'You are not her,' he whispered.

Before I could figure out what that meant, he fell down to the ground, his defence circle off. He threw his staff away. It fell with a soft plop on the overgrown lawn. My chusit, who had been struggling to drink his mantra, suddenly had the whole juicy treat laid out in front of it. It started to suck with complete abandonment. Jugnu screamed in agony.

'Kill me!' he said, withered and weak. 'I don't care anymore! I just want to join her!' He shuddered. 'I didn't kill your dasyu! I didn't!'

'You were at Prem's place earlier tonight! You were there, don't lie. Pick up your staff! Fight! Shakti's piss, fight!' I cried out in frustration.

But he lay still on the grass, a sacrificial lamb waiting to die, the chusit sucking on him happily.

'I didn't … do it,' he whispered.

I took a deep breath and called off the chusit, although I kept my boneblade levelled at him. His staff lay untouched on the ground.

'Thank you,' he said, sitting up shakily. He sat cross-legged on the grass, took out a vial from his pocket and sniffed a drop of charak, his hands trembling. His baby-blue eyes dilated almost instantly.

'Talk.'

'I ... I had seen your friend at Lavu's house so I tracked him down, pretty sure he had something to do with her murder. But by the time I reached his place, I saw this ... this monster standing over his body. It was a woman, but hardly a woman. Her hair, it was all spread out ... and ... and snakes oozed out of her head. Ferocious, scary snakes. That's what confused me when I saw you. I mean, frankly, your hair,' he gestured with his hands around his head, making crazy circles, 'is kind of all over the place, you know? Anyway, that's why I hit you with my firefly, to reveal the true you. But you are not her. She had a greyed body and an ear-splitting screech. She was putting small sharp things into his wings. I ... I couldn't bear it, that screaming. Your ... your friend ... he was screaming too ... so loudly. She kept on shrieking something about a Key. So much pain! I couldn't bear it ... I cannot bear violence at all, so I turned and ran away. I ... I didn't know what to do and didn't want to go home, so I came here. I thought partying would calm me down.'

'You saw Prem being attacked and ran away?'

'What could I have done? Have you seen my powers? That monster would have finished me off like this,' he said, snapping a twig in half.

I nodded and sat down next to him, taking out a beedi and lighting it. Cowardice is good survival strategy.

'And Lavanya Mohan? You didn't kill her either?'

'No, no! I was worried about her, so I went a few hours later after she had had some time to cool off. I went to her apartment and saw someone leaving from the balcony. Then I saw Lav ... Lavu's body on the floor with blood all over her.' He started to cry.

'Lavu?'

'Lavanya is … was, I mean …' he said, his voice breaking, 'my girlfriend.'

'Your girlfriend?'

'Yes. It … it had just become serious. Just a week ago, she proposed to me with a ring. We were going to get marr … married …' He waved his right hand in my face to show me an intricate monster-sized ring with huge diamonds on it, in the shape of a net. 'And then she went weird … and told me to stay away from her … she yelled at me at the party … she just … Later, when I was worried about her, I went to her apartment and f … found her … like *that*. Lavuuuuuuuuuuuuuuuuuuu!' he bawled suddenly.

'Pull yourself together.'

'Do … you know … who … who killed her?'

'No, up until five minutes ago, I thought it was you. You didn't exactly earn my trust by attacking Prem and me when we entered Lavanya's apartment.'

'I … I panicked! I didn't really want to kill you. I thought you were the killers, so I yelled out the first mantra that came into my head. Unfortunately, it happened to be mayan fire. I had only just learnt that. I used it without realizing it … it would burn … everything. My dear, darling's things.' He was almost my age in years, but in experience he had so much to learn.

'Do you know why she was killed?'

He shook his head. 'She was working on some assignment. I didn't ask her much about her work. I was … I was just so thrilled when she asked me to go out with her. Someone like her! But … if only I had known. I could have saved her! That's why I went to Prem. I wanted to somehow find out who had killed her.'

'So you were looking for revenge?'

'No, no! I don't want to kill anyone! I am a vegan for god's sake! I detest violence!'

'You are a Vama, for Matsya's sake!' I cried out. 'It kinda comes with the job!'

'If I had a choice, I would never have become a Vama. I … I wanted to be an artist … but my uncle … he … he forced me to …' He took a deep breath. 'He's not someone you can say no to. If you met him, you would know what I mean.'

'Vajrin Mahendra?'

He nodded glumly.

'Do you think your uncle might have something to do with Lavanya's death?'

He shook his head again, his brown hair flopping on his forehead. 'My uncle may be many things but he's not a killer. He liked Lavu. He would never kill her, especially since he knows my feelings for her. In fact, he has been really worried about me ever since he heard about Lavu's death.'

'I … see,' I said slowly, even though for the life of me I didn't.

'And do you know anything about this Key that the monster woman mentioned? Did Lavanya ever mention it?'

'No. Never heard of it until I saw that horrible chudail!' He shuddered. 'What she was doing to that dasyu! There's so much violence in this world!'

He bent down over his charak to take another sniff. I had heard enough. I got up and left. Whatever Jugnu was, he wasn't the killer I was looking for. He just seemed to be in all the wrong places at all the wrong times. Prem had been raving about a woman who was going to give him a break in the movies. The one he had claimed to be in love with. I needed to find out who had called him.

Dawn was breaking in the sky beyond, a grey, tired dawn, just like me. I called up Grrhat and told him about Jugnu and the monster chudail. Grrhat hung up with a curt: 'We will free your boyfriend tomorrow morning.'

It was over. Nikhil would be free to go. Hopefully, if the man had any sense, he would stay as far away from me as possible. Like any sane man should.

I reached home, dead on my feet and sad. Just before I slept, I took ten smells and put them on the terrace. As a bonus like I promised, I added two new ones – a bottle of perfume from France that Dakini had gifted me and a pair of dirty socks. At least someone had helped me, right?

'Come, Anantya, let's go,' he whispered. Anantya knew he was afraid. They shouldn't be here, but she didn't want to leave. She wanted to see. She wanted to see what Mama and Papa were doing down there. She peeped through the banisters from the stairs, third from the top. It was stuffy, dark and damp. At first, she couldn't see anything. There was a lot of smoke in the room, making her eyes itch and water. She wiped away a few tears impatiently. The smoke was from a fire that burnt at the end of the room. The room was in the basement, so there was no outlet for the smoke.

She saw Papa first. He had his back towards her, but she could see it was him. She knew him by the way he wore rudraksha beads in his ponytail. But he was not wearing his dhoti. She cringed. Then he moved and she saw Mama. Mama was lying flat on a really big, square, flat stone, her hands and legs apart. There was a circle all around her. She had no clothes on. Riju came up behind her. 'We will get into trouble, Princess, let's go,' he whispered. She didn't care. Quiet as a mouse, she crept down the stairs. One. Two. Three. That was when she saw the others. She had seen them before with Papa in his chambers, talking about important things. Sometimes Papa had let her sit on his lap while he spoke to them. Papa would often proudly tell them that, one day, she would become a real beauty, a pride for a tantrik. She always smiled then.

None of Papa's friends wore their dhotis. Their pee-pees hung down, looking like swollen cucumbers as they walked around her mama's naked body. All of them looked ugly, not like her mother. Tell them to wear their dhotis, she wanted to cry out to Papa, but something stopped her. All of them came and stood around Mama outside the circle and used their pee-pee to throw smelly susu on her body. Her body was drenched and she started to laugh. Anantya wrinkled her nose as the smell made her want to pee too. Papa got into the circle and lay on top of Mama. He began to move like he was sitting in a boat, which was really funny to look at. She almost giggled. His friends were all looking on, all of them touching their pee-pee, then their chest and then their forehead, one by one, muttering mantras.

'C'mon, let's go,' said Riju, trying to pull her up. She didn't want to. She wanted to see what was going to happen. Papa moved for a while longer. She wanted to know if Mama was hurt, but she wasn't. She started to laugh again. Laughing out so loud that her laughter echoed in the room, making Anantya clamp her hands over her ears.

Then one of Papa's friends put his pee-pee into her mama's mouth and started to rock up and down too. Oh how she hated him! She wanted to rip off his pee-pee then! Mama didn't laugh anymore. Instead, she bit him hard on his pee-pee. Good, Mama! That's what she herself would have done. The old man cried out and fell back, the others rushed forward to pick him up. Papa hit Mama hard on her face. Her mouth was full of blood and she spat out a lump of meat. Then he climbed on top of her and started to move harder, like he was riding a horse. Mama began to wail and shout and scream.

'Mama!' She ran down to help her. Papa turned and saw her, but instead of stopping what he was doing to her mama, he ordered his friends to catch her. She ran and ran and ran! Oh, how she ran!

'Anu!' Riju cried, but she didn't look back. A big, fat man fell on her, making her fall face first on the ground. Only, it wasn't the fat *man, but Prem's leathery wings, bloodied by the holes drilled into them, that folded around her and started to squash her in a tight grip which was growing steadily tighter. She couldn't breathe. The wings squeezed harder. She screamed, but no sound came out. Breathless and suffocated in the dark, in a corner, almost like being in a womb, almost like...*

'Umphgh!' I cried out, trying hard to move my limbs. Something held me in a stranglehold. I opened my eyes to find two shadowy figures standing by my bed. I struggled to free my hands and reach for the bedside table, but I couldn't move. A blanket of velvety smoke had wrapped itself around me tightly. Only my face was free of it.

'If you don't stop struggling, the betaal will squeeze the life out of you,' warned a cold, hard voice.

I froze, lying absolutely still. The betaal was a malevolent creature that sucked on a living body's juices, and it was best if it thought I was dead.

'Good. Freeze her mouth,' ordered the cold voice.

A man dressed all in black loomed above me. His gloved hand inserted something that felt like ice into my mouth. In a second, I could no longer feel my tongue, or my mouth for that matter. As his gloved hand came towards me again, this time with a blindfold, I saw the glint of a purple 'T' imprinted on his right shoulder. The symbol of Tazaak. The two Tazaak thullas picked up my unresisting body, wrapped in the betaal, and walked out.

'Search this filthy place and see if you can find it,' ordered the same cold voice over whose shoulder I now lay.

We headed out and I was roughly stashed into the boot of a vehicle. The car drove away with a silky, smooth purr. I wanted to struggle, but the betaal was still clamped clammily around me. Without my boneblade and without a mantra, there wasn't much I could do except wait and find out what the Tazaak wanted of me.

'Is she in here?'

It felt like a womb, a comfortable little hole where I could simply forget all my worries and tensions. At the back of my mind, I was aware that it was all the betaal's doing. It numbs the skin and the brain and quietly sucks on the shakti before feasting on the soul of the human, leaving the flesh a shrunken shell. Being a tantrik, I ought to have been able to put up some resistance and stayed in control, but the one on me seemed to be particularly effective. Or maybe I was just really tired. So the human voice I heard felt distinctly intrusive and annoying.

'Yes, Justice.'

'Has she been stripped of everything magical?'

'Yes, Justice. We have all her things collected and stored.'

'And I see she has become quite comfortable in the betaal you gave her. Women are so weak. Undo her blindfold.'

I squinted even though it wasn't very bright. The room was dimly lit by fire torches on the walls. In front of me stood a couple of men, one of whom, I assumed, was my kidnapper. As for the other, although I couldn't see him properly at first, I knew who he was.

'Hello, Miss Tantrist,' said Kanthak. 'It's good to see you here … again, may I add?'

Justice Kanthak, the head of the Tantrik Authority or Tazaak in Delhi, was only a little taller than I was, had a slight slouch and his protruding pot belly added an extra dimension to his crisp black dhoti. He looked like someone's kind uncle at first glance. Behind that gentle smile was the ugliest soul I had ever seen. It was his ruthlessness that made him such a good Justice for the policing authority of CAT. With a genial smile, he would cheerfully pass a death sentence. Kanthak held his cane in a light grip. It was carved in the same style as the logo of the Tazaak – a 'T' motif in intertwined vines.

'Memo maumi manmak,' I replied.

'Unfreeze her tongue. Just a drop, I don't want her tongue to become too loose. And remove the betaal.'

A thulla forced open my lips and I felt a liquid scald my tongue. Fire unfurled on my lips. I heard a mantra being uttered and the betaal left my side. That was when my skin started to scream. I winced as my cells came alive, all of them hurriedly trying to reposition themselves as the memory of a body returned.

'Aargh!'

'Welcome back. As I was saying, we missed you here, Anantya.'

'You could …' I swallowed to get rid of the annoying stinging sensation at the tip of my tongue. '… have dropped in for a … cup of tea …'

'What can I say? I got busy with my many responsibilities. Taking care of a region as big and important as Delhi is quite time-consuming. And there's no dearth of troublemakers.'

Kanthak was a chatty one. I had known him in Kaula Ashram in Banaras. At the time, he was a snivelling nobody, desperate to fit in. Unlike the other tantriks at the ashram, he had chandaali blood in him, which made him a pariah in the tantrik world. His complex drove him to ensure that he missed no opportunity to prove his loyalty to the Kaula clan. He demonstrated his zeal by finding innovative and brutal ways to punish those against the ashram. He was an attack dog for them, loyal and ferocious. His fealty had been rewarded five years ago when he was appointed Justice of the new Tantrik Authority when the Central Association of Tantriks came into being. Since then, arrogance and insecurity had combined to make him one of the most ruthless tantriks around.

'Uh huh, all that ass-licking must take up a lot of time,' I said.

Justice Kanthak beamed from ear to ear as he nodded. 'Perhaps you would like your face to be covered by the betaal this time, huh?'

'Perhaps you would like to tell me why I am here, unless you want another notice from the RC.'

Kanthak's plastic grin froze in place. The Rights Commission had been giving him trouble. Before the Non-Tantrik Rights Commission had been established two years ago, he had had a free hand to deal with the prisoners as he pleased. No questions asked. But then, too many of the arrested sups had either gone missing or died. And too many fingers had pointed to Justice Kanthak. He had denied all of the accusations, but in order to squelch the rumours, CAT had created the Non-Tantrik Rights Commission. Since then, it had inundated the Tazaak with innumerable notices querying random arrests.

'Oh, they don't care about murderers,' he whispered in my ear and grinned, showing me shiny, plastic, pointy teeth. His breath smelt of tumble-dried garbage. 'Murderers don't get any mercy. But the Tazaak goes by the book, even for human killers.' He leisurely walked to the far side of the room and returned with a red, hand-bound diary. 'On account one, Miss Tantrist, you have been accused of stealing a precious artefact from a Miss Lavanya Mohan, a neech residing at Greater Kailash.'

'Excuse me?'

He ignored me and continued, '… on account two, you have been accused of poisoning her, stabbing her and causing her death, as well as arson by mayan fire.'

'WHAT!'

'Do you deny any of the charges?'

'Of course I do!'

Kanthak leered at me with big, shiny pointy teeth. 'But we have proof, Miss Tantrist. The police recovered a tantrik skullcup from the premises. I think this is yours.' He held up Lala, my ritual skullcup. 'Would you even bother to deny it?'

So that's where it was! When everything around you is going up in flames, you tend to miss a couple of things. I had wondered where it had vanished to when I readied my satchel yesterday.

'No. I mean, yes, this is mine,' I answered.

There was no point denying it. Kanthak's insane grin showed that he knew that too. Everything that a tantrik uses for a ritual has an imprint on it, as unique as a fingerprint. I'd had Lala for four years now and had used him in far too many rituals to remember the exact count. The imprint would be as strong in the skullcup as a DNA stamp on my own child. He had probably tested the skull before he sent for me. He was vicious, not stupid.

'Thank you for recovering it,' I said. 'I wondered where it was. But I didn't kill Lavanya. I was trying to stop whoever killed her.'

'I see. Why did you go to Miss Lavanya's flat?'

'I am investigating a case in which she was involved. I went to interview her and discovered that her door was open. When I went inside, I saw someone escaping through the balcony who attacked me with mayan fire.' I deliberately kept Jugnu's name out of it. The boy was stupid but did not deserve the Tazaak hounding him. 'Lavanya was already dead when I entered. I started a mantra to douse the mayan fire or it would have consumed the whole building. That's when humans entered and I decided to leave. As you know, it's never a good idea for an active tantrik to meet a human. I didn't want to tarnish the image of tantrism by getting arrested by the human police.'

He turned the skullcup around in his stubby hands. 'Is there a witness to your story? Were you accompanied by someone?'

I didn't want to name Prem either. He was a dasyu and he was dead. Tazaak would refuse to accept the testimony of a pashu, only talking magical animals to them. And a dead one wouldn't help anyway. So I shook my head. Even the Tazaak couldn't ask the dead to testify, well not this Justice for sure.

'Who is your client? This person you are working for?'

'I am sorry, but I cannot reveal his name without permission.'

'Hah!' He smiled. 'You become ethical when charged with murder?'

'How come you haven't done a post-mortem on Miss Mohan's body, yet?' I countered. 'A soulprint of the body will clearly prove that it wasn't me that killed her.'

He snorted. 'Soulprints are costly. CAT funds only cases where tantriks are involved.' He leant closer, giving me another whiff of his striking breath. 'What are you, Anantya Tantrist? A woman who no one cares about now, a woman who pretends to be a tantrik? If you can find someone to finance the soulprint, we will do it for you. CAT will certainly not do so.'

I chewed my inner lip. There was no way to prove I hadn't killed Lavanya Mohan. Tazaak's motto for anyone who was not a tantrik was: guilty until proven innocent. The only way I could prove my innocence would be through a soulprint on Lavanya Mohan's body. Unlike an object, a soulprint of a corpse was an advanced ritual. Although it would prove that I wasn't Lavanya's murderer, it would cost not only money but also time.

'Money is not a problem,' I countered. But time was. 'I need to get out of here.'

'Oh, that will take time. Even if you find the money for a soulprint, it will take at least a week or more to get the approval from CAT. And then, another three weeks to get our results. Until then, you will be our guest here. And would you know where this artefact that you have stolen from Lavanya's apartment could be?'

'I don't know. I have never seen it in my life.'

'Aha. That's not what the gentleman who accused you told us. According to him, you stole Indra's Key from Miss Mohan and showed it to him.'

'And may I know who has pressed these charges on me?'

'Of course. We go by the book here.' He sneered. 'It's industrialist Lord Qubera. As you see, he has a much more established reputation than scum like you, Miss Tantrist.'

'Augh!' I kicked the air, which hurt like hell since I had to raise my chained leg to do it. That two-faced fatso! I could cheerfully throttle him with his bloody bling.

'Will you stop that? You will get all of us consumed!' squeaked a voice to my right.

'You should have thought of that before you did whatever crime you did!' I snapped.

'I was falsely accused! I was!' it screamed back.

'Me too! I didn't do it! That rotten tantrik made me do it! You cannot bind me here for his actions!' moaned another voice from my left.

Great. This is some fine shit to fall into, Anantya. Two of my fellow prisoners thought they were as innocent as newborns. There were four of us in all, chained to a thick, dead teak stump. Our arms and legs were bound to its branches. A triangle was drawn around us, about three feet away, giving us just enough space to stretch our legs, but not much else. I wasn't sure, but I guessed that there were five or ten more of these stumps around me in the dungeon. From time to time I heard a groan or a gasp. Most of the time though, it was just a sullen silence.

The prison was an endlessly long underground cave in the Tazaak quarters. I wasn't quite sure where it was located, not having had the pleasure of visiting it before, and having been brought in blindfolded. I had been caught twice before by Tazaak's long arm, but had managed to grease palms at my first arrest, and the second time, I had managed to prove my innocence. This time however, the crime was murder and that was an offence for which even Kanthak could not be bribed. Golden goose, self-centred eternal! I should have known. You just cannot trust a daeva. Something about living for gazillions of years makes you a selfish goat. Could that fat daeva be so dense as to think I had actually stolen it? No. I knew he was smart. He was covering up something by blaming it on me. But what?

'I did what I did because I had to,' said the fourth hand in our little chain gang around the teak stump.

He had his back to me on the opposite side of the trunk. He was a quiet one. We would have become friends if I hadn't been busy racking my brains to figure out how to break out of this dungeon. Breaching the triangle's outlines was not a problem for any tantrik, but no one would do it because that was the only thing that separated us from the betaals that patrolled the darkness, eager for living flesh to consume. If any one of us somehow broke free of the shackles and attempted to escape by stepping out of the triangle's lines, all four of us would be consumed by the betaals until one of the guards was alerted. And I knew that the guards in this place were known to be fast asleep when a prisoner was being devoured.

'If you don't let me in, I will call Swami Netrahin and see to it that you are removed from this post immediately!' bellowed a familiar deep voice from somewhere to my right. It was too dark to see anything, but I felt a lightness as the betaals were called to heel. A few seconds later, Dakini entered.

'Antz! Oh, my jewels!' she hollered, wrinkling her nose and stepping into the triangle to hug me. 'Zee called me an hour ago. I can't believe these people put you into this rotten place instead of a prison for tantriks. And they've tied you up like a pashu! Wait till the Rights Commission hears about this!'

She wore a bright purple T-shirt today, showing ample brown cleavage. 'Urg! What is that smell! Here, let me make it better for you.'

Dakini fished out a bottle from her glittery tote and sprayed it on my face. Then she went around the tree trunk and did the same to my hapless fellow inmates. Lilac. Her favourite perfume.

'Now that I can breathe,' she said, touching her bosom dramatically, 'I have got you a lawyer, the best one I could find at such short notice. Now tell Anil everything you know and we will get you out of here.'

'Somewhere more private?' I asked, showing her my chained hands.

A burly guard came forward and unshackled me. 'Don't try any tantrik tricks on us,' he warned me. 'My chief is ready with the betaals if you do.'

We were taken to a triangular room, a yantra with walls and ceiling. There was no way in or out of this place unless it was magically opened. They had had the decency to furnish it with some plastic chairs. I sat down with a sigh, only then realizing just how exhausted I was.

'You say that Lord Qubera blackmailed you into taking this case? By kidnapping Nikhil?' asked the lawyer, Anil Mussadi, a pale, glossy-haired man.

He took notes as I spoke about my meeting with Qubera and the assignment, although I only gave him vague outlines. I hid the fact that Indra's Key would lead to untold miseries if it fell into the wrong hands. No need to put extra pressure on the fellow.

'Dahling Antz, Niks is all fine!' said Dakini. 'He called this very morning to get an appointment with me. He mentioned that he couldn't call you since he had to go to his aunt's in Jaipur for something urgent over the weekend. Are you sure this Lord Qubera has him?'

'Of course I am sure, Daks! I mean the last I saw of Nikhil, he was frozen into a golden statue in Qubera's fancy mansion. He's lying for some reason.'

'Miss Tantrist,' said Mussadi, tapping his pen on his notepad, 'we will need proof of it. Until now, we only have your word which doesn't really amount to much.'

'I. Do. Not. Lie,' I emphasized, bringing my face close to his pale one.

He didn't flinch but I could see a vein tick in his forehead.

'I don't judge that,' he said softly. 'As your lawyer, my business is to save you from a long term in prison. The only thing I am concerned about is getting solid proof of what you say. As of now, we have your word against Mr Qubera's and that will not get us anywhere. Now if you were a tantrik—'

'I *am* one!' I cried.

'—a *recognized* tantrik, we could have appealed against Lord Qubera's charges and tried to get you bail. But being a respected member of the society, he has much more sway than you have, I'm afraid. A she-ta—'

'You can say it, Mr Mussadi. I won't bite your head off. Not today,' I answered.

'The rights of a tantrik who is not male are not recognized by CAT as you very well know. Which means that you are an illegal tantrik as far as the Tazaak are concerned. Therefore, you are guilty until you prove your innocence, Miss Tantrist.'

I had figured that much. Getting absolved of the murder charge wasn't a problem really. Lavanya's post-mortem would clear me. But if they pinned the burglary on me, I would get a sentence of a few years under the Mayan Act. Being a woman, I wouldn't be in the nicer jail they reserved for male tantriks, but in the hell-hole where they piled up the mayans and pashus and all the other sups.

'The only hope we have is to take your case as a special one under the manava section,' said Mussadi.

'But I am not a human, I am a tantrik.'

'Well, you are a human if you are not recognized as a tantrik,' he countered.

He had a point. I nodded assent. They prepared to leave after assuring me that I still had a chance for bail.

'Oh my hotpants, almost forgot,' said Dakini as they were leaving. 'Zee gave me this note to pass on to you.' She handed me a piece of paper. 'It's from your friend Madhu.'

Madhu? I unfolded the note that seemed to have been scribbled in a hurry.

Anantya,

I believe you. Everything you said. I cannot do a long letter, so here it is. You were right. It's not over. There has been another incident on Sunday night. A dead man and his daughter found in a girl's school, Little Sunflower in Moti Bagh. The girl was a student there and the father, a teacher. It was somewhat different from what we have seen in the last three cases. Both the bodies were found burnt. The police are writing it off as a fire accident.

I wouldn't have connected it to our case, which I officially closed today and transferred to the Authority, but I came across a witness's account. The guard. He was dead drunk at the time. He claims he heard shrieks and then ran outside to see a divine being with wings fly upwards. Then he saw a black pyramid form in the school ground before the whole thing burnt down. There is no other evidence that this was connected to the three sacrifices. I specifically asked, but there was no moonblade or cellphone this time. The burnt bodies were the only thing that remained. The police have closed the case and the family has been told it was an accident.

There's more. Riju Das's body and his cellphone were stolen from Shukra's lab last night, about an hour before midnight. No one knows where they went, but his lab assistant (remember that girl with Shukra?) is missing too. I don't know what a dead body can be used for, but I have heard from you that tantriks can use it for things I don't want to know about. Could it be possible that someone is trying to use Riju's dead body? And that it goes missing an hour before the fourth incident cannot be a coincidence, can it?

I tried to talk to Nandan to let me reopen the case for this new incident or let me look into Riju's missing body, but he told me to lay off. It's in the Authority's hand. And guess who CAT has appointed to look into the case. Swami Narahara. You were right, Anantya. They are trying to close it. I don't trust that guy.

I cannot follow up on this as I am on surveillance 24x7 (Nandan can be a real bitch). All I can do is write to you and beg you to continue your investigation. I hope you are not too pissed off with me for leaving you with your father at the Kaula Ashram. The guy didn't look that much of a villain.

Still your friend,

Madhu

I folded the note carefully. So I had been right.

'Is everything okay?' asked Dakini. 'You look pissed.'

'Do you have a beedi?' I asked.

'Will a filtered cigarette do? I know you like the cheap version, but dahling, I don't—'

'It will.'

I took her lighter, burnt the letter and then lit the cigarette. A deep puff later, I looked at Anil Mussadi.

'Mr Mussadi, I think you'd better call Justice Kanthak. I would like to confess to the crime that Mr Qubera has accused me of.'

I ignored the surprise on their faces and inhaled deeply before blowing out filtered smoke. It just wasn't the same as a strong unfiltered beedi. Watered-down things never were.

'You are a *tantrik*?' cried out the sup on my left in disbelief. I was back in the dungeon, with my limbs bound to the dead branches. 'But you don't have white seed. How do you perform your tricks?'

'That's just pile loads of shit. Tantriks don't need white seed. We need shakti to do magic, which most of the males take from the woman they are fucking,' I answered, paused and then continued in a melodramatic undertone, 'Some also use mayan blood.'

He shivered and then exclaimed hurriedly, 'DontkillmeIdonthavepowers.'

'I will think about it,' I said in a serious tone.

He shivered again. 'Why are you in a mayan prison if you are a tantrik? Why not in those fancy prisons they reserve for magic weavers like you?'

This one came from the one standing behind me, the one who had confessed to his crime and said that it had been necessary. He was a smart one. I couldn't make out which kind of a sup he was but the term 'magic weavers' was used in the jungles and I had never heard it in the city. An outsider. He had a whispering voice that was soft and husky.

'Yeah, well. I can tell you about gender discrimination, but you'll just call me a prickly bitch.'

'So CAT doesn't recognize female tantriks?'

'Nah,' I answered, tracking a betaal that hovered right in front of me, outside the triangle. Betaals look like a couple of meters of black velvet cloth hung on a hanger. Some of them look different though, more like black velvet draped over a live wire.

'Men have had the power and the fun for far too long. I don't think they are keen on sharing it with others, especially with natural holders of the shakti, the ones they want to control.'

'Are there others like you? She-tantriks, I mean?'

'Dude, that's a question too many when I haven't even seen your face. Who the hell are you?' There was silence. I got pissed and pinched the mayan on my side.

'Ouch!'

'Pass this on to the nosy bugger who stands behind me.'

He didn't get the chance. With a soft swish, all the betaals were recalled. A few minutes later, I was dragged out and tied to a pole in the interrogation room, the same triangular room in which I had been with Dakini.

'I assured him that you confessed you stole the artefact that belongs to Lord Qubera's vault and that we are ready to pronounce our judgement on you,' announced Kanthak as soon as he entered, bristling. 'But Lord Qubera wants to offer you a chance. As per the new laws, we are bound to try and reconcile differences rather than instantly mete out punishments, which is all a waste of time, if you ask me. So the thing is,' he paused both for breath and to show me his disgust, 'Lord Qubera would like to speak to you once, alone. If you agree to his terms, he just might withdraw his charges against you. I don't know how you do it, Anantya, but this is a really lucky break for you.'

He spat out the word 'lucky' as if he wanted to crack it

with an old-fashioned nutcracker. I glowered at his back as he left, wishing I could burn things by staring at them angrily. But no, today's anger was reserved for an elephantine eternal. A trembling Lord Qubera entered the room. Did I say trembling? I should add he was trembling with rage.

'Tell us where it is!' he commanded.

'I won't,' I answered. Simple, succinct and stupefying. That's me.

'Excuse me?' His chins wobbled with displeasure. 'As your liege, your daeva, and the being who's paying your filthy bills, I command you to tell me now!'

A barky, short laugh escaped me before I could control it. 'Are you high on piss? After what you have done to me? Got me to look for the Key only to get me arrested for stealing it? Now you expect me to also tell you where it is?'

He turned away, walking to the other end of the room. He was breathing noisily. I wondered what was wrong with him. Qubera was not at all like the person I had met before. The last couple of times, he had been impeccable in his brocades and layers of gold. Today he looked like a hobo with unkempt hair and filthy, torn clothes. Even his wide, solid gold bracelets and other jewellery were missing. Qubera looked ... different, as if someone had taken what used to be the daeva I had met and put him in a gas chamber with rats. He walked towards me, slowly, almost like he was crawling. His eyes were pinpoints of glittering black and his jowls shook.

'Tell me where it is and you will be saved from getting torn to pieces like your little dasyu shit.'

The threat hung in the air like a cloud of poison gas. I felt a strange calm descend on me. I knew now with whom I had to avenge my friend's death. Daevas. Should have stayed away from their business.

'Like you killed Lavanya?'

'Oh yeah, her too. It was kind of fun. Do you know how your winged friend cried and begged me to stop when I slowly inserted poison into his delicate wings?' His vast expanse moved with a surprisingly graceful coiling motion as his face lit up with remembered sadistic glee. My head exploded with hatred and I burnt as if with a fever.

'Why?' I hissed, the word oozing out of me, like pus. I had to know before I sent the bastard back to his plane of existence.

'Oh, didn't I tell you? So rude of me. I apologize.' He smiled creepily and bowed low, almost falling over on his fat face. His smile expanded and his eyes glittered. 'I killed him because of you.'

I sucked in a painful breath.

'If you hadn't let your filthy dasyu poke his nose into businesses that weren't any of his, he wouldn't be dead right now. It's all your fault. You let him die while you were busy getting sloshed at Bedardi.'

'You disgusting eternal fuck! I am going to rip off your fat limbs!'

'Hah! How do you plan to tear off my fat limbs? With hatred? Hah! The only reason you haven't gone the same way as that pet of yours is because you have something you can trade your life with. Tell me where the Key is and I will let you live your sorry life. You see,' he bent close to me, his face almost touching mine, 'I can set you free.'

He touched my nose softly with his right index finger and smiled, showing dirty, yellowed teeth. I opened my mouth wide and bit his finger as hard as I could. There was a satisfying crunch and a surprised gasp. I spat out a piece of flesh, swallowing some blood and tendons, and then shouted the first mantra that came to my mind:

'*Sachcha Jhootha Jivah Dikha!*'

The Jivah mantra was a truth potion for the body. A mantra that compelled the being to reveal its true self. The mantra hit Qubera straight in the stomach and he fell backwards with its force. He burst out laughing, the sound seeming to emanate from a huge, empty barrel.

'You asked for it, you stupid neech!' He turned a deep shade of grey and started to kind of fall apart, disintegrating into weird black blobs. It was when the blobs started to wriggle that I knew this was going to be trouble.

'Jussssstiiiicce!' I yelled at the top of my lungs, struggling against the mayan rope that bound me. 'Where in Chandi's name are you? Aren't you supposed to protect those in your fucking jail?'

The blobs had now become worms that piled themselves on top of each other, rather like slimy, shiny goo and formed themselves into a humanoid shape. I might have said female, but I wasn't too sure. Then two boobs popped up on her chest. Woman, definitely woman. Shiny fish scales settled all over her body, her eyes were slits of yellow. A naga, but then how did she disguise herself as Qubera and manage to evade the jail's anti-maya charms? The charms were meant to cancel maya, mantras and potions. If she hadn't done anything like that, how did she disguise herself? She stood up, her skin becoming smooth and buttery like a baby's.

'Jusssssssssstice!'

'Thisss,' she said, bending down and picking up a couple of worms that were still wriggling on the floor, and swallowing them whole, 'wass not a good idea.'

'What in Bhairava's name are you?'

Her face was angular and sharp and her features beautiful. She had a supermodel-like body and a face that was clearly stunning, but if you had asked me to describe her features, I wouldn't have been able to. They were beautiful, but they also defied definition, as if her face was an amalgam of many pretty faces.

'I like you, you know?' Her voice had changed. It had become huskier, like she had a blocked nose and was whispering. 'You think different. For a tantrik female, I mean. Most of the oness I have met are just dull drugged dollss for their consortss.' Her tongue flickered out, naga-like, every few words, as if she was tasting the air with her tongue.

'Had you told me where the Key was nicely, I would have spared your life, might have even let you go unharmed. But now? Now you have pissed me off. And the only thing I do when I get pissed off is strike!'

She interlaced her thumbs and raised her cupped palms above her head and her whole body turned into hundreds of small holes from which emerged heads of worm-like snakes. Holy shakti shit. She flung the worms towards me. I saw them coming in slow motion, flying horizontally, their little black heads towards me. I was bound to a wooden pole with rope, there was no escape from the attack. I looked around desperately, looking for something that could save me. Nothing. Nothing, except the scampering pitter-pat of a panicking rat that I could barely hear over the pulsating buzz of the worms. I just about had time to turn my head away from the onslaught.

'Ugh!' The arrow-worms hit me like soft nails. Pinches really, but all over my body. My neck, forehead, chest, stomach, legs were covered with the live darts. The pole creaked as I struggled and toppled to the ground with a loud clank, my back still tied to the pole.

'Aaah!' The worms had just bit me; it was like a million

scorpions stinging simultaneously. The smell of raw blood, not oozing as from a wound, but boiling over, filled the room. Poison. Great, so the worms were poisonous too.

'Now tell me, Anantya, where … iss … the … Key? I give you a choisss.' She was bent low towards me, her hair falling over her perfect face. 'You tell me and I will kill you instantly, or I will take a long, long time to do it.'

'Sure,' I ground out through clenched teeth. The poison spread in my body, giving off a stench of rotten, pus-filled flesh. 'Kill me now!' My blood heaved in panic, running through my veins like it had a mad dog after it. The quiet pain of poison spread like hot lava. The only reason I was still breathing was because she wanted something from me. The Key. Not a good time to be honest and confess that I hadn't a clue in hell where the bloody thing was. Where on earth were the guards and Kanthak? Was he involved in this?

The snake bitch kicked me in the stomach, then shrieked and let loose another army of her worm-nails at me. I couldn't see them this time, but heard the soft swoosh as they came. The new lot hit my back and thighs.

'Ugh!' I groaned, not wanting to give her the satisfaction of hearing me scream. Softly again, like pinpricks. But I knew the bites would come, and with it, the poisonous stench.

'Do you remember where now?' she whispered softly in my ear.

'It … has,' I grunted, biting my lip hard as the worms bit into my flesh in sync, '… slipped … my … mind.'

A rodent crept towards me cautiously, its whiskers twitching. He wanted a bite as well. Well, get in line, little one. The mouse, having made up its mind, scurried towards my face, sniffing. I lunged, stretching my neck with what was left of my strength, and bit deep into its fleshy, hairy body.

Naughty, impatient mouse. You should never trust tantriks, not until they lie completely dead. (Sometimes not even then.) The she-monster flipped me over with a hard kick to my side. Excruciating agony zinged through my body.

'Wha—' Before she could react to the fact that I was holding a mouse in my mouth, I bit hard on its neck. Blood squirted out on my injured face, neck and into my mouth, almost choking me. I thought of the first mantra that came in my head, making a nine-petal lotus mudra with my still tied hand.

'Ghoom aa phata jaa!'

Oh well. Not the best I could think of, and the spell wasn't directed very well, but it would have to do. My head was woozy and I couldn't really cook up a better mantra. The Visphota mantra hit her in the stomach, which bloated and blasted its contents outwards. She smiled the same freaky smile as her stomach splattered on the walls around us. The blood and skin hit me on my face, but I welcomed the black stench of it. Unfortunately, it didn't have much of an effect on her. Her body was destroyed, but she had broken up into hundreds of mini snakes, all of which were now slithering towards me, angry, hissing, like poisonous rattlesnakes.

I closed my eyes and yelled, 'Juuuuuuuuustice! Where the fuck are you?'

The snakes reached me, riled and rustling. I felt their forked tongues laser all over my body, face, neck, arms, legs and torso, striking as a group. They aimed for the nerves this time. My brain shut down. My vision bloodied and I could taste rodent blood mixed with my own on my tongue. The mouse was tastier and smelt like decayed roses, I thought as my eyes clouded with the colour of blood. Suddenly all the madness stopped, the rattling silenced. There was nothing on me, nothing at all. I lay in the darkness, silent. Waiting, hoping that the bloody Justice would show up soon. Like now.

'What happened to her?' A familiar voice. Not Kanthak, someone else. Someone I wanted to kill. Although mentally my hands clenched into fists, in my weakened state, I couldn't quite pull it off physically. I opened swollen eyes and Grrhat's reddened face swam into view. The blood in my ruptured cornea was giving my visuals an interesting scarlet tint.

'She was poisoned.'

I saw him take off his pants.

'No!' I said feebly. Or thought I said, because no sound emerged from my lips. Dark, smelly, hot liquid spurted on to my face and neck, my breasts and legs. Bloody rakshasa had just peed on me. Didn't I say I had a vial of rakpiss in my snakebone locket? Yup, rakshasa's piss. Yeah. Has healing qualities for wounds and poisons. It is as rare as a thoroughbred rakshasa. Rakshasas were about to get rarer still when I killed off this one now. Grr-fucking-hat.

My wounds sizzled as the rakpiss hit them. My body was on fire, burning up, my veins felt distended, as if they were going to burst. My gut wrenched hard and I opened my mouth to puke. When the nausea subsided slightly, the muscles began emitting their SOS. I lay back feeling the pain flood into every cell. Worst. Hangover. Ever.

'I am out of piss! Quick, give me some more water to drink!' he cried.

I could hear more murmurs and movement. I thought I could feel both rough and sleek skin against my body. A little while later, I felt more hot liquid on me.

'Hot,' I managed to say, coughing out another stream of foul liquid on whoever was stupid enough to stand near my face. I burnt all over, like I was being cremated alive by a prankster with a warped sense of humour. My eyes flickered open again to see Grrhat scrutinizing me anxiously. With all the strength that I could muster, I clenched my hand into a fist. *Pow!* The punch landed on the side of his jaw. He reeled back, shock in his red eyes.

'Some thanks for saving your ass,' he cried.

'You used me as bait *and* you peed on my face,' I answered gruffly, swallowing against the pain of speaking. I sat up, propping myself on the wall behind me.

'Your fault completely, you stubborn chudail!' he shouted.

Kanthak and his Tazaak men stood around us, interested.

'Can we get a moment alone?' I requested, looking at Kanthak. For a minute there, it seemed like he would refuse, but he nodded curtly. The man looked subdued. It must have deflated his ego to have me attacked inside his prison by someone who wasn't officially approved of.

'Are you here to get me out?' I asked, holding my head as still as I could. It felt like the contents of my skull had been replaced by mouldy rags that threatened to unravel with the slightest movement.

He didn't hear me. 'Who the hell asked you to confess?' he exclaimed. 'Can't you for once do something predictable? I mean, you are innocent! You've not stolen the Key. Then why own up to something you didn't do? You've completely messed up our plan ... what an idiot—'

'Did you catch that crazy snake bitch?' I asked.

'She ... escaped. Vanished like smoke.'

'Can't do anything right, can you?'

'Look who's talking!' exclaimed Grrhat. 'All you had to do was lie low in the prison and chill while I sorted out this mess. But nooooo ... you had to go and do something insane!

What kind of a charaki admits to a crime they haven't committed?'

'I wanted to meet your boss, that slimy daeva, and kick his ass.' I had a huge craving for a beedi, but there wasn't going to be one of those until I was out of here. My body was sore and tired. All I wanted to do was sleep.

'Well, you got someone's ass kicked for sure. Yours.'

'And I resent being used as bait for a bitch. Qubera was the one who asked Lavanya Mohan to take Indra's Key out of the vault, wasn't he?'

Grrhat had the decency to look abashed. He flexed his muscles and then inspected his black nails before meeting my eyes again. 'She wouldn't have come for you if you hadn't confessed. I came as soon as I was told of your confession. But by then, she was already here. You have no idea what we are dealing with here, have you? Even Lord of Men is scared of her, for daeva's sake!'

'If you had told me what we were dealing with in the first place, I would have found her long before you did. Why use me as bait?'

'Because someone had to be used,' he answered, shrugging. 'When Lavanya Mohan was killed on Saturday, Lord Qubera became desperate. He knew that the monster would come after him next to find the Key. He didn't want that, so he called up the Tazaak and told them you had stolen Indra's Key from him. The monster couldn't reach you in the Tazaak prison, and it would also buy him time to find the Key. But—'

'But he waited. He knew the monster was loose but waited until Lavanya Mohan died. Until, my friend, Prem, died. All he cared about was to save his own fat ass.'

'It's not like that, Anantya. He's really scared. The Key

needs to be kept away from this mad woman. I don't know why it's so important. But that doesn't matter now. As soon as I heard about your confession, I went to Lord Qubera's office. Vajrin Mahendra had come there to meet him. I told Mr Qubera about your confession. He ... he smiled and told me that the case was off. He asked me to get you released from the prison. He is dropping all charges against you.'

'So he's found the Key?'

'He told me the Key was back where it belonged.'

'You mean in Qubera's vaults or with Indra?'

Grrhat shrugged. 'Don't know and don't care. I am glad this is over. In his kindness, he has even provided your bail for Lavanya Mohan's murder charge.'

'Because he knows it's that mad monster who killed her,' I said. Then I giggled, a tad hysterically. 'Heheh. D'you know the funny part? She came here to the Tazaak headquarters and confessed that she killed both Lavanya and Prem. But I am still the one who needs bail for it. That's justice for you.'

'Listen to me, Anantya,' said Grrhat, his eyes glittering. 'She wants that Key. Really, *really* wants it. Now that you have announced that you have it, she will return for you. She still thinks it's you who has the Key.'

'So I am still the bloody bait for your Lord Qubera, eh?' I got up, wincing. Hot needles seemed to dig into my joints. 'Don't worry, Grr. I won't serve your Lord Qubera's royal hide to her. I have my own friend to avenge. And the next time she won't find me so helplessly unprepared.'

I steeled myself to the agony of walking. While Grrhat took care of the paperwork, I fantasized about all the ways in which I could kill the bitch. She had attacked me. She had killed Prem and attacked his family. I would be darned if I let her get away with all that as I played sacrificial lamb, or worse, hide in a hole somewhere hoping she would lose my scent. If I had even a little tantrik blood in me – and I had a lot – I would find out where she was nesting and attack her. Fuck the case. Fuck the coward Qubera shutting me off from the case. This was personal now. I had to find that Key and flush her out of her lair.

96

I like days when you are so tired that you can feel it leaking off your bones. Those are the days when even the nightmares don't come. I slept like a swatted fly on a hot summer's day. It was only when I woke up around noon, completely stiff and with a parched throat that last night's craziness came crashing back. I got up, wincing as pain radiated through my nervous system. Bloody snake bitch! I applied some more of the rakpiss that Grrhat had given me on my sores.

The house was messier than usual. I had returned home after my incarceration to see my satchel lying on the ground, split open, its contents spilt, and some vials broken. That was not all. The haveli had been turned upside down and inside out. I had set up some protective charms around the haveli and fallen on the bed, exhausted.

Now I sat in the middle of the mess, cross-legged, put on the septifocal goggles and said the Drishti mantra to test all seven planes. The physical walls of the house fell away as the coloured ones came alive. Violet, indigo, blue, green, yellow, orange and finally red. There was no one here but me. Even Zee was missing.

I wondered where I should start. Somewhere out there, the Cult of Chaos had already done the fifth sacrifice successfully on Monday night while I had been preoccupied fighting the snake bitch. However, tonight I could stop them. I could save the sixth girl from being sacrificed. I had to.

I started to put my satchel together again, throwing things into it – skullcup (politely returned by Kanthak), liquids to heal, acids, blood vials. I refilled my snakebone locket with rakpiss and rakta, and buckled my belt, putting the boneblade into its scabbard. I was ready.

'Maula! Yeh zamaana hi kharaab hi. Izzatdaaron ki haveliyon ko raond dete hain. Chain se jeena namumkin ho gaya hai.'

I ignored Nawab Sahib and started to prepare a cauldron for a potion. If I wanted to find and finish that manic bitch, I needed some armour. That schizo was a nagin – half-snake, half-woman. Zee, himself a naga, had often warned me that nagas were one of the most cunning races among sups. But the more powerful of them, as in humans, were the female of the species.

Whatever kind of nagin she was, she was way more powerful and potent than any sup I had met. Even Grrhat was quaking in his boots yesterday at the very mention of her. Only pure spirits had the power to remain in their adopted forms, unaffected by any anti-maya spells. So perhaps she had a little spirit blood as well – apsara or gandharva? Or was it something else altogether?

A drop of the last ingredient, frozen jaws of a warrior wasp, accidentally splashed my face, burning my cheek. I swore hard, wishing Zee were here.

I found potion-making tedious, to say the least. It required precision and patience, both of which I lacked at the best of times. Today was not a particularly good day. I randomly sprinkled a few drops of mercury, hoping it wasn't too much. Then I added poison ivy thorns, a few rose petals for the fragrance and, finally, the mashed liver of a horse. The extra squirt of rakpiss.

The squirming viper in my hand tried to attack me, its forked tongue flickering. 'I have survived more of you than you can imagine,' I whispered, holding him by the scruff of his slippery neck. I forced it to open its mouth and drained its poison sac into the cauldron.

'Venom for venom, death for death,' I whispered, slashing its throat, letting its blood and entrails fall into the concoction. I slashed my index finger and let some drops of my blood fall into the vat. The place was beginning to smell like a rotten corpse. I added a whole bottle of bhang and a few marijuana leaves. The anti-venom potion seemed almost ready. All I had to do was invoke some rudrahs, the spirits that instilled fear, to energize it. I took a deep breath and tugged at my shirt to let some air circulate over my skin. It protested with a spark.

It was as if the very air was crackling with shakti. That was good for the potion, but not for any living being – too much shakti, and before you know it, sups start behaving erratically, like running naked in the streets in their true forms. Then the tantriks will go on a rampage to kill them and before you know it, the whole country will be headed for a chaotic civil war. Perhaps that was exactly what the Cult of Chaos was hoping for. I started to whisper the mantra for rudrahs when my phone rang. I had failed to answer Prem's call, and the next time I saw him, he was dead. So now I rushed to the phone, drying my hands on my pyjamas to release their static. It was Madhu. I pressed the green button. A jolt of electricity hit me hard and sent me flying backwards. I fell with a loud thump.

'Ugh!'

My fingers tingled with residual energy. I pushed the speaker phone button, this time with a long, wooden stick.

Madhu's bloodcurdling scream rang through my empty house.

I kick-started Chhotu and rode like a bat out of hell to see two guards stationed outside his home. Before they could even start with their questions, I curled my hands into fists and, without any mantra, hit one in the middle of the neck and the other in the stomach. That felt good. They fell to the ground and I ran up the stairs, three at a time, my heart pounding hard. Madhu's flat was on the third floor of an old DDA apartment building. I pushed open the door and entered the living room. It was empty, in a neat little way. No signs of a scuffle at all.

'Madhu!' I yelled, my boneblade in hand, ready to battle whatever was there. I had been here before, but had never gone beyond the living room. It led out into a kitchen and a toilet, and then at the far end was the bedroom. I peeped into the almost-closed bathroom door and heard sobbing. Madhu's voice like I had never heard before. At least he was alive, was my first thought, and then cringed at the thought of seeing him vulnerable.

He crouched in the corner of his bathroom, between the basin and the toilet, quivering and as dark as a betaal. He was naked, his eyes were glazed and he was mumbling to himself. His whiskers, wet with tears, drooped sadly.

'What is it, Madhu?' I asked gently, as I hurried towards him.

'Hghughmfgffp!!' he cried, his hands waving madly, like he was trying to ward off an invisible fly buzzing around his ears. He stared ahead, eyes unseeing, unfocused. That's when it hit me. I flicked down my septifocals over my eyes and muttered the Drishti mantra. A fat rudrah buzzed around his ear, sucking out the juices from his skull. I whispered a mantra, placed the tip of my thumb on the base of the little finger and rescinded the rudrah, sending it back into the spirit world.

'Ugh. What—' Madhu managed to say weakly. He then looked down at himself, and at me, and screamed, 'I am naked!'

'Good observation.' I smiled.

He scrambled into his clothes as I wondered how the hell my rudrah had found its way to Madhu's house to haunt him.

'As soon as you answered the phone, I felt a crazy need to scratch my head. And then I don't remember a thing,' said Madhu when he had rested a while and recovered enough to eat something. Could it be possible that the phone had teleported my rudrah to Madhu? If yes, then … Shukra's theory on the night we met in the forest rang in my ears. The cellphone at the pyramid's apex, an open line to amplify the electricity. But what if the cellphone was acting as a portal to send the spirit to someone somewhere? Could a spirit be transferred from the yantra to some other place? As far as I knew, it wasn't possible. But … it had just happened with Madhu, hadn't it?

'… labelling it an accident. I feel so helpless, Anantya, I don't know what to do. You have to figure this out. With the new moon night only a night away …'

Then I remembered Vajrin's party and the iMagic he had unveiled. Wasn't that based on the same principle? That people could receive positive shakti through the phone? Wasn't that what the technology department at CAT was researching, the same department that both Riju and Nasty belonged to. Then they would know. They would also know how to go about it. What if Riju had been killed not because he was responsible, but because he knew something more about the way these sacrifices had occurred? Nasty. I had to find out where the sixth sacrifice was happening tonight.

'Is Shukra on the case still?' I said urgently.

'No. Both that Amritananda fellow and the Authority threw him out faster than you can say "hey" after the CBI handed them the case. Poor guy was so in love with them. Ever since his assistant went missing along with Riju's cellphone and his body, he refuses to even answer my calls.'

'All the more reason to see him,' I said. 'Now Shukra may be willing to listen to my theory. I need his help in this.'

I could hear surprise in Madhu's silence. 'But ... but if he's not even seeing me, what are the chances that you will get through to him?'

'I can make my presence felt when I need to.'

'Are you saying you *want* to work with him?'

'No, that's not what I am saying.'

'You are not?'

'I am saying I *have* to work with him. Want doesn't come in the picture. I have no choice here, Madhu! Give me his address.'

The door opened with a small swish, even before I had the chance to ring the bell. I cautiously stepped inside, boneblade in my left hand. It was bright, too bright. I stood in an endlessly long marble corridor. The floor was buffed to a high, mirror-like polish. I took another careful step and sensed someone move somewhere to my right. I whirled around, ready to attack and then stopped. My face, complete with the halo of frizzed hair, stared back at me. For a second I stared, fascinated by how wild I looked: crazy hair, filthy clothes, loony eyes, chapped lips. Well, I was busy saving the world, wasn't I? My face, neck and chest were pockmarked with red scars where the nagin's worms had attacked me.

Shukra's house was unlike anything I had seen. It was in the very posh Golf Links. The house stood out among the old-style bungalows there. How could it not? It looked like an elongated, white dice with huge, black holes for windows. No driveway, no garden, just one massive cuboid. Somehow, it suited His Grace. Perhaps it was just my instinct, or maybe his house was indeed bloody weird, but I was on red alert.

'Hello? Shukra, are you there?'

Are you there? My voice echoed hollowly, sending shivers down my spine. The corridor seemed endless. After about ten metres, the floor suddenly gave way, and I fell. *Phchack!*

'Ugh! Empty brains of a bhains!' I exclaimed.

The liquid, about a foot deep, was shallow and sticky. I sat up, wiping the sticky gunk off my nose so I could breathe. The muck had begun to harden instantly, solidifying around me. I tried to get up, but the dirt-coloured snow was holding me fast. Instead of feeling cold, it was heating up.

'Naraka's piss!'

'Hot ice to be precise.'

His Grace's voice came from behind me. Using my hands and elbows I levered myself up, breaking the mould of ice. It was solid, but not rock solid. More like crushed-ice solid – difficult, but not impossible, to break free of. I grunted with the effort of tugging the encrusted bits off my clothes and body. Fumes rose from it.

'In chemistry terms, it's just a mixture of baking soda and vinegar boiled together. However, a lot of your charlatan colleagues who use it call it Devil's Snow, or even sacred ash from the mounts of Kailasha! I can never understand why it's easier to believe in magic than to understand the science behind it. All you need to do is ask the right questions and conduct the right experiments.'

His Grace, Shukracharya the seventy-sixth, stood in front of me, a boy in a grown-up's clothes. He was dressed impeccably in a white shirt and black trousers with suspenders and a long tailcoat. He looked like an underfed butler.

'Is this how you welcome all your visitors?'

'No, madam. Only those who sneak into my house.'

'The door opened by itself before I could ring the goddamn bell!' I said furiously.

'I realize that.' He offered a white-gloved hand and pulled me out of the trench. 'Now would you like to leave unescorted or should I call the police?'

'Look,' I answered, gulping. It was harder to say than I had imagined. 'This is urgent. I ... I need your advice.'

'My advice? You need my advice?'

I nodded. 'There is no one else who can solve this for me.'

He turned on his heel, striding away, crooking a finger at me like I were a bloody underling. But, as I had no choice, I followed, grimacing. I noticed that he was wearing warm shoes. The temperature dropped to freezing, making me shiver. Curiously though, the ice seemed to be melting on my body, although I didn't feel its wetness.

'Is this normal?' I asked, pointing to the puddles from the liquid dripping off my clothes.

'Haven't you ever had a chemistry lesson?' He exasperatedly readjusted his glasses on his nose bridge. '…'course you haven't. They don't teach tantriks anything but how to become charlatans.'

'You mean like the ones you love? The Kaulas?'

His nostrils flared.

Back off, Anantya. You don't want him to throw you out.

'As I was saying,' he continued in his uppity way, 'hot ice turns into liquid at freezing temperatures and solidifies when it gets warmer.'

'Wow!' This reaction was not in response to his boring chemistry lecture but to the chamber we had just entered, a vast, high-ceilinged room beneath what appeared to be a massive glass dome. It was so high that I had to crane my neck to see all the way to the top. Weirdly enough, there had been no sign of a dome on the outside. The room was bright with the sunlight streaming in. The chamber had a lighthouse quality to it, tower-like, and vertically larger than it was wide or long. There were six parallel rows of wooden tables labelled with alphanumeric codes, laden with various kinds of beakers, bottles and test tubes systematically positioned along their centres. Microscopes and hi-tech gadgets were tidily set up against two of the walls. Needless to say, it was nothing like my lab. It was neither dusty nor messy. Each jar was spotless and meticulously arranged by size and the serial number of the experiment. Clean and tidy. Just like Shukra.

'Obviously, the entrance you used is a decoy; it serves to fool a trespasser into believing he's had easy access. Just like the ceiling you are staring at is not real. It's an optical illusion. So is the building's shape. You might have wondered whether it is rectangular or cuboid. It's actually a cube. It's the black lines that make it look rectangular. Now you know why I remain convinced that real magic is nothing but science that you haven't quite figured out, not yet.'

'You know,' I replied, walking around with my eyes still glued to the glass dome. *That had to be real!* 'You are right about that.'

'I am?' asked Shukra, surprised. He extracted a small square of tissue from a drawer in the desk closest to us, wiped his spectacles with it and replaced them on his nose, blinking at me owlishly. 'I mean … you believe me?'

'Of course, when have I not?' I beamed at him, ear to ear. He stopped, slack-jawed with surprise. 'You have me convinced completely. Which is why I came here today. For your help.' I waited for that to sink in, and continued, 'You remember how when we met for the first time at the site of that second sacrifice, you mentioned something about spirits being nothing but concentrated pockets of electrical energy, but ignorant tantriks choose to see them as demons?'

'Y … es?' he hesitated, unsure where I was going with this. He sat on a small stool and changed out of his shoes into a pair of fuzzy slippers. With cartoon rabbits on them. I forced myself to keep a straight face. 'Well, I am now certain that you were right all along,' I answered, mustering a smile, giving my blood a rapid spike of saccharine.

'Seriously?'

'Yes,' I said, absentmindedly fingering one of the jars on a table near me which seemed to contain someone's heart in a semi-solid state. 'And I have figured out how the powers of Kolahal or his mistresses were being called into that pyramid and where all the mistresses were being directed.'

'I am listening.'

'As soon as the ritual ushered in the demon's mistress into the yantra from which it couldn't escape—'

'Within the closed circuit you mean?'

'Sure, whatever. Soon after the mistress entered there and killed the two humans with electric charge, it escaped somewhere. What we couldn't figure out was where, right?'

'My theory so far has been that the electric ball, or the demon mistress as you put it, was flung back into the atmosphere.'

'But what if the demon mistress didn't go back into the atmosphere, but was actually directed through a channel to something? A storehouse of all this mass of electricity?'

He came and stood opposite me. I leant on the table, playing with a metal rod I had just picked up.

'There was no opening,' he countered, shaking his head. 'We didn't find a channel there, remember? Both the humans were dead, and the circuit was completely closed, except to the sky.'

'That's where we were wrong! You remember how you thought that the mobile phones we discovered at each of the sites were actually amplifiers? Something that multiplied the electricity entering the triangle?'

'Yes.'

'What if it wasn't an amplifier but a channel? A passage through which the danava, or as you would put it, the electric charge, could pass through? Could that be possible?'

'A conduit for highly concentrated electrons?'

'Higher concentration and power than anything that science has ever discovered!'

He abruptly spun around and ran.

'Hey!' I followed him, confused.

'Turn right, that's not a path but a wall,' he yelled without looking back. I swerved almost in time, but still managed to ram my shoulder into the wall that had been painted to look like an open door.

'Ow! Bloody Indraprastha!' I exclaimed.

'… and that carpet. It's water.' The warning came too late. I fell in with a huge splash and clumsily rose, soaked and livid. As he had the grace to look apologetic, I didn't give in to my urge to murder him on the spot.

'Is anything in your place what it seems?'

'Only for those who have eyes. You guessed right, though. The asura who made Indraprastha's palace of illusions, Maya, is my ancestor. This house is a dedication to his now rare and obsolete art style. Optical illusions will be everywhere. Although now I think I may have gone slightly overboard.'

'Slightly? Do you have an extra vat of rakpiss to patch up the people who injure themselves here?'

'Not somebody's urine, but I do have one of the finest first-aid kits in the world. Would you like to see it?'

'No.' I rubbed my shoulder. 'Just tell me if what I just told you is possible and I would like to leave your maze of madness, still in one piece.'

'Actually it is,' he said.

We were in his study now – just as brilliantly white as the lab. It was more of a gallery than a room, and made of polished marble slabs. The walls were almost entirely covered with white bookshelves that held books on a vast range of subjects; their covers lent a touch of colour to the room. The walls and books were real. At least the ones I touched were. There were more tables here with pickled human organs in jars. We stood in the middle with a broad white table between us.

Shukra was studying a mobile phone wrapped in plastic. It was the same model as the one at the sacrifice site. He carefully peeled the plastic away with his white-gloved hands.

'Now we can see a transmitter here, which is what I confirmed that day too. But I am not sure how this electric charge was relayed to and fro by someone on the other side.'

'Is it possible for demons to go through a mobile phone?'

'Theoretically, yes. Combinations of electromagnetic rays or even electrons can pass through if the mobile phone is a transmitter. It's a fairly simple wireless energy transfer, nothing new to science. The power source transmits energy into one device. This energy is then received by an antenna which is a receiver. However, the wave of electricity sent in this way will grow weaker and diffuse over distances. We call it leakage.'

'That explains the static electricity in the air these days,' I said, bumping into the table behind me in my excitement. Something clattered on it. I turned around to see a wobbling jar containing a brain floating in a green liquid.

'Can the spirit be sent somewhere and somehow stored?'

'It can be stored if the receiver absorbs it and directs it into something.'

'What kind of a receiver would be required? Would a cellphone do? Riju's cellphone?'

Shukra shook his head. 'The receptacle has to either be very big so that it can catch the emitted electric impulses or, if it's smaller, really close to the transmitter to ensure that all the relayed energy is captured. With a device as small as a cellphone or an antenna or a receiver, it's quite improba—'

He stopped mid-sentence and stared at the bare desk for a second, muttering, lips pursed. Then he whooped. 'Hang on, hang on!'

He flip-flopped quickly to a corner that was kitted out with electronic paraphernalia and checked something online on a sleek computer screen. 'Impossible! Feat of science!'

'What?'

'Riju's phone. It was a satphone!'

'Umm ... a phone that was sitting?'

'Really, Miss Anantya,' he said patronizingly. 'You need some lessons in technology. A *satellite* phone! It all makes sense!'

'Not to me, it doesn't.'

He leapt up, slapping his forehead. 'Why didn't I think of it before?'

CRASH! The jar with the brain fell, spilling its contents on the polished marble. A green puff of smoke rose towards the ceiling. It was in the shape of the brain.

'Horns of a horny horse!' I exclaimed, guiltily withdrawing my hand from the table. I had been absentmindedly fiddling with the jar.

'That,' said Shukra witheringly, his glasses magnifying the reproach in his eyes, 'was the venerated remains of one of the six immortals of Ashwanath from China! It has been in my family for generations! You—'

The brain quivered on the floor and then, with a soft poof, turned over and died.

'The satphone,' I asked, trying to distract him, 'how can it be a receiver?'

For a second his eyes clouded over. They were big and black with just a dribble of blue.

'A satellite phone, madam.' He deliberately turned his back on the bleakness of the desiccated brain. 'It means that when someone called his phone, the transmission would be directed to a satellite, not to a terrestrial cell site, and then beamed back to his satphone. Now a satellite is big enough to receive an electron charge and reflect it back as a beam. So yes, what you suggested is possible. The spirit, or electrons, could have been transported from the sacrifice site to a satphone via satellite.'

'And in each of the triangles, the cellphone was always switched on to Riju's phone, right?'

'Yes. That's true.'

'Cool. So that's how the demon's mistresses are being collected, through satphones,' I said, half to myself, parking myself on a high chair.

'However,' Shukra continued, 'if Riju was receiving this electronic demon through his phone, and it was all going according to plan, why does it continue to happen even though he's dead?'

'Because it wasn't Riju who was receiving the demon's powers … It was Riju's phone, yes, but it was Nasty.'

'Nasty?'

'Oh. Swami Narahara, I mean. The satphone belonged to him, not to Riju. It was planted on Riju the night he died.'

'But … when the fourth death happened—'

'It was back with its owner already. With the help of your assistant who was actually from the Kaula Ashram.'

'My assistant? Oh.'

'I finally remembered where I had seen her before. When Madhu and I visited the ashram, we saw her at the reception. She was one of them, Shukra. She worked at the Kaula Ashram, although she looked quite different that day. How did you meet this assistant of yours?'

He stared at his cutesy slippers for a while before looking up, pushing up his glasses. His hand shook. 'She came to me in response to an advert. Her credentials were good … so I didn't bother doing a thorough check. I desperately needed help. Before I could figure out what had happened to Riju, his body and his phone both went missing from my lab. Along with my assistant.' He sighed and turned away.

We stayed silent, lost in our own thoughts.

'It … they are fake, Anantya!' His slight frame was shaking, angrier than I had ever seen him before. 'The Kaulas, I mean. It's not the pursuit of true science that drives them, but a sordid game of power! I was with them for only half a day, only half. I spoke with Maharishi for a few minutes. All he was interested in was how to cover up Riju's death and the sacrifices to ensure that the Association didn't get a bad name. He sounded so … dry. And the same with the Authority. When I heard that Swami Narahara had been asked to head the investigation, I met him to offer my help. He … they dismissed me out of hand. I thought I had made friends with the Maharishi that day. But that was also just an illusion, wasn't it?'

'Yes, it was,' I said. 'Which is why we need to prove that the sacrifices are still happening. The Association will try to bury the case because it's giving tantriks a bad name. We need to prove to them that Narahara and perhaps others from the Kaula Ashram are involved. We need proof. We need to catch the buggers tonight, red-handed. But for that, we need to find out exactly where the next sacrifice will happen.'

And hopefully save a girl from certain death. I chewed my lower lip. There was something I needed to remember. Something that seemed to be slowly crawling towards me as I went from one disaster to another.

'How do we find out where the next sacrifice will be?' I looked around his lab, searching for inspiration. What was it? I picked up a soft, cuddly ball from the shelf behind me and played with it.

'There has to be a pattern, an order in the chaos,' I whispered to myself.

'My lab will turn into chaos if you don't put that bomb down,' Shukra answered.

I looked at the squishy ball I held. 'This is a bomb?'

'A very powerful one,' he answered, carefully extricating it from my hand and placing it in the powder box from which I had taken it.

'Why don't we go to my kitchenette?' he said, firmly placing his hand on my elbow and steering me as far away from the study and his precious shelves as he could. He made two cups of tea for us and we sat at a round white table to drink it. I was still soaking wet and cold and the hot tea felt good, even though it was a weird concoction without milk. 'Green tea,' he said when he saw my expression.

'There has to be a pattern,' I muttered, sipping the sorry ass tea and biting on an unlit beedi. Shukra was apparently allergic to smoke. The kitchenette was a cosy room, with contemporary-style sofas next to a tall window. Along the opposite wall was a long shelf, above a counter and a sink, all predictably in white. The afternoon sun shone brightly into the air-conditioned room.

I began pacing, but that was a mistake. The room was too crowded to tolerate any pacing, what with Shukra's long limbs, the shelves and the sofas presenting hurdles at every turn. I sat down heavily on the sofa. 'Do you have a paper and pen?'

'No. But I do have a tablet here,' answered Shukra. He took out a small notepad-sized device.

'Okay. Make a list of all the places where the sacrifices have happened until now. There have been a total of five, starting on Thursday night which was when I was having that miserable dat ... I mean duck for dinner.' Not that Shukra noticed. His fingers were tapping on the screen silently. I chewed on my beedi, wishing I could light it.

'It started on that terrace at Kotla Mubarakpur. Then the second sacrifice happened in the Pusa Hill Forest. That was followed by the warehouse near Ghata Masjid—'

'The fourth,' said Shukra, still typing, 'happened inside the school in Moti Bagh and then another one at the other school in Kishan Ganj last night, again disguised as an accidental fire, which Madhu told me about earlier today.'

'Can you print out a map of the city and mark the spots?'

'I can do better than that; I can add them on an interactive map online. Give me a minute.'

He did some more tapping on the screen in his hand. I stood behind him, peering into his device. He was using his fingers instead of a pen to write things down. I had never seen this tablet thingy before. It looked like a small diary. Technology was as mysterious to me as tantrism was to others.

'Here you go. It looks like a child has drawn a circle around central Delhi,' said Shukra. 'Can't anyone get even a geometric circle right nowadays?'

'It's too random to be a circle, but it does look like a pattern.'

'I would say the sixth sacrifice will take place somewhere east.' He pointed on the map with his bony finger. His finger was on the Yamuna near the place where they had built the disastrous Commonwealth Games Village some years ago. Then I finally remembered what had been bugging me all this while.

'Give me a pen!' I exclaimed, smacking him on the shoulder.

'Ouch! Here,' he said, handing me a fountain pen.

I uncapped it and began to draw a line on the tablet screen.

'HEY!' he screamed, grabbing my hand in a surprisingly strong grip. 'What in Einstein's name do you think you're doing?'

'I want to draw a line,' I told him, wriggling free.

'You cannot write on a tablet! Don't you know that?'

'Well, you were writing on it!' I exclaimed.

'I was using my finger! Wait, let me take a printout for you to write on.' After some more tapping, he brought me a paper map with the five dots. I drew five lines across, joining them in a pattern. Two triangles. Voila!

'Two intersecting equilateral triangles, one up, one down!' exclaimed Shukra. 'It's what is called the Shiva-Shakti yantra or the Star of David in Judaism. Both here and in Judaism it is associated with an archaic form of magic.'

'Thank you, Encyclopaedia,' I answered. 'I don't know about others, but this is the most powerful yantra in tantrik circles. The cult has been creating a fucking yantra on half of Delhi itself. Do you know what that means?'

'That the electron spirit might be a big guy?'

'No, idiot! It means that the spirit can drink in and consume whoever is within this yantra. It's the biggest ritual food one can give to their god. No wonder ...' I got up, the piece of paper falling off my lap. 'No wonder the moonblades were so excited. Half our city will become a shamshaan if this devil comes into our plane.'

'It will be like a nuclear bomb in the centre of Delhi. Nothing will survive.'

'Oh. But I bet it's not exactly like a nuclear bomb. More like an electric shock?'

'Nothing,' I said, coming close to him and standing on my toes. I barely reached his chest. 'Nothing,' I emphasized, speaking slowly, 'which is inside the circle will survive. The spirit will eat away all humans and sups within.' I poked his chest with my index finger as I said each of the last four words.

'Okay.' He shrugged. 'If you believe it, I am ready to go along for a while with your reasoning. Who is this demon again?'

'A pissed-off thing called Kolahal. Now that's what I call a double whammy. Kolahal enters the world and the first thing he does is destroy one of the biggest cities in Asia. He doesn't really like civilization much anyway. From what I have learnt, the leader who will be the vessel for this danava will not be able to control him after sometime. So Kolahal enters, destroys a city and then brings chaos to others after eating the soul of the stupid tantrik who is bringing him in. Somehow, the whole thing sounds stupid enough to be something my half-brother will fall for.'

'But why would Narahara want to do that? Destroy the city? Isn't he in a good position in the Association?'

'We will find that out soon,' I answered, putting another dot, right in the middle of the two intersecting triangles on the printed map. 'And this is the bindu. The central point of the yantra that will open the door for Kolahal to enter this world. The seventh sacrifice where the danava will consume half of Delhi.'

I stared at my drawing for a while, imagining power-hungry Nasty in that role. Shukra had a point. Did he have a good reason to destroy half of Delhi?

'I know that point. It used to be a cemetery on Raisina Road.'

'A cemetery? That would be ideal for the last ritual then.'

'Does that mean that this tantrik,' asked Shukra, 'will be at this point, this cemetery, tomorrow at midnight?'

'Yup, but we will finish this before that. We will meet him tonight. You were right, Shukra. The sixth incident will happen in the fields between Yamuna and the Commonwealth Village. But this time, we will be waiting for whoever is orchestrating this. Waiting to catch Nasty and his gang red-hangggg—'

My tongue felt like wet cotton snagged on thorns. I reached for the side of the sofa with my left hand, but lost my grip and keeled over. The floor rose to meet me as I fell flat on my face on the smooth marble. The last thing I remember was Shukra's stick-thin figure as he loomed over me with his face in the shadows and his slippers, his soft, ridiculous-looking, expensive slippers near my face. Seemed like I had been poisoned with green tea. How clichéd.

It's dark and a ghostly chill pervades my body. I can feel something cold holding me tight, promising to never let me go. Each breath is painful. I attempt rapid shallow breathing to reduce the pain. (It exists, the House of Belles.) The thought lingers, echoing inside my freezing mind. I try to open my eyes, but my eyelids are glued shut. There are colours here, just not for the eyes to see. (We located its successor.) It's cold, so cold. My blood freezes, becoming blocks of ice in the veins. (She's alive. The apsara is still alive.)

Who...

Kaani.

Am I dead?

No, you are on another plane. The space reserved for my ancestors. The space of Kinnaras.

Bladebirther?

Yes.

Couldn't you have just called me? That might have been easier for me.

That phone thing is too cumbersome. I have to wait for you to pick up. This is easier. Kinnara plane is so much easier. You cannot refuse my call here. Haven't you tried it before?

No.

Oh. It must be painful for you then. You being a manava.

Like hell, yes.

Oh.

Got to say, this is the worst communication method invented in centuries.

Oh.

Can we speed up our conversation, Bladebirther? I am in a lot of pain here.

Oh. Yes. That's true. You asked about the House of Belles, the last owners of the moonblades. I managed to find one of their successors who is still alive. An apsara of old times. You might get to know about the moonblades from her and who she gave them to.

Who?

I don't know who she gave them to. You will have to ask her.

Who is the apsara?

Rambha Devi.

The actress?

No, I told you she's an apsara. She is an old one, that one. But now she dances for the ghostly theatre.

You mean Bollywood?

Yes. The same. Really demeaning for someone who has an apsara's blood in her veins.

Oh. Thanks, Kaani. I will send you your payment. But you know what?

Yes?

Next time, please call me instead.

The chill abated, replaced by a bright light. So bright that I had to squeeze my eyes shut. However, something cold held them open.

'Ugh! Bri ... ght!' I muttered.

'Ah, good. The dilation is decreasing. Thought you had died for a while there. You went quite cold,' said Shukra accusingly, his nose almost touching mine. Between our faces was a little torchlight, which was flashing annoyingly into my eye.

'Can you ... switch ... that off?'

'Sorry,' he said, hurriedly switching it off and helping me up. I sat miserably on the sofa, fighting an urge to throw up. My head throbbed and my tongue felt like it had been sand-papered.

'You should have warned me that you have an epileptic reaction to green tea,' he said.

I turned sharply with an acid retort. Bad idea, the urge to puke won through, and spilt all over his pretty slippers.

'Oh ...' he exclaimed. 'D212!' A small metallic mouse whirred in squeaking and, in a matter of seconds, cleaned up the mess. Even the ridiculous slippers were back to looking brand new. Explained the marble polished to a high finish.

I placed my head between my hands, feeling wretched.

'Here, have this pill. Might help some.'

I slowly, very, very, slowly raised my head to glare at him. He was grinning delightedly. It took me a while to find my tongue, which had been lost in all the wool that was stuffed in my mouth. The Kinnara channel was one form of communication that I would avoid like the plague if I could help it.

'So are we now going to catch Narahara in the act? I have something that I have been meaning to tell you about him.'

'Do,' I said, cutting him off. My tongue felt weird. 'Dhe are dhoing to dheet thomeone famouth firtht. Thetter dhear your betht Diwali dreth.'

He surveyed me with all four eyes, his eyebrows leaping into his hairline. 'And you will go like this?'

'Yeth. Will uth tharm thoo get thin.'

'Hah … I see. And who will interpret if you speak this way?'

I hit him by way of reply.

Shukra quickly researched Rambha Devi, the actress, and dramatically informed me that she had been quite famous in the Hindi cinema of the sixties and seventies. Not because of her acting, but because of her raunchy posters which showed ample cleavage, skimpy clothes and a body to die for. One of the articles had even revealed that the actress had been involved in a sex scandal in Mumbai where four people had died. After that, she had taken voluntary retirement from films and moved to Delhi in 1978. Since then, she had lived more or less like a recluse, away from the media glare. She had to. After all, someone was bound to notice that it had been fifty years since her heyday, and the woman still looked like she was in her twenties.

If what Kaani had told me was true, Rambha could be anything like several thousands of years old. That wasn't all. An apsara was a spirit, who, like a daeva, lived in the spirit world. But unlike a daeva, who needed to possess a human body to stay in the human world, apsaras had the ability to shape-shift and take on any form they wished, on any plane. They were not bound to one physical human body. If Rambha Devi was a true apsara, she was more dangerous than even Kolahal. Unlike Kolahal, she didn't need a human body to inhabit, and was powerful enough to destroy anything that annoyed her. So why would she want to bring in Kolahal into our world? Apsaras were loyal to daevas, the new gods. They hated the old ones, didn't they? I hoped so.

After a heated argument about the dangers of mobikes on the roads of Delhi, I was finally able to convince Shukra to ride pillion with me on Chhotu. Shukra, his long legs and I straddled Chhotu and headed first to the haveli, where I quickly completed the potion I had started on and packed some chudail antidote for the nagin. Just in case. An hour later, we reached Gurgaon. Rambha Devi may have retired, but she lived in a sprawling estate in a ramshackle bungalow surrounded by an unkempt garden. As soon as we rang the bell, we were greeted by two cheerful girls dressed in printed silk dresses.

'Can we help youuuuu?' they chorused, bowing in the style of Chinese kung fu movies (Zee would have been thrilled – he is an ardent Chan fan).

'We are here to meet Rambha Devi,' I answered, thankful my lisp had gone.

'You have appointment?' they said. When I shook my head, they chimed: 'Then not posseeble!'

'Well, it's rather urgent you see,' tried Shukra.

'Not posseeble!' the girls repeated, bowing again. The door shut on our faces.

'Of all the—'

'Wait, let me try again,' said Shukra patiently. He rang the intercom buzzer.

'Not posseeble!'

'Tell her that we have a message for the successor of the House of Belles!'

There was a long pause. Then we heard some whispers.

'Not poss—'

I took out my boneblade, ready to blast the door open with a mantra when it opened again. In front of us stood Rambha Devi who looked sexier than I remembered from

Vajrin's party, in a take-me-here sort of way. She wore a translucent, white dress with underwear that was neon pink and didn't like to stay hidden. Her long, wavy hair fell like silk around her shoulders. She looked younger than she had at the party, her eyes kohled with a winged eyeliner and accentuated with fake eyelashes. The two kung fu imports standing behind her suddenly looked ugly in her sheer presence. I probably resembled manure.

'I am Anantya Tantrist, a detective. I want to speak to you about a case I am working on,' I said, bringing my chin up, so that I didn't need to stare at her fuchsia bra.

Something like surprise flitted across her face, but I probably imagined it. She smiled politely, her eyes a mesmerizing light green.

'Agugu ... gug,' said Shukra who was standing by my side, mouth open and drooling. I elbowed him in the ribcage.

'Guuuh! Shuk ... rah!' he managed, his eyes bulging. 'Simply marvellous to geek—'

'May I ask why you disturb an old lady's peace?'

Shukra uttered a strangled cough, trying not to stare at her perky breasts.

'We just have a few questions for you about moonblades,' I answered.

She took a long drag from a cigarillo-holder held between her beautiful fingers with its long emerald-green nails. 'Well, you had better come in,' she replied, elegantly exhaling smoke from her cherry-red lips, 'and tell me more about this.'

We walked through a narrow corridor leading into a softly lit room with red walls and black sofas. No sunlight was allowed in. On the mantelpiece opposite the door was a large framed photograph, spotlit with a yellow lamp, of Rambha with a beautiful young girl. I recognized Mohini, the girl who had been at Vajrin Mahendra's party a few nights ago.

'That's my daughter. They grow up so fast,' said Rambha, gracefully gesturing to us to take a seat. All the other walls were covered with larger-than-life photographs of her. In each one her choli was progressively smaller than the last, and her pose increasingly more Kamasutra than the last. Shukra sat beside me, stiff and stupefied, his eyes darting from poster to poster. And here I was hoping that he would be able to cross-question her.

'Would you care for a glass of brandy?'

'No, thanks,' I replied.

Shukra, to my surprise, nodded a yes. He took the glass and downed it at one go, like he was parched. A female servant discreetly refilled it. He emptied the glass again.

'So, what can I do for you?'

'You can tell us more about this,' I replied, showing her a moonblade. I had retained two; one was with Tazaak now; and two were missing, probably with Nasty.

'The crest on the hilt, the two intertwined roses, is it from your House, the House of Belles?'

'Let me take a look,' she said, holding the blade carefully in her hands. She moved her manicured finger over the carving on the blade's handle.

'How curious,' she muttered.

'What is?'

'This is really well crafted, but I am afraid it is a mere imitation of my crest,' she said, still fingering the blade. She beckoned to the girl who had served us our drinks, and was now standing unobtrusively by the door.

'Roiyi, show them the house crest please,' she told her.

Roiyi had flawless, dewy skin and wore a barely there

gown. She stood in front of Shukra and me and parted her legs. Then she lifted the gown she wore, showing us her inner thigh. Shukra gasped. Roiyi had the same crest tattooed on her skin. Two roses with their stems intertwined. This was slightly different, however. One of the roses was breaking off.

'My house's crest represents a heart full of joy and love, but also a heart full of sorrow,' said Rambha. 'It has been our ancestral curse if you will, falling in love and getting our hearts broken.' She laughed softly at her own joke. 'I guess it comes with the profession. Since you know about the House of Belles, I presume you know about me?'

'Yes, I was told. You are an apsara. How old are you?'

'That's a rude question. Let's just say I have been around a long time. I have seen times when we ruled over the hearts of kings. Now, everything is so different. And the House of Belles is nothing but a dead memory, even though I continue to live. Now all I can get with my dancing skills is an item song in the movies,' she said, indicating her portraits nonchalantly.

'This moonblade does not belong to you?'

'I am afraid not. I do own the original seven moonblades, the famous ones that is. They have been in the family for generations, but I do hope you realize,' she said, tossing the velvet bag carelessly on the sofa beside her, 'that these are clearly fakes.'

'They are?'

'Of course,' she said, with a dismissive motion. 'They are a dime a dozen out there. The Seven Sisters is a very popular hoax. Everyone knows their history and their power. Every tantrik out there is after a blade that can get them to possess a daeva. There are hunters by the hordes out there looking for the real thing, and counterfeiters by the hordes as well. I get a few sellers and buyers every month. It's most amusing.'

'And yours are safely with you?'

'Obviously. Mine are safe in my safe.' She smiled at the pun, her perfect lips curling slightly.

'Would you mind showing us your originals?'

'Miss Tantrist, your nerve makes me want to laugh. You enter my house unannounced and make personal demands. However, I still entertain you, purely for my amusement. You ask me questions rudely and I answer sincerely. Now you expect me to open up my precious vault and show you my priceless ancestral blades, without you having furnished a single proof of your credentials whatsoever? How do I know that you won't steal them? That you are not after that ultimate goal of possessing a higher spirit? Do you imagine that I'm naïve?'

'Anantyaaaa,' said Shukra in a loud stage whisper, grabbing my arm, 'she's right. It is all wrong. Let's leave. I have to peeeee!'

'Wha—? Stop it!' I said, furious.

He tugged at my sleeve again, shaking me. I turned to him angrily, but stopped. Shukra looked unwell, his face a little too shiny, droplets of perspiration beading his high forehead. He stood up, swayed unsteadily and collapsed in a heap on the sofa. Then he leant his head on my shoulder, took a handful of my hair and sniffed.

'Your hair smells of pork pickle,' he said, giggling.

I jabbed him hard in the ribs with my elbow. He fell back, his back arched, his head lolling, his spectacles askew.

'Mr Shukracharya cannot hold his drink, can he?' observed Rambha. Her eyes glinted.

'Yes, well,' I said, getting up. 'I am sorry we wasted your time. I thought I was returning something that was precious to you. I will dispose of the blades after our investigation is over, since they are useless anyway.' I stretched my hand to take the blade from her. She hesitated, just long enough for me to notice.

'Actually,' she said, gripping the velvet cover of the blade, 'now that I think about it, why don't you sell it to me? It will be most amusing for me to sell fake moonblades to the next hopeful buyer who comes my way.'

'No, I would rather destroy them.' I tried to take it from her, but her hands gripped the sheath.

'I insist that you give it to me,' she said.

'I insist that you return it to me,' I responded curtly, reaching over and taking it from her hand.

'Give them to me!' she shouted. She grabbed for the moonblade, her face black with fury like a veil of storm clouds had fallen over it. Shit. I had managed to do the one thing I shouldn't have. Piss off an apsara.

'I have to peeee!' wailed Shukra, rising from the couch and then flopping back into it.

'These are the real ones, aren't they?' I said softly, wondering how fast I could reach for my boneblade. I was no match for an apsara should she decide to kill me. But I hoped that we could reach some kind of truce here.

Rambha sat down on the sofa, her bowed head between her hands. 'Yes ... yes they are.'

I took out my boneblade and pointed it at her. 'So you are the one who gave it to all those men. You are responsible for the deaths of those innocent girls.'

'What girls?' she asked. 'Indra forbid! Of course not! The blades were stolen from my vault. All seven of them. I ... I don't know how.' She covered her face with her hands and this time a sob escaped her. She got up, wiped her kohl-smudged eyes, and said, 'I ... I didn't know what to do. I couldn't go to the Authority. By Urvashi's hair, if word of this gets out, I'll be ruined! I have been looking for them. Discreetly. Asking all the right people. I … I didn't know that the blades were being used in these deaths.' She shuddered and took a gulp of the brandy, then signalled her maid for a top-up.

'Do you know who took them from you?'

'Not yet.'

'Where were they kept?'

'In … I … I can't tell you!'

'Miss Rambha, I am trying to save a sixth girl from being butchered by a moonblade that belongs to you. You are the only one who can save that innocent's life!'

'They are …' she gulped, 'were in my house safe.'

'Who else knows about your house safe?'

'No one but me.'

'Any of your servants?'

She shook her head.

'What about your daughter?'

Her kajal-smeared eyes narrowed, her red lips thinning. 'What about my daughter?'

'She doesn't know?'

'I would like you to leave her out of this,' she answered curtly. 'She has gone through bad days and is now building a new life for herself far away from the world I am stuck in.'

'Where does she work?'

'Not that it's any of your business, but she works with Vajrin Mahendra,' she answered proudly. 'She's not in my line of entertainment, and is already making a space for herself in the corporate world. She's involved in one of his personal projects,' replied Rambha, getting up. 'Now I would like you to leave. I have some appointments for which I have to get ready. I hope you will restore my moonblades to me as soon as your investigation is over.' She escorted us outside. I held Shukra who had wrapped himself around me like a wet snake. I had a feeling that she was hiding something from me, but exactly what that was, I wasn't sure.

'Oh and one more thing,' she said just before bidding us goodbye, 'if I were you, I wouldn't worry too much about these sacrifices being successful.'

'Oh. Why?'

'Because the moonblades can only carry out a sacrifice to invite a danava into this plane. Once here, the danava needs a human vessel to survive in,' she said, her lips stretching into a smile. 'In the past, a rishi's or a true aghori's human body could handle it, but present-day tantriks are just not powerful enough.'

'You sound rather confident about that fact,' I commented.

'It's my business to know,' she answered with an enigmatic smile.

'Madam,' whispered Shukra, 'are you really … truly an apsara?'

'Don't I look like one?' she responded, patting Shukra on his head affectionately before curtly nodding to me.

I bit my lower lip. I hadn't said anything about what kind of a thing, danava or otherwise, was being summoned with the moonblades. Had she just assumed it, considering the moonblades were meant for that purpose? Or did she know more than she was letting on?

After Shukra had peed and puked all the brandy out, he apologized. I gave him a mint, which triggered a series of thank yous.

'You think she gave the moonblades to Narahara?' He blanched as the strong flavour of the mint hit him.

'Maybe. We can be sure only after we've taken Nasty down and interrogated him.'

'You think it might be someone other than the Kaulas?'

I shrugged. 'There have to be more people involved in the Cult of Chaos. But Nasty is the only definite lead we have for now. Let's go to the sacrifice site and hope he is there too.'

'There will be no need for that, Miss Anantya,' he answered, looking at his phone.

'Excuse me?'

'When I last met Swami Narahara, I was deeply disillusioned by his attitude, and decided to not trust him anymore.'

'Well, good decision, Shukra, but—'

'Patience, madam.' He raised his hand. 'Hear me out. I used a rather nifty tool – a small tracker. You see, I tagged him!' He clapped his hands together triumphantly, and looked at me. 'Oh. You don't see. I "tagged" him, madam. Which means that with an app on my smartphone we can find out where he is.'

'What's an app?'

'Oh dear.' He looked away. 'Let me just say that we can find out where he's standing right now by looking into my phone. Hang on, let me show you.'

'Really? That will put poor gandhas out of business.'

'Might as well, since they do not exist.'

'Are you serious?'

'Yes, the map will show us. Give it a second—'

'No, I mean, you really don't believe in gandhas?'

'Of course, they don't exist. There's no scientific proof of it.'

'I ... see.'

I wondered what Rajni Gandha, his wife, Gulabo, and their four children would have to say to the fact that they didn't exist because someone from the scientific world hadn't written about them. I may need to introduce them to our friend here. I smiled at the thought of Rajni explaining his existence to Shukra. Perhaps he would just feed His Grace lizard poop smells by way of self-introduction.

'So what's Nasty up to?' I asked, forcing myself out of the pleasant daydream to the task at hand.

'He's there, Anantya,' Shukra replied, his eyes and his glasses glittering with excitement. 'Near the river bank where the sixth sacrifice is supposed to happen.'

२०

The only sign that the sun had set was that the grey sky turned darker. Red rashes ripped over the thick mantle of the still night sky. Charred clouds belched a dry thunder every once in a while, no light, only sound. A putrid breeze drifted in from the Yamuna, which lay somewhere ahead of us. Chhotu chugged along through it all like a brave little soldier. Dry air whipped my hair and face, prickling and sharp like daggers. But it was Shukra who suffered the most. Every once in a while he would whine about how my 'unruly' hair was getting on his nerves.

'You drive like a maniac!' screamed Shukra in my ears.

I wondered whether I should abandon him and his stupid smartphone right there, and figure out how to save the world by myself. It would be simpler.

'If you hadn't insisted on giving me directions, we could have taken the flyover,' I answered, proud that my voice was calm, even though what I really wanted to do was shove a cauliflower into his big mouth to shut him up. It was the new me, this trying to reason first.

'Is it my fault if he decided to take the most convoluted routes? It's only an app, you know. Not magic.'

The app thing that Shukra used on his phone, made him, if possible, more irritating than before. Every time he saw the Nasty dot on his phone screen, he would get frantic and

285

screech: left, right, no, no, straight now! Each time I turned, he would change his mind. Frankly, Rajni would have been more efficient. We took by-lanes, rode through backyards of people's homes (once plunged headlong into a naala) and finally reached an open area. It was on the banks of the Yamuna, adjacent to the DND flyway that could have brought us here half an hour earlier if someone had had the intelligence to tell me where we needed to go. I stopped Chhotu where the road ended, dismounted and glared at Shukra, smoothening my hair. Unruly, he had called it. Well, his was plain stupid.

'Why did we stop?' he asked, the pale glow from his phone making him look like a ghost.

'No road, Your Grace. Would you be so kind as to take the number eleven bus?'

He blinked owlishly, uncomprehending. Of course. His Grace was too high up to get low humour. 'Walk,' I said, 'we walk from here.'

I had wanted to leave Shukra behind. Dealing with a corpse was one thing, but I wasn't too sure how he'd cope coming up against a powerful tantrik who was very much alive and extremely dangerous. But he had insisted. And since he was the one who got us here, I had given in. Before setting out, he had figured out a way to record everything that was going to happen tonight. He had given me a long-winded lecture about a detective camera with night vision and something about a net, most of which whizzed over my head. While he droned on, I tuned out conveniently and began to think about my strategy for tonight. I hoped that I would have to kill Nasty to save the world. That would be nice.

'So where is he?'

'Somewhere here…' said Shukra, looking into the phone, '…about … yes, about 250 metres away from us in that direction.' He pointed straight into the river.

'Under the waters of Yamuna?'

'Oh. But … but that's where the GPS is pointing.'

'Your GPS is a delusional, manflesh-eating aghori,' I snapped.

We waited while he stared at his pale screen.

'It's moving again,' said Shukra after a while.

I followed Shukra through a field of marigolds. The air was a nauseating combination of the sweet stench of stagnant water and marigold. The mulch beneath our feet began to grow as we walked on it. Every step made a loud squelch. And because I had been looking down, concentrating on being careful with each step, and keeping behind Shukra, making as little noise as possible, I was surprised at the sudden darkness that had descended on us. Dark, damp and dangerous. It was as if we were not under the open sky, but in a room full of smoke and haze. I could barely see my feet.

'Looks and smells like a mantra,' I said, sniffing and taking out my boneblade.

'It's only marsh gas—' Shukra tripped and fell into a puddle with a loud splash.

Squelchch!

'Bhains!' I whispered, signalling him to switch off his screen. The noise had come from somewhere ahead of us. 'Stay here.' I took a step ahead.

'I am coming too,' he whispered back.

'Have you ever fought with mantras or anything?'

'I am the seventy-sixth descendant of Shukracharya. I know duelling.'

'With mantras? Magic?'

'Of course not,' he answered, offended. 'Learning tantrism has been out of fashion in our family since the late nineteenth century. I have been taking fencing classes since I was a child. I have even participated in a fencing tournament in Europe and own an ancient rapier.'

'Kali help us. Stay here.'

'Who will record your brave fighting if I do?'

'Oh.' He had a point there. 'Fine, come. I will give you a suggestion though. Try to stay alive.'

'I will—'

There was a loud, wailing scream. The still night vibrated with its panicked urgency.

'Shakti's shit!' I exclaimed, running blindly towards the direction of the scream. I heard Shukra following.

A small derelict cottage materialized ahead, a hazy monster wrapped in mist. A solitary light from a hanging lantern bravely slashed at the black mist. I saw Nasty looming over a shrunken figure. He held his staff with the Kaula triangle aloft in his right hand. In the other hand, he held something that wriggled. Was it a girl? My head swirled with a creamy madness. Before I realized it, I had plunged forward, slashing my finger and shouting the Vayusa mantra.

'Hawa hawa, tez ho ja!'

The blast of air hit him with gale force on his back. He pitched forward, face first, his broad body slamming into the ground.

'Leave her alone or the next curse won't be a breeze.' I ran towards them, kicking his staff aside and lifting the girl, hoping she was okay. She turned out to be a goat.

'RED CUNT!' he screamed. He turned sharply, sat up, looked into the darkness behind me and said, 'Seen enough? Do it ... NOW!'

For a second I thought he spoke to Shukra, who ought to have been somewhere behind me, recording the whole thing. *Wheench! Wheench!* High-pitched noise filled the murky air. I whipped around in time to see the white, whining tendrils that hit me like red-hot whiplashes. The lashes felt like fire and ice together, searing deep into the flesh of my back and buttocks and binding me. Pain exploded in my head as I struggled against the fire-ice wisps. They didn't budge, holding me like carnivorous vines. A shadow walked towards me.

'Miss Tantrist, I always find you causing trouble,' sneered Justice Kanthak's silky voice, his teeth protruding from his mouth, pointy and plastic. His right hand, which held the staff, twisted to control the thongs that bound me.

'Mmmmhauph!' I tried to spit. The fire-ice vines wound around my lips, like they had read my mind.

'Are you all right, my lord? Praise the goddess, I decided to accompany you tonight.' Kanthak helped Nasty to his feet.

'You didn't have a choice, Kanthak,' Nasty barked. 'You were ordered to. I hope you prove to be useful and put her in prison for the rest of her filthy life. Bloody cunt attacked me!'

Nasty turned towards me viciously, pointing his staff at my neck. The triangle's point pierced my skin. I struggled against my bonds in furious helplessness.

'I will cut you,' he sneered, 'into small pieces and throw you into the Yamuna for the fishes. And do that one thing father has been wanting to do with you for years now.'

'Mhhhapyp!' I replied, daring him.

'I … umm … my lord, that may not be a good solution,' Kanthak whispered from behind Nasty.

'What? You saw her! She tried to kill me, the heir of the Kaula Council! She must have been planning this for months with those Vama dung. How dare you even try to take her side?'

Vamas? What Vamas?

'I am only doing my job, my lord,' protested Kanthak. 'She needs to be tried by the Tazaak. The Association will want to—'

'You turncoat pashu! I don't care what CAT wants! She is working with Vamas! She's a Red!' bellowed Nasty.

The Justice of Tazaak stepped back, afraid. 'I am on your side, my lord,' Kanthak pleaded, wiping his face with his free hand. 'There are benefits to taking her alive to CAT. Think about it. The things she might be able to reveal about the Vamas. And all that credit will go to you.'

There was an ominous silence as Nasty thought this through. 'You could be right.' He turned to me, crouched on his haunches and stared into my face, his eyes blazing with hatred. 'So, cunt … are Vamas that much better at sex that you sold yourself off with the sacrifice of little girls?'

'MMMufffff!'

'I think … ummm … what Miss Anantya is trying to say is,' said Shukra's voice from behind us, 'that you cannot really blame her for something without giving her a fair chance to defend herself.'

'You!' Nasty snarled as Shukra came into the range of the lone lantern. 'I will kill you right now, you snotty asura!' He pointed his staff towards him.

'Muuumffh, mayyy!' I cried, helplessly. Why was he still here? He could have made himself scarce if he had been even half as smart as the little goat. No one would have known he'd come with me tonight. Why the hell did he have to show himself?

'Umm … just to point out one thing before you, you

know, continue with your plan,' said Shukra, standing unarmed but calm, facing Kanthak and Nasty, both of whom had their staffs pointed at him. 'This is being broadcast live online, so you might want to do this with a smile.'

'What?'

'What?'

'Maauf?'

'You see, I have a camera fitted on my chest,' he pointed to a small dot on the lapel of his jacket, 'which has been recording for exactly fourteen minutes now and uploading everything you said and did online. Let me assure you, the quality of this video and audio will be very clear. It started to record at the time that Mr Kanthak here "arrested" Miss Tantrist and Mr Narahara started to spout a string of colourful expressions. Now if you don't release us or decide to kill both of us, the link to this video will be automatically sent to CAT's email ID as well as to prominent media houses of the country. Oh, and don't think about breaking this one, I have two others on my body which are recording this from different angles. The only person who can stop this is me. So, Mr Narahara, I suggest that if you want your chance at election to the Kaula Council, I advise you to refrain from harming either of us. I don't know what your father would say to the media about you murdering your half-sister.'

Narahara's face drained of colour. He lowered his staff, his eyes mutinous.

'He … he's right, my lord,' said Justice Kanthak. 'We cannot take the chance of him maligning you, especially in public. We should follow the law.'

'Good,' said Shukra. 'So now that we have agreed to be civil, give Miss Tantrist a chance to speak.'

Nasty's face looked pinched. I would have laughed out loud if the fire-and-ice vines weren't gagging me.

'I will have you arrested for doing the Black when this night is over,' said Nasty threateningly before signalling to Justice with a curt, 'Do it.'

'Ouch!' I muttered as Kanthak sadistically yanked at the tightening vine, ripping it off my face. It still bound my body.

'Where are they?' he asked me.

'Who?'

'Your Vama gang!' hollered Nasty. 'The conniving blood thieves! Your partners! The ones who have done these sacrifices! The ones who killed Riju!'

'If you tell us where the others are and help us catch them,' said Kanthak, bending down to speak to me as I was still bound and on the ground, 'I will personally make an appeal to CAT to be kinder to you.'

'I am working with no Vamas!' I cried. 'You think I will help someone sacrifice girls? It's his deed.' I pointed my chin at Nasty. 'He's the one whose students have been involved. Are you so desperate for power, Nasty, that you will kill millions of innocent people to summon this danava of yours? Even destroy your own clan and everything you have stood for?'

Nasty's face turned red as he roared, 'I AM NOT DOING THIS!'

'NEITHER AM I!' I yelled back.

Nasty was apoplectic with rage. 'Then why did you come here tonight? How did you find out that there will be a sacrifice here?'

'I figured it out. I figured out the yantra you are using. The Shiva-Shakti yantra created to take in half of Delhi itself!'

'Hah! We had that figured out this morning itself,' replied Nasty.

'Then why haven't you stopped the sacrifices from

happening? Aren't you supposed to end this? Why are the sacrifices continuing?'

'I am trying to!' roared Nasty. 'I am trying to stop it! What do you think I have been doing? I have been chasing the Vama responsible for this. That Mattreya. I know he's somehow involved. I wanted to catch the Red tantrik red-handed. The sacrifice smells of Vama shit! I know it!'

'Mattreya has nothing to do with it! The people who are dying are all Kaula students.'

'He has hired them! He has turned them to his Red ways. I have been trying to catch him night and day, ever since he…' Nasty gulped, 'since the night Riju died.'

'Riju? You killed him! And then stole his body.'

'What? Riju's body is still at the CBI lab. This asura was supposed to send it to the Tazaak headquarters. It hasn't reached us. But that doesn't matter! It's the leader who matters. The one who is behind it all. Tonight I will catch him. The Vama who leads this group, the one who wants to bring in this danava along with you. Mattreya!'

'Why are you so sure that Mattreya's the one?' I asked.

'Because the Vamas want to somehow prove that they are better than Kaulas. They want to destroy our reputation. They hate us. They have been politically trying to up us in CAT sessions too. Since the Kaulas have already brought in one daeva into this world, successfully and without any human sacrifice, they want to do this too. This stinks of Vamas! Except their choice is a danava instead of a daeva. We followed rules, regulations and etiquette. That's the kind of tantrism we practise.'

'You have, lord?' asked Kanthak. 'Brought in a daeva? Who?'

'That cannot be revealed. Only the top brass in the Council

know,' answered Nasty, his rudraksh ponytail swinging as he shook his head. 'We did it without any danger to manavas. The daeva is safely trapped in a human body and under strict observation. These Vamas got to know about it and want to do the same. They are using Kaula ex-students so that if this goes horribly wrong, the blame will fall on the Kaulas.'

'So all this sacrificing is nothing but a one-upmanship contest of whose dick is bigger?' I cried, furious. 'You would put lives in danger to prove that you are the biggest dickheads in the world?'

'It's not so trivial. The very control of the sups depends on us. If the Vamas win this fight, the sup world will be divided. The tantriks will be divided!'

'Not everything is centred around you, you twat—'

My anger was cut short by the distant gurgle of a jeep or station wagon. We all stopped talking together, listening. The jeep had halted somewhere in front of the shack. We couldn't see it.

'You,' barked Nasty, pointing to Kanthak and picking up his staff, 'stay here, and give this one a drop of amrita. We will deal with her boyfriend later. I will catch the Vama shit and make him sing.'

He sneered in my direction one last time and vanished, becoming a shadow in the dark. Kanthak took out a little bottle from his pocket and opened it, smiling his plastic pointy smile. Amrita. The truth serum. *Shit*.

'No!' I protested as he forced open my mouth. The last thing I remember was Shukra running towards us like a loosely packed bundle of sticks, his gangly limbs flying.

'Madness strikes the moonblade, which smells a pail of blaaaoood … A pile of smells, a dash of flesh, it takes what it so laaaaoooooves!'

'Shut up!' Kanthak whispered furiously, slapping me. I pursed my lips real tight, but the song started to sing in my head instead.

'Madam, you are truly ghastly at poetry,' observed Shukra who sat on the other side, bound by mayan rope.

I felt my own lips pressed against my gums.

'Mhemhemhe,' I giggled. Nothing could be funnier really. It was all clear now. We came after Narahara who was following us, but then someone else had come too, and no one knew who they had come after. I giggled again.

'Gave her too much…' muttered Kanthak, '… if you hadn't shoved me.'

'You should not pour a bottle of this potion directly into anyone's mouth!' answered Shukra. 'This is potent stuff, Mr Kanthak. It affects not only the nervous system but studies have shown that it also messes with human memories. Now whom should we hold responsible if she ends up permanently braindead? Mind you, she may not have had anything sensible there to begin with, but still. You are accountable for her well-being if she's under your arrest.'

I wanted to rub my dry lips with my hands. But my hands didn't seem to want to obey. Oh, well.

'How come it hasn't had any effect on you then, huh? I did put a drop in your mouth too.'

'You think I wouldn't be sensible about this in my line of work? I take anti-venom pills every day, just in case—'

'Avens!' I exclaimed, looking up. The dark sky was heavy with black shooting stars that seemed to be plummeting to earth and in our direction. 'Avens!'

'Miss Tantrist seems to be pointing to the ravens above.'

'What about them?'

'Well, I guess you should know. We saw three or four ravens three days ago at a sacrifice that she claimed was a disguised yatu—'

'BingofAvens!'

'Yes, yes, I am telling him. Well, this yatu told her that he and his group had been spying on the sacrifices, because his king told him to. If these are the same ravens, your boss could be in trouble as they seem to want the sacrifice to go through. I think that is what Miss Tantrist is trying—'

The black shooting stars fell all around us and on us, falling and crashing and biting and pinching and shouting, all crying. Loud and soft, cool and hot, high-pitched and rumbling cries. The meteors turned into snakes and bit at my flesh, little pecks at first and then great, gobbling bites.

'Eat, eat,' I whispered, my lips free but dry.

A long shadow of glistening black feathers stood before me, staring at me with large, amber eyes. He came stealthily, silently, but I felt him coming. He smoked near me, his soft feathery hair tickling my face as his sharp beak came close to my eye. *Craaawk!* A sharp searing pain shot through my ear. Then, like a luminous shadow, he melted, taking the black shooting stars back into the sky.

The sky rumbled, livid and dry, cracking and spitting red lightning everywhere. I closed my eyes and the lightning turned orange on the screen of my eyelids. The sky rumbled again and a powerful lightning bolt shot at me. It was a lousy shot, really. I moved, but it had already fallen somewhere behind me.

Drunkenly, I pulled myself up from the ground. My face was wet with blood and my clothes had been ripped to shreds, but my hands were now free. In the gloom, I saw two bodies lying on the ground. Shukra and Kanthak. Their faces were bloodied and bitten. I quickly bent over Shukra to check his pulse. It was weak, but there. I put a drop of the rakpiss from my snakebone locket into his mouth, doing the same for Kanthak. Enough to keep them alive.

I wasn't sure what the hell those ravens had bitten me with, but it had completely cleared the effects of amrita from my head, even if it left me weak. I had to find the strength to stand up and walk to the front of the shack. Yellow light from a patio lantern lit up the bare courtyard. There was no mist here, although the sky was still cloudy and rumbling ominously. A triangular yantra had been drawn in the middle of the flat ground, blazing in the darkness. At the centre of the yantra stood a man in a black dhoti over a naked girl, her face and womb covered with red kumkum that looked black in the yellow light. The moonblade glimmered in his hand, paperthin, lit like a neon light in the shape of a sharp C. I could almost feel its yearning, its craving for sacrifice and blood. He crouched and aimed for the girl's womb. I ran, faltered, fell and scrambled to my feet.

'No!' I screamed, taking out my boneblade.

'Thought you were dead,' said a rough whisper. It came from the shadows everywhere. I could feel the voice on my skin like someone was grinding thorns beneath it. The man stopped, his head snapping around in my direction, his eyes desperate.

'Help us! She's forcing me!' he cried.

In the glow from the moonblade, I saw fear etched on his face. He looked up and mutely pointed to something in the sky. *Swish.* Like the whisper of a breeze, fat vines rained down on me, binding my hands in a snap. They were not vines, but snakes, long, fat ones. I saw Nasty then. Bound by snakes as well, he was suspended spread-eagled in mid-air, over the centre of the triangle, hovering about five feet from the ground, above the man and his daughter. He was naked, his body motionless and grey, as if he was dead and decomposing. The bites on his body looked familiar. They reminded me of the bites I had seen on Prem's body. The bites I had seen on Lavanya's body. The bites I had felt in the prison. The bites that came from the nagin.

'You? How?' I exclaimed, struggling with the snake-vines. A couple of them looked up, their hoods flared, their ruby-red eyes staring into my face, stony and still.

'Not right now, darlings,' the nagin cooed to her snakes.

I still couldn't see her, although her voice whispered close to my ears. A vine of slithery, shiny snakes twisted together in front of me, dancing in a series of eights. Finally, the nagin stood in front of me, butt-naked and nauseatingly beautiful. I struggled, itching to grab her. The last time around, she had left me for dead. Had she followed me to figure out where her precious Key was?

She smiled at me and casually flicked her polished fingernails. Three snakes shot towards my face, their mouths wide open to take a bite. I fell over backwards as the slithery snake vines still held my ankles in a deathgrip. She put her right foot on my neck and pressed. 'You will have every inch of her.' In the light of the lantern, I saw the tattoo on her naked inner thigh – two intertwined roses. The crest of the House of Belles.

'You are … gah!'

'Hang on a sec,' she said. Her voice had changed now, from a rough whisper to a modulated husky tone. She turned to the tantrik. 'Go on, Anwar. Why did you stop? Don't you want Kolahal to come into this world? Don't you want him to create a new world for all of us? Don't you want to become immortal? To give everyone the fair chance they deserve? Just as we all had imagined.'

'Yeah right,' I spat from behind her, squirming to break loose from the reptilian ropes. 'Immortality for her, not you, Anwar. She's the one who will get powerful. You will just die like your other friends. And there's no coming back after you have become a corpse!'

'Shut up!' she screeched, her voice turning harsh again. Her snakes flared their hoods and hissed in unison. Then as if a lever had been switched in her body, she grinned, the smile spreading on her face like someone had physically stretched her luscious, red pout. 'You know I don't need any immortality, Anwar, don't you?' she crooned, doing a crawly pirouette around the triangle.

'But how will you do it? You haven't found the Key!' he exclaimed, struggling to hold the moonblade, which seemed to have developed a mind of its own.

'Oh, I did, I did!' she exclaimed. 'Didn't I tell you? I found the Key and a beautiful surprise for our true god! Our leader will be ecstatic when he sees that one. It's him, it's him! I got Indra himself! What an irony it will be. To sacrifice a false god for the true one. Won't Kolahal be pleased? To use the shadowblade, the last of the moonblades on the one who imprisoned him! It's perfect!' She giggled like a girl and stopped twirling. She softly moved her hand to a snake in her hand. 'Will you do it already or do you want to be the one forced to feed on your daughter's flesh? Even *that* Kolahal will enjoy. For, you know, that's the other option we had considered. Before I managed to get the moonblades.'

'No! I mean, yes,' he answered, 'I will do it. I will donate her blood to Kolahal's cause.'

I rolled over, the squishy bodies of the snakes rolling with me. The snakes that held me hissed angrily and bit my shoulders as a warning.

'No, don't!' I cried as he picked up the phone, which had started to ring, his hands shaking. 'Jai Kolahalnath!' he whispered into the phone. He listened for a few seconds, his eyes hardening. He placed the phone on the apex of the yantra carefully and came back towards the girl, his moonblade turned downwards, like a claw.

'*Aum Ain Hreem Shreem …*'

He held the moonblade above the child. It shimmered, a crescent moon on a grimy night. With a soft swish it sank deep into the girl's guts. Her scream rent the night.

'Noooo!' I shouted. Hundreds of tiny wormlike snakes flared their hoods on my body, ready with deadly poison if the mistress gave them a signal. They tightened their python-like embrace. I gasped for breath. My locket jumped up and hit me hard on the forehead.

'*… Kolahaley Namaha.*'

I bit the locket vial open. Rakta trickled into my mouth. Twisting my fingers into a mudra, I screamed the Agni mantra:

'*Jal bhun bhasm ho ja!*'

Snakes flew in all directions as I blew them up like a suicide bomber.

'YOU BITCH!' screeched the nagin, coming at me like a dissolving nest of vipers. 'I will eat you alive!'

I grabbed the spray can of chudail antidote from my satchel, glad I had taken the time to brew it. Spritzing with the spray can in one hand, and wielding the boneblade in the other, I screamed the Visphota mantra.

'*Ghoom aa phata jaa! … Aum Ain Hreem Shreem …*'

Her body inflated and exploded as her insane screech

filled the air. Snakes flew in all directions, hissing angrily. A dark, smoky form floated upwards. It seemed to grin in the black night. *It's not over*, it whispered, *I will come back for you*. The form vanished into the dark night as the snakes melted away, leaving me free and crawling on all fours.

Freed from the snake vines, Nasty's heavy body fell on top of Anwar with a resounding thump. Anwar screamed for help. But the damage was done. The girl thrashed, blood gushing out of her, like a fountain of black water. The sky lit up with shimmering lightning, vertically above the yantra, forming a pale, translucent film around it. I lurched towards the triangle, willing my feet to move faster. The earth shook as the power of Kolahal infiltrated the world. The final section of power to complete him. The sixth mistress.

'Anantya, nooooooo!' someone cried from behind me. I didn't stop. There was only one thought in my mind. To save the girl. To not let this happen, ever again. Even though I could be too late.

'*Kha jalaa, sokhna, nimagna!*' I shouted, pressing my treta ring to a bleeding bite-wound on my shoulder. The earth rumbled and the pyramid started to solidify as I leaped into the triangle. The walls were crystallizing. The darkness suffocated me. My body shrank, its fluids being siphoned out. A whirling charge rotated within the enclosure, round and round, faster and faster, in anticipation, in excited circles. I saw the girl, lying dead. I saw Nasty, groaning. I grabbed his hand. His body felt strangely light, like it was the shadow of his body. I could feel the sixth mistress, its power and excitement pulsating with desire as it fed on the blood of the girl. The phone on the apex of the triangle blinked, a small biscuit of light as the mistress was summoned to it. *I grow stronger. Just one more night and I will be alive again. The seeds of anarchy and pandemonium, my sisters, my wives! Our wait is over!* It is kind of ironic, isn't it, to solve a case and then die just before telling anyone what really happened?

'Is my lord dead?'

'Who cares if your oaf of a lord is dead or not? I saw Miss Tantrist jump into the tetrahedron! If something happens to her, I will donate your nitwit brain to psychological research.'

'What's this pyramid?'

'It's a tetrahedron,' Shukra answered automatically. 'A sheet of electricity formed by static directed from the sky.' Then, after a pause, 'Not that it matters.'

Shukra! Through the pain, I smiled. I struggled into a sitting position on the rubble as the pyramid in front of me collapsed like a pack of cards. Shukra had just broken the yantra.

'Who's there?' cried Shukra as I tried to stand up. 'I have asuric weapons!'

'And when do you,' I whispered, my voice hoarse, 'plan to use them?'

'Miss Anantya!' Shukra came running towards me. 'How are you still alive?'

'Bad … habit.'

He hopped out of the triangular yantra, touched my arm and recoiled. 'You are electrified! Marvellous. How did you survive it?'

'Tantrik magic,' I replied mysteriously, getting up and dusting my body. I could have told him the truth. I could have told him that I had jumped out of the triangle just in time, micro-moments before it closed completely. That I had used the Nimagna mantra to deflect a part of the danava to my ring to protect myself. I had been lucky, I guess, but I was bitten, bleeding, bone-tired and hurting everywhere. I could do with a laugh.

'Not possible! You're lying,' he exclaimed, taking the bait. 'I will figure it out, Miss Tantrist, one way or another.' He pushed those steel-rimmed spectacles up his thin nose.

I smiled tiredly and stood up, managing to reach the steps of the shack before I collapsed again. With shaky hands, I took my locket, now almost empty, and drank a mouthful of rakpiss. Someone groaned behind us.

'Kanthak,' I said, 'I was able to save one out of the three. The wrong one. And the dangar may need a few drops of this.' I had a few more drops of rakpiss. Kanthak grabbed the bottle and hurried to Nasty. 'Just a few drops, mind you. I don't want to waste precious piss on my shitty half-brother.'

Shukra hesitated, standing in front of me, wringing his long, bony hands. 'Saving Swami Narahara was a good thing to do, Miss Tantrist.'

'Call me Anantya, will you? I wasn't trying to save him. I wanted to save her. I—' A lump formed in my throat. Too many people had died because I had failed to get there on time. Too many.

'It's not your fault, Miss ... Anantya. You tried. You even jumped into a pool of electricity to save people, though that was foolish of you. But Narahara. You hated him. To save someone you hate is good.' He went to where Nasty lay, with a slobbering Kanthak tending to him.

Nasty. Who would have thought that I would save my half-brother from dying tonight? Two hours ago, all I could think of was finding him guilty and killing him. I giggled, getting hysterical. Imagine. He thought I had been guilty of killing Riju, and I thought it was him. All the while someone had been working those sacrifices smoothly, killing the little girls. I felt like a complete idiot. The possible answer had changed but the questions hadn't. Who had killed Riju Das? Who from the Kaula Ashram was running this? Who was the leader? Was it like Nasty had been saying all along, that someone from the Vama clan was trying to destroy the Kaula reputation? Mattreya? Was he the one behind it?

Who was the nagin working with? Now that was a bolt from the blue. Two cases, both connected. Hah. I should have paid more attention to Qubera's ramblings on the night that he kidnapped Nikhil. He had mentioned something about the Key opening up the sky and unleashing a bad guy named Vritra. Vritra, the God of Chaos. Kolahal, the God of Chaos. It was the same god, the same bloody danava just different bloody names. I hate demons and all their fancy aliases. It's just so irritating! Why does everyone need to have ten different names for the same demon? Stupid. And I had slipped up, not made the connection.

No wonder the nagin had been desperate for the Key. They could bring in all the six mistresses, all six of Kolahal's powers into the world, but the final sacrifice would be unsuccessful if the leader's body died when the demon came into it. She had needed Indra's Key before the seventh sacrifice. And if she was telling that dead man the truth, the Key was with her. *I found the Key and a beautiful surprise for our true god!* Nagin's ecstatic, mad voice rang in my ears. Indra. What could be a better tribute? Kolahal would love to feed on his arch-enemy as he entered the world.

I needed to find the nagin. The nagin who had killed

Lavanya and Prem. The nagin who had been the perfume factory in a tube dress in Vajrin Mahendra's party. The beautiful nagin who had made everyone's heart beat with desire. The brave nagin who had volunteered to let the vampire drink blood from her body. The mad nagin who had attacked me and killed many others for the cult. The nagin who was also an apsara's daughter.

Mohini Devi. No wonder the anti-maya charms in Tazaak's prisons were too feeble to stop her. She had the blood of a powerful naga *and* a fucking apsara. She was Rambha's daughter. She could become any creature she chose to, a true shape-shifter. And she could shoot little baby snakes like arrows from her body. To top it all, she was a psychopath, hell-bent on bringing in a vengeful demon into the world. Bones of an ass. How do you kill such a creature?

I laughed and lit up a beedi, puffing long and hard on it. I had about twenty hours before the last ritual began. Twenty hours to find her, hopefully kill her and secure the Key.

Twenty hours. I slapped my face to wake myself up. There was no time to rest. No time to agonize over how I had failed a young girl whose body lay in the yantra in front of me, butchered by a bloodthirsty moonblade. Ignoring the weariness that was creeping into my bones, I got up and shouldered my satchel.

'I have to go,' I told Shukra. His face was still covered with pockmarks where the ravens had pecked him, but he looked all right otherwise. 'You go home.'

'Where are you going?'

'To meet Rambha.'

'Rambha? Do you still suspect her?'

'No. Now I am sure.' I stopped and hesitated. Then I took a deep breath and started to walk. 'Well, you take care,' I said casually.

'Oh no,' he answered, quickly catching up with me. I could hear his now-torn baggy trousers flapping on his thin legs. 'You are not going anywhere. Not without me.'

'No drinking today,' I warned Shukra, boneblade in my left hand and a mandala in my right. We inched together towards Rambha Devi's dilapidated bungalow. It was an hour past daybreak, not that you could tell by the grey sky. The air felt dry, so dry that I had to lick my lips every few seconds. Even walking generated sparks.

'Come on, Anantya, I don't—' answered Shukra, holding the boneblade that I had given him like he was preparing to dice a tomato.

'You should have stayed home,' I whispered furiously for the umpteenth time. It was one thing to help me out in the case – and for that I was thankful – but Shukra was obviously a complete dodo when it came to physical combat. But he was adamant. He wanted to be part of this. He still believed that the demon was nothing but electric current, Devi help him. He wanted to stay with me so he could prove it.

It ought to have been Justice Kanthak doing this, arresting Rambha and finding out where her crazy daughter was. He was part of the bloody Tazaak. He was responsible for the unruly, murderous sups at large in the city. But he had quietly slunk off into the night, taking Nasty with him. His excuse? *Swami Narahara is wounded and needs to heal*. Idiot.

'Stay behind me,' I warned Shukra again. I had already scanned the place with my septifocals to make sure there were no spirits or other invisible creatures around. All around us was clear, which didn't really mean anything. When we had stopped over at my house to quickly replenish my satchel, I had added an extra dose of chudail venom for the daughter. But if I had to fight Rambha, I didn't know what would work. The apsara herself was strong enough to grind us into a chutney if she wanted to. And I had no clue how to deal with an eternal of her stature. All my teacher Dhuma had ever taught me was to stay away from eternals. Good advice that. Even destroying a daeva was simpler than doing in an apsara. You throttle the human the daeva was in and kick the spirit back to Amravati, the spirit plane. It would still be alive, after all it was an eternal, but it wouldn't trouble anyone on earth. But an apsara was tricky. An apsara didn't need a human body to stay on earth. Travel between the spirit world and the human one was as easy for apsaras as taking the metro to Jangpura from Khan Market. Hopefully, I wouldn't need to physically fight her.

Instead of ringing the bell, I lit up my beedi, using the lit matchstick for a mantra.

'*Jal bhun bhasm ho ja!*'

The door was blasted into pieces as the firebomb hit it. Behind the rubble stood the two girls who had answered the door on our previous visit. They were surprised in the act of handling two suitcases as big as themselves.

'What's the meaning of this?' cried Rambha, striding towards us with a cigarette in one hand, her translucent floral print gown billowing behind her, an enticing yellow bra showing through. 'Leave or I will call the police.'

This was no time for small talk. I pointed my boneblade in her direction and shouted the Jivah mantra:

'*Sachcha Jhootha Jivah Dikha!*'

She stopped mid-puff, her eyes widening slightly. For a second nothing happened. And then she sort of vaporized.

Her body disintegrated into grains of light, millions of diamonds, to make a mosaic of a woman. The glow lit up the red-walled corridor. I shielded my eyes with my hand. This is what humans knew as divine light, these mad, crazily lit creatures. Even in her divine avatar, she looked cross. But at least it was definitely her.

'What is the meaning of this?' The words sounded like an echo of whispers all around us. *'Meaning of this?'*

I saw the kung fu duo quivering behind her. My bet was they hadn't ever seen this avatar of their mistress. A huge grin broke through my cracked lips.

'Just wanted to be sure you are not your crazy-ass bitch daughter.'

The dim corridor had just one soft light reflecting off the red walls and her diamante body. She stared, her eyes cold diamonds of light. Perhaps I had overstepped my limits this time and she would blast the puny humans that we were into smithereens. But then she nodded and turned back into skin and curves and beautiful breasts. Rambha Devi's long lashes fluttered and came down on her cheeks.

'I understand,' she said softly.

'Where is she?'

'Mohini?' she asked, although she knew damn well who I meant. She took a long drag from her cigarette. 'How would I know? She's an adult now and doesn't tell me where she goes.'

'And does she tell you who she kills? Or do you figure that out yourself?'

'Are you implying that my daughter has killed someone?' Her voice became whispers again, as her body started to shine like millions of diamonds under the floral gown.

Shukra put a tentative hand on my shoulder as if to warn

me. 'Anantya ...' But he hadn't seen Prem, his wings pierced and in shreds, nailed to the rock. He hadn't seen Lavanya. He hadn't seen the naga bitch.

'I don't imply, Miss Rambha. I know. And if you want to keep your dear Indra in this world, I suggest you tell us where she is.'

'He's safe!' she exclaimed. 'Nothing will harm him. I spoke to him last night.'

I could smell the sweat of fear and unease on her.

'You made bloody sure he would be killed when you gave her the moonblades.'

'I didn't. She ... she stole them,' she whispered, resuming her human form. She tapped her cigarette with a manicured finger and said, 'She ... I just wanted to keep her safe.'

'You mean by letting the raving, murdering bitch roam free?'

'No. No! You don't understand. I didn't even ... maybe ...' She licked her lips and looked behind us and then said, 'Would you like to come in and have a drink? I ... I ... my lips are really dry.'

I hesitated, wondering if it was a trap, but then I needed to find out where Mohini was. And Rambha could tell me. She poured herself a large peg of whisky in the living room, and offered us some. Shukra vigorously shook his head this time.

'I ... I have saved your world,' she said, downing the whole glass in one greedy gulp. 'She cannot bring in the monster without the Key.'

'She has the Key, you drunken dolt!' I exclaimed. We were in the same living room as the last time, except for one change. All the furniture was now covered in cellophane. It looked like Rambha had packed her bags for a long vacation. 'She told me so herself when her snake buddies were trying to eat my eyes.'

'No. No. She doesn't. She cannot. He said it's back, back where it belonged.'

I remembered the same words from someone else's lips. Grrhat. It is back where it belonged, Qubera had told him.

'Back with my lord,' Rambha added.

Back with her lord. Back with Indra. 'You just signed your lord's death warrant,' I said, but she wasn't listening.

'She cannot. Simply cannot.' She shook her head and her silken mane danced around her shoulders. 'She's difficult, but she's good. She will not harm my lord. She is just … headstrong. It's the naga blood in her. It whispers to her. Her father …' She looked at me then, but her eyes were far away. 'He was a successor of King Kaliya. Naga seed. Strong enough to give me a baby. *Me*. It was such a surprise to become pregnant with her, those few decades ago. Most unexpected. I hadn't had an offspring since the old war. She is so powerful. More potent than apsara or naga. I dreamt of making her the head apsara for Indra. But she … she is just different. We are apsaras, it's in our blood to excel at dancing, singing and seducing, and all the arts that please daevas. But … but she kept questioning, "Why do apsaras need to serve daevas? Why can't they rule? Why must Indra rule them all?" She was just a child. I thought she would get over it. When she was involved in an accident where some neechs in Mumbai were killed, we … we moved to Delhi. Then I got a chance. A year ago, the Kaulas brought in my lord Indra successfully in a human body. He was here on earth. So I put her into his service, thinking she would grow to love my great lord.'

'You mean you offered her to whore for Vajrin Mahendra.'

It all made sense. Mohini was serving Indra. Mohini was working as a secretary to the powerful businessman, Vajrin Mahendra. Vajrin Mahendra had a debt to pay to the Kaula clan because they had brought him into this world. Hadn't Nasty said as much? Which meant Vajrin Mahendra was Indra. No wonder Nasty could browbeat him like that at his own party. Vajrin Mahendra had probably invited Mattreya to his party deliberately. To piss Nasty off – and he had certainly been successful there. Yes, Vajrin Mahendra with his silken soft curls, chiselled face and perfect body. Indra would not come into anything less than a perfect human body. That would answer a lot of things.

'Whore? As a partner! A lover! To be loved by a daeva is the highest, purest form of being for an apsara.'

'I … see,' I answered. No wonder Mohini had hated her life enough to want to kill half the world with it. Apsaras. Amazingly idiotic creatures! Wanting to serve. Bah!

'For a while I thought she had grown to love him as I did. But … but it was all a lie. A month ago,' she looked at me, her eyes full of sadness, 'I found that the moonblades were missing from my locker. I knew she had taken them. You see, I had told her about their powers when she had come of age. I had one of my maids follow her and discovered that she was having sex with a puny little tantrik she had met in Lord Mahendra's home. My maid traced them to a slaughterhouse in Masihgarh where they met almost every day. It was then that I found out about their little group of tantriks. About a dozen of them, all filthy, all greedy, all ugly neechs. Cult of Chaos they called themselves, worshipping and sacrificing to this old danava, someone that my lord had unseated millions of yugas ago. Someone who still wanted to avenge himself on Indra.'

'Vritra. Or Kolahal,' I answered for her.

She nodded. 'The same. All of them were burning with a desire to bring him in. Other than the moonblades for the ritual, they needed a way to strengthen their own leader, this tantrik my daughter was sleeping with. I had told Mohini about Indra's Key. The Key that protects the wearer and transfers the powers of Vritra to whoever opens it. It's an old legend in our community.'

'But unlike others who thought it was just a legend, she knew it was true. And she knew where to find it too,' I finished for her. 'Qubera. Once you found out about this little plot of hers, you planned with him to take Indra's Key of Light out of his vaults.'

She paused, lit up another thin, brown cigarillo and took a long drag, as the kung fu twins quickly replenished her glass. 'Yes. I had no choice. She's my flesh and blood. If she found the Key and brought in Lord Indra's enemy with her stupid cult, it would ruin her. My lord is not very forgiving to those who worship another. Especially an enemy of his.'

'So you let her go ahead with the plan—'

'But made sure she would fail,' Rambha finished for me, elegantly tapping her cigarillo.

'We hired Lavanya Mohan and asked her to take the Key out of the vaults and keep it safe from my daughter.'

'Except your plan went horribly wrong, didn't it? Mohini found out about Lavanya.'

'Yes.' She sighed and took another gulp of the whisky. 'Mohini's smart. She changed into me and coaxed out Lavanya's name from Qubera. And she killed Lavanya before I could find out where the Key was now hidden.'

'And Qubera had already hired me too,' I said, tapping my boneblade on my lower lip, 'because he didn't trust you completely. He wanted to be sure that Lavanya didn't meet your daughter.'

'It was a mistake. Hiring you. I told him I would talk to her.'

'But you didn't, Rambha. You let her kill Lavanya Mohan and then my friend, Prem,' I said softly, feeling the slow burn of anger in the pit of my stomach.

'That dasyu slave of yours? He saw me when I went to Lavanya's apartment to look for the Key. I tried to warn him, but he was stupid. Mohini found out about him soon.'

'And you let your lunatic daughter kill him.' I stood up, shaking. Prem's torn body flashed before my eyes, his beautiful wings in shreds. Rambha shrugged.

'I tried to save him. The dasyu was so smitten by me, poor little thing, but I couldn't.'

'HE WAS MY FRIEND!' I shouted, lunging at her.

Shukra grabbed my waist. I took a deep breath and stopped. Rambha remained seated, looking at me with calm, cool eyes.

'Tell me something, Rambha the apsara, if you love your Lord Indra as much as you say you do, why didn't you tell him about your daughter's real motives? As his liege, isn't that your duty?'

'I spoke to him only yesterday and warned him that there were people trying to harm him.'

'Did you happen to warn him that these people are your daughter? The woman who is in his bed every night?'

'There is no need to tell him that. She is harmless. Just a bit misguided. It's that neech lover of hers, that cult leader, who has filled her head with these silly ideas.'

'Misguided? She's a raving lunatic, you imbecile! Your daughter is planning to kill your king. Tonight. Sacrifice him to her god, Vritra. Sacrifice your useless king and half this city with him.'

She languidly blew smoke from her cigarillo, her lips forming a small red O, and rose, straightening her floral gown. 'He will be safe enough. He's an eternal.' She combed her fingers through her luxuriant hair. 'Even if the ritual is successful tonight, and Vritra comes, all he can do is send Lord Indra back into the spirit plane, back to Amravati. Vritra will consume the neech vessel he possesses within a week and then it will be complete chaos for a while here. I will bring Indra back to Earth from Amravati. My lord will restore the balance and send Vritra off to Patala again. He will be the new god again. The god who saved everyone.'

'And you will ask him to pardon your daughter in return? For what's a few million human and sup lives in exchange for being your dear king's favourite apsara? We are mere rats to you, aren't we?' I said it softly, ignoring the anger that burnt in my belly.

'Yes, a few neechs will get destroyed, but what of that? They breed like flies anyway,' she answered with a dismissive flick of her manicured hand. 'A small disaster like this will not drive them to extinction. My daughter will realize that it's futile, leave that filthy neech lover of hers and drop the cult like it's cursed. And she will come back to me.'

'No, Rambha. You are wrong there. She won't come back to you.' I replaced my boneblade in its scabbard and moved to stand in front of her, arms akimbo. 'You see, I intend to kill her.'

Rambha laughed, a husky sound that warmed the cold nights. 'Don't be silly. You may be good at this tantrik thing, but she's too powerful for you. You will just end up dead instead.'

'Oh, don't worry about me.' I smiled sweetly, my eyes glittering. 'You pack your bags and run like the chicken you are. I will find a way. I will find a way to send her back to Naraka with her lover and that demon god of hers.'

२२

There are days when I wish I knew a mantra that would make Chhotu's ancient engine go a little faster or that I had the siddhi to teleport myself to another place, or better still, to fly. Unfortunately, siddhis dropped out of tantrik knowledge and tantriks are yet to develop mantras that work with bikes, however ancient the bike may happen to be. And that is why, even as the world was threatening to end around me, Chhotu chugged along at thirty kilometres an hour, laden with me, Shukra and his long legs.

'Vajrin Mahendra is Indra?' Shukra shouted right into my ear, his broad hands clutching my waist in slight panic.

'Yeah. He looks arrogant enough.' I wiped the sweat off my face. The heat was sweltering. Weirdly enough, although static dryness had increased, my skin felt clammy with a layer of oily dirt.

'I thought Narahara was just being creative when he spoke about bringing in a daeva. How is it even possible?' he asked, shouting out the last question into my ear, even though we had stopped now.

The city had awoken as usual today. Rush-hour traffic crawled on the road from Gurgaon to Delhi. A long line of cars stood ahead of us. Ironic. Even on a mission to save the city, one has to first contend with traffic jams. I smiled at the thought that even Vritra would be stuck in traffic in his human body.

'Impossible is what you haven't learnt to do yet,' I answered wisely. As the traffic started to move, a car zipped past us, honking impatiently. I had to swerve hard and screamed a mouthful at the driver.

'Perhaps Vritra will be doing us a huge favour by destroying humankind,' I muttered under my breath. I didn't know why I was so hell-bent on saving Delhi's ass anyway. Humans and Delhi were both weird and irritating. Maybe I should follow Rambha's example and take a holiday in the Himalayas, sit with aghoris and smoke chillum.

'I always believed that daevas were nothing but manifestations of human fear,' Shukra screamed from behind me. 'Like fear of lightning becomes Indra. Fear of water becomes Varuna.'

'Yeah right, and Qubera is the fear of going bankrupt? You are weird,' I told him as I parked the bike, a little away from Masihgarh cemetery. It had taken us more than an hour to reach the spot where, if Rambha was right, the cult had been meeting regularly.

'You stay here and guard Chhotu.'

'No way, I am coming too,' he answered, pushing his glasses up his nose. His face was dirty as was his hair, which stood straight up on his head, making him seem even taller.

'Do you have any weapon-like thing other than your confusing logic? You hold a boneblade like you are cutting your birthday cake.'

'I don't like the knife, but you do need someone to record what you do inside,' he replied, pointing to the three cameras on his body, one hidden in the lapel of his once-white shirt, now brown with blood and mud, one on his chest and the last on his waist, hidden in his suspenders. I shrugged. It was almost eleven in the morning and I was too tired to argue. Better get this over with.

'Your skin, your decision.' I slung my satchel and did a quick check of my yugma locket, treta rings, the septifocals on my head and the boneblade at my waist. Sweltering, dry heat made my blouse cling to my body. My lips felt raw and dry. I was ready. As ready as I could be.

Amrit Kasai's warehouse was not too hard to find, a mere hundred metres from where we had parked. Like a gandha, we followed the oily, sweet smell of stinking, rotten meat. The lane where it stood lay empty and quiet, except for the buzz of flies. The place itself was more of a shop than a warehouse. A small signboard hung over a wooden door, swollen with age, dangling by a single rusted hook: *Amrit Kasai Since 1921*. The walls were oily and caked with years of soot and abuse. Flies covered the wooden door like glittering black sand. I pulled the septifocals over my eyes to survey the seven planes, just to check that the flies were really what they seemed to be. There were no sups or spirits there. Neither were there any humans. Nothing but flies.

The door squealed on rusted hinges as I pushed it open. The flies flew at my touch, starting to buzz around my face and hair. I glanced back at Shukra questioningly. If he didn't want to come in, I would understand. His thin frame shook slightly, a disgusted look on his sweat-streaked face. I could have sworn I heard his heart thump loudly. But he nodded. Neither of us spoke. We entered as quietly as we could, the insistent buzz of flies sounding unbearably loud.

It was dark, damp, hot and rotten inside. Before my eyes adjusted to the darkness, I could smell the rotting flesh. The floor was cemented and sticky. I took a step and stopped. There was nothing there. Nothing alive. But the place still strummed. A constant, alive panting. Like a dog slobbering on a hot summer day. The shakti vibration hit me inside my ribcage, making my heart thump harder, blood pounded in my head. A powerful presence, but not a living presence. Not good. Oh, so not good.

I heard a metallic click and a small, white beam of light shone behind me. Shukra had just switched on a torch, and held a handkerchief to his nose. In its light, we saw the blood on the floor, sticky black in the white light. It was still fresh. Flies buzzed around. Shukra directed the beam to the source of the congealing red river. A huge black bison's glazed eyes shone in the light, its horns curved and pointed. The blood on its throat – slashed and half open – had already dried up. Its forehead had a streak of red vermillion. *Sacrifice*. A bloodied cleaver lay to one side on a block of wood. The corpse was already rotting. But it couldn't have been more than a couple of hours since the beast had been killed. I readied my boneblade and inched ahead cautiously. The butcher's shop didn't look like it had been used much recently. Blocks of flat wood lay on either side of us, still greasy from decades of meat-chopping. Meat hooks hung from the ceiling. Weirdly, only the heads of cows, goats and pigs hung from the hooks, their eyes dead and vacant. The heads looked like they had been deliberately preserved, because the rot hadn't yet set in, although the flies didn't spare them either. Their eyes seemed to follow us as we crept forward.

'Be careful,' I muttered, though of what and why, I wasn't sure. Something here was alive. With my septifocals over my eyes, I glanced around again, checking the periphery often, muttering the Drishti mantra. Nothing. Nothing that was a spirit or a sup. Despite the septifocal goggles, I felt blind. At the far end of the room, we reached a small door. As I turned the handle, a bolt of shakti surged through it, almost like electricity, sending a frisson through my hand. I heard a loud clank behind me. Shukra stood frozen. His torch had fallen to the floor and was sending disco streaks of white light around the dark room as it rolled away.

'What?'

For once, Shukra was speechless. He mutely raised his hand and pointed towards the door through which we had entered. The bison stood there, its eyes black and blank, its broken neck dangling. Entrails hung from its fat stomach, long tubes and a blob of rotten flesh. Its nostrils flared but no breath came out of them. The corpse bison slammed its front hoofs on the floor and charged, its glistening, sharp horns curved like twin cleavers, heading straight at us.

'Run!' I screamed, pushing Shukra's frozen body to one side as I flung myself to the other. The bison's huge horns sliced the air between us, hitting the wall behind me with a thundering thunk. I rolled and got to my feet on its right. The bison backed up a few inches, not even dazed by the collision and immediately turned to come after me. As I ran towards the door, I could hear its hooves thudding angrily behind me.

'It's dead!' Shukra screamed.

'Don't think it knows that,' I yelled back.

Just then, I slipped, and the dead beast's horn slashed my arm, ripping through cloth and flesh. I let myself fall and roll over as the pain seared through my bicep. I continued to roll in the sticky congealed liquid on the floor that was the bison's blood. I took a fistful of its blood and touched it to my boneblade. The bison swung its head from side to side. A cloud of flies emerged from its neck and face. It pawed the floor before charging at me again.

'*Ghani bhavati!*' I cried.

The blood on the floor froze, making the bison skid and slip before finally falling on its side with a loud thwack.

'Shukra! The cleaver!'

Shukra picked up the cleaver and flung it, swinging it in a full circle before letting go. It flew through the air, and sank into the gaping wound in the dead bison's belly. With the momentum of the cleaver, Shukra lost his footing on the frozen blood and shot straight into the bison's intestines, which were frozen as well. *Thwonk*! The bison's stomach heaved. I hurriedly shook Shukra who seemed disoriented after ramming his head on the frozen, rotten beef.

'... thank you for the Nobel prize,' he muttered. I unscrewed the rakpiss vial in my yugma locket and put a drop into his mouth.

'Get up,' I said urgently, 'it won't stay down for long.' Already, the bison quivered, its blank eyes staring up at us. 'Now!'

As Shukra lurched to his feet, I pulled his arm around my shoulders, yelping as he brushed against the open wound on my arm. Gritting my teeth, I led him towards the rear door. The handle had been charmed against any intruders, which was why the zombie bison had risen as soon as I touched it. The carcass got to its feet again, already unfreezing from my spell, its head swinging from side to side.

'Hurry!' I cried, half dragging Shukra who was still concussed. He was too tall for me to support, and heavy, I knew I couldn't hold him up for much longer.

I could hear the bison's pounding hooves behind us, but didn't look back. The bison was just a whisper away when Shukra tottered, and I lost my balance. We had reached the doorway that had activated the zombie bison, and I shoved Shukra through it as I fell. I twisted in time to see the bison's horns gleaming dully in the dim light. The door behind me swung shut and I fell with my back against it, facing the bison. I levered myself with as much thrust as I could manage and vaulted upwards and backwards through the door. The bison's horns came within an inch of my leg as my feet flew. Crash! The bison's horn tore the plaster off the wall by the door as I dropped down into darkness and onto something bony.

'Oof!' Shukra groaned. I scrambled to my feet, boneblade still in my hand. Thankfully, the drop hadn't been too far. Just three or four steps down.

'You smell!' Shukra cried, putting his hand over his nose. He was right. The place stank, like a pond of puke and dead flesh.

'Balls of bull,' I whispered. Grey light filtered through a small vent in the high ceiling into what appeared to be a storeroom.

Etched into the door at the opposite end were three snake heads. Their six eyes stared at us malevolently, glittering red like rubies. I took out some sifter powder from my bag and blew it on the door. This time, I wanted to be more careful about curses on doors. The white powder remained unchanged, falling like snow on the floor. I pulled Shukra upright and pushed open the door.

We were in an empty chamber, with medieval fire torches on either side that lit up a wetly glistening stone sculpture at the far end. The chamber itself was only about fifty feet in length, but with a very high ceiling. The sculpture, a monolith of the three-headed cobra, rose to the ceiling, its hoods spread across the chamber. Its black body gleamed in the flickering light, and twisted along the walls with the end of its four-foot-wide tail curving into the centre of the chamber. The statue was a beautifully executed work of art, exactly matching the tattoo I had seen on the first man who had sacrificed his daughter. The symbol of the Cult of Chaos. The sign of Vritra or Kolahal, the God of Chaos.

The entire ambience was that of an underground tantrik temple, a mysterious cavern with dampness clinging to it like a wet undergarment. Except for the mound of flesh piled in the middle of the floor. The chamber reeked of rotten flesh, blood, stale food and death. The offal in the middle lay exactly where the statue's tail ended, in a fire pit. Liver, trotter, heart, kidney, lungs, testicles, tongue, intestines and other organs lay in a mouldering heap in the pit. Animal organs, offerings for the God of Chaos. But that wasn't what made me catch my breath. Next to the stinking pile of meat lay a body, a human body on a clean, white sheet. A human male body. Riju Das's body.

'Isn't that—' whispered Shukra.

'Riju,' I whispered back. For some reason, even though we were alone, we whispered. Our whispers echoed sibilantly around the chamber.

'But why did someone bring his body here?'

'Do you remember the bull corpse that said hello to us outside?' I asked. Shukra shuddered. Even in death, Riju had a soft smile on his face. 'We have to take him out, Shukra,' I said. I didn't want my friend's body to be used by a power-crazy tantrik and his nagin girlfriend. 'Help me,' I said, gesturing to Shukra to grab hold of the poor man's feet, while I got ready to lift Riju's shoulders.

'Anantya, wait!'

I was so blinded by my need to save Riju's dead body from being misused that the only thing that struck me as being out of place was the ugly ring on his index finger. A monster-sized thing in the shape of an intricate net, inlaid with huge diamonds. I didn't, for example, notice that his body wasn't stone-cold as any corpse ought to be (and mind you, I have seen many corpses). I didn't notice that his body wasn't decomposing, which is what it should have been doing, considering his death had occurred three days ago. But I did see the sparkling ring. The same monstrous ring that Lavanya Mohan had given to Jugnu before she had died. I frowned.

Riju Das opened his eyes. 'Hello, Anu,' he said, smiling his warm, rabbity smile. 'I was wondering when you would show up.' The realization hit the pit of my stomach, strong, aching and powerful.

'You! You are—'

'My lover and the leader of our cult,' a husky voice said from behind us.

Mohini sauntered into the room, flawlessly beautiful. She stretched out her palm and I heard a slithering sigh. Black snakes bound my arms and torso. My boneblade fell to the floor with a loud clatter. The snakes raised their heads in front of my face, their hoods flared, their long, black tongues flickering. Behind me, I heard Shukra struggling, as someone attacked him. I heard a thud and a groan. Shukra had fallen.

'Today you will get to bite her,' Mohini cooed. 'I promise.'

The snakes opened their jaws wide, their long fangs moist with poison. That was the last thing I remember seeing before they lunged at my face. Everything went white and then turned red. I felt warm tears on my cheek. Why was I crying, I wondered before I realized that they weren't tears. Blood was pouring from my eyes.

My eyes screamed in pain. Something cold was poured into each of them, but the burning didn't stop. I blinked furiously. Blood and tears oozed out. If only I could rub them a little. Someone forced them open. 'It's done, chief. Her eyes are open.'

Blurry red shapes formed. One turned into Riju Das, surrounded by stars and spots. Ugh. My lower back was against something round and moist. The rest of my bed felt like a pile of bones. My hands were stretched behind my back and secured with thin ropes. Mayan ropes. And I was naked. Unharmed, but very much naked. I scowled and squirmed to free myself. A groan came from under me.

'Hurts,' it cried. Shukra? Shukra! He was my 'bed'. The soft thing I felt on his bony body must be his buttocks. Great.

'You're good?' I whispered.

He groaned something I couldn't quite catch, but at least he was still breathing. Riju Das stood over me, gazing down at me. His cheekbones stood out sharply in his face, as did his ribcage above his concave stomach. His hair had turned snow-white, and there were saggy pouches under his eyes. He had lost a lot of weight since I last saw him. Perhaps being dead for a while did that to you. His chest and shoulders were covered with bruises, blue and black and dark red, like someone had pushed him down a long flight of stairs. He wore a crisp black dhoti and around his neck hung a locket with two vials intertwined in the shape of a snake. The yugma locket that my mother had given me.

'Anantya, you must forgive my darling Mohini,' he said, casually waving his left hand at me with Jugnu's enormous ring on the index finger. The other hand was clasped around Mohini's narrow waist, brushing her right breast. He moved his hand to squeeze her breast and looked up at her. 'She's over-enthusiastic with her poisons.'

Mohini gave Riju a slobbery smile, something akin to love in her beautiful liquid eyes. He rose on tiptoes and kissed her bow-shaped lips with a loud smacking sound. She's so much taller than him, I thought, wondering why they hell I should notice such things when I was about to die.

'Get a room, you two,' I mumbled.

There was an angry hiss as Mohini turned to me, her smooth skin growing scaly. Snakes shot out from her, threateningly swiping at me. Shukra cried out in pain or terror, I wasn't sure which. I turned my body a little so that we were almost sideways, though I was still on top of him.

'Don't waste your precious soma, my darling,' said Riju, rubbing her breast in a hypnotic up and down motion. 'We will need it in the new world!' Another slobbering session happened. This time, I wished that they had poisoned me first so that I didn't have to see it. The three-headed cobra stood behind them, six disapproving eyes glaring from his massive height. The danava looked like he had a leery smile on his face. Two guards stood at the entrance through which we had entered. I could just about see their beefy muscles from the corner of my eye. The only way to escape. *Jaadugar tu jaadugar…*

'Umm, mind if I take that call?' I asked politely.

Riju chuckled softly. Mohini scowled.

'You have always been funny, Anantya.' He reached for my satchel, which lay in the far corner of the chamber. Too bloody far from my reach. It wasn't the lack of clothes that made me feel naked. It was the lack of my boneblade, my mother's locket and the septifocals. Riju brought my phone towards me, still ringing.

'Oh, we have to hear this. Your naga friend, I think.' He put my phone on loudspeaker.

'Anantyass?' Zee's voice echoed in the chamber. 'I found the poisonsss, the one that Riju partakesss. It isn't poison to die. Is a rare poison. From the fangs of a blueblooded nagin. It stuns, not killsss. It stopsss the heartbeat for a day and a night before the body becomessss alive. Your friend might be alive and—'

'I think Anantya already knows that I am alive … Zee, isn't it?' said Riju, cutting him off. He threw the phone in the darkness behind him where it broke with a dull clatter. 'And she is smart enough to have figured out how I remained alive. Now, where were we?'

'You were about to tell me how you took to the Black and started to sacrifice little girls,' I answered. 'Was it this poisonous nagin's moist vagina that convinced you?'

Angry snakes popped out from Mohini's long, flowing hair. What can I say, I am good at pissing people off.

Riju threw back his head and guffawed. 'Anu, Anu! So amusing. Darling, let me take care of my old friend here. Go and get our special guest ready for tonight. We should leave soon.'

Mohini gave me one last bristling look of pure hatred and walked towards the three-headed cobra sculpture, disappearing under a door there.

Riju sat on his haunches, his full, moist lips close to me, his teeth gleaming in the firelight of the torches. The yugma locket touched my breast as he bent over me. He brushed a strand of hair off my face, his fingertips soft. 'You got me into this, Princess.'

'Me?'

'Yes, you. If you hadn't rejected me all those years ago.' He smiled and bent down to kiss my nipple. My stomach roiled with disgust. 'Always so perfect, you were,' he whispered, lightly running a finger on the mounds of my breasts and then on my stomach in circles. 'Did you even realize how I worshipped you, Princess? All those years we were together at the ashram, all I wanted was to touch you, breathe you, take you, make you mine.' He ran his finger lightly on my lower abdomen and touched the hair on my vagina. 'But that could never happen, could it? You were a high-born and I was a low-caste nobody. But then you fell in love with that ... that filthy worm, who was lower than me. I was so hurt, so angry. I had no choice but to tell your father about it.'

'You?' I spat the word out, anger burning up my eyes. 'You were the one who told him? I thought you were my friend.'

'*I thought you were my friend*,' he mimicked, laughing, as he rose to his feet, dusting his hands. 'You are delusional, Princess. No one in the ashram was your friend. Even Neel, your lover. Like me, like your father, all he wanted was the moist shakti that oozed from between your legs. But you were so infatuated with that idiot. It made me retch when you first told me about him. You couldn't see beyond his vapid, pretty-boy eyes. It gave me such pleasure to hear his screams from the ashram's dungeon. His screams when Kanthak tortured him slowly.'

'Why? For the Council's favour?'

His laughter filled the darkness in the room. His eyes had darkened into pinpoints of black. 'I never wanted a Council seat. Who wants to sit around gossiping with a bunch of oldies? I wanted to learn, to know true power. I wanted to learn the darkest arts of tantra. I wanted to become more powerful than the bunch of fools that run the Kaula Ashram.'

'Then why didn't you leave? Kaula couldn't have taught you the Black arts.'

'Do you think the White tantriks don't dabble in the Black arts? Oh there are hidden nooks in the ashram where these arts are whispered from ear to ear. From master to apprentice. A secret within a secret ashram. Only a select few are chosen for their intensity and ambition to take it further. I was one of them. I learnt the Black arts from my true master who learnt it from his. I had to hide my true purpose, so I won Narahara's trust, became his pimp, his puppy. He never suspected me. Even when I gave him a few pointers to the rituals, Black rituals, that were used in iMagic, he didn't realize what I had told him. Stupid, he has always been so stupid. Do you think he would have been able to figure out how to bring in a daeva into this world without my help? It was I who showed Narahara the way to bring Indra into our plane. I who told him about the rituals. He took my advice behind closed doors, but before the Council, he took all the credit. And I let him. The Council didn't matter to me. What mattered was true power. I want to take tantrism into a whole new direction. I want to delve into the juicy powers of tantrism, the power that strums in this universe. But you know about that, don't you? After all, you dabble with the Red yourself, don't you?'

'I don't murder girls,' I snarled.

'You kill goats instead,' Riju said softly. 'How is that so very different? Red is but a hair's breadth away from Black.'

I wondered whether I could use my shakti without any blood. It was hard, harder than I had ever cared to learn. And with the mayan rope around my hands, there was no way I could even use a mudra. Could I reach my bag somehow? Shukra groaned under me.

'A thin line is all that separates the bad from the good, Riju.' I had to keep him talking. As long as we were chatting, he wouldn't kill us.

'Lines and limits, boundaries and borders.' He spread his thin bruised arms and got up to face the monstrous sculpture of Kolahal. 'They are all fake, Anantya! Created by us, created by false gods to make some feel more important than others. The lord of chaos comes tonight to destroy all these artificial lines. There will be no more shackles, no more secrets, no more walls between rich and poor, human and sup, Kaula and Vama, woman and man. It will be an equal world. Everyone will be the same. Everyone will be together.'

'You are an idiot. The only way the world will become fair and equal is when everyone is dead. Look at us. I am tied up and you are free. How does that make us equal? Free me and we might be equal.' I twisted my wrist, feeling a slight give in the mayan rope. Shukra's wrists were thinner than his large hands would suggest. If I could just slip my hand out from his. Shukra mumbled something, but I couldn't quite hear him.

'Tonight, I promise you, Anantya. Tonight all of us will be free. In the rule of Kolahal, true equality will come. Everyone will fear him. Fear him enough to follow his wishes. The true god will make everyone equal.'

'Your true god will just eat everyone up.'

'Every change comes with some sacrifice. Tonight, it happens!' He did a kind of a jig. 'Oh, you don't understand,

Anantya. I have been seeking him for years! Indra was just a small experiment and now he will also become an offering to my lord Kolahal.'

'I have to hand it to you. Your plan of creating a yantra on Delhi was quite impressive.'

Keep him talking. Keep him bragging. If only I could slip my fingers out now. Just that much. If my left was free, I could do a quick mantra. But my hand slipped back into the rope. I started to try it again, flexing my hands and wrists as far apart as I could, my lips pursed to keep me from crying out as pain shot through my injured arm. Shukra's bound hand wriggled with mine now, as if he had begun to understand.

'Wasn't it? It was brilliant. Grand enough to please my god. A yantra in the heart of Delhi.'

'To use a satphone to bring in a god is also quite an achievement for a tantrik,' I said. 'How did you do it?'

'Smart, Princess. Do you think I would give away my secrets to another tantrik? Even to one who will die in a few minutes? Of course not. But as it's your dying wish, let me just say that I used the same chip we had developed for iMagic. It opens a channel, a secure one, to bring in our god. His powers escaped the yantra every night and I would be standing by with my satphone. Waiting for his blessing, his mistress. And each one was juicier than the last.' He puckered his lips and blew a kiss at the room.

'Better than even Mohini? How did you get her?'

Riju gave a wide smile, pleased. 'My god sent her my way. I was lost in the darkness of ignorance, serving Vajrin Mahendra's petty wishes. That is where Kolahal sent her. As soon as we laid eyes on each other, we knew. Hate bound us together. Hate of the privileged, of those born rich and royal. Those like you.'

As if on cue, Mohini slithered in towards us, cobra-like, her body scaled and moist with anticipation. Riju caught hold of her waist and suckled on both her breasts, finally giving her a long, sloppy kiss. My wrists were busy trying to set themselves free.

'Both of us had been abused and rejected by those in power,' he said, surfacing from the snog to get some air. 'Every night, after she had whored her body for Vajrin Mahendra, she would come to my room. Together we would plan how to kill him. But we wanted to do more than just kill him. We wanted to bring in a new world, an equal world. I introduced my darling to Lord Kolahal. She told me about the moonblades and Indra's Key. I couldn't believe they were real. It was fate! And so we began to plan in earnest. Mohini stole the moonblades from her mother. I had already recruited from Narahara's students and was training them. We were all ready. All we needed was the Key. But before Mohini could convince Qubera and take it, her mother played spoilsport and warned Qubera. Then you came into the picture. After that, the plan got derailed for a while.'

'Yes, I reached Kaula Ashram. So you had to die.'

Riju smiled. 'You were always the smartest of all Amritananda's children. If only that idiot could have seen that. Taking poison was the only way you wouldn't suspect me. Of all the people, it was you I distrusted the most. You have an uncanny habit of smelling trouble. Always have. Except when you are sentimental. When you get emotional, your head stops working. So I spoke to you when you were leaving the ashram. But I knew it wouldn't be very long before your logic kicked back in. When Mohini told me that you were also involved in the hiding of Indra's Key, I knew you had to go. Mohini sent you a nice gift outside Bedardi

Bar that day, but somehow you managed to give our cobra the slip. That's why she went after that dasyu puppy of yours. Poor Mohini,' he said, cupping and caressing her breast, 'it has been a very stressful time for her, hunting for the Key, chasing you and giving me the nagin poison to stage my death. It's been quite an adventurous week. But it has all been worth it, hasn't it, my darling?'

Mohini's skin shimmered in the flickering light. She started to slither and twist in excitement as did the snakes that had popped out of her hair. Shukra groaned again. Riju tenderly brushed a strand of snake off her face.

'Let me guess the rest. Mohini steals your body from the morgue and sets you free. But how did you find out where the Key was?' My hand was almost free. Just one more tug. *Come on, Anantya. Time to kill the bastard.*

'You want to tell her that, my darling?'

Mohini nodded and sexily gestured to someone standing behind us. A broad, muscled guard entered my line of vision. He held a man in his arms. Vajrin Mahendra, inert, naked, his body gleaming with oil.

'He told me,' said Mohini, cackling with laughter.

'A man in love is stupid, but a daeva in love is a complete idiot!' cried Riju giddily, laughing at his own joke. 'He confessed! Told her that he had found the Key on his nephew. Mohini was sleeping with him. He was smitten by her. It was all so easy. With the simple promise of telling him where the original thief was, Mohini brought him here. So now we have a sacrifice for the lord as well as Indra's Key to make sure that he has a strong vessel to come into.'

Mohini started to laugh again, her shrill screeches echoing in the dark chamber. 'He thought that an apsara could never be disloyal to his royal ass,' she screeched. 'Just because my mother has been his whore all her eternal life, he thought I would be too! Arrogant asshole!'

Suddenly, my hand was free. I could do a mantra, although not a powerful one because that would require rakta. Without my locket, I had no blood. Except my own.

Riju came up to Mohini again and kissed her nipple. 'Let's go, darling. Let's call our lord!'

I made a mudra with my hand, put in all my loathing in the mantra, and screamed:

'Bhool bhaal khel khal sab dho daal!'

My body warmed up, my blood curdled as the Yupati mantra spread in the room, its silky stinging smoke creating a dark mass of confusion. A couple of screams were followed by a loud thud. I knew the confusion mantra wouldn't affect the nagin too much, but the guards would be bewildered. I rolled onto my stomach, bringing Shukra on top of me. 'Come on, Shukra! Wake up!' But all he did was groan. I crawled to the corner, where my boneblade lay on top of the satchel.

'That's it! I am killing the bitch!' cried Mohini. I heard the hiss of snakes as Mohini shot her babies at us. The inky blackness hid the direction they came from.

'Take her, not me!' cried Riju as a shadow moved and grabbed hold of him.

I tried to rise using my left hand to leverage myself, but Shukra's body weight was on me. I fell back on the ground just as the snakes came hissing. The tiny snakes bit me on the face and breasts and legs. I cried out.

'No!' cried Riju. 'Wait, darling!'

'What? You want to save the bitch?'

'No, darling. I have a better idea. Why don't we feed them to your cousins? That will keep them busy too.'

Mohini bared her teeth in an evil grin, her eyes glittering.

'Oh, yes,' she said breathlessly. 'Let's do that. I get so turned on when you get these crazy ideas.'

The guard behind me held my hands roughly, retying it with mayan rope. Then suddenly I was in the air, suspended from the high ceiling by the ropes which tied Shukra's feet and mine together. We hung upside down, our hands hanging down, over the pit where the pile of offal lay. The mayan ropes began to dig into my ankles. Shukra groaned in pain. The smell of rotten flesh, blood, stale food and death was too much to bear. But there was nothing I could do.

Riju bent down, close to my ear and whispered: 'This one is especially for you, Princess.' He straightened and looked at Mohini. 'Call them, darling. Kitta, take Anantya's bag and blade. We don't want her to escape again, do we?'

Mohini made a hissing sound and then signalled to the guard to pick up Vajrin Mahendra's body. They left through the door we had entered. Leaving me alone with Shukra and the six-eyed monster statue. I wondered who Mohini's cousins were. Or did Riju want to kill us with bad smells?

A soft, slithering sound made me glance towards my feet. For a second it looked like the three-headed cobra god was crying. Fat, long, black tears fell from its six eyes, glittering and falling with small plops on the ground. The tears rose and hissed. Aha, the cousins. The tears were cobras, their bodies thick, black and powerful. They slithered towards the pile of offal in the middle, attracted by the smell. There were ten, then there were twenty, thirty and after that I lost count. The three-headed cobra cried poisonous tears and the snakes started creeping towards us, their small, reptilian eyes gleaming, their long, forked tongues flickering.

'Stop moving!' said Shukra crossly. 'It hurts.'

'Welcome ... back ... sleeping ... beauty,' I grunted, pushing my body sideways, so that we swayed together like a pendulum. Some of the cobras raised their bodies, one foot, two feet, three feet high, depending on their size. They swayed with us, their hoods spread and their bloodshot eyes steady on our faces. One jumped up high, trying to bite, but had miscalculated and fell back. 'Open your eyes and look.'

'Snakes!'

'Valid ... observation,' I cried. We swayed from one end of the chamber to the other, the only way to keep the cobras from biting us. Our heads were about four feet from the ground, so only the bigger ones could reach us. 'If you don't want to die, move with me!'

The thin mayan rope creaked. My ankles were bruised with the weight of my body. A cobra jumped up, its mouth wide, its fangs bare. It took in a mouthful of my hair, just inches from my ear. The monstrous three-headed cobra still wept poisonous tears. There were probably hundreds of them by this time. How many uncles and aunts did Mohini have to breed so many cousins? I will have to ask Rambha about that. Right now, though, I should be thinking about how to get out of here. Mayan ropes were good with stopping magic, but not strong enough to keep us up and away from the cobras for too long. They made ominous creaking sounds at our feet. The floor below was already covered with a live rug of slimy black that seemed to be growing. If we fell, we would be well and surely dead. Not instant death, mind you, but nice and slow, and excruciatingly painful. No wonder Mohini had so taken to the idea. My only hope was to swing far enough to reach the entrance. And then perhaps we could get away with just a few bites. Fat chance, that. The carpet of cobras increased in size beneath us.

'Eek!' screamed Shukra, wriggling, so that we started to circle instead of swinging from side to side, getting dangerously close to the mound of cobras in the middle.

'Swing, you idiot!' I cried again. We swung harder, like a strange pendulum, to and fro.

The entrance door blew open.

'Where is my ring?' the tall shadow screeched.

'Help!' I cried, dizzy from the swaying. A tall man held a staff in one hand, its tip glowing with blue light.

'Where is my Lavu!' he cried again.

'Jugnu! Fire!' I managed to scream as the rope broke and Shukra and I crashed headlong and head first into the pile of angry black cobras. I fell hard on my face, squishing a snake or two beneath my body. A cobra rose to attack me, going straight for my nose. I crouched and swung my leg, which was now free, at the cobra.

'Now!' I cried. Shukra wrenched his hand and we were free, but for the hissing snakes that is. Shukra and I stood back to back. I held my left hand up and cried.

'Raksha bhaksha kavacha!'

I held my hand up, feeling the tingle as shakti burst from my palm to create the shield of magic. An invisible wall grew before us, but without a mandala, it was a weak, fluctuating one. Around us stood death, dark, slithering, against the shield like black spikes, their red eyes staring.

'First tell me. Where's my Lavu?

'Lavu? What's that?' whispered Shukra, reaching over to brush off a snake that had just climbed on my shoulder. The Kavacha mantra was one-sided; I could attack the snakes, but they couldn't get at me. As long as the shield held. I could already feel the hissing behind me as the cobras readied to attack.

'My uncle,' said Jugnu in a boyish voice, 'he snatched the ring Lavu had given me. He was so angry about it. He kept asking me from where I had got it. Why would he take that last gift away from me?'

'I can't tell you if I am dead, can I?' I cried, turning and kicking a snake in the face. The snakes shrank back as I whirled to face them, but there were too many of them and my Kavacha was sliding off as the shakti behind it weakened. I wouldn't be able to hold them off for much longer. Jugnu just stood there for a few seconds, straightening his dishevelled hair, and then muttered a mantra. A ball of blue fire emerged from his bone staff and billowed at the snakes slithering towards us.

'More!' I cried, holding Shukra's hand and running, squishing snakes underfoot. The Kavacha mantra died as my feet moved drunkenly, much slower than I had thought. The poison was beginning to take effect. I flicked one from my shoulder and Shukra seemed to be wriggling to get the snakes off him. 'Lots more!'

The smell of burning flesh filled the chamber. Balls of mayan fire rolled around us, green, purple, blue, red and orange. I flew the rest of the way to the steps at the entrance. The mayan fire spread quickly, wild and furious.

'Run!' I cried, grabbing a frozen Jugnu by the arm and pushing him through the doorway ahead of us. Together we ran towards the main entrance, as the blue fire started to eat the door of the cavern of horrors. We ran – straight into the path of the bison, standing a few feet from the door, head down, its horns pointed straight at us.

'Great,' cried Shukra as the bison kicked its leg and started to charge. Shukra and Jugnu fell to one side as the bison came towards me head-on, its eyes small round blue balls. I jumped up and grabbed an overhanging meat hook, pressing my body to the ceiling and as high up as I could. The horn of the beast scraped my shoulder.

'Run! Run!' I screamed, ignoring the pain and trying not to give in to the dizziness caused by the poison. I swung down, still holding the meat hook and, using the momentum, jumped as far as I could, landing on both my feet and then plunged on towards the door leading into the street, behind Shukra and Jugnu. I was the last one out of the gates of hell. Blue mayan fire reached the gates just a few seconds later.

'We … need … to … put out … the fire,' I said, panting.

The poison was beginning to kick in. I wished I had my locket or some rakpiss with me. Bloody bastard hadn't even left me my clothes. Jugnu recalled the mayan fire, as Shukra and I collapsed on the muddy ground in the alleyway. The sky was still a murky grey, with raw, red rips. My eyes watered and my sight reddened. Shukra bent his face to my thigh and sucked. It tickled.

'What?'

'Poison,' he spat, 'needs to be taken out.'

'Where's my ring?' asked Jugnu, standing over us and pouting like a two-year-old, his wavy hair thick with sweat and dirt.

'Your uncle has given it to his secretary who will use it to create a highway for a hell god to enter.'

'Mohini? Why? Why does everyone want my Lavu's ring?'

'It wasn't hers, you silly toad!' I cried with my remaining strength. 'It belonged to your bloody uncle.'

'You lie! It is mine. I want it back.'

'Then go and get it from your uncle,' I replied, nodding a curt thanks to Shukra and standing up. I waited for the dizziness to pass. 'Shukra, let's go.'

'You can't! Tell me where he went. I followed him here and then lost him.'

'They just left to destroy the city and if we don't stop them, it will happen soon enough.' On a garbage pile in a corner of the alley, I noticed some rough jute sacks. I picked up two, threw one to Shukra and draped one over myself. We looked like vagrants.

'Well, do you have a phone?' I asked Jugnu.

He looked a little blank, but then took out his phone. I took a deep breath and called the one man I didn't think I would ever need to call. Thankfully, Jugnu had his number.

'Riju's alive,' I barked into the phone as soon as Nasty picked up. 'He's the leader of the cult. Not Mattreya, but your … our dear Riju. He has Indra now and he plans to finish what he started. How do you plan to stop them?'

'I don't,' came an equally curt reply.

'What? This is the Association's responsibility. You can't let innocent people get killed! You have to do this.'

'You don't order me, woman,' he yelled back. 'I have more than enough on my plate.'

'Your Indra will be consumed tonight by Vritra. If you want to save his sorry ass, you had better come.'

'Do you think we are all idiots? We already know that. I

didn't know who the leader was, but that doesn't matter now. What matters is stopping Vritra from coming in.'

'And how do you plan to do that?'

'The Council has gathered at the ashram to perform a ganachakra tonight. It's going to be massive. We aim to contain the damage that the demon of chaos will bring in with him. The only thing you can do now is pray and wait for the cleaning. And Anantya,' he paused, as if hesitant to say it, 'stay away from the yantra tonight. It's no use putting your life in danger.'

'Like hell! Your ganachakra will not be able to stop people from dying! If Vritra enters the yantra tonight, a lot of people will die before your ganachakra can recall him. That's a stupid, time-consuming process. We need to stop him from entering this plane.'

'We can't. We have to take that chance.'

'You guys are nothing but lumps of cowardly bullshit!' I cried and disconnected the call. Bloody Kaulas. Staking half of Delhi's population on a stupid ritual like ganachakra. To think that this could be solved with fancy sex in a circle! While two daevas fought each other, they would conveniently bury their ugly heads in the sand. Typical! The Kaulas' ritual was a cleaning-up session after the party had ended. Which meant the Tazaak would stay out of it as well. That just left me and I needed to see a nagin burn for all those she'd killed. Which meant I needed help from Dhuma.

There are ancient powers even older than the oldest of daevas. Tantriks know of them, just like they know, or at least the smart ones do, that they need to be left untouched. These spirits have always been here to create and destroy, provide life and take it away. The goddess of death is one of them. She lives, floats and breathes in the outskirts of every village, every civilization, waiting in the darkness, waiting for the world's time to end so that she can feed on it. Shamshana Kalika is her name, but don't say it aloud. For she will hear and answer, and come to you and the ones you love. Shamshana Kalika was the only power that could possibly prevent the holocaust tonight. The only problem was that this goddess loved death too much to stop it.

'Doing shava sadhana to control a danava is like putting out a bonfire with burning lava,' said Dhuma as soon as I had told her about the plan. Her ash-covered, pendulous breasts swung as she rubbed a potion into the wounds on my back.

The skulls suspended from the thatched roof tinkled like wind chimes as a boiling waft of air drifted in through the window. The sun was dark and ominous. It was some hour of the evening.

'But it might work, right? She's the only one who could possibly stop Kolahal. Dhum, we are desperate. This is the seventh night. The new-moon night. The danava will devour half this city. Think of the countless people who could die. You once told me, poison fights poison best!'

'A pinch of poison is enough for a snake-bite. Not a whole vat of it,' replied Dhuma, hitting me hard on the head with her jhaadu.

'But we can control her, right? We can put her in me, in a shell, and that will keep her powers contained.'

'Control? Hah! You are talking about Shamshana Kalika here! She cannot be controlled by the living. She will swallow your soul before you can even close the door.' *Thwack!* She hit me again. 'Foolish girl! To her your life is like that of an insect. If you fail, she will gobble you up and not even belch. If you succeed, she will still eat you. You want to die?'

'Umm … madam,' said Shukra, who had been sitting quietly in a corner in Dhuma's hut. 'I don't mean to interrupt, but it looks like this skeleton wants to tell you something.'

One of the skeletons behind Shukra was repeatedly hitting him on his head with a human thighbone. Shukra took the bone from its hand, his eyes firmly rooted to the floor, and handed it over to Dhuma. He had been feeling slightly out of place ever since he laid eyes on Dhuma. Nakedness disturbed him, I think. It had been the same when we'd come out of the cult's hellhole. Was he a virgin, I wondered.

'Chitti, what do you want?' asked Dhuma, placing her hands on her fat grey stomach.

The skeleton's jaws moved agitatedly, making various clacking sounds.

Dhuma nodded. 'Yes, yes. How interesting.' She leapt up suddenly and began dancing exuberantly around the fire in the middle of the hut, playing a small damru. 'Can be. Can be!' The low flame burnt with a reddish flame. 'Can be. Can be. Will it bring the truth out? Can be, can be. Will it feed the hungry mouth?' She swooped to scoop ashes from a bowl on the side and threw it into the fire. It flared.

Crash! Shukra, who had tried to unobtrusively scuttle away from the flame and the impromptu performance, fell into a pile of skulls. Dhuma stopped mid-step and gave me a blank stare. 'There is a way.'

'How?'

'We bring Shamshana into a corpse instead of you. That way she will not consume your soul and it will give you more time. But she has to be in the yantra when the danava comes. She has to be inside there, you understand?' When I nodded, she continued, sitting on her haunches and shaking her head vigorously, dreadlocks dancing, 'How much time do we have?'

'About five hours until midnight,' answered Shukra, his head still bowed.

'And for how many hours do you need her to come?'

'Until midnight. That's when he comes,' I answered.

'She won't like it. She will piss and claw. She will want more blood.' Dhuma shook her matted locks again and turned to what looked like a pile of rubbish in another corner of the shack, although I knew it was her ritual stuff. 'No one likes to possess those that are already dead, especially she. She will …' She continued to mutter, scratching her head, rummaging through the litter. 'You will be next, you know that, don't you? She will never forget you.'

I nodded, chewing my inner lip. There was no other choice. Even if I had my boneblade and the satchel that Riju had taken with him, I would still be powerless to overcome the combined strength of both Riju and Mohini at the ritual spot. Not singlehandedly. Riju had become a powerful Black tantrik, who also knew the Kaula tricks. Mohini was a monster, a powerful and cunning one, the perfect killing machine. Bringing in Shamshana was an act of sheer desperation. But the world as I knew it was ending, and I had to do something crazy, right?

During my training days, I had found out about shava sadhana, a complex tantrik ritual performed by sitting on a corpse – symbolizing life over death. I had watched it being performed a couple of times when Dhuma had had a midnight party with a bunch of her friends, but I had never actually participated in the ritual myself. I didn't even know how to do it. Dhuma had withheld some tricks of the trade from me.

She hollered something and Chitti, to Shukra's alarm, stood up and walked towards her, clattering away. Dhuma and Chitti sank deep into a strange conversation, her hoarse voice mixing with his clickety-clack. I waited. Shukra was unusually silent.

'You there,' she said, pointing at me after a while, 'we'll need thirteen healthy goats. You understand, no sheep, only goats. Get them here within an hour.'

I nodded, turning to leave. Something tugged at the jute outfit that I still had on.

'You are not leaving me behind, are you?' whispered Shukra, his glance taking in Dhuma and Chitti, before turning back to me. His eyes pleaded.

'Clingy baby!' Dhuma said, without looking at him. 'Yes, you go too. Get me a corpse. Fresh and juicy, freshly dead. Not something a day old. Just a few hours old. It needs to be full and beautiful, no body parts missing. Like you would want to eat it as soon as you saw it.'

The colour drained from Shukra's face.

'This Black magic, Anantya, I am sorry but this…' He waved his hand around. 'I … I cannot help you with this.' He looked pasty green and physically ill.

A series of clacking noises filled the hut, distracting us. Chitti held two long thighbones in his skeletal hands and was beating them together. The hut's assorted skulls and bones started to clatter simultaneously. As the noise got louder, the decibel level rose, reaching higher and higher into the darkening sky.

'It has started,' I said, excitement burning through my body.

'Corpse? Where will I find a corpse?' Shukra muttered as we started to walk towards Chhotu.

'I will drop you off at a morgue. Steal it,' I suggested, giving him a large jute sack. 'I will see you here in an hour. Come on, you wanted to help, didn't you? Just do this.'

Finding thirteen goats took longer than I had anticipated and, since the city was getting set to celebrate a festival, turned out to be really expensive too. Brains of a bull, I wish someone would pay me for saving the bloody world tonight.

'FOUL MITE! DILUTED BLOOD!' Dhuma's angry screech carried through the dark night. The air felt heavy, as if solidifying already. I tried to hurry to where the voice had come from, but when you are handicapped with herding thirteen goats, it takes a while to get anywhere.

'… should have gone myself! To trust an asura to do something right is like whispering a tantrik secret to a pig!'

'What happened?' I asked as I reached the spot where the ritual was to be performed.

Dhuma stood in a circle made of ashes and bones. In the middle was the temple. A temple dedicated to Shamshana Kalika. It wasn't a temple by conventional, or even tantrik, standards. It was a heap of dead and decaying matter. Bones, pieces of flesh that were mulched with cow dung, faeces and piles of garbage. It was all there, the dead and the dying, the rotten and foul, everything piled up to invoke the harbinger of death. The mound was about two feet high, shaped like a small boat in the middle of a vast, drowning ocean. Just the way she liked it. A thrill passed through my bones again. To me it was something more than just trying to save the world for sure. I wanted to see her. I wanted to feel Shamshana Kalika myself. How on earth had I become so self-destructive? Or, from another angle, so desirous of power? I didn't want to analyse it too much. Not yet.

Dhuma stood in the centre, next to the pile, and shouted, 'Rotten mutton head! He brought a babe's corpse!'

'A baby's?' I exclaimed.

'Two-year-old girl child. That was the only whole corpse,' said Shukra, gulping and shaking. 'The only one that I could find. All the rest looked like accident victims. Nothing was … complete …'

'I understand. Thanks, Shukra. Dhum, can you still do it?'

'… will become a laughing stock. Messed-up asura …'

'Dhum! Can you still do it?'

She paused, a jhaadu in one hand and the damru in the other, legs apart, breasts swaying dangerously.

'I will do it,' she scowled. 'No other option. It gets too late. She will torture us for doing this to her. Hound us forever, you understand? Because we ask her to get into this baby's body.'

I nodded.

'I … Miss Anantya, I don't think I can—' Shukra looked squeamish. He rubbed the tip of his nose. 'I don't believe—'

'Why don't you leave?' I completed his thought for him.

'I would still like to help you.'

'You don't need to see this. Wait near Chhotu. I will come when this is done.'

He gratefully left. I had a fair idea of how he felt. I had felt the same when I performed a sacrifice for the first time. Not everyone could carry the guilt of killing. Not everyone could digest what we were about to do. Murder left a permanent scar on the soul, be it human or animal. Riju's question rang in my ears. Is it so different? Killing a beast from killing a human? Red tantrism or Black tantrism? Not that the Kaula methods were any better. Kaulas raped women to harvest their shakti. It appeared that you couldn't get that kind of power without extreme violence.

Dhuma squatted on top of the pyre of rotten and dead things and shat on it to mark the beginning of the ritual.

'*Om aim hrim klim shamshanaye Kali vicche,*' she cried, starting to beat the damru to the rhythm of her mantra. '*Om aim hrim klim shamshanaye Kali vicche. Om aim hrim klim shamshanaye Kali vicche.*'

'*Om aim ...*'

Just beyond the line of the circle, on the anvil of death, I began to sacrifice the line of goats I had brought with me, letting each one's blood flow into the furrow looping outside the circle of bone and ash around the pyre that Dhuma had created. *Meeeh! Meeeh!* All the tethered goats awaiting their turn were terrified and pleading. They could smell the metallic tang of blood and fear, the smell of a sacrifice. Two down. Eleven to go. Every one of them wanted to live, to survive, to breathe. *Meeeh! Meeeh!* I closed my mind and ears, and continued to use the blade on their necks mechanically, sure, deep, one by one. It was dark now and the blood looked like a shiny, black, lubricated river.

'*Om aim hrim klim ...*'

As I struck with the boneblade, blood and gore splashed on my hands, and crept up my arms and chest and hair. The smell of blood and entrails enveloped me, absorbing my being, so I could barely see where the blood and goat flesh ended and where I began. Eight. Five more to go. The mantra reverberated in the thick, curdling air, rising up like mucous in a blocked nose.

'*... shamshanaye Kali vicche ...*'

I picked up the dead flesh and threw it onto the growing pile in the centre. I wasn't sure just how long I had been doing this. It felt like years, an eternity, forever. Hacking and picking up the dead sacrifice before tossing it on the growing stack in the centre. *Thawk!* Thirteen. I rose and walked into the circle of bones, carrying the final goat carcass. Although the pile was just a few feet away inside the circle, it felt like a long walk. Dhuma danced and hopped, muttering the mantra, calling Shamshana's name. I placed the last of the goat flesh on the mound. It was done.

'It's time!' cried Dhuma, her voice alive with excitement. She signalled me to bring the corpse. My limbs, body and hair were all soaked in blood. I gently removed the jute bag that covered the body of the two-year-old, freshly dead. A mere infant, a little girl. Her body felt heavy. I half dragged, half carried her, feeling exhaustion grip my bones. Dhuma flicked her hand to indicate I was to sit with the corpse on my lap. Sit on the pile of dead things. I obeyed without question, the corpse heavy on my lap. The blood from the freshly killed goats below my buttocks soaked through my sackcloth outfit.

'Shamshana Kalika! I call upon you.' Dhuma started to hop and dance around the pile of rotten things, chanting, her damru beating rhythmically. 'I call upon you who is alive with life. You who changes and creates. You who dies and destroys …'

The saccharine smell of garbage and rotting flesh rose, heavy and heady. I breathed deeply, without recoiling, the pure smell of the foul and terrible. I had never felt more alive as I did then, breathing in the freshly drained blood, holding the baby's white, bloodless, stiff dead body. The living and the dead. Who would she choose to come into?

'… come here tonight! Kill and consume the evil that breeds! Bite the flesh, drink the blood, copulate and create. Destroy and devastate! Revive and rejuvenate! Drink up the dead, the freshly spilt blood! I call upon you! Shamshana Kalika! I call upon you! Bless us! Bless us with creation! Bless us with destruction! Shamshana Kalika!'

The skeletons lying around the pyre stood up, like white

puppets. They began to drag themselves, crawling at first, and then as the energy of death suffused all, walking, and then running and dancing, round and round me until they became a wall of intricate lacework. Some danced on their legs, some hopped, some stood on their heads, some walked on their hands, some crawled on bare rib cages. Together they swayed, as one, welcoming Shamshana Kalika into the circle, singing odes and long-forgotten songs in a cacophonic clickety-clacking chorus, all of it out of tune. They danced around the circle as Dhuma danced around me. She picked up a bucket of blood and threw it on the corpse. Blood splashed over me. I delighted in the fresh tanginess of it as the sweet, all-consuming smell arose. Dhuma set the pyre on fire. The burning stench emerged as one being, one goddess, as blood, as life, as death, as universe. It rose all together, dancing and mingling and crawling and clinging to the skulls and bones and hands and souls. Together it rose, dancing to an ancient tune, the song of death and change, of destruction and creation, of fire and ashes, of blood and bones. It rose as the silent song of Shamshana Kalika.

The corpse on my lap grew heavy, bloating up and becoming a mountain. It became light, a bundle of feathers (or was it me growing heavier?). I became cold, dead and heavy. I started to burn, the fire raging both within and without. It was so cold that my blood froze. I held the baby with my fingertips, offering it to the fire, the rotting pile and the rising stench of death. Giving it over to become lighter, to burn, to become a vessel. Inviting Shamshana Kalika into the small bundle of dead bones and flesh, inviting her into the world. The baby turned black as the fire consumed its dead flesh. I burnt too, for the corpse was alive and my body was dead. I felt my soul travel through the baby and me. A connection formed between us, a bridge that connected us together, now and forever. Rising with the stench of burning blood and the whoops of delight of the skeletons and Dhuma's frenzied cries, came a bloodcurdling scream. The sound rent the leaden night sky and removed the cloak of darkness to show the shining stars for a split second. It vibrated through everything in the shamshan, changing the very forms of beings. It was the call of Shamshana Kalika.

'It … it has fangs as well,' observed Shukra, peering into the baby's mouth. He had forced open her upper lip with a pen. 'They weren't there when I brought it in. I double checked since that crazy woman wanted a corpse without anything broken.' He looked at me expectantly, over the top of his steel-rims, his eyebrows up, his eyes questioning.

'She has turned into a baby monster and that's what you point out?' I answered.

The two-year-old corpse was alive now, too alive for my comfort. Her burnt skin had solidified into shiny black scales, like a dwarf wearing black armour. In addition, she had sprouted fangs (as Shukra had just helpfully pointed out), long protruding teeth like a mouthful of sharpened nails. Although Shamshana couldn't use her mouth to do much except scream and chew, she could express herself with me very well. *Shamshana I am called. You called me into a babe's corpse. I was cut into little pieces. Then fed into the tandoor.* The whispering in my head were waves of thought which felt like spurts of blood. When Dhuma had done the ritual she had warned me that we would be connected, that Shamshana would join with my soul and I would be able to feel her desires and read her thoughts right in my head. What Dhuma had conveniently left out was that it wouldn't exactly be a civil communication. Shamshana's jumbled thoughts and demands (there were many, they were persistent) exploded in my head like a series of screams each louder than the last. *I promise to save you for the last. You shall die, but slowly, your human skin roasting on the embers of yesterday's fire.*

'Her name is Shamshana. Don't call her "it",' I muttered, trying to distract myself from the horrific visions she projected into my mind. *My child's eye was poked with a needle by my drunken husband. Just because my son was trying to stop him from bashing my brains in.* Several television screens. Several channels streaming together at various volume levels played simultaneously inside my head. *Come closer, I will tell you a secret. But then I will have to kill you. Ring-a ring-a roses. My eyes are blood and posies.* And you couldn't turn any of them off. I closed my eyes, wishing away the headache. How in Kali's name would I fight Riju and Mohini together with so much noise in my head? *Bones. That's the bare truth. The only thing that remains of you. The purest.*

'And I think she wants to chew on a bone.'

'Bone?' Shukra looked down at the baby crocodile thing he awkwardly held in his arms.

I tossed Shamshana a random bone of an animal, and turned back to continue rummaging through my lab supplies for a deer's belly button. We had pit-stopped at the haveli to prep for tonight's battle. As I had no clue what we were going to face in the seventh ritual, I hadn't the faintest idea how to equip myself, so the preparations were haphazard to put it mildly. I quickly changed, buckled on a belt as a makeshift scabbard for the new boneblade (it lacked the power of Kaani's boneblade, but would have to do) and threw vials into my new bag, things I may or may not need. Rakpiss, maya potion, darzit, sifter, a new mandala for defence. *He dripped acid on me, drop by drop, slowly. It burnt and burnt and burnt, so slow, so slow. And he laughed.* I harnessed Shamshana in a rucksack. *I was raped repeatedly by them. Three they were, all my friends. My body was left to rot in an open drain.* Zee was missing, which was good. It meant he may yet outlive the night, unlike us. *He stripped me bare in the snow and stuffed my face with snow until it turned red.* Shukra had changed out of his jute suit into a fitted, white nylon overall. A long, needle-like blade hung from his waist. A rapier, he told me. He still looked dazed, like he was in a waking nightmare – mouth open, brows furrowed, wide-eyed. Poor fellow. Less than twenty-four hours ago, he had been convinced that aliens didn't exist, and had just spent the night drinking with the worst of them. Dhuma could be a tad overwhelming.

'You should leave. We may not come back at all,' I said to him. *The vultures came when I was old and tired. Each fed me a drop of water, hoping it would burn me like poison.*

'Leave where? Everyone I know dies tonight if this electron intimidator enters our city. It is only logical that I try and stop it.'

'Do what Nasty and his crew are doing. Stay away from the yantra.'

'And leave you alone?'

'I have her,' I said, pointing to the backpack that held Shamshana. *The butcher knife hacked me into little pieces. I didn't even see who was holding it. I will do the same to you. Maybe tonight. Maybe not.*

'No.' He adjusted his glasses and placed his hand on the hilt of his rapier. 'If you don't mind, I would like to accompany you on this mission to try and restore the balance of the universe.'

My father burnt me and fed on my meat. I nodded, hitting my forehead with a fist. Shamshana screamed from inside the bag. At first I thought it was inside my head but then I saw Shukra wince and cover his ears. *I am afraid of the dark. It was darkness that brought the rats. The rats that bit me, first slowly and then frenzied.* A thin veil separated my mind from Shamshana Kalika's vast consciousness. I felt like an insignificant insect. *My tongue turned black and swollen and I bit into it and swallowed it.* Standing at the rim of a black, bottomless abyss, trying not to get sucked in. I closed my eyes for a second. *No, I can't speak. But you can still hear my screams.* And opened them again. If this is what it meant to become a vessel for a powerful spirit, Riju would go crazy as soon as the demon of chaos came into his body.

We started towards Kolahal's nest. The bindu. At the dead centre of the two intersecting triangles of the Shiva-Shakti yantra. In an academic sense, I appreciated what Riju Das had done. He had exceeded the education given at the Kaula Ashram and taken the tantrik art to a whole new level, combining it with technology. But what good is power if all you want to use it for is to destroy things around you? *The sky cried tears, but no one was there to wipe them away from my festering wounds.*

'Static has increased!' shouted Shukra, jerking his hand away from my waist as a spark flew from the touch.

'Could be the chemistry between us,' I said, giving his thin thigh a squeeze.

Even through Shamshana's screaming in my head and rocking in the haversack between us, I felt Shukra's acute discomfort. I smiled evilly, pushing Chhotu to her limit. The roads were empty, thanks to TV broadcasts in the evening that had warned people to stay indoors, and not use their cellphones and electronic gadgets as this immense increase in static could be lethal. It was as if they knew that he was coming. Dry storm or a demon god. Same difference. *I was just taking a midnight stroll when I was hit by lightning. It tingled like hell.*

I parked Chhotu and dismounted. A squirming Shamshana strapped to my back, my boneblade in my left hand, and even though I held a mandala in my right hand to defend myself, without my yugma locket, I felt naked. Or more like lucked out. My head pounded, overwhelming whispers pouring in. *I thought I would be terrified but it was comforting, like taking too much of aspirin.* The darkness behind the veil felt welcoming. Ignore it. Keep it together, Anantya. *Keep it together? But I couldn't find the fingers I had chopped off.*

Shukra followed, apprehensive but determined, duelling sword in his right hand. Rapier, I corrected myself. The spot for the seventh ritual had been a cemetery before it had been sold to a real estate builder. *I flew like an eagle when I jumped off the seventeenth floor. Even my tears flew sideways.* Was it only yesterday that Shukra and I had joined forces and worked out the hot spots for the ritual murders? I had been so sure at the time that I would solve the case that very night.

Madhu, who had visited the site earlier in the day, told me that the place was empty except for a few workers and security guards. At the centre of the walled enclosure, a large foundation pit had been dug with massive structural columns rising up in preparation for the multi-storeyed project. Could I be mistaken? Madhu had asked me this a couple of times. Yantras don't lie, I told him. If Riju Das had to create a true Shiva-Shakti yantra on Delhi, he wouldn't have too many sites to choose from in the area. All around it were office buildings usually bustling with activity. This was perfect. An abandoned, old cemetery imbued with the power of spirits. A place of the dead was perfect to usher in a danava. It had to be this. *I died without knowing if she was sleeping with him. Even when I gouged out her beautiful eyes with a knife, she denied it.*

The logo of the real estate company loomed in front of us, a gigantic splash of colour on a corrugated wall, thirty feet high. It looked like just another innocuous construction site in the heart of the city. Except for the ravens. Hundreds upon hundreds of them cruised the skies overhead. Cackles and caws and croaks and squawks filled the leaden sky with cacophony. They sang in a million voices of the joys to come.

The tall gates of the site were wide enough to allow two sixteen-wheeler trucks to pass through together. It was lit by a small bulb, like a diya in a vast cave. Shukra gasped; just then, I too saw the corpses. There were six of them, scattered in front of the gate, probably construction workers or guards. The bloated bodies were riddled with holes and puncture wounds. The ravens feasted on the flesh now. *My own dog lapped at my open wound when the burglar sliced my belly open.* Their distorted shadows fell on the uneven ground, grotesque and hideous. I signalled to Shukra to stop. Shamshana Kalika climbed out of the backpack, clutching fistfuls of my hair to do so.

'Aaaaaaaaaaaaaaaaaaayyyyyyyyyyyyyiiiiiii!' Her thin bloodcurdling scream trilled both inside and outside my head. The ravens perched on the cadavers turned together as one, their beady eyes staring at us, unblinking. The others, flying in the sky, homed in on us like missiles. Shamshana clambered onto my head, and screamed again, a battle cry to announce us. 'Aaaaaaaaaaaaaaaayyyyyyyyyyyyyiiiiiii!'

'Uh-oh,' I said.

Swiip. Swiip. Swiip. Ravens dive-bombed from the sky, darker than the darkness, smoke trailing behind them like swirling dark cloaks. The flapping of their wings was one sound, as was the clacking of their sharp beaks. Yatus. One or several, I wasn't sure. I jumped towards the corpses, into the stream of light from the lone bulb, cut my finger with my boneblade and, pointing to the shadows on the ground, screamed:

'*Kaali parchhayee chipak jaa!*'

'Craack!' The shadows congealed like black ice on the ground. Some of the ravens stopped mid-flight, strangely frozen in the air, their shadows stuck to the ground. I had managed to freeze some of them, but there were just too many of them. As I crouched and executed a neat roll without dislodging Shamshana from my head, or tripping over the corpses, I could hear the sharp clacks of beaks. They clacked and clawed and pecked, aiming at my shadow, biting and piercing my ears and hair and back. Their screams dug into my flesh and ears. Shamshana screamed and clawed at one, Shukra sliced with his rapier at a bunch of them. It was of little use as the thin metallic blade passed through the insubstantial shadows harmlessly.

'Shukra, torch on the wall. Now!' I yelled, rolling over and over as the ravens came at me from all directions. *Even though I wore so many coats, the knife slid through my chest, carving out my heart.*

I fled to the other side of the light bulb, the clacking deafeningly loud. Attacking them physically was pointless. I had to capture their shadows.

'*Kaali parchhayee chipak jaa!*' I screamed again. Splat! Another bunch of them froze as their shadows solidified. *It was a dark night when my soul seeped out. I was so scared I shat.*

My head throbbed. Shukra switched on the torch and directed its beam to the gates behind us. '*Kaali parchhayee chipak jaa!*' I screamed. Some more of the shades froze.

'We don't have time! Take Shamshana to the bindu. Take her!'

'What about you?' he yelled, pouncing on a wriggling Shamshana who was clawing at a raven's shadow and biting it with her fangs.

'I will follow. Go! Now!'

Shukra threw the torch to me. It landed nearby but there were too many ravens between us. He ran towards the gate, holding a squirming Shamshana. More ravens pursued them, striking and pecking, cawing and cackling. *'Kaali parchhayee chipak jaa!'*

I readied my boneblade again to attack more shadows when there was a loud crunch and I was plunged into complete darkness. Darkness consumed the area, and the yatus whose shadows I had bound, freed themselves with a soft swish. They flew towards me, clacking their beaks, their eyes shining in the blackness.

'No shadows. No kills. She-tantrik,' clacked a heavy voice behind me. I turned, but could see nothing. 'You not see me,' it clacked again. I felt cold fingers crawl on my neck. *Meat. I was desperate for any meat. Even if it meant eating my own child. He wouldn't ever know, would he?* It clacked loudly again. 'But Shadow King sees your shadow still.' A sharp pain rose in my shoulder as if it was pierced by a long stake. I winced. Clack, clack! As my eyes adjusted to the darkness, I saw the shape of the Shadow King, a huge grey splotch. The several hundreds of ravens had somehow merged to make a gigantic, black, dinosaur-sized shade, its eyes as big as plates, towering over me, its long beak clacking continuously. *My beard was trimmed and my head placed on the dinner plate and then I was photographed.* It hadn't yet torn me to pieces, just given me a small peck. It was playing.

'You. You are the one who freed us so that I could stop the ritual yesterday night.'

'Yes,' it clacked, spreading its wings, formless shadows of long feathers and cawed. 'Me set you free.'

'Then why stop me now, Shadow King?' I asked, groping around with my fingers. Wood, I needed wood. *I used a stake instead. There's something artsy about piercing my heart with a stake.* But where do you find wood in a construction site?

'The evil tantrik holds the shadows of me clan.'

'Let me go and I will release the shadows.'

'Too late,' it clacked, its beak opening wide. 'Be ready to die.' It jabbed, a gigantic raven pecking at a puny rat. Clack! I rolled to the side, onto my shadow, just as its shadowy beak landed, melting through my buttocks, a cold wave. It was my shadow it could harm, not my body. Clack! Clack! I kept rolling and then scrambled to my feet, and then ran, weaving and zig-zagging to avoid its beak. Clack! Clack! *I prayed for him to stop, begged him too, but he continued to put that* thing *in my anus.* The Shadow King jabbed my shadow thigh.

I pushed open the gate and squeezed in, falling on the muddy ground, crawling. The giant raven hopped on my shadow, and I flew, landing face first on a pile of rubble, roots and dirt. Clack, clack! I turned and skidded down the heap, ignoring the sharp pain in my ribcage. Clack! The Shadow King pecked hard at my shadow, hitting the exact same place on my thigh. I fell on my face, and kept rolling. Clack! *I injected myself with coke to run away from the monsters pounding in my head.* Anything, even a piece of rotten plant or stem would do. Stem! Root. I was lying on a pile of roots. I turned and rummaged in the dirt, making sure I kept moving constantly. Clack, clack! Stone, dirt, metal, root. Root. I grabbed the piece of root, a foot-long gnarled root of an old tree that must have been felled for this construction. I yanked it out and, with a single stroke, pierced the eye of the Shadow King, screaming.

'Aum hreem bhuta aa, kar de kreem chhaya kha!'

'Crawwwww ...' The Shadow King screamed as it bled, smokey-grey blood. It disintegrated into smoke and scattered like dry leaves. A lightning bolt flared as it shot down from the sky into the cavity of the dark excavation pit. *I smell them. They desire, oh how they desire blood. We do too. Would you stop us from taking it, Anantya?* The path on which I stood circumvented the foundation crater, about the size of a cricket ground and nearly thirty feet deep. Partially built steel and concrete pillars emerged from the ground like a monster skeleton. I gingerly hobbled down the ramp into the hellhole below, one step at a time. Where was Shukra? Where had he hidden Shamshana? As if on cue, Shamshana's bloodcurdling scream echoed through the emptiness.

'Aaaaaaaiyiyaaaaaa!'

'Anantya, Anantya,' crooned Mohini's voice.

The sky above screamed again as veins of lightning tore the clouds overhead. A red web built up, like the veins of a monster. Metallic fingers rising from the cavity lit up like white fire, reaching up to the sky. In the middle was the yantra. An equilateral triangle, shining brightly.

'You silly stubborn thing. Where are you hiding?' The voice came from the guts of the cavity, sharp, screechy. 'We have your little puppy. Do you want him back? Do you, do you?'

Shukra hung suspended in the air above the triangle, trussed up in coils of snakes. Mohini stood on one side, her arms extensions of the snake bodies which held Shukra. She wore a figure-hugging bodysuit in black, hair falling on her shoulders in a wave. Riju stood within the yantra, gazing down at Vajrin Mahendra's perfectly sculpted, clean, oiled, naked body. Blood had been liberally splashed on his face and body.

'Like my handiwork, Princess?'

I took out a beedi and put it to my lips and lit a match. A long puff later, I cried out,

'Jal bhun bhasm ho ja!'

The flame shot out at Mohini. Before the nagin could even react to the Agni mantra, Riju jumped up and turned around. He pointed a finger in my direction. Red zigzags of lightning issued from his bare hands. The electric charge shot through me. My body shuddered, froze and I staggered.

'Not nice, Princess,' said Riju, turning back to his work as if he had done nothing more than swat a fly. 'Mohini was just trying to be friendly. Darling, tie up Anantya with her puppy. I think our lord would like an appetizer before he can have the real deal.'

'I … tried. She ran away,' gasped Shukra, twisting to look at me apologetically.

Mohini's snake-fingers zapped through the air and coiled around me. The snakes tightened their hold, squeezing me as an anaconda would its prey, until I gasped for breath. She flicked her hand and, like an airborne log, I flew and hit my head hard on a pillar. She smiled.

'Who is he talking about, Anantya? Did you get someone else?'

My head rang and I fell on the ground outside the yantra, freed of the snakes for a moment. *The worm ate me slowly, for years, gnawing at my skin, my blood vessels and then my bones. Chuk, chuk, chuk. I still remember the sound it made inside my body. Chuk, chuk, chuk.*

'Someone who will ...' I gasped, speaking through bloodied lips, '... wipe that smug smirk off your face.'

Mohini's eyes squeezed into pinpoints. Her snakes picked me up again and tossed me like spaghetti a few times until all I could hear was the sound of bells tolling inside my brain. Then she tied Shukra and me to a pillar at the apex of the triangle.

'Like who?' Riju looked up again. He had been etching with a thin needle on Vajrin Mahendra's chest. The shape of the three-headed cobra came alive on his beautiful body. 'The Kaulas are busy having sex while the Vamas don't give a shit whether we take over or not. The humans think it is a desert storm. Who will she get? Just tie her up, darling. It's time we called Lord Kolahal.'

'These pillars ... good conductors of electricity,' whispered Shukra in a shaky voice. 'As soon as the electric demon strikes, we will be the first to burn.'

Where the hell are you, Shamshana? I have a meal ready for you.

Here. Close. Coming.

'Shamshana!' I screamed into the dark night. As if on cue, Shamshana's spine-chilling cry rang through the night again.

'Aiyiyiyiyiyiyaaaaaaa!'

'Who is Shamshana?' asked Mohini, flicking her hand so that the snakes coiled tighter around me.

'Your death,' I answered, smiling sweetly, spitting blood. She was close to me. I could feel it in my bones, or rather in my vibrating head. *It was the vibrator. I should have kept it on low when I used it.*

'What was—' began Mohini. Shamshana was crawling, walking, waddling. Her nose caught the scent of her prey and she started to hunt. Somewhere close. I focused and called her, pleaded with her. Drink her blood, Shamshana! Now!

'Ignore her, Mohini. It's time to do this. Leave these two here and go.'

Riju picked up the moonblade and raised it to the sky. In response, the sky rumbled and spewed layers of sheet lightning connecting to the moonblade itself.

'*Aum Ain Hreem Shreem Kolahala Namaha.*'

The moonblade gleamed in the darkness, darker than night itself, like black lightning, sharp and shining eerily. He pointed the last moonblade to the sky and the clouds parted.

'*Aum Ain Hreem Shreem Kolahala Namaha.*'

The tiny snakes that wound around me started to bite my arms, face and legs. Shamshana scuttled like a crab, crawling, giggling. Her mouth watered in anticipation. She hurtled towards her prey and started to bite. Shukra, who had been strangely quiet beside me, screamed. When I tasted his blood in my head, I knew that Shamshana was attacking the wrong one.

'Not him, you idiotic piece of dead meat,' I screamed with my last breath. 'Attack them! *Them!*'

'What is that?' asked Mohini, walking towards Shamshana. Mohini tore something from Shukra and held it up against the sky. 'Is this what was coming to help you, Anantya?' she said, holding her up. 'A monster baby?'

'*Aum Ain Hreem Shreem …*'

Shamshana, displeased at being deprived of Shukra, attacked Mohini, starting with a big chomp on her luscious pout. Mohini screamed in surprised terror.

'*… Kolahala Namaha.*'

Lightning uncoiled in the sky. It struck Riju who stood with his arms spread wide, accepting; lighting him up like a red beacon with its touch. Lightning bolts struck the iron pillars around us, which set them thrumming with electricity.

One of the bolts hit Shukra, who had a seizure and fell shaking and frothing to the ground. The ground shook, one big mass of flesh, rising as it powered up in submission, readying for a new master. In the throes of his strange religious fervour, Riju raised the seventh moonblade, the shadowblade, blacker than black, and plunged it into Vajrin's inert body with one deep stroke. Vajrin screamed. Mohini attacked Shamshana with all her strength, recalling her snakes in her distraction. Suddenly, I was free.

'I will kill you!' she screamed, lunging for Shamshana as the ground below us trembled.

I crawled towards my boneblade that lay a few feet away where it had fallen when Mohini captured me. Swaying drunkenly, I lurched towards Mohini who was strangling Shamshana's small corpse body with her snakes. A beefy hand fell on my shoulder.

'Let's leave!' hollered the beefed-up wrestling champion in Shukra's voice.

'What the hell happened to you?' I shouted. The lightning had done something to him. He had become twice his size. 'No, idea,' he shouted back. 'Let's go! Now!'

'No! I can still stop this!' I cried over the screaming whirlpool of electricity that rotated around Riju, who stood, with his arms spread wide and screaming: 'Come to me, my lord!'

'It's too late!'

'I have to do something! Go!'

I shoved him and turned back towards Mohini who was throttling Shamshana with her bare hands now. Only the top of her little dead head was visible, the rest was covered in writhing snakes.

I put the weight of my body behind it as I aimed my

boneblade, not at Mohini but Shamshana. I pierced her flesh directly beneath the chin. With the thrust, the blade bit deep enough to decapitate the tiny body, taking the head clean off. There was no blood, of course, because corpses don't bleed. Claws of smoke escaped her tiny body, engulfing and permeating me. Mohini turned to look at me in surprise, her lips and face swollen and blackened. The last thing I remembered was Riju standing there, his eyes glittering, his arms spread.

২৬

A black hole loomed over my mind, the veil had vanished. In the far recesses of the blackness a distant memory glimmered faintly, Dhuma's last words:

'If Shamshana doesn't destroy the danava in this corpse body, you offer her a new vessel. Your living body. Cut open the corpse and take her power inside you. Don't let anyone else kill the baby, for then Shamshana will be free from our spells, free to destroy at will. Once she's inside you, try and come back to me as fast as possible. She will consume your soul within an hour, for that's her nature. Do that only if you are desperate and there's no other way. You understand?'

I understood that this was the end of me. Dhuma, I am sorry, I had no choice.

As if in a play, I watched myself, wholly detached. I saw my hands grab Mohini and rip her neck open, biting and eating the poisonous snakes that erupted from her breasts. I savoured the black blood, with Shamshana laughing maniacally all the while. Mohini's eyes grew large in terror. Through my many eyes, I saw Riju Das. He was inside the yantra, his delirious eyes turned skywards. I ran towards him. The sky darkened, flashed red and white and then black again. Black lightning poured over Riju. I crossed the yantra and sprang at him as he stood there, his arms spread, his body blackened as Kolahal entered him through his mouth. I

367

bent down and grabbed his left hand, biting the middle finger so hard that the Key, Indra's Key, dropped with a small clink on to the muddy platform.

'Wear it!' I screamed to Vajrin Mahendra, tossing the ring towards him. He dragged his bleeding body towards the ring, picked it up and slipped it onto his finger. The walls around us, of the triangular yantra, darkened, becoming blacker than darkness itself. I opened my mouth, my many mouths, and leapt on Riju, flattening him with my body. That was when he noticed me. Stunned, he tried to push me away. But I opened my mouth, wide and wider still, and bit him. His nose, his face, his shoulders. Kolahal's dark blood leaked out of the holes that I punctured in his body. Riju screamed. Shamshana Kalika drank Kolahal's spirit and powers. Sucking on the God of Chaos. I drank his black blood. Riju's body disintegrated and melted, like gooey chocolate, spreading on my mouth, my body. Without a vessel to hold him, Vritra fell back into the abyss above, losing his consciousness, screaming in helpless fury as he was sucked back into whichever hell he had come from. I let go then. It was over. I fell back and breathed, the veil parting open.

'Anantya!'

'Dhuma,' someone whispered, maybe it was me. My hand curled over the yugma locket that I had snatched from Riju's liquidized body. My mother. I had to find her and ask her why she hadn't told me she was alive. But how could I? Shamshana was still hungry and wanted to feed. Feed on my mind, my thoughts, my memories, my anger, my rage, my suffering and my blood. If she didn't get out of my body soon, my head would explode. Someone, a giant-sized someone, picked me up like I was a ragdoll and began to run. My body flopped limply on his shoulder. There was so much pain. My head throbbed and my teeth did too. My thigh bled and my head, oh my head.

The black hole edged up, slowly, surely, swallowing everything all around until the pain, the panic, the disgust, all ceased to matter. I became the blackness, the vastness, the black hole. I felt the others, their memories, wishes, thoughts, desires, all churning in the darkness. I felt overwhelmed, surprised, pleasured, insignificant. Someone far away called to someone called Anantya. They screamed her name over and over again.

'We burn her.'

Was that Dhuma? What did she want to burn now? But the thought was melting away, drowning in other voices, the many other voices around me in the darkness. Screams and whispers and laughter and cries of pain. Something hot touched my skin. Someone's skin was on fire. There was pain, to which someone else screamed. There was a dark womb around me, warm and moist. I liked it here. I didn't want to leave. Ever. Someone yanked me by the hair, by the soul, by the feet. I was turned upside down and thwacked on my buttocks.

'Your work in the world is not done,' she whispered. Who the hell are you? I don't take orders from anyone, I said crossly. If I want to stay here, that's my business.

'Someday, my daughter, my mother, my sister,' she whispered. 'We will meet and you will know. Someday I will tell you who I am. But not now. Leave now. Go back to the light. Your work in the living world is not complete. Not by far.'

I didn't want to leave, but bloody hell, even my soul didn't heed me. Pain struck me, like millions of boiling gashes as light blinded my eyes. The taste in my mouth was raw, that of blood and oil and debris. I licked my lips and cried. Two faces swam over me. One was Dhuma, her crooked teeth shining in the darkness. The other I didn't recognize at first. His face was covered with shaggy hair. And then I remembered. Shukra. Something had happened to him.

'Kolahal?'

'Gone back,' answered Dhuma, 'and so is the nagin and that greedy pig friend of yours. Both gone to hell with the danava.'

'You saved the city, Anantya,' said the beefed-up Shukra in Shukra's old voice.

But I wasn't done. 'Shamshana?' I croaked.

'Took all my skills to get her out of you. If this crazy asura hadn't brought you here in time, you would have gone with Shamshana. Now rest.'

Finished. I lay back. The Cult of Chaos was over. It was over. My city was safe. As were my people.

২৬

It took me a week to return to my senses. By then, the world had reverted to its usual shitty self. I reached the top of the hill and hobbled to the other side, which fell off into an almost vertical precipice. The sun was only just setting and the cool evening breeze brought with it a hint of monsoon. I placed the cassette player, bought from a raddi shop, on a flat rock and pressed play. A sentimental Bollywood love song from the seventies filled the air. I lit up a beedi. Soppy and whiney, just the way he liked them, I thought, blinking back tears. Damn this wind. I ignored the slight fluttering of wings behind me. I knew his family was there, but I didn't want to talk to them. Not just yet. *Prem Chhokra, this one's for you.*

Smoke from my beedi drifted over the cliff. It reminded me of the abyss that I had looked into recently. Heights would never scare me again, not after having teetered on the brink of that one.

Shamshana. I knew she and I were connected. We would always be now. Shit of an ass.

My last conscious memory of the horrid night was Riju's blood on my body and lips and my unquenchable thirst for more of it. Shukra had later told me that he had picked me up and carried me to Dhuma (*you kept screeching in my ear – it was worse than the ear-splitting honking on Delhi's roads*), who had then started the ritual to extract Shamshana from me.

371

Meanwhile, he had called Madhu who had then anonymously tipped off the local police about Vajrin.

The inspector who followed up on the information found industrialist Vajrin Mahendra almost dead, lying in the pit of a construction site on Raisina Road

Mohini Devi, the billionaire's glamorous (now ex-) secretary, was found dead at the same place. She had been brutally butchered (lizard's piss, did I do that?).

Jugnu had gone on record to say that Mohini had kidnapped his uncle and tried to kill him when the ransom demanded was denied. The inspector took all the credit for the raid and became the hero of the hour. Madhu, who had opted to remain in the shadows, located my satchel, septifocals and boneblade along with Riju's black magic paraphernalia at the site. He had quietly dropped off the entire lot at the haveli before the Tazaak descended on them. I still hadn't sifted through *that* pile, but I was in no hurry now.

After darkness had consumed the sun (metaphorically, I mean; night, you know, happened), I placed the envelope Grrhat had brought from Qubera's office at the opening of the cave and left. The money was tainted with a friend's blood, something I so didn't need. From the excited fluttering behind me, I knew Prem's parents had discovered it. Perhaps it would buy them a few months of maya potion and freedom. Along with the cheque, Grrhat had also brought me an apology for almost getting me killed (*but you did solve it, right?*). That I had gladly kept – along with half a litre of rakpiss, which I extracted after forcing him to drink tharka, a drink made of desert cactus thorns. He had screamed all the way to the best rakpiss I'd ever had for my rasayana lab. (No, no, it was not sadistic. Tharka is seriously the best way to make rakpiss. Though, come to think of it, brahmi would've worked just as well. Wonder why I didn't think of that.)

Later in the evening, I paid Vajrin a visit to find out how he was doing. He had smiled his incredibly beautiful smile, thanked me and had the creepy balls to offer payment for saving his ass. I walked away, pissed. What was it with daevas and offering money? Did they think any ass-filth could be wiped clean with wads of paper? Jurassic dodos.

I set my septifocals on my head, caressed the boneblade resting in my scabbard again and kicked Chhotu to life, appreciatively breathing in the heavy, moisture-laden air. *The rains will start! The rains will start!* Maiyya's chant rose in my heart, as I reached Bedardi Bar.

'Where were you!' exclaimed Shukra, pouncing on me as I reached the doorway to the pub. The mostly humanoid crowd was jostling to get into the bar and resume their real forms.

Despite his new bouncer-body, His Grace quailed at the unruly mob. 'This place, it's *teeming* with ruffians. Why can't we go eat at a normal place?' He eyed Maiyya with suspicion as she squatted on the sidewalk under the streetlight, along with a couple of her cronies.

I waved at her, winking. 'There's a Thai restaurant in Rajiv Chowk I've heard about—' he said. I burst out laughing. 'I've heard their duck is not that great,' I answered, taking him by his marvellously hairy, muscled bicep and guiding him to a less crowded area opposite Bedardi. I took out a beedi and offered one to him.

He shook his head. 'You shouldn't. It causes cancer, you know.'

'Oh, but I can magic it away,' I said, laughing again and taking a long drag as he eyed me with a frown.

'Anantya. I … I wanted to say something,' Shukra started gruffly. 'I realize there's a lot going on in the world that I do not know. I … I want to thank you for making me see things in a new … way.' He finished lamely, looking down at his feet.

After the initial shock had worn off, Shukra had researched into what had happened to him. Bio-electricity, was his explanation. *That night, the air was full of asuric ions, ions that are genetically aligned to my race's DNA. My body acted like a sponge in the electric spectrometry triggered by the lightning storm. The reaction made my body change. Become … more alpha.*

In tantrik terms, his asuric nature had absorbed some of Vritra's demonic energy. He had broadened and beefed up in a matter of seconds. His hands and feet were large to begin with, but they had become even bigger. Hair had sprouted all over his body and face. I wondered if his gentle nature would gradually change as well, and become more like Vritra. But he had enough on his plate right now, and didn't need to worry about that possibility. He wore his new body like a child who was stuck inside a suit stolen from his father's wardrobe. He had had to order new clothes (several sizes larger) and now, on a daily basis, combed and gelled his mane of hair and used product to tame his facial and chest hair. And only shakti knew where else. (I didn't want to think about it, my hormones went a little crazy. What? I like hairy men!) I made an effort to stop staring at his magnificently bearded face and tried very hard to put a leash on that line of thought. That beard on my breasts. Doing it with him … it … this would just mess up something that might be … on its way to becoming a friendship. Complicated, that.

'You sex?' Someone tapped Shukra on his shoulder. It was a darba, disguised as a handsome human. I had seen him in the bar a few times, a lecherous old sup with two heads and a dangling thing.

'I am sorry, no. My name is Shukracharya, the seven—' he said, adjusting his glasses.

'I don't think he's asking you your *name*, Shuks,' I said. 'He's with me, dodo. Skunk off, will you?'

'Oh, didn't realize he's yours,' answered the darba, scuttling away.

'What did he mean?' asked Shukra, blinking owlishly. His nose, I noticed, had broadened like the rest of him. The steel-rimmed glasses now looked a lot smaller on him. I stepped back, giddy and horny. ('You sure iss not a date?' Zee's jeer from last night rang in my ears.)

I shook my head. No, this wasn't a date. At Bedardi, all dates went only one way.

'Come, let's go inside,' I said, steering him by his arm and entering the bar. 'Try not to faint, will you?'

He didn't, but came close. He froze in the middle of the busy floor where sups, mayans and pashus danced in their various ways, with their various limbs in various positions. I made a beeline to the bar, dragging the shell-shocked Shukra behind me, signalling to Maaki over the gyrating party animals for two strong soma-on-the-rocks. His Grace gulped his down, asked for another and downed that as well. Understandable, if you had never really met sups in your life. I lazily scanned the bar, spaced out and definitely *not* looking at the widescreen television on the wall opposite me, which featured my worm of a half-brother. He had become a poster-boy tantrik for the Delhi media nowadays. As touted by CAT and the Kaula Ashram, he was the swami who had successfully averted the storm by holding a massive all-night yagna on the ashram premises in Banaras. As a result, the Kaulas had become more popular than ever. The government had appointed them as their official spiritual guides. They were now consulted before any documents were signed or acts passed. The ashram was so pleased with Nasty that he was given a probationary seat on the High Council. He was the youngest person ever to have achieved this honour. Father would surely be pleased.

I, on the other hand, got a visit from the mighty Kanthak himself. He condescendingly informed me that the Tazaak had decided to drop all charges against me for the alleged murder of Lavanya Mohan, classifying it as an 'unfortunate accident'. Swami Riju's death had been dubbed a suicide and that case had been closed as well. He had taken the two moonblades from me to make sure Tazaak kept the entire set of all seven blades 'safe' until their rightful owner, Rambha, could claim them. (Rambha, her suitcases and the kung fu girls had vanished overnight without a trace.) Just before he left, Kanthak handed me a show-cause notice for suspected illegal tantrik activities with an aghori, 'Madame' Dhuma, a week ago in a shamshan ground on the outskirts of Delhi. It had come to the Tazaak's notice that I had been indulging in blood sacrifices on a new-moon night. I was to attend Tazaak court and explain to them exactly what I had been up to, and why. He told me that Swami Narahara (now Rishi Narahara) would be there to support my cause as my half-brother. I ripped up the notice and slapped it on Kanthak's callused palm. His astonishment gave me momentary pleasure. However, I would still need to attend the bloody court. If I wanted to live in Delhi, I had to keep on the right side of Tazaak. But then, I could have just as easily punched his face and, although that would have given me greater pleasure, it would have been a greater offence. Hey Kali, I was growing older and wiser.

I sat with my back to the wall, lazily looking at two kravyads, sups with fiery breaths, hanging upside down from the ceiling and drinking up live fire from a hookah.

'Do you suppose I will ever return to normal?' Shukra asked, rubbing his hand over his chiselled chin, worriedly.

'You don't like this?' I asked, amused and a tad sharply.

'It's ... it's a bit too ... macho, you know? I seem to make my colleagues nervous—'

I couldn't help grinning. An asura with the natural ability to absorb power wanted to reject it, while an ambitious human had butchered six innocent little girls to get his filthy hands on it. Why wasn't I surprised? I wondered what Shukra's ancestors would say about that.

'So who was this boyfriend that Riju mentioned, ifyoudontmindmeasking?' he finished hastily, embarrassed and slightly tipsy now.

'That's a whole other story. A long, long one,' I answered, surprised that the memories didn't hurt too much. I could think about Neel without my heart splintering again. I let the memories drift over me, while I sat still. After the vastness of Shamshana Kalika's dark and chaotic ocean of misery, somehow my misfortunes felt small. Perhaps that was why I had stopped having those nightmares as well.

Shukra was in a chatty mood. Now that the Kaulas' science had been shown up as crap, he wanted to dedicate his life to research the various species of sups and how tantrik science could benefit them. He was determined to make an in-depth study of (to her utter horror) Dhuma, Rambha (if we could ever find her) and his own ancestors. I listened to him, rapt, my heart beating, chewing my lip, wondering if he would like the idea of a sex-date. Wondering if he was a virgin. Wondering how coarse or fine his beard was. Wondering if I should take advantage of his drunkenness and take him to my place with an offer of green tea.

My phone rang. It was Madhu Tripathi. A late-night call

from him always meant a difficult case with which he was desperate for my help. I looked back at the hot asura opposite me, glowing in drunkenness, ready to be taken to a dark corner and ravished, and then at the flashing light of my insistently ringing phone, which now held the promise of a new game. Kali's shit, why must life give you such hard choices?

Of muses and kind people

It was just another Tuesday when Anantya Tantrist first sneaked into my mind. Thankfully, at the time, I stood in front of a whiteboard where I quickly managed to jot down the first elements of her world before she faded away. From that day onwards, Anantya has grown in my mind in infinite ways, throwing ideas, images, thoughts and words at me, sometimes at really, really bad times, much like Shamshana Kalika does to her in the last scene of this book. (See Anantya, that's my revenge!) I remain fascinated by her survival skills, her sheer will and the crazy adventures she has. Thank you, Anantya, for choosing and trusting me as the medium that would bring you to this world.

A tight hug to my husband Ashwani Sharma for patiently taking me out for walks and for showing me flowers on days when I had written nothing (and on other days too). To Dad for his workaholism and Mum for her retellings of myths over the phone. And the rest of the Delhi family for continuous support and love. A special thanks goes to all the initial readers who helped me with frank feedback, prompt emails and sometimes a shoulder to cry on: Ashwani Sharma, Varun Taneja, Uthara Narayanan, Kanishka Lahiri, Kanchen Rajanna, Safrina Nishad, Manasi Subramaniam, Madhulika Anchalia, Shantanu Ray Chaudhuri and Ashwini Seshappa.

To Ajitha G.S. for listening to me with a straight face when

I accosted her at a literature festival and told her how Anantya wanted her to be the editor of the series; for saying yes and cuddling and hugging every word of the book. The kind George Mathen for taking out time to meet a fan, treating her to coffee and making a spectacular cover for her book. To Karthika V.K., editor supreme, who calls Anantya 'our girl', HarperCollins India for believing and taking a chance on something that is new and untried in the market; Kanishka Gupta for the fastest acceptance in the history of literary agents (a day). And copy-editor Usha Surampudi for mutilating a doormat at home in order to simulate a tantric sacrifice and get it right.

An awed bow to the masters of words from whom I learn every day: Terry Pratchett, Neil Gaiman, Ursula K. Le Guin, G.R.R. Martin, Isaac Asimov, and many others whose names might have dropped off my memory charts, but their words haven't. To books.google.com and archives.org, where I found the most incredible out-of-print titles on tantrism and the occult. And for help, guidance, technicalities of the trade and selfless support, I am deeply in the debt of Ashwin Sanghi, Samit Basu, Zac O'Yeah, Krishan Pratap Singh and Sharath Komarraju. To the diligent reader who stayed with Anantya and me to these final pages, thank you.

Finally, to tantrism and its creative power, the Goddess, without whom nothing would be.